*Techies, Trials & Terrorists*

# Techies, Trials & Terrorists

∞∞∞

## The Transient Generation

Jim Lynch

Techies, Trials & Terrorists Copyright© 2020
All Rights Reserved By Jim Lynch

All rights reserved. No part of this book may be reproduced in any form or by any electronic or mechanical means including but not limited to information storage and retrieval systems without permission in writing from the author. The only exception is by a reviewer who may quote short excerpts in a review

**Copyright©: 2020**
**ISBN:** 9798625811989
**Imprint:** Independently published

## Dedication

This book is dedicated to my eight children and their spouses and to my fifteen (and counting) grandchildren. I hope you all grow to understand that where we are headed is rooted in where we have been. Please learn to forgive one another, to forgive yourselves and forgive me for my overly repetitive advice.

# *Prologue*

In Pennsylvania, Fox Babcock glances over at his naked girlfriend. They are engaged to be married but Fox prefers to think of Evelyn as his girlfriend. He doesn't attach much meaning to the word, fiancé. When they get married things will be different. For now, not much has changed.

Fox is amazed by how fast Evelyn can fall asleep. Almost every night as soon as her head hits the pillow she is out. If there is a more romantic or erotic end to their evening she will still be asleep first. *Does Evelyn lead a guiltless life?* That can't be true. Maybe she has never killed anyone, but she must have some regrets, some guilt. But Fox doesn't know what Evelyn's regrets might be. By contrast, he *has* killed someone. In fact, Fox has killed two people. He assumes that Evelyn suspects as much. However she has never asked him about it directly. Maybe that helps her sleep soundly.

∞∞∞

In California, Simone Muirchant rolls over in her bed. She is sleeping alone. She likes it this way. Simone has been sleeping alone most nights for more than a dozen years. When she gets out of bed each day she is immediately her own woman.

But occasionally Simone has trouble sleeping. This is one of those restless nights that come along seemingly without provocation. The recurring emotional encumbrance is back. Simone is burdened by her belief that her ex-husband, Frank Babcock, has actually had someone killed. That victim was one of her former lovers.

However, Simone is unaware that her own son, Fox Babcock, is also a killer. Simone despises violence of all types, especially mass violence. She has been an anti-war activist throughout her life. Inexplicably, too many of the men in her life have known violence in one form or another. She doesn't know why this bizarre incongruity keeps cycling through her life. She thinks of herself as a peaceful person. But she is not at peace with herself.

∞∞∞

In New York, Mickey Johnson throws his arm over his sleeping wife, Sydney. He loves her, and he respects her restrained ambition. Syd can have whatever successes she wants in life. Mickey is happy that she chose to be the mother of their three children. Syd is his lighthouse in the storm. She is vigilant even as she sleeps peacefully. Like the lighthouse, Syd is always there.

Mickey has never told anyone about his simmering hatred. He hasn't told Syd. He won't tell his best friend, Jack Birdsong. And he certainly would never tell Simone. In some ways Mickey's hatred is ironic. Paradoxically, a little over a year earlier Mickey had helped *save* the life of Frank Babcock.

But although he tries to repress it, Mickey wants revenge. Mickey is convinced that Frank Babcock is responsible for the homicide of Wayne Johnson a decade earlier. Wayne was Mickey's father. Now Mickey constantly harbors feelings of vengeance. He guards his passionate inclination, carefully. For the longest time he tried to believe that Babcock was innocent. But in the past year he has come to think differently. He has given in to his apprehensions. Now Mickey is convinced that Babcock commissioned Wayne Johnson's murder. And now it has become an obsession. His attempts to control or repress his own coarse thirst for retribution are failing. His once stalwart value system is disintegrating with hatred. He scares himself.

∞∞∞

Gradually across the country the Babcocks and the Johnsons get out of bed and start their messy meshed days.

*1991*

# I

## January 1991

"Margot will be leaving earlier today, Burke. She'll be down with the baby momentarily. Make sure that Jedd has 6 ounces of formula at 8 AM. Play with him and keep him stimulated after his morning bottle. He'll be ready for his first nap around 9:45. Then call me at the office to let me know that everything is okay."

∞∞∞

Ten month old Jedidiah Babcock was so very precious to Nicole Silver. But as precious as her infant son might be, Nicole resented Jedd's father with an equal passion. She thought that all of the legal maneuvering around Jedidiah's birthright was a total nuisance. Silver and her sometimes lover, Frank Babcock, were now drafting a fourth version of the legal stipulations surrounding young Jedidiah's upbringing. They had been working on this document for several months even before Jedd was born.

Nicole Silver is a young woman who knows herself quite well. She knows what she desires and she knows what she disdains. Nicole is also adept at doing whatever it takes to ensure that her own cravings are fulfilled. And yes she is truly fond of her son Jedidiah. However it isn't the normal love between a mother and her child. It is more like an affection for a precious possession. Nicole feels a covetous ownership of her son rather than a normal nurturing maternal love. She is vaguely aware that this is true but she doesn't care. She is glad that other people are jealous that Jedidiah Babcock is her baby. She realizes that every person in her law office hates her passionately. She is regarded as the slutty associate attorney who turned ultra-uppity the moment she knew she was pregnant with the big boss' baby. The others in the office refer to her alternatively as either "a bitch on wheels" or "a bitch on heels," depending upon what she wears to the office that particular day. Since Jedidiah's birth she has never worn the same outfit twice.

∞∞∞

"Don't worry about it, Nicole. I've got it under control," Burke Finnegan knows that Nicole's litany of instructions is not meant to sound motherly. Silver's directives are meant to convey that she is in charge.

"But call me at 10 AM anyway. I want to hear that things are exactly as they need to be. It'll only take a few seconds."

"Fine. I'll call you at 10:00." Finnegan tries to keep a pleasant tone in his voice, but he is simply one of the ever growing contingent of hired help who despise Silver. However the strapping ex-cop hopes that Silver will finally hire a new nanny, today. It has been 15 days since she fired the last one. Finnegan is a personal security expert, not a babysitter. Frank Babcock is paying him double his normal security wages for every hour he spends nurturing Jedidiah during the day. It doesn't matter.

During the evening and nighttime hours, Nicole's sister, Margot Silver, helps out with the baby. That earns Margot an opportunity to live in Frank Babcock's four bedroom five story townhouse on the upper east side of Manhattan. Margot Silver has been living there for seven months. Her older sister Nicole has lived there ever since she got herself pregnant.

Burke Finnegan began his day at the townhouse shortly before 7 AM. He watches as Nicole Silver moves rapidly through the main floor – the second story of the Babcock residence. He knows that she is teasing him. It is part of her qualifying routine as a mean-spirited bitch. Silver has an affinity for short tight skirts that look even shorter on her pixyish body. And there are times that Finnegan feels like grabbing her, bending her over his knees and spanking her as hard as he can – or at least until she learns how to treat people with some modicum of respect. Normally he is never one for fantasies. However this is one that he often replays in his mind. During the last two weeks, reddening the rear end of his employer's significant other is a vision that has helped keep him sane.

"I have no idea what time I'll be home this evening so do me a favor and cancel the nanny interview. Ask the woman if we can reschedule for next week sometime. If Frank calls, tell him to call me at the office."

## January 1991

She thinks for a moment and then adds; "Or at least see if you can get a time and a number where I can reach him. He's somewhere in Europe, on his way to Saudi Arabia, but he hasn't had the decency to tell me what hotel he is staying in. I have no idea what's wrong with that man."

Silver's tone is officious. She has not yet turned thirty but she wants to appear more sophisticated than her personal acumen and achievements would suggest. Finnegan believes that the only goal this little tart has attained so far is that she has gotten herself knocked up by a billionaire who wants another son. However Finnegan acknowledges that Silver has managed to bring this child into the world on the twenty-fourth birthday of Frank Babcock's first son. This is a remarkable feat. But Finnegan has a strong sense that regardless of other treasures which Silver might acquire, the title of Mrs. Babcock is not going to be among them.

Silver is now standing in front of an oval mirror near the front entrance to the townhouse adjusting her short black hair. It is razor cut and layered. This coiffure has recently replaced her dated mullet look. Silver hopes her new hairdo will make her look softer and more feminine, without surrendering any of her sway. Instead its shorter length causes a more severe bearing to emerge. Burke Finnegan thinks she looks like a Nazi. He believes that no amount of mirror primping is going to help.

Meanwhile Silver takes her time with her lipstick. She knows that Finnegan is watching her from behind. She also knows that Finnegan carries a revolver in a holster at the small of his back. Something about that excites her.

∞∞∞

Twenty minutes after Nicole leaves the townhouse, her sister Margot comes down the back stairway carrying 10 month old Jedidiah Babcock. There is a telling physical resemblance between the two sisters, but that is the extent of their similarities. Margot is much more nurturing in the way she holds her nephew. She swaddles young Jedidiah in a receiving blanket and a warm comforter. She holds the baby close to her chest and moves slowly to avoid jostling him. Although she doesn't visit the same expensive salons that her sister frequents, Margot's warm soft smile is framed by a slightly longer and more casual hairstyle. In stark contrast to Nicole's demeanor Margot's mien is reflective of a carefree insouciance tempered by an appealing inner warmth. Her daily attire normally consists of jeans and various informal tops. However this morning Margot is wearing a plain short sleeved black dress, with a knee top hem.

∞∞∞

"I'm sorry I'm leaving a little earlier than usual, Burke. Jedd is awake and he's as cute as a button. He was gurgling like crazy when I changed him. I think he'll be talking very soon." She carefully transfers the baby from her arms to the waiting hands of the security agent. "See ... see what I mean. His eyes are wide open. He's looking right at you. He's so alert." Margot has placed the baby in Burke's hands but she has not yet let go. As a result she is standing less than a foot away.

"You're right ... real cute kid. Looks more like his father, I think. So what has you up and out so early, another job interview?"

"You got it. This one seems more promising. I don't think they'll require as much experience as the last couple of opportunities."

As much as Finnegan detests *Nicole* Silver, he thinks that *Margot* Silver is a nice kid. The only problem that Finnegan has with Margot is that she is too laid-back. She graduated from NYU eight months earlier but still has not secured employment of any kind. In the interim Margot is also taking a few graduate courses at her alma mater. *That's part of the problem*, he thinks. *Kids these days just keep going to school. Pretty soon they're thirty years old and know nothing about the real world.*

"These companies have to realize that everyone has to start somewhere. Good luck with the interview. I'm sure you'll do well."

"Thanks, Burke. By the way, you know that Jedd has to be fed at eight. Right? I'm sure Nicole left Jedd's schedule on the fridge magnet as she usually does."

Margot is not hurried. Yet she doesn't linger. When she sees that Burke has everything under control, she kisses Jedidiah on the cheek, and says, "Aunt Margot has to go bye-bye now. I'll be back tonight. I love you little man."

Finnegan wonders if Jedd's mother was as affectionate with the child when she left twenty minutes earlier. Somehow he doubts it.

∞∞∞

When Nicole Silver gets to the midtown office of Babcock, Gordon, Ellis and Turley, she immediately enters her small office and begins to reread the latest version of her prenuptial agreement with Frank Babcock. The very

## January 1991

fact that it is even called a prenuptial is a farce. By now Nicole realizes that Babcock isn't really interested in marrying her. The agreement reads more like a guardianship accord between two parents following a divorce. The document begins with a statement that Nicole Silver attests to the fact that she has not engaged in sexual relations with anyone other Frank Babcock for eleven months prior to the birth of Jedidiah Babcock. It further stipulates that both parents are in agreement that genetic testing has determined that Jedidiah is the biological progeny of Frank Babcock and Nicole Silver. The document is all about custody, control and money.

The proposed accord contains an extensive discussion of the Babcock family trust. And there is also a lengthy set of agreements about the care, supervision and guardianship of Jedidiah Babcock. The document contains multiple paragraphs which start out with the term "If the parents should marry ..." and several balancing paragraphs that begin with, "If the parents are not married ..." There is much verbiage dealing with the upbringing of Jedidiah Babcock. There's less language around the ramifications of the breakup of a prospective marriage.

Nicole Silver has a hard time getting her head around many of the specific requirements that Babcock has insisted on putting in the contract. A good example is Babcock's insistence that after the age of twelve Jedidiah is to be raised on Long Island and that he is to attend the same all-male Jesuit high school that his father attended. Silver knows that Shenandoah High School in Garden City is one of the most prestigious high schools in the country, but there are many other excellent secondary schools. The entrance requirements for Shenandoah are quite rigorous but Frank Babcock sat on the Board of Trustees of the school for many years and still maintains a passing friendship with the long time President of Shenandoah Jesuit Community, Father Thomas Dunham. The school is also the recipient of a $75,000 annual grant from the Babcock Foundation.

Frank Babcock also stipulates that Jedd must attend an Ivy League College other than Columbia. When Silver asks Babcock about the contingency plan for the possibility that Jedidiah won't be accepted at one of these schools, Babcock merely states that "denied acceptance isn't a possibility."

Included in their agreement is a child support accord that gives Silver and Babcock temporary joint custody of Jedidiah until such time as they marry, die or enter into a subsequent agreement. The covenant puts no travel constraints on either parent with respect to traveling with or without Jedidiah. All of this language seems highly unusual and unnecessary in light of the fact that the parents are currently living under the same roof and have an acceptable – albeit not intensely intimate – sexual relationship. However there is also a provision that requires Silver to agree that they will raise the child as a Christian and that he be is barred from attending any non-Christian religious services until he is at least 14 years of age.

Another stipulation deals with premarital finances. This stipulation is what makes the other articles worthy of consideration for Silver. In addition to full financial support for Jedidiah's every need, Babcock pledges an annual stipend of $1 Million to be paid to Silver for her care and protection of Jedidiah. This amount is an addition to funds for a nanny, as well as for food, housing, education and security, all of which are directly billed to Babcock. The agreement also states that prior to their marriage Frank Babcock and Nicole Silver will cohabitate at Babcock's residence on the east side of Manhattan. The contract specifies that both parties agree that regardless of the duration of such living conditions, and irrespective of any ongoing sexual relations between the parties, neither party will petition any court of law to consider such living arrangements a "common-law marriage." It further states that these housing considerations and other activities are merely "an arrangement of convenience" for both parties.

The additional $1 million stipend is more or less a salary – although Silver detests that word in concept – paid to Nicole Silver for taking care of her own son. The stipend is an annual sum scheduled to be paid in twelve monthly payments on the first day of each month. This particular stipend will be superseded and replaced with a similar stipend paid in the same amount to Silver from the time she would marry Frank Babcock until the time when they would divorce ... if either of these events ever do occur. However in the event of a marriage between the parties, the monthly payments would be rescheduled to be paid in one lump sum annually on the anniversary of the marriage. This stipend remains constant through each year of such a yet-to-be-proposed marriage, and would be discontinued if and when such a marriage is terminated in a divorce or upon the death of either parent, with no payment due for the year during which such an event might occur.

In signing this agreement Silver would also surrender rights to any claim on other personal assets of Frank Babcock and/or his estate, including any and all wealth or assets that might accrue during a prospective marriage.

## January 1991

Meanwhile, the substance of Babcock's personal last will and testament has never been shared with Silver.

Most of the initial haggling over the verbiage in the contract is incidental rather than substantive. Silver has insisted, for example, that the word "salary," used in the initial draft, be changed to "stipend." She has also required that none of the legal work behind the agreement could be done by any lawyers at Babcock, Gordon, Ellis and Turley other than herself and Babcock himself. She also postulated that no one at their law firm would be provided with copies or drafts of the agreement. Frank Babcock immediately agreed to this simple sidebar because he maintains his own staff of personal attorneys. These personal attorneys are never involved in any of the work of Babcock, Gordon, Ellis and Turley and vice-versa.

A more substantive proviso in the prenuptial agreement which Silver finds to be particularly irksome is the unilateral fidelity clause. This clause demands that Silver remain faithful to her marital vows – which are also spelled out legally in the text of the contract and in advance of the marriage. This clause also contains specific and onerous financial consequences if it is ever proven that Silver has been sexually interactive with another individual during the course of her prospective marriage to Frank Babcock. Meanwhile, there is no such clause regarding Babcock's potential infidelity.

Oddly enough the unilateral fidelity clause only covers the period of time *during* the prospective marriage but says nothing whatsoever about any sexual activity that Silver might choose to engage in prior to marrying her child's father. This is the first definitive clue that Silver has received indicating that Babcock has no real intention of marrying her any time soon.

Silver is currently collecting Babcock's monthly "stipend" payments even before the marriage begins and is free to engage in relationships with others. However once she marries Babcock, she will have to wait until her first anniversary to collect her next million dollar payment, and she will need to be completely faithful in order to collect it. That pattern then will repeat itself annually. However, if she signs this agreement and doesn't marry Babcock she will at least be assured of receiving $83,333.33 a month for the foreseeable future. This is in addition to her salary at the law firm and her living expenses at the townhouse. In the short run this is not such a bad deal after all. It also provides her with the possibility of digging in deeper at a later date, and offers her a certain modicum of social freedom in the interim.

## *Techies, Trials & Terrorists*

After all of the revisions spanning the past 17 months, and after rereading the latest version of the prenuptial agreement one last time, Nicole Silver is finally ready to make her decision.

∞∞∞

# II

# January - February 1991

CNN is remarkable. They are bringing the world the first real-time televised war! And the good guys are winning! There has been a remarkable turn in world events. While most of the planet's geopolitical attention has been captured by the crumbling of Soviet domination in Eastern Europe, 120,000 members of the Iraqi army have invaded neighboring Kuwait.

∞∞∞

In August of 1990, under the direction of Iraqi dictator, Suddam Hussein, the occupation and annexation of Kuwait took less than two days. Saddam Hussein immediately claimed Kuwait as the 19th province of Iraq. This claim was then rapidly nullified by United Nations resolution # 662.

Hussein's invasion of Kuwait was condemned promptly by nations on all six inhabited continents around the world. Even traditional adversaries such as the United States and the Soviet Union were linked in their denunciation of Suddam Hussein.

Live reporting on the Cable News Network began almost immediately. CNN and other networks followed activities both in Kuwait and in Iraq extensively throughout the end of the year. They covered real time political responses as well.

Saddam Hussein vastly underestimated the resolve of American President George H.W. Bush and the readiness of the United States to defend its Middle East allies. As Bush orchestrated a coalition of nations, he also urged the United Nations Security Council to pass several additional resolutions. These included resolution # 665 which imposed a shipping

## Techies, Trials & Terrorists

blockade and a maritime embargo; # 670 which reinforced the blockade by confirming that it applied to air traffic and shipping lanes and # 678 which authorized the UN coalition to use all necessary means including military force to bring Iraq into acquiescence with previous resolutions. This final resolution included the issuance of a January 15$^{th}$ 1991 deadline for full compliance.

Bush got all of this done within 6 weeks of the invasion of Kuwait, while concurrently deploying more than 100,000 troops to defend neighboring ally, Saudi Arabia, against a follow-on invasion by Iraq. As the world waited for Suddam Hussein's response to the deadline, CNN covered the action from inside Baghdad, Iraq. Never before had the media attained such uninhibited access to war.

∞∞∞

"I thought we would be getting together this evening. I know the circumstances are unusual, but I need to know if and when Abdulrahman will be able to meet with me."

In exasperation, Frank Babcock listens intently to the response on the other end of the phone and then replies, "Patience has never been my strong suit." He hangs up the phone in his room at the al-Haddād Kingdom Hotel in Riyadh, Saudi Arabia and flips the TV back on.

Between these scheduling frustrations, Frank Babcock is watching pirated CNN coverage of the ongoing bombing in nearby Iraq and Kuwait from his hotel suite. The local Saudi network has appropriated feeds of the Gulf War that CNN is broadcasting back to the United States. The Saudi network is airing these feeds in selected hotel venues within the kingdom. The coverage is amazing. It includes live videos and pictures from cameras mounted aboard U.S. aircraft. These feeds show real-time attacks on Iraqi targets. It reminds Babcock of some of the video games that Fox used to play with his Russian friend Sergei Zubkov when they all lived in Great Neck, on Long Island.

Although the major media networks such as CBS, NBC, and ABC are giving thorough coverage to the conflict in the Middle East, CNN is now the only network news organization with a correspondent still situated inside of Iraq. CNN correspondent Peter Arnett continues to send bureau reports to CNN anchor Bernard Shaw from inside of Baghdad's Al-Rashid Hotel even as the air strikes begin hitting the city. Arnett and Shaw are becoming

## January - February 1991

household names overnight back in the United States and the historical scourge of war is now visible to everyone in real time. It is truly remarkable!

"Amazing, absolutely amazing." Babcock says it out loud, but realizes he is talking to himself. He takes a soft drink from the minibar. There are no alcoholic options.

∞∞∞

*Immediately after the January 15th 1991 deadline, the UN Coalition unleashed Operation Desert Storm which began with a colossal air offensive targeting Iraq's Air Force and anti-aircraft facilities. Within days, tens of thousands of sorties were flown from Saudi Arabia; from air craft carriers in the Persian Gulf and from ships in the Red Sea.*

*As the total destruction of Iraqi Air Force was winding down, the UN targets shifted to Iraq's command and communication facilities. President Bush and the rest of the UN coalition correctly assumed that Iraq's military defiance would crumble rapidly once Iraqi command and control was crushed.*

*The final phase of the air offensive consisted of sorties targeting military positions throughout Iraq and Kuwait. The principal objectives of this phase of the airborne initiative were the destruction of all of the Scud missile launching devices; Iraqi anti-aircraft defenses and research weaponry locales. During this phase Iraq was able to launch a limited number of Scuds at Israel. However they were mostly inaccurate and ineffective. They were fired from an extreme distance carrying a diminished payload. The United Nations coalition suffered less than 50 aircraft losses while flying an astonishing total of more than 100,000 sorties, and dropping more than 88,000 tons of explosives!*

*Within the first week of the air campaign, General Norman Schwarzkopf, the head of United States Central Command proclaimed that Iraq's nuclear test reactors had been totally destroyed. Before the end of the second week Schwarzkopf announced that the coalition had achieved "total and complete air supremacy in Iraq." The Iraqi Air Force had been decimated. President Bush then issued an ultimatum to Suddam Hussein to remove his troops entirely from Kuwait by February 23rd or risk having them annihilated by Schwarzkopf's ground forces, which now included more than a half million US troops gathered in the region along with another 250,000 coalition troops. In effect, Schwarzkopf had an astounding total of 750,000 troops at*

## Techies, Trials & Terrorists

his disposal. President Bush expressed a willingness to deploy them, if necessary!

∞∞∞

Meanwhile Frank Babcock has been in Riyadh for two days and is growing frustrated by the fact that his meeting with Abdulrahman al-Haddād has now been delayed three separate times.

Babcock also has no idea what to make of Masira al-Haddād. She is well educated and speaks the English language impeccably. As part of the al-Haddād family, she is meant to be treated with respect, but Babcock thinks of her as someone who has been sent to entertain him. He is fairly certain that her intentions are not sexual, although she does not wear a hijab to cover her face and hair when she meets with him in his hotel suite.

Once they leave the suite and are together in public, Masira dons a black Burka. Also there are always male companions on these occasions although Masira is clearly the person in charge of the itinerary. She has already introduced several additional family underlings who have graciously met with Babcock. Together Masira al-Haddād and the others have taken him to a few local tourist attractions and treated him to dinner at the finest restaurants in Riyadh. But Abdulrahman al-Haddād has not yet confirmed the time of their meeting. And no member of the host family of al-Haddād discusses the looming war in any detail. Any discourse on that topic would be led solely by the family patriarch, Abdulrahman al-Haddād.

∞∞∞

*Babcock had met Abdulrahman al-Haddād at an art gallery party in New York City two years earlier. Although both men were among the world's hyper-wealthy, they had never known anything about one another until that evening. As it turned out al-Haddād and some members of his extended family were in need of legal representation for significant property acquisitions that they were making in the United States. Al-Haddād had invited Babcock to Saudi Arabia to get to know him better and to introduce him to some of his family members, but it was becoming apparent that they had chosen the wrong time for this meeting, even though it had been scheduled three months earlier. This was after the initial incursion into Kuwait by Suddam and his Republican Guard troops.*

∞∞∞

## January - February 1991

But now after all of the delays and excuses, Babcock wants to leave. He isn't sure how to go about leaving without offending his host. Then the more he thinks about it, the crazier that notion seems to him. He isn't the one being rude. It is Abdulrahman al-Haddād who is out of line. Babcock is not used to being slighted or having his business interests treated as inconsequential. But he continues to wait and watch live video clips of fighter planes zooming off aircraft carriers and dropping bombs on targets in the sands of Iraq. He is totally unfamiliar with this feeling of helplessness.

∞∞∞

*The law firm of Babcock, Gordon, Ellis and Turley specialized in working with family owned businesses as well as with trusts and individuals with eight and nine figure portfolios. Babcock's role with his own firm was principally that of rainmaker. The circles Frank Babcock traveled in were often shaded, shielded or sheltered by soft emerald clouds. And frequently green rain drizzled down on Babcock thereby helping his law firm flourish and prosper.*

*The law firm also handled much of the legal work for the recently founded and funded hedge fund, Black Inoculum. Although he was not deeply versed in complex investing and hedging strategies, Frank Babcock was a principal partner in Black Inoculum because of the substantial sums he plunked down to get the fund started. Most recently he was spending more time understanding the intricacies of the Black Inoculum investments than he was with the legal work of his law firm.*

*Almost all of the legal work being done at Babcock, Gordon, Ellis and Turley was being done by Gordon, Ellis and Turley and a few young associates. In fact, Frank spent nearly as much time with his personal attorneys as he did with the attorneys and clients of his law firm. But this time he was visiting Saudi Arabia expectantly readying his firm for another green shower. On this particular business trip he was, in essence, representing both his law firm and his hedge fund.*

∞∞∞

*Frank Babcock's personal wealth was now well in excess of 3.5 billion dollars and was growing by the minute. In reality, income from his law practice made very little impact on his vast multigenerational wealth. Babcock was a lawyer by professional training but a billionaire industrialist and investor by legacy, inheritance and birthright. The Babcock family* fortune had been originally amassed by family members dating back nearly two hundred years. In the early nineteenth century Frank's great-great grandfather – James Byron Babcock, JB to his friends – made a killing in the fields of metallurgy and mining. JB's fortune was new wealth at the time. Then future generations of Babcocks preserved and grew the principal fortune, throughout the nineteenth and early twentieth century.

Intriguingly, generational wealth which had once been spread across several successor families became reconsolidated as family members began to die off without leaving direct line heirs. As recently as the mid-seventies, two of Frank Babcock's maiden aunts died and passed on their aggrandized wealth to the last living Babcock. Frank Babcock, himself, had been successful in positioning the family fortune in growth markets. Whether through astute investing or dumb luck, the Babcock family fortune continued to grow at abnormally exponential rates.

Frank Babcock had two children who were born in the 1960's. Francis Xavier Babcock Jr (A/K/A Fox Babcock) was born in 1966 and was currently in his final year at Johns Hopkins Medical School. Maureen Babcock was born in 1967. Maureen died in 1982 as one of the first female victims of the AIDS virus. This happened at the height of the frightening epidemic that had engulfed the country in the early 1980's.

Later it was revealed that Fox Babcock was not the genetic son of Frank Babcock Sr. In a complex twist of circumstances Frank Babcock had finally learned that Fox's genetic parents were Mickey Johnson and Simone Muirchant. Babcock had married and divorced Simone twice, and he regarded her as a two time loser. Two times she was Simone Babcock and now she had decided to go back to using her maiden name.

∞∞∞

While he waits for some news from Abdulrahman al-Haddād, Babcock continues to watch the Gulf War on CNN. It begins with a far-reaching assault on the Iraq Army from the air. The coalition's aerial bombing campaign is now in full swing and Iraq is enduring major repercussions due to its Kuwait invasion. The Iraqi death toll is already estimated to be in excess of 10,000 soldiers. Some news bureaus estimate the number of Iraqi casualties as being substantially higher. There is little discussion of civilian casualties other than the broad use of the term, *collateral damage*.

∞∞∞

## January - February 1991

"I'm sorry it took so long for us to meet again, Mr. Babcock. As you know recent political turmoil is quite consuming in this part of the world." Abdulrahman al-Haddād was educated in London and his grasp of the English language is superb. He speaks softly. "We have held several family meetings over the last several days. Maybe we should have scheduled a better time for your visit, Mr. Babcock."

"It's Frank, please call me Frank." Babcock is a bit irritated by al-Haddād's sudden repeated formality.

"Yes. Regardless, my apologies." The Saudi businessman is about 6 inches shorter than Babcock and he is accompanied by four other Saudi's who stand two to either side and one step behind the patriarch of the al-Haddād family.

"However, I will tell you that we would like to engage the services of your firm in conjunction with many different financial issues in your country. The aggressive nature of the Iraq incursion into Kuwait has led us to consider moving more of our liquid financial assets to the United States." It is the first and last commentary on the war that would be made by a member of al-Haddād family during Babcock's visit. Frank Babcock is rapidly learning that, in their own land, the al-Haddād family, like most Saudi families, are reserved in their disclosures.

∞∞∞

*The al-Haddād family was in the construction business and they had been forced to subcontract business through the family of Mohammed bin Laden. The bin Laden family was very close to the House of Saud. Consequently King Saud had made the bin Laden family extremely rich through the nearly incestuous relationship between the families. The fifty-four children (mostly his 25 sons) of Mohammed bin Laden controlled more than 80% of the construction that was done in the Kingdom of Saudi Arabia. The al-Haddād family was trying desperately to establish a first-hand relationship with the House of Saud and to end their dependency on the bin Laden family as the middle men. The current arrangement frequently placed the interests of the al-Haddād family at odds with the bin Laden family, when payments were withheld or delayed or unilaterally renegotiated.*

Babcock was already aware of a good number of the US based investments on the part of the al-Haddād family. Not unlike the bin Laden family, they were heavily invested in aerospace, casinos, movies and real estate. A good number of their investments were in New York, Nevada,

# Techies, Trials & Terrorists

*Florida and California. The al-Haddād family was much like the bin Laden family in another way as well. Many of the members of both extended families led different religious and social lives when they were outside of the Saudi Arabian homeland. Inside the country they observed strict tenets of the Muslim creed. However during their time in the western world, many of the members of the al-Haddād family became hard-drinking, club-going, party animals who threw their money around to acquire whatever goods or services they desired. And of course all of this avarice was fueled by the flow of oil. The oil traveled beneath the surface in Saudi Arabia, through the ruling House of Saud, then through the benefactors of House of Saud including the bin Laden family and by extension the al-Haddād family.*

∞∞∞

"I'm glad to hear that we will continue to investigate ways in which we might help each other. And I fully recognize that these are most trying times for both of our countries." Babcock tries his best to remain cordial.

"My family and I recognize the good will you have shown us by keeping your commitment to travel to our country even during a time of war. However the exact timing for our meeting is not now optimal. We will have short term impediments to doing business in our usual manner. Hopefully these obstructions will be erased in the next month or two. I hope you understand that meaningful discussion of this business will need to wait until that time."

"I understand, fully." Babcock lies. He doesn't truly understand. He knows that Abdulrahman al-Haddād should be able do whatever he pleases with his money, whenever he wants to do so. But Babcock also wonders if al-Haddād is being constrained by either the bin Laden family or by the House of Saud.

"In the meantime the al-Haddād family would be most interested in extending you every convenience and courtesy during your visit here in Riyadh as well as during your planned trip to Mecca."

Abdulrahman al-Haddād pauses briefly and then continues.

"My daughter, Masira, has an excellent understanding of our family's position in the kingdom, and I'm sure she will express the al-Haddād family's vision of the future to you as she takes you around to see our city and our country. My son, Tariq, will also accompany you for parts of your journey. Tariq is studying medicine like your own son. But Tariq is just

*January - February 1991*

beginning his studies at the Cambridge School of Clinical Medicine. He will be returning to the UK in two days."

∞∞∞

Babcock recognizes that the al-Haddād family is a curious lot. Before going to Saudi Arabia, Babcock did his homework. He learned many things about the family. Although Abdulrahman al-Haddād is only 55 years old, he is considered the patriarch of the family. He has been married six times but currently has four wives – the maximum allowed by Islamic Sharia Law. He has divorced two of his previous wives. In total he has nineteen children by nine different women including his four current and two previous wives.

Three other woman have borne him children out of wedlock but they are still considered his children. At first, Babcock found it hard to believe that a man could have nineteen children. He was astonished to learn later that this number only accounted for the male progeny and that al-Haddād has also fathered seven known female offspring. However, of the female children, only Masira al-Haddād and Yarah al-Haddād have received an American or European education. They are also the only females to play any role whatsoever in the al-Haddād family business. They receive this deference simply because they are the daughters of Abdulrahman al-Haddād's favorite wife, Shiekha.

One of the ex-CIA men who tutored Babcock about the background of the Saudi families and culture described the al-Haddād family as being like the Beverly Hillbillies of the 1960's CBS' sitcom. He likened Abdulrahman al-Haddād to "Jed Clampett," and said that most of al-Haddād's sons reminded him of Clampett's half-witted son, "Jethro."

This same briefer was familiar with the Saudi players and tended to think of them all in the same manner. He indicated that the bin Laden family and even the sons of ruling House of Saud were all similar to the al-Haddād and the Clampetts. Instead of hillbillies he referred to them as "sandbillies." He said that the Beverly Hillbillies and the Saudi Sandbillies both were basically ignorant people who ultimately owed their enormous wealth to the fluke of luck that had them residing on top of enormous reservoir of oil. At the time Babcock wondered whether or not his ex-CIA briefer was subliminally projecting a belief that Babcock owed his own wealth to the fluke luck that he was born atop a huge reservoir of inherited wealth as well.

∞∞∞

## *Techies, Trials & Terrorists*

The meeting with Abdulrahman al-Haddād is quite brief – less than 20 minutes. Frank Babcock is flummoxed by the total lack of productive dialogue. However he is also made aware that al-Haddād has done his own homework on the Babcock family. There are a few not-so-subtle references such as the mention of Fox Babcock's medical studies and a later reference that is made to his younger son, Jedidiah, being nearly a year old. This leads Babcock to conclude that al-Haddād is truly considering doing business with him. Otherwise why would he bother to check him out so thoroughly? Maybe the Gulf War is simply providing some kind of convenient hiatus while al-Haddād is completing his due diligence. Babcock has no way of knowing and he is not the type of person who likes being kept in the dark on any topic.

∞∞∞

# III

## March 1991

Mickey Johnson is flying home from a successful four day business trip to Atlanta. He is looking forward to spending time at home with Syd and their three children. Mickey has a fourth child. His oldest son, Fox Babcock, lives in Baltimore and is studying medicine. Fox is engaged to be married to a fellow med student, Evelyn Webb.

Mickey is a man of ample means but he is not in the same economic strata as his long-time nemesis Frank Babcock. Whereas Babcock is a trust baby who has inherited a consolidated family fortune, Mickey Johnson is a self-made multi-millionaire, who has earned a more modest fortune through hard work and entrepreneurship in the commodities markets.

∞∞∞

The trip home from Atlanta looks as though it will be longer than anticipated. Mickey's plane has waited out a passing storm on the ground at Hartsfield Atlanta International Airport. After being 17$^{th}$ in line for takeoff, they are now finally airborne. Mickey hopes to have a couple of cocktails and then grab an hour of sleep on the three hour flight. He is glad that the FAA has recently banned smoking on all domestic flights, because he is sitting in what used to be the smoking section of first class. But he has some business that he wants to take care of before taking his coveted nap.

Mickey's carry-on luggage is a proud new possession, a Mac Portable made by Apple Computer. Fox gave it to him as something he could use to "learn about computer applications." But Fox has warned him that the Mac Portable is already "a two-year old machine using four year old technology."

## Techies, Trials & Terrorists

Fox told Mickey that it would be obsolete before the end of the year. Regardless, Mickey thinks the machine is magnificent. It is small enough to carry onto the airplane and it sports a front-mounted handle for this purpose. The Mac is loaded with a preformatted 3.5" hard drive and a preinstalled operating system. This means that you don't have to be a genius to use the thing. It also has an attached trackball and a 9.8" 1-bit, 640 x 400 pixel viewing surface. This active matrix screen is crystal clear for reading. Mickey regards it is a real beauty ... his first ever laptop computer. Fox thinks it's a dog. He told Mickey he will replace it whenever Mickey's user skills advance enough to realize the limitations of the machine. Fox says that Apple already has upgrades planned and that there are newer machines in the mix that will soon be available for a steady stream of continuous releases.

As soon as Mickey whips out his laptop and turns it on, an older woman sitting next to him asks him, "What is that thing? Is it a computer? It looks pretty small to be a computer."

"Yes it's a computer. And it's fabulous. I can type all my business notes and do all my calculations on it. And it only weighs 17 pounds!"

"How does it work?" The older woman appears to be in her late sixties, maybe even older. She's wearing a good bit of make-up to hide her wrinkles but looks to be cultured and well kept. She smiles easily and she speaks as though nothing ever bothers her.

"I'm not sure how it *works* ... I just know what I can *do* with it. It has word processing software and spreadsheet software preloaded inside of it, so I can simply turn it on and I'm ready to go."

"Don't you have to plug it in somewhere?"

"After a while, yes you have to plug it in to recharge the battery. It has a lead-acid battery that lasts for about ten hours between charges."

Mickey retrieves an earlier paper that he was working on and shows the older woman how the saved document begins painting the nearly ten inch matrix screen."

"Wow that's rather ingenious. I wish they had these things in my day. I used to type rough drafts myself, but after a while my assistant used these newer computers and word processing thing-a-ma-jigs, and she did most of my typing for me. But then again I retired a long time ago."

Mickey has neither the interest nor the inclination to ask what she means by "a long time ago." So he simply smiles and waits until she turns

## March 1991

her attention to the window. Then he goes back to working on his document. However he does find it ironic how this older woman thinks of him as being technically savvy. He knows that he can't come close to Fox's computer acumen. Nor does he have the depth of IT understanding that Simone Muirchant possesses. Mickey is determined to step up his game in that regard because he believes that IT skills will be extremely important for the future of his other children, Cody, Noah and Jessica, who are seven, six and three respectively. Before too long he stops working and orders his first martini. Not much later he nods off to sleep.

∞∞∞

Simone Muirchant is traveling back to New York from her rebuilt California residence. Her home in the Marina District of San Francisco suffered major structural damage in the Loma Prieta Earthquake sixteen months earlier. The reconstruction has been significant – essentially a rebuild in place. Simone is happy that this particular chapter of her life is now behind her. Her ex-husband, Frank Babcock suffered a heart attack during the earthquake, but he recovered and moved on with his life. She has barely spoken to him since shortly after he left the hospital following the quake. Conveniently Babcock did provide funding for Simone's new start-up data-storage company. However Simone doubts that Babcock truly understands his investment. She knows that he is merely demonstrating gratitude for her part in saving his life following the tremor. But throughout the financing arrangement Simone never worked directly with her ex-husband. Babcock simply made certain that details were taken care of appropriately.

Simone has not heard from Mickey Johnson either since the earthquake. However that is about to change.

∞∞∞

Simone sees Mickey first. She has just retrieved her bag at turntable 7A for the flights from San Francisco. Mickey's flight from Atlanta is delivering its bags to turntable 8A directly adjacent to those from her transcontinental flight.

"Mickey! Mickey! ... Crazy seeing you here! How are you?" She walks over to where he is waiting and rather deliberately but enthusiastically kisses him on the cheek.

"Hi Simone. Not so crazy for me. Remember, I still live on Long Island. What brings you back this way?"

## Techies, Trials & Terrorists

Mickey's response is a bit flip and much too casual, but he never knows exactly how to respond to seeing Simone. She is the idiomatic embodiment of someone who always "turns up like a bad penny."

∞∞∞

Mickey Johnson and Simone Muirchant have one enduring common interest. Mickey has come to realize that he is never going to be able to purge Simone from his personal life. He has resolved to put up with their inevitable but intermittent crossing of paths. Simone has been an intricate part of his life since 1965. When Mickey was a 17 year old high school student, the sultry Simone had been his seductress. She had introduced him to the ways of the world. Now, she is his shackle, someone who binds him to the world of the past, even as he hopes to explore the vibrant new world of the future.

∞∞∞

"I'm only in town tonight. Then I'm driving over to New Jersey to see about some additional data storage real estate. After that I'm heading to Baltimore to see Fox and Evelyn. Do you believe it? Fox will be twenty-five on Friday. Where does time go?"

And so there it is – the major ongoing connector of their lives – their son, Fox Babcock.

∞∞∞

Mickey wants to get his bags quickly and leave. He doesn't want to get into a prolonged discussion with Simone. However that option apparently is not in the cards. Simone already has her one suitcase. It is an interesting piece of luggage in that it has two wheels built into the bottom of the suitcase and a short collapsible handle that sticks out of the top of the valise. Mickey has seen several of these popping up in airports over the last couple of years. Mostly they are being used by stewardesses and female passengers. Mickey wonders why it took so long to invent this kind of travel luggage and why it is only being used by women. He just read an article in an airplane magazine that said these bags – called "rollaboards" – were designed by an airline pilot in 1987. He assumes that the pilot was a man.

∞∞∞

"Twenty-five years old but I've only known him for about 10 of those years. He's a great kid. I don't know why you ..." Mickey stops himself. This is *definitely not* what he wants to do – right here, right now. He doesn't want to discuss his son, with his son's mother, in the baggage retrieval area of La

## March 1991

Guardia Airport. Painfully however, Mickey's one checked bag has not yet come down the conveyor belt, and Simone stands next to him in high heels with her rollaboard suitcase jauntily angled on its hind wheels and leaning almost weightlessly against her hip. As Mickey stands awaiting his checked bag and clutching his laptop, he realizes that Simone looks terrific especially considering she has just taken a long flight. But the Simone dilemma has *never* been about how she looks. Then again, maybe it *always* has been about how she looks. That's how it all started for Mickey, 26 years earlier.

∞∞∞

"I'm worried about Fox, Mickey. This is the second time that he and Evelyn have postponed their wedding. They've been engaged for a year and a half, and they still don't have a date scheduled. Do you know if they are having problems?"

"No, I don't think so Simone. Why do you ask?"

"Call it a mother's intuition. That's all. I thought that maybe you know something that I don't. They were supposed to be married in July and now they've moved the date back indefinitely. I don't hear from Fox as much as I used to. While I was in India, I got a letter from him almost every week."

"That's a long time ago. Fox was in high school then. Right?"

"Yes, but what does that have to do with it?"

Mickey is now wondering how he has allowed himself to be drawn into this conversation. Fox is amazingly well adjusted considering the fact that neither of his biological parents were around much during his formative childhood years.

"Simone, I don't want to be confrontational." He hesitates and then adds, "But don't you think that Fox's '90's approach to the marriage commitment is more thoughtful than your own might have been in the 60's? He's not ready to rush into anything. From what he says, Evelyn is cool with that also. I think that these are two intelligent kids ... future physicians, mind you ... who know what they want and when they want it. Right now they both have additional things on their plates."

There is still no sign of Mickey's baggage being released. There are now fewer bags coming down the ramp but Simone seems in no hurry to leave him.

"Still, don't you think it's strange that they both have their own places? They haven't even moved in with each other yet and they only live a few blocks apart."

## *Techies, Trials & Terrorists*

Mickey senses that the conversation is growing even more bizarre. When Simone was engaged to Frank Babcock back in 1965, not only was she not living with him, she was also sleeping with another man ... namely himself. And ... oh yeah ... there was also the matter of Simone sleeping with Mickey's father, Wayne Johnson. Many years and numerous skirmishes and struggles have come and gone between the Babcocks and the Johnsons since then, so Simone's current concerns sound nothing short of eccentric.

∞∞∞

"No I don't think it's strange at all. Maybe they both want some personal space."

"Then why get married at all?"

"Look Simone, I have no idea how to answer that. All I can tell you is that when they stayed at my house over the Christmas holidays, they seemed quite content and involved in each other's lives. They were happy. They did everything together the whole time they were on Long Island. Even when Fox went out to see his old Shenandoah buddies, he took Evelyn with him."

∞∞∞

Simone Muirchant has gone back to using her maiden name. Her legal name had been Simone Babcock since her first marriage to Frank Babcock in 1965. She never changed her name throughout her divorce and remarriage to the billionaire. She didn't even change it after her second divorce. However when she returned to the United States after spending nearly a year and a half in meditation and missionary work in India, she tried to get by only using her first name – Simone. Effectively she was "Simone" to everyone, although technically she had still never legally altered her name in any way. Occasionally she had been compelled to sign her name as Simone Babcock on certain official documents that required her full lawful name. Then in early 1990 she finally filed the paperwork in court to reembrace her maiden name of Simone Muirchant. Recently, she had completed her MBA at Berkeley after taking courses intermittently since she first returned to California in 1985. Her diploma was issued in the name of Simone Muirchant.

None of this took into consideration the fact that for eighteen months when she was on her spiritual quest in India, she used the name 'Sangmu,' which was her Buddhist Dharma name, given to her by one of her spiritual advisors.

## March 1991

*Try as she might to get away with using only her given name, the 49 year old was back to using the full name – Simone Muirchant – she had used for the first 24 years of her life.*

∞∞∞

"Well I'm glad to hear that you think everything is alright. I'll let you know what I think after I see him next week." Simone implies that their chance encounter in the baggage area might possibly be rebuilt into a more lasting discourse. But before Mickey offers an agreement or rebuttal, Simone quickly changes the topic while Mickey woefully waits for his checked bag.

"Well at least we can be happy about the fact that the foolish war in Iraq has come to a quick conclusion. I was quite worried there for a while that Bush was planning on occupying Iraq and that we would end up with a Vietnam-like mess all over again."

Mickey goes for the bait.

"You have to admit, Bush did it the right way. He simply used overwhelming force. Once Suddam refused to yield, he simply obliterated his military. After the aerial assault, the ground fighting was over in three days. One hundred hours of ground fighting and Iraq folded like a cheap suit. Hussein is now out of Kuwait and we have a permanent cease-fire."

∞∞∞

*War had always been an issue between the two ex-lovers since 1965. That was when 23 year old Simone seduced the nearly 18 year old Mickey and tried to dissuade him from fighting with the Marine Corps in Vietnam. There were numerous sexual escapades during the final three months of Mickey's high school years at Shenandoah High School in Garden City. Simone was an assistant to Father Thomas Dunham the Jesuit priest, who at the time served as the president of the all-male school. Most of their torrid trysts took place a few miles away in the sweaty heat of Simone's Mineola apartment. Even a quarter of a century later there was some residual warmth from the passionate ardor and sizzling intensity of those moments, which neither of them could ever fully expunge. However these were even more important moments to Simone. She often felt that those few months were some of the most exciting days of her life.*

∞∞∞

"The problem with war … any war… is that people die needlessly. The war might have been short in duration but that 'overwhelming force'

## Techies, Trials & Terrorists

you mention, simply killed a lot more people a lot faster. Iraq also claims that the US bombed civilian targets. They say that the civilian victims are almost equal to military casualties."

"Less than 150 Americans were killed. And we don't seem to know the total number of Iraqi soldiers yet, but I've heard that it could be almost 25,000."

"They're still human beings, Mickey. That's the bottom line. It's an awful lot of carnage and bloodshed."

"You seem to forget; we didn't start the war. Americans don't *start* wars we *finish* them."

"Very few people died when Iraq took over Kuwait. It was more of a political boundary shift – one that the US should never have contested. A few months later thousands upon thousands of human beings died. I've heard that the number of dead Iraq citizens could be much higher than your number, by the way."

"Well we should both be glad ... that at least now ... it's over."

Mickey is looking for an escape route from this conversation and he finally sees it coming. The last three bags from Atlanta are coming down the ramp and one of them is his. He grabs his luggage bag at the bottom of the ramp even before it hits the rubber rimmed sidewall of the baggage carrousel. It is a powerful left-handed grab with support from a right arm that is still partially debilitated from a Vietnam War injury.

"Nice talking to you, Simone. I've got to run." He starts to walk away. Then in an attempt to be friendlier he turns back toward Simone and endeavors to kiss her goodbye – on the cheek. His approach, is an awkward one. Simone turns her face at the last second and the kiss lands on her lips. The kiss and her lips are invitingly soft. It lasts a full second and is way more intimate than Mickey had planned. He isn't quite sure who is kissing whom.

Mickey turns around and walks toward the door without saying another word and without looking back. Simone watches every step Mickey takes until he reaches the doorway. She is ready to leave also but she simply watches and remembers. She knows who owns the kiss. Mickey Johnson, she fathoms is the sexiest man she has ever met, even if he is pretty thick-headed about war.

∞∞∞

# IV

## March 1991

Syd turns, looks at her husband and says, "She's really not such a bad person, Mickey."

"I never said she was a bad person. I think that she has never understood what her life is all about. She's a person who adopts one cause after another without any rhyme or reason."

"Can you really say that? It's been a long since you first met Simone. And there were many years when you didn't even talk to her. So whenever she suddenly reappears, how would you know what makes her tick?"

Sydney "Syd" Johnson knows that she is meandering into a field of emotional landmines. Throughout her nine and a half year marriage to Mickey Johnson, she has avoided most personal discussions regarding Simone. And above all, she has eluded conversing about Mickey's private feelings toward Simone.

They had cleared all of the important details before they were married. There are no past events in Mickey's relationship with Simone that Syd does not know about. However in the ensuing years they have tried to keep the emotional impact in check. During the few times that Syd has met Simone she has taken a liking to her. Syd admires Simone's business acumen and feels a little sympathy and compassion for her convoluted personal life.

∞∞∞

"I never said I hated the woman. I simply said that she's been nothing but trouble for me throughout my life. I don't think of her as a bad person as much as I think of Simone as a bad person for me. Besides why are you sticking up for her? I don't get it."

"I'm not sticking up for her. I just feel a little sorry for her that's all. You must realize that she's still madly in love with you."

Syd has been parked outside of the airline terminal while Mickey was waiting for his bag and conversing with Simone. Syd is the one person in his life who keeps him grounded and focused on the important things such as marriage and family.

"That's crazy, Syd. I don't think that Simone is capable of love. I doubt that she ever has been capable of loving anyone. But don't get me started on her. Remember there are no secrets on this topic between you and me. So why go back over this turf now?"

"I don't want you to be angry. I just think it might help if you understood Simone a little better. Then you'd be able to get a sounder grip on chance meetings like the one this evening. Remember Mickey, Simone is the mother of one of your children. Shouldn't that help you get past some of your difficulties with her?"

"Well right now, my difficulty comes with understanding you. Why are you so reluctant to criticize Simone?"

"Because I also love you that's why."

"That makes no sense, Syd. If you love me, I would think that you would dislike Simone. I would guess that most women might even be a little jealous."

"I hope you realize by now that I am not like most women, Mickey." She offers him a sincere big smile as she speaks and Mickey senses that she might be ready to issue one of her characteristic multi-tiered rippled laughs.

"Alright, I certainly agree that you aren't like most women ... at least on most topics. But how can you sympathize with Simone on this topic?"

"Because I realize that she loves you. She probably always has loved you."

"How would you know that?

"Trust me, women just know these things. We can tell."

"So first you say you're not like every woman ... but now you are?" That is enough to get Syd's rippling high pitched laugh started. She is an extremely self-confident woman and is never afraid to issue a snicker of self-deprecation.

## March 1991

"Of course ... I'm a woman ... I get to have it both ways. That's my prerogative."

Mickey immediately relaxes and allows a slight chortle of his own.

Syd's laughing begins to abate but she still speaks through her beautiful wide smile. "I understand that feeling because I love you too. The good news for me ... I guess... is that I know you love me and I know that whatever affectionate feelings you might have had for Simone are buried in the distant past. Therefore I can be sympathetic with her for her loss."

Mickey is still smiling almost against his will when he utters his one word rejoinder on the whole topic. "Women!?!"

They leave La Guardia Airport and arrive back at their Mill Neck home in less than 45 minutes. It has been a long day for Mickey. He feels like it's close to midnight and it isn't even 8 PM yet. As he walks in the door he is greeted by his daughter, Jessica, and by Kathy McDonough, Mickey's mother-in-law by his first wife.

∞∞∞

*Don and Kathy McDonough were the parents of Mickey's first wife Barbara. For many years they had lived across the island on the south shore in Rockville Center. But that had recently changed. In light of the fact that Barbara had been their only daughter and had died childless, the McDonough's had enthusiastically embraced Mickey and Syd's children as though they were their own grandchildren. It was one of the warmer liaisons among the many unusual family relationships in Mickey's life.*

*However when Don McDonough died suddenly the previous year, Mickey and Syd made an important decision. They had been searching for a good nanny for quite some time but in light of the fact that Syd was not working outside of the home, the need was not a dire one. Instead they asked Kathy McDonough if she would like to come live with them. After Don died Kathy had no other relatives living on Long Island. And although she had numerous south shore friends, she jumped at the opportunity to spend more time with her semi-adopted grandchildren. Four months after the funeral she moved into a guest room in Mickey's house. Syd went out of her way to make Kathy feel comfortable and from the outset it was a harmonious relationship all the way around.*

∞∞∞

## *Techies, Trials & Terrorists*

Ray and Violet Spataro were Syd Johnson's parents. They had lived in many different venues throughout the world but had lived in Missouri, an hour outside of St Louis since Ray's retirement. The Spataros had frequently visited Mickey and Syd on Long Island for various holidays. They loved seeing their grandchildren, and they were contemplating moving east when Ray had a sudden heart attack just this past November. Ray died about seven months after Don McDonough had suffered the same fate. So now Violet Spataro was also living at the Johnsons' home. Accordingly, Mickey was now living with his wife, three children and two mothers-in-law. His buddy Jack Birdsong told him that he would be nominating him for sainthood. To make matters even more intriguing, Kathy McDonough was Irish-American and Violet Spataro was African-American.

∞∞∞

The plan for the evening called for Kathy and Violet to watch the Johnson children while Syd picked Mickey up from the airport.

"How was your trip, Mickey?" Kathy asks.

"It was short and it was long. Short because I made it down and back in four days and long because I feel like I was away for two weeks. But we got the branch review done thoroughly, had dinner with a few key customers and appointed a new branch manager. All in all, it was a successful trip."

"I'm glad to hear that." However Kathy would not have been glad to hear about Mickey's chance encounter with Simone Muirchant. Neither Mickey nor Syd brings it up.

∞∞∞

It hadn't always been smooth sailing for Mickey and the McDonoughs. Barbara McDonough died in February of 1973 from metastasized melanoma. In the years following their shared loss, the McDonoughs encouraged their son-in-law to date other women and hoped at some point that Mickey would re-marry. But over time they drifted apart slightly. Mickey was a single man and his in-laws didn't want to intrude on his lifestyle. When Mickey became engaged to Syd the McDonoughs were happy for him. They were invited to the wedding but gracefully declined the invite – again wanting to avoid the possibility of being a source of any discomfort for Mickey with his new wife and in-laws.

When Mickey and Syd began to have children, the McDonoughs were delighted. They began to see more of the Johnsons and were readily accepted

## March 1991

as "part of the family" by Syd Johnson and by her parents. However the relationship took a major hit when the McDonoughs learned that Fox Babcock was actually Mickey Johnson's son. This in essence meant that Mickey had cheated on their daughter back when they were dating in high school. The McDonoughs eventually forgave Mickey but they looked upon Simone Muirchant as nothing short of a witch, who had poisoned some fond memories. Kathy McDonough's feelings on the topic hadn't changed since the passing of her husband. She loved Syd and she loved Mickey. But she despised Simone Muirchant, even though she had never met the woman.

∞∞∞

Mickey picks up his three year old daughter, Jessica and kisses her.

"Did you miss Daddy?"

Jessica nods her head up and down and then wraps both her arms around her father's neck in a tight hug. Mickey puts his daughter down and Syd takes Jessica by the hand.

"So where are the boys?"

"They're back in the family room with Violet. I shut the door so the drums won't drive us all crazy. Frankly, I think Violet knows how to handle the boys better than I do."

"Nonsense Kathy. You both are saviors for Mickey and me. We don't know what we'd do without you two." Syd is overstating the situation to make Kathy comfortable. In reality they are all still adjusting to the relatively new living arrangements.

∞∞∞

Mickey leaves Syd, Kathy and Jessica and walks straight to the family room at the rear of the house. He is greeted by the sounds of his oldest son Cody tapping lightly on his drum set while Noah sits listening to his boom box. MC Hammer is rapping "U Can't Touch This," while Noah lies on the floor even though the two sofas are unoccupied. Meanwhile Violet sits in one of the four arm chairs in the spacious family room. She tries to watch the news on TV over the general hubbub. The scene is incongruous but tranquil in its own way.

Noah bounces up from the floor the moment his father enters the room. But his brother Cody, Noah's senior by eleven months, just keeps tapping away on his drums, as though he's looking for some secret rhythmic sound. He isn't loud but he is certainly focused. The Irish twins are more into rap music than they are into anything more mainline, but at the tender age of seven, it's difficult to identify anything more than simple enthusiasm from Cody's drumming.

"Grandma said that Grandpa used to play the drums."

"See that Cody. You knew something that I didn't know." He turns to Violet. "Is that right, Mom?" Adding to the general household confusion, Mickey calls both of his mothers-in-law "Mom." However Syd refers to her own mother as "Mom" while calling Kathy McDonough "Kathy."

"That's right. Ray played drums with a few of his buddies for about five years when they were all stationed in Germany in the 60's. But they did a lot of oldies stuff ... the pre-Beatles stuff, a lot of Rock and Roll. You know, Elvis, Buddy Holly, Chuck Berry ... that kind of stuff."

"See, I didn't know that. I knew he loved his music and I think I remember him saying something about a band in the army, but I never remember him saying he was a drummer."

"Well, that's Ray. He never talked much about himself."

"Did you like his music?"

"It was pretty good, I think. But it wasn't what I grew up with. When I was a child, all I knew was gospel music. We all sang when we went to church, and we sang the same songs when we went home. That was all before I met Ray, of course."

∞∞∞

Violet Spataro was an African American, a descendant of an American slave. Her deceased husband, Ray Spataro, was a white skinned Italian American and a career army officer. Both of their children, Sydney Johnson and Jermaine Spataro, exhibited mixed racial physical attributes. However all three of their grandchildren were white skinned and ethnically unperturbed at this point in their lives.

∞∞∞

"Well then I guess we can say for sure that the kids get their musical inclination from their mother's side of the family." Mickey reflects with a smile. "I can't sing or play a note."

Violet laughs in a sincere but hearty manner. "I think your children have many gifts from both sides of their family, and I ain't talking 'bout no drums and no boom box neither."

## March 1991

Mickey is amused by his mother-in-law's use of a double negative – or what actually amounts to a triple negative. Violet Spataro is a college educated woman, capable of speaking the King's English, American English or African-American English, depending upon whatever emphasis she wants to exert. Not only is Violet well-educated, she is also quite intelligent and has an affinity for controversial discussions with people she trusts. Violet and Mickey have recently discussed the very topic that is now making him smile. It is something that Violet refers to as "Ebonics."

Violet characterizes Ebonics as African-American vernacular English. She claims that her pronunciation and grammar are, by definition, correct, whenever she is using *that* language. Violet also contends that it is pure racist hypocrisy for someone speaking the King's English to criticize someone speaking in Ebonics. She asserts that these critics wouldn't be so bold as to disparage someone speaking in French or Spanish. If nothing else it makes Mickey think. It makes Mickey wonder.

∞∞∞

Within a few seconds, Syd, Kathy and Jessica also wander back into the family room.

"Please turn that down, Noah." It is a concession on Syd's part to her husband so that he won't have to make the request personally. The single loudest noise of the cacophony in the room is Noah's boom box. Noah quickly complies. Cody also stops tapping his drums.

Mickey had contended that the drums and the boom box were not age appropriate Christmas gifts for their sons but Syd had prevailed. Subsequently the boys became more passionate about their music over the ensuing winter months. However Mickey's tolerance for the loud music is more limited than that of the other household members. He is looking forward to the warmer weather when he hopes that Little League baseball will displace rap music as his sons' preferred pastime.

Mickey walks over closer to Violet. She still has her attention partially deflected to the news on TV while her grandchildren are amused with their musical devices. They both watch as the news anchor updates the latest news from across the country. In Los Angeles an emerging story over the last couple of days involves local protests over the beating of a black man named Rodney King by police officers. King has resisted arrest by the police. However video evidence also demonstrates that the LAPD has clearly used excessive force.

## *Techies, Trials & Terrorists*

"The problem is that the cops don't understand that this issue is not going to die out. It is only going to get worse once the political activists start riling up the local folks out there." Violet has lapsed back into the King's English. She is clearly angered by the television coverage of the crime but she is also rational in her assessment of what probably occurred.

"This man Rodney King was driving over 100 miles an hour through a residential area, so he's not a saint. But they'll probably make him out to be a martyr. This is the kind of thing that keeps our country divided. Do you think these cops would have beaten a white man so maliciously?"

Violet's question is meant to be rhetorical, but Mickey decides to tackle the question anyway.

"My guess is that these cops were probably pretty pissed off at having to chase this guy and then they might have been afraid simply because they were in a poor black neighborhood. None of that is meant to condone anything that happened. And to answer your question no I don't think they would have beaten him so severely if he had been white. It's atrocious."

Even as he gives this answer, he vividly recognizes the irony of the fact that his own father, a New York City cop died from a mugging at the hands of a recently paroled black criminal ten years earlier. The other adults in the room, are silently aware of the image that is probably in Mickey's mind also. In an uncharacteristically assertive manner, Kathy McDonough, grabs the TV remote and changes the channel.

"Let's see if we can find something more positive to watch."

No one argues with her, but it is easy to see that Mickey's two mothers-in-law are not on the same page.

∞∞∞

# V

## March 1991

Nicole Silver arrives back at the Babcock townhouse at 11:15 PM. She is obviously intoxicated. Burke Finnegan is obviously irate.

∞∞∞

Nicole had told Burke Finnegan that she would return home before 5 PM. This was important to Finnegan because he had his annual St Patrick's Day dinner with several other former police officer buddies scheduled for 7:30.PM. Finnegan was now infuriated that he was alone with Jedidiah Babcock on an evening when both Margot Silver and Frank Babcock, the other two townhouse residents, were both out of the city. However at least Margot was due to return before midnight.

∞∞∞

"*Shorry* I'm a teeny weeny bit late. I don't know what got into me." Nicole Silver slurs her words. She allows an alcohol induced grin to cross her face. She is wearing high heels and having a difficult time standing in them. Silver was raised as a Jew. However, she is wearing a Kelly green leather skirt and a white blouse trimmed in green. She's also wearing a large button that says "Kiss me I'm Irish." It is slightly askew on her blouse.

Finnegan is totally incensed. Silver hadn't bothered to call him and he was legitimately worried about her before she walked in the door sloshed. When he watches her start her little giggling routine he grows even more furious. Just as his temperature begins to boil over, Silver trips and nearly falls hard against a coffee table in the second floor of the town house. Finnegan catches her face in his hand, as Silver's knees hit the floor. He stops her forehead about an inch from the table. She looks up and then laughs in his face. He pushes her head back so that she is now sitting back on her thighs with her face still looking up mockingly at his face. Then she suddenly reaches out and grabs at his crotch.

"*Lesh shee* what you've got, *Frrinnegan*." Her intentions are unmistakable despite her slurred words and Finnegan pushes her away. However, Silver thrusts tightly toward her target to the point where Finnegan has little choice but to slap her across the face in order to protect his genitalia. Silver goes down briefly but bounces back up. Again she lunges at Finnegan's crotch, this time with both of her hands. In defense Finnegan bends down and grasps Silver by the wrists. In the process he ends up sitting on the same coffee table that Silver nearly hit with her face seconds before. Now he is gripping both of her wrists in both of his fists while she wiggles in an attempt to get free.

"You're an inconsiderate pretentious little bitch! You know that?" Burke Finnegan is convulsing. He has had enough. This bantam-weight slut is not going to treat him like her personal servant any longer.

While Finnegan is still holding her down by her wrists, Silver rolls her eyes up at him and says, "Fuck you, Burke." Then she spits at Finnegan but is barely able to get her saliva past her own chin. Regardless, this sets Finnegan off completely. He snatches her off the floor until she straddles his body while he was still sitting on the coffee table.

Finnegan doesn't wait for her to spit again. He simply uses the strength of his own physical anger to flip her body over so that she is face down with her head and feet near the floor and her middle section across his lap. One of her high heels falls off in the process. He proceeds to yank her skirt up over her hips. He also jerks her hose and panties down below her knees. Silver offers more refutation with a tirade of expletives than she does with any physical resistance. The first hard smack of Finnegan's open hand against Silver's bare ass, causes the slight young mother to spasm in pain. She recoils with a hard head jerk and a slight knee lift, as her other heel falls to the floor. But Finnegan's raw power continues to restrain the young woman's overall escape attempt. The second smack is harder and the third smash in quick succession brings about tears of pain to replace her earlier outburst of invectives.

## March, 1991

Silver is forced to endure a thorough spanking of nearly a dozen open handed but severe smacks, until her rear end is beet red in color and nearly numb with pain. She is sobbing miserably in defeated embarrassment, when her sister enters the townhouse from the stairs leading up from the curbside walkway.

Margot is totally dumfounded. She hears her sister's yelping and crying the moment she passes into the parlor area just past the foyer threshold at the top of the outside stairway. The anguished sobbing continues as Margot hustles through the short foyer/parlor and onto the second floor. She isn't sure what she will find. However the scene she stumbles upon shocks her into disbelief. She witnesses the last two blows that complete her sister's spanking and then watches as Burke Finnegan pushes Nicole Silver down off his lap and onto her knees on the floor. Margot watches in stunned disbelief as her sister stands up and yanks her underwear back into an upright position and then pushes her skirt back down.

"What is going …?"

"He tried to rape me." Nicole Silver sounds more embarrassed than threatened as she makes the hollow-sounding accusation.

"That's not true at all and you know it." Finnegan snaps back in firm rebuttal.

Margot glances at her sister and quickly determines that she is obviously quite intoxicated. Her hair is totally disheveled and her make-up is a runny mess across her face as she tries to wipe away her tears of agony and embarrassment. Also Margot didn't expect to find Finnegan still at the townhouse, and she immediately wonders who is watching Jedidiah. The last concern is quickly answered by the security agent.

"Your slutty sister just arrived home about 15 minutes ago and attempted to seduce me … correct that … she grabbed at my dick. She's the one who sexually assaulted me."

Burke Finnegan is fuming mad. He is spitting out his words, while both women listen in stunned silence. "She was supposed to relieve me almost seven hours ago. I put Jedidiah to bed at 8 PM. He's been sleeping upstairs since. I'm leaving now."

"What about Jedd?"

"You're *his* aunt and you're *her* sister" He looks disgustedly over at Nicole Silver who has now slumped into an arm chair in chagrinned discomfort. "I trust you will figure something out." Then he adds, "And I'll call Frank to tell him I'm not returning." Then he points at the older sister without looking at her again and adds. "I don't ever want to see that worthless pig again."

Before Margot could respond Burke Finnegan walks through the foyer/parlor and the front door and then down the exterior stairway. Within 30 seconds he is gone.

Back on the second floor, Margot looks at her older sister in dismay. It isn't as though Margot is unaware of Nicole's edgy lifestyle, but she now looks at her sister in a new light. Nicole doesn't appear to be at all concerned about Jedidiah who is hopefully still sleeping comfortably on the fourth floor.

"What the hell happened here, Nicole? What did you do to Burke to get him so crazed? It's hard to believe he got as mad as he did. Is there some kind of sexual perversion between you two that I don't know about?"

"So why is it *my* fault? I thought you were *my* sister. You should be on *my* side." The older sister begins to gather her wits about her and attempts to straighten her hair with her hands, and then she begins running her hands across her skirt and blouse in a primitive attempt to return her apparel to some form of dignity.

"Should I call the police? 911? Should I call Frank?"

"Frank's in Atlanta. He can't help, anyway. The cops won't do anything either. They'll just get their jollies out of making a report." Even as Nicole spoke her sister could see that she was thoroughly drunk.

"You're sloshed, Nicole. Go to bed."

Nicole takes out a wide toothed comb and attempts some sort of additional grooming that lasts less than five seconds before she stuffs the comb back into her pocketbook. Then she puts her feet back into her heels and walks towards the foyer and front door. With her back to the main room Nicole hears Margot yell after her, "And who's supposed to take care of Jedidiah?" The next sound is the slamming of the front door.

∞∞∞

It is still St Patrick's Day, although March 18$^{th}$ is minutes away. Nicole Silver decides to return to the party she left an hour earlier. She stands out on Madison Avenue trying to catch a cab, without much success. She sees another woman hailing a cab in front of her. Nicole steps further into the street in order to draw the attention of potential taxis. Silver is oblivious to the speeding black Cadillac limousine that is racing up Madison Avenue circling past a slowing cab near 53$^{rd}$ street. She steps right into the path of the Cadillac and is hit flush by the car. Her body is slammed back into a row

## *March, 1991*

of newspaper boxes and a telephone booth on the corner and her head hits the curb hard. The Cadillac doesn't stop after it hits her. Instead it continues north on Madison Avenue and speeds away.

∞∞∞

# VI

## April 1991

It is a beautiful Saturday morning and Syd Johnson is out shopping for clothes for her two young sons. The boys are with her. Mickey's two mothers-in-law are also out for the day, and his daughter, Jessica, is napping in an upstairs bedroom. Jack Birdsong is visiting.

"Don't you find it more than a little bit strange that Frank Babcock's enemies always die early deaths and he never gets pinched?"

"I'm not sure how I should answer that, Jack."

"Come on Mickey. Why are you always so ambiguous about that asshole? He's as dangerous as they come. He's a murderer. He killed your own father."

"We don't know that for sure. All we know is that he wasn't in town when my father died. The cops have thoroughly investigated Dad's death and have continuously said it was a random mugging. No one has ever implicated Babcock in any way other than to say he had a motive. And I don't want to rehash that right now. That was nearly eleven years ago."

"Alright, then there was the murder of the two degenerates that molested Babcock's daughter. They were found beaten to death in the Long Island Sound, not far from the old *Babcock Manor and Gardens.*"

"That was *also* nearly ten years ago, and Babcock was in Boston at the time. Besides those degenerates probably had more than a few people who wanted to see them dead. They got what they deserved."

"Maybe so. And these other murders might be ten years old, but this is something brand new. Now you have the mother of Babcock's child being

## April 1991

killed by a hit and run driver and the cops are questioning Babcock's security guy. Rumor has it, by the way, that the victim's sister walked in on the security guy as he was flogging Babcock's old lady."

"I wouldn't characterize Nicole Silver as Babcock's *old* lady. The newspapers said that she was only twenty-nine years old. Babcock has got to be in his mid-fifties."

"Fifty-six to be exact. That was in the newspapers also."

"So how do you know this security guy they're questioning was screwing Silver?"

"I didn't say he was 'fucking' her. I said he was 'flogging' her."

"Huh? What are you talking about Jack? This guy was beating her?"

∞∞∞

*Jack Birdsong and Mickey Johnson were lifelong friends. They went to Shenandoah High School together and they also served together in the Marine Corps during the Vietnam War. Birdsong had spent four years as a POW in a Vietnamese prison before his release in 1973, while Mickey had returned to Long Island in 1969 after a three year tour in Southeast Asia.*

*Later, Birdsong and Mickey each earned their college degree by taking night courses at Hofstra University. After their respective graduations, Mickey pursued a highly successful career in the commodity markets in NYC.*

*Meanwhile Birdsong worked as an investigator for the Defense Intelligence Agency before leaving government service to form his own investigative agency. Birdsong had developed a strong network of law enforcement and government intelligence professionals as part of his business assets. However, by far, his closest friend in life was Mickey Johnson. Their friendship was unshakeable. They were more like brothers than friends.*

∞∞∞

"Well, Mickey, here's what I'm hearing. Babcock never wanted to marry Nicole Silver. He just wanted her to have his kid. The baby, Jedidiah Babcock, was born last March."

"Yeah. I'm aware of that much. He was born on March 15$^{th}$, twenty-four years to the day after Fox was born."

"Right, we've discussed that before. So stay with me on this. Apparently Silver and Babcock have been haggling over some kind of custody agreement with respect to their kid."

"I thought that they were going to get married. Why would they need a custody agreement?"

"You may have thought they were going to get married and Silver may have thought that also, but Babcock apparently had no such interest. Although he probably led her along a bit. Technically, this custody covenant was being drawn up as part of a prenuptial agreement."

"So where does the security guy come into play ... the guy who was supposedly *'flogging'* Silver?"

"Well this whole thing is a long story. So I want to make sure you have the time to hear me out. I also have a few written notes that I've taken from conversations with my cop buddies and various sources, so I'll need to refer to these notes."

As he says this Birdsong pulls a lined yellow pad out of his briefcase. The two men are sitting in the study on the first floor of Mickey Johnson's expansive Mill Neck home. They have yet to open their first beer of the afternoon.

"I'm not in any hurry, Jack. Just tell me what you know."

"Alright let's start with the security guy. He's a retired cop and has worked for Babcock for a couple of years. His name is Burke Finnegan and he owns his own agency and employs other ex-cops part time. He is well liked and well respected within the NYPD. His largest client by far is Frank Babcock, although my sources say that he still works for Babcock. Finnegan is being represented by a Harley, Webster and Quill. This is the same firm that has represented Frank Babcock in the past, so the assumption is that Babcock is footing the bill. If Babcock is footing the bill he either *believes* that Finnegan *didn't* kill his girlfriend. Or he *knows* that Finnegan *did* kill his girlfriend. Either way, Finnegan isn't saying anything, probably because Babcock wants it that way."

"So what's the story between this guy Finnegan and Nicole Silver."

"No one knows for sure. Most of the guys say that Finnegan hated Silver's guts, but now some of them are having their doubts."

"Why is that?"

"Well, on the night that Silver died, she had been out at an upper eastside St Paddy's Day shindig with some young jet-set party animals. Ironically half of them are Jews. Silver is a Jew also by the way." He lets that much sink in and then continues. "Anyway, a female friend of hers who was at the party, drops her off in front of her townhouse a little after 11 PM. For

44

## April 1991

one reason or another Silver leaves the Babcock townhouse less than an hour later and is run down by a black Cadillac while she is trying to hail a cab. It is almost exactly midnight when the hit and run takes place."

"Was she heading back to the party?"

"No one seems to know much about that. But it's not as important as what happened in between 11 and 12 PM. That's where this all gets very interesting."

"So tell me what happened."

"It's all pretty fucked-up actually. Most of what I've been told hasn't been in the papers or anything. But trust me, it's not just cop talk. Cops sometimes make stuff up and glamorize things that aren't important just for the sake of making good stories. But this is serious shit. They aren't screwing with this information at all, as far as I can tell."

"Alright Jack, so tell me what they *think* happened in between."

"The cops have one eye-witness to some of this and are trying to piece together other facts along the way. So this broad, Nicole Silver has a younger sister. Her name is Margot ... Margot Silver. Apparently Margot is also living at Babcock's townhouse and has been living there for many months ... anyway, she helps out with watching after the baby, Jedidiah, or at least that's the story for now. The guys downtown think she's a straight shooter. They put a lot of credibility in what she has to say."

"So what is she saying?"

"Margot says that Finnegan hated her sister, Nicole. But ... now get this ... when Margot comes home on the night of the 17th, she finds Nicole bare-assed over Finnegan's lap and the guy is really spanking her! At first she thinks it's something kinky, you know, some sort of sadomasochistic sex-thing."

"Well, was it?"

"Who knows? Margot is telling the police that they both bolted out of there moments later and that Finnegan was super pissed off, but sober, and that her sister was blotto-drunk. Margot told the cops that Nicole accused Finnegan trying to rape her. Now, for whatever reason, Margot doesn't believe that this is true. But Margot doesn't rule out the possibility of Finnegan being angry enough to run her over twenty minutes later. By the way, according to Margot, Finnegan left first, in a fit of rage. He was fully dressed when Margot found him whacking her sister's ass. Then about fifteen minutes later Nicole Silver stumbles out the door as well, even though

Margot told her to go to bed. Meanwhile Silver's baby, Jedidiah Babcock, is sleeping upstairs on the fourth floor of the townhouse."

"So none of this is in the papers or on TV, Jack." Mickey pauses. "All that the media has reported so far is that the cops are questioning one of Babcock's security agents and the victim's sister. The cops are saying that the hit and run accident appears to be a random act of violence."

"Sounds like what the cops said when your father was killed also."

"Let's leave my father's death out of this for the moment."

"Okay but I'm still worried that our boy Babcock is a bigger problem than you know."

Birdsong lets his statement sink in. However Mickey angles away from that assertion and revisits what the media outlets are saying.

"There also are a few reporters who have sympathy for Babcock losing his fiancé."

"That's such bullshit. Nobody … except possibly Margot … believes that Babcock was ever going to marry Nicole Silver. If he was going to marry her he would have done it already. And that's probably why *most* of the reporting is running against him. It's amazing that they don't have more about him in their files. This guy is as rich as Croesus, but outside of his tight circles he is relatively unknown or at least well below the radar."

"One of the newspapers said that they were planning on getting married at the end of the year and that they had both signed a prenuptial agreement less than a month before she died."

"That stuff came from the sister … from Margot. She kind of hero-worshipped her older sister at one point. She was probably just trying to counter all of the tabloid releases showing pictures of Babcock out on the town with another woman. You have to wonder how these paparazzi guys get these pictures. I guess that our boy's shadowy nature is about to get probed bigtime."

"Yeah, you have to wonder. They have pictures of Babcock on the same night at a St Patrick's Day party in Atlanta. Why would they even be following him, especially if …?"

"Almost seems too convenient wouldn't you say?"

"Except for the fact that, the picture that I saw in the paper showed a damn good looking woman shoulder to shoulder with Babcock in Atlanta. Doesn't appear that Frank is terribly worried about any prenuptial agreement with Silver."

## *April 1991*

"Well that's what all of this tabloid noise is now about. This story isn't going to go away. And you can be sure that the public interest will eventually lead the reporters to some other decade old events."

∞∞∞

# VII

## April, 1991

Fox Babcock re-reads the story in the *Enquiring Nation* magazine. He feels terribly bad for his father. Frank Babcock has always made a point of doing his best to stay out of the newspapers. He has avoided interviews with financial magazines and business publications for the simple reason that he's always valued his privacy more than what the publicity might do for his professional reputation. And now *this* has happened. Francis X Babcock Jr is staring at the picture of his adoptive father, Francis X Babcock Sr. on the cover of one of the largest weekly tabloids. Fox simply fumes at the picture of Frank Babcock and a woman named Amber Reaper. The caption under the picture is entirely unfair. "Billionaire Parties with Buxom Blonde Playmate while Fiancé lies in Coma." The storyline is even more unbalanced:

> Ultra-wealthy lawyer, industrialist and hedge-fund honcho, Frank Babcock, a formerly reclusive billionaire, is now where he doesn't want to be. He's in the news. Babcock, who for many years has gone out of his way to avoid the press, has now been spotted partying with a former Playboy Playmate at an Atlanta nightclub. Meanwhile his fiancé and law partner, Nicole Silver lies in a coma in a midtown Manhattan

## April 1991

> hospital *after being struck down by a hit and run driver on Sunday evening. Ms. Silver, who is the mother of Babcock's young son, Jedidiah Babcock, recently became engaged to the philandering philanthropist. According to our sources they were planning a wedding for this September.*
>
> *Frank Babcock was seen leaving the Rainbow Suite at the Pot of Gold Club in the Buckhead section of Atlanta with former playmate Amber Reaper following a St Patrick's Day party at the famous Irish pub. Neither Reaper nor Babcock could be reached for this story, but several other well-heeled patrons of the club were spotted in the Babcock party including two wealthy Saudi Arabian princes.* THIS JUST IN AT PRESSTIME: *Nicole Silver has died of injuries sustained in the hit and run accident!*

It is a deplorable excuse for journalism. Fox Babcock throws the newsweekly on the end table near his own fiancé, Evelyn Webb. Without saying a word to Evelyn, he then walks over and picks up his Motorola cell phone from its charging base. He extends the aerial and flips down the talking piece. He punches in the unlisted number for Frank Babcock but the call goes to an answering device. He had talked to his father earlier but he wants to repeat his outrage and restate his support.

"Hello, Dad. It's Fox again. I just re-read that despicable article in the *Enquiring Nation* and wanted to tell you again how sorry I am that you have to put up with all of this at such an awful time. Please know that Evelyn and I are thinking about you and that we wish you well. Call us if there's anything we can do."

Fox then turns around and angrily asks Evelyn, "How can these people get away with this nonsense?"

"Don't let it get to you, Fox. Your father can handle himself. He'll be fine. I do feel sorry for Nicole. I didn't care for her much, but no one should die that way. I hope the police find out who did it."

"Yeah, that's one thing. But I'm still annoyed at these vultures at *Enquiring Nation*. This article is only 200 words long and it contains about a half dozen lies and a few more half-truths. First of all they knew that Nicole had died long before they went to press, so their closing tactic is gross and just plain cruel. Secondly, my father was not engaged to Nicole. Thirdly, they had no plans to marry in September. They had no plans whatsoever, about getting married. Dad said that Nicole was pushing him to sign some kind of agreement but he never signed anything. There was no engagement ring, no set wedding date ... no anything. Trust me. He wasn't going to marry her. But he certainly wanted her to take care of Jedidiah. He certainly wanted to maintain the status quo. He had no reason whatsoever to want to kill Nicole and besides my father is just not that kind of man.

"Then they say that Nicole was Dad's law partner. Now I don't want to speak ill of the dead, but Nicole was little more than a clerk in my father's office. Just because she passed the bar doesn't make her his *law partner*.

"Then there's this whole business about a coma. They make it seem like she was hanging on for days. She died four hours after they brought her into the hospital."

"What's the story about the woman in the picture?"

"I asked Dad about that earlier ... as discreetly as I could possibly ask. He said that he was with a couple of his clients, who were Saudi businessmen ... but certainly not princes ... and that Amber Reaper was with one of these guys. They all walked out of club together and Dad was on one side of Reaper and this Saudi guy ... someone named al-Haddād ... was on the other side. The paparazzi simply cropped the photo to get the story they wanted to get. They were probably following the Saudi guy because he frequently dates models and Hollywood types. End of story."

"That's rotten."

"It sure is. To make matters even worse, the picture of my father was taken a couple of hours before Nicole was run down. He was back in his hotel that night by 10:30 PM, so he couldn't have possibly been 'partying while his fiancé was in a coma.' It's all just pure unadulterated bull shit. I have no idea how they get away with it."

"Do you think that they just do it for the money? Or do you think they actually derive pleasure out of making other people suffer?"

"I have no idea. You're the one who's going to be the psychiatrist. You better get used to this stuff. It won't be long before you have people like this sitting on your couch looking for help."

∞∞∞

## *April 1991*

Fox Babcock and Evelyn Webb were both in their final year of study at Johns Hopkins Medical School in Baltimore. They had been engaged for more than a year and a half but had not as yet set their wedding date. At one time both of them had wanted to pursue psychiatry as a chosen specialty. However about halfway through his curriculum, Fox had decided that he wanted to focus more on neurology and surgery. He now had aspirations of a career as a neurosurgeon. Evelyn had continued to focus on her psychiatric curriculum.

Fox also walked a tightrope in another area of his personal life. He was close to both Frank Babcock and to Mickey Johnson. He considered each of them to be his father. He grew up as a Babcock, living on the north shore in a family estate known as Babcock Manor & Gardens. He was 14 years old in 1981 and in his freshman year of at Shenandoah High School when he learned that he was not Frank Babcock's genetic offspring. Yet as part of a messy custody settlement, Frank Babcock was allowed to adopt Fox as his son. This was facilitated in part by the fact that all parties to the agreement had thought that Fox's natural father was Wayne Johnson, who was deceased at the time of the adoption. For the next four years Fox was led to believe that Wayne Johnson was his father and that Mickey Johnson was his half-brother. It wasn't until Christmas vacation during his first year at Harvard University in 1984 that Fox found out that Mickey Johnson was his biological father. Mickey himself only found out a few weeks earlier. Six plus years later, Fox was still managing to hold onto tight personal relationships with both men. And even though Simone Muirchant was the source of Fox's own identity issues, he still loved his mother also. He knew that she was fundamentally a good person.

∞∞∞

Evelyn begins looking for a splash of solace in a sea of contempt. She knows that Fox is still seething at the *Enquiring Nation* people.
"If nothing else good comes of this mess, at least you're now talking a little more to your father. Things are still good between you and him. Aren't they?"

"Sure they've always been good. Nothing's changed. Lately he's been traveling a lot and certainly we've been busy around here. I haven't seen him since the Christmas holidays, but I've talked to him several times. It's not like we've been completely out of touch. But when he calls back, I'm going to see about getting together with him, either up there or down here."

"I hope you do it soon. He might need your support more than we think."

"My father is not a man who needs much support from anyone."

"Are you sure? I know he told you not to bother coming up for Nicole's funeral, but I doubt that many other people were there to support him."

"People from his law firm went with him to the services. Thank God they got that out of the way before the media vultures stepped it up. One thing about Jews is that they don't waste much time burying their dead. Nicole died on a Sunday night or actually in the wee hours of Monday morning, and she was buried on Tuesday morning."

"Aside from the media circus, how's Frank handling the loss of Nicole? We might not have cared much for her, but your father must have felt something for her. After all she had his baby."

"He liked her enough. But he was never going to marry her. For whatever reason he's avoided getting too close to any one woman at this stage of his life. I wouldn't be surprised if there are other women that he's been seeing besides Nicole."

"Why do you think that?"

"Because he can. I'm sure he feels that there's no reason not to. Realize that Nicole was someone willing to have his child, and he wanted another child, plain and simple."

"Does that bother you?"

"Not really. I could never ask for more than what Dad has done for me. Remember he was there for me when others were not. He was also good to Mo before she died. I'm sure he'll be a great father to Jedidiah as well. I can't think of anyone else who is more misunderstood. He can always count on me and he knows that. But Dad's history with women is complex."

"What do you mean?"

"As far as I can tell, my father has never had a woman who truly loved him for who he is. My own mother was married to him twice and I'm not sure whether she ever loved him at all. I'm not sure she knows what love is. But Mom's a different story ... one that I don't want to get into right now." Fox takes a deep breath and then continues, "After he finally moved on from Mom ... I mean after their second divorce and all of the court proceedings ... you have to realize that Mo died in the middle of all that ... well after the

## April 1991

second divorce, he married Diane. I'm sure Diane thought about the money more than she thought about anything else. She was an alcoholic loser."
Fox shakes his head and continues. "That's probably a generous assessment. I could never see what he saw in Diane. He paid her off pretty well when they split and the next thing you know Nicole is pregnant with Jedidiah. In my opinion ... Nicole had his baby but her focus was on his wallet. One thing about being wealthy ... you never know."

"What is that supposed to mean?"

"I think that most people – whether they want to admit it or not – act deferentially toward wealthy people. It's hard to tell how people really feel. My father is a private person, who is now suddenly at the center of a media controversy. I'm worried that this is going to get worse before it gets better."

"And you're the only one he can truly trust?"

"Something like that."

∞∞∞

# VIII

## *June 1991*

"How are you holding up, Frank. I'm aware that you cherish your privacy so these must be trying times for you." Dr. J. Hamilton Brophy, the elite Park Avenue psychiatrist has been treating Frank Babcock off and on for almost six years. Their relationship is strictly professional and their connection is still based upon unilateral trust. However Brophy has upon occasion asked Babcock if he wants another professional therapeutic opinion with respect to his social issues. There is no specific diagnosis for whatever ails Babcock, and there is no specific remedy for his unspecified quandary or quandaries. However he is certainly more in the public eye of late and that in and of itself is reason for their sessions ... currently weekly sittings ... to continue.

"To tell you the gods' honest truth, I'm doing much better than I'd have thought I'd be doing. The media stuff is more entertaining than bothersome. But the cops can be a real irritant."

"Haven't you simply stonewalled them like you did in the past?"

"To a degree yes. But they're starting to join forces with the media through calculated leaks. This is getting messy so I'm trying to be a little more cooperative."

"And how's that working out for you?"

"Not optimally, that's for sure."

"Have they already hung you in the gallows of public opinion?"

## June 1991

"That's far too eloquent a summary of their belligerence. It's hard to believe that the paparazzi actually believe that I had something to do with Nicole's death. It's just preposterous."

"I did see the article hinting at some kind of affair between Burke Finnegan and Nicole Silver. Where did that come from?"

"To hazard a guess, I'd say it's a police leak. Finnegan still works for me and he has my lawyers protecting him. I've talked to both Finnegan and Margot ... Nicole's sister ... and they both told me essentially the same thing. Nicole came home drunk and abusive and she ran back out the door shortly thereafter."

"The article claims that Margot told the police that she came home and found Finnegan in bed with Nicole."

Babcock half smiled with his mouth, while his eyes remained impassive. "Well we might as well clear the deck here. I'll tell you what I've been told and what I believe."

"That would be helpful."

"Alright to start with, Finnegan detested Nicole ... and he wasn't the only one, by the way. So anyway, Finnegan had an annual St Patrick's Day dinner scheduled with his friends. Nicole was supposed to be home by 5 PM. When she didn't show up or call, Finnegan didn't know whether to be worried or to be pissed off. When Nicole came home smashed, she tried to make a play for him. Given some of Nicole's history this is quite conceivable."

"How old is Finnegan?"

"I don't know for sure. I'd say late forties. He's definitely younger than me."

"So what happened when Nicole made her play for Finnegan?"

Again Babcock offered up his impassive-eyed half smile. "He spanked her?"

"What does that mean?"

"It means just what it sounds like: he spanked her. When Margot came home, she found Nicole laying across Finnegan's lap with her rear end exposed, and well ... he was spanking her."

"With his hand or with a paddle or something else?"

"What's with you shrinks? What is it? Do you get off on this story or something? From what Margot told me ... and Finnegan confirmed, he was smacking her naked ass with his open hand. He stopped when Margot came into the room. And then Nicole bolted shortly thereafter."

Babcock enjoys his attempt at turning the table on his psychiatrist, but he is not at all bothered by his disclosures.

"We can change the topic, Frank, if you want. My interest is only to get you to let go of any anger that you may have built up as a result of all of this."

"I'm not angry about any of this. I'm more annoyed. And before we change the topic, I might as well tell you whatever else I know about that night."

"Okay fine. One clarifying question though? Did Burke Finnegan also leave right away?"

"Yes. That's right. Finnegan left right away ... immediately, according to Margot. Nicole left about fifteen or twenty minutes later."

"So what else do you want to tell me about that night?"

"I just want to say that I don't think any of this had anything to do with Nicole's accidental hit-and-run death. There is no connection whatsoever with what happened in my townhouse and the accident on Madison Avenue."

"Except for the fact that everyone agrees that Nicole was intoxicated, right?"

"Yes. That was certainly a contributing factor to the accident."

"A lot of the women in your life have had trouble with alcohol. First Diane and now Nicole. Was your first wife a heavy drinker also?"

"Simone? No, Simone has her own problems, but drinking isn't one of them."

"How about you, yourself, Frank. Do you ever wonder if you have your own drinking problem?"

"Not really. I use alcohol from time to time, but I never let it use me. That's not to say that I've never overindulged. Surely I've done that. But ... it's never been a problem. If someone told me tomorrow that I had to give it up entirely, I'm sure I could do it. This is foolish stuff, Hamilton. Let's move on to something else."

Dr. Brophy shuffles a few notes that he holds in his lap and then asks, "Can we go back to the household staff for a second. You mentioned that Burke Finnegan is still in your employ. What about Margot Silver? Is she still working for you also?"

"Yes, she has continued on as Jedidiah's nighttime nanny. Now that Nicole is no longer with us that has become a real need. I've got another

## June 1991

woman ... a little older and very reliable ... that has taken the daytime nanny work. Her name is Josephine. She's not a live-in, but she's very good. Finnegan has gone back to his normal security stuff."

"So how is this all working out for you and Jedidiah?"

"It's working out well. Josephine is more of an in-charge type. Margot is a sweet kid. She's still quite upset about losing her sister, but she's still going to school, taking a few graduate courses during the day. She had been looking for a job, but for now, she's working for me. She's different from her sister .... more attractive, actually."

"Do you now have a sexual interest in Margot?"

"No. Of course not. She's just a kid."

Brophy finds this pronouncement to be peculiar. His patient has made a habit of dating much younger women.

"Do you have a hard and fast rule on what makes a young woman 'a kid?' According to my notes, your first wife, Simone, was 7 years younger than you. Then Diane was 11 years younger and finally Nicole was 27 years younger. There seems to be a pattern of younger and younger women in your life. And none of the other women that you have mentioned over the years was anywhere near your age. Am I right about that?"

"That's true. But trust me I have no romantic interest in Margot Silver. But I'll say this about that. If my own shrink is sniffing around about this, the paparazzi are probably not far behind. What a great story that would be. I can already see the cover story in the *Enquiring Nation:* 'Babcock *buries* Nicole Silver then *digs* her sister, Margot.' Looks like I'll be coming here to see you for a few more years after all."

"I think your hiding some of your anxiety behind sordid humor, Frank. We're almost finished here today. But next week let's discuss the inevitability of either the police or the media putting together (1) the unresolved violent death of a man who was sleeping with your first wife; (2) the unsolved murders of two street people who accosted your daughter and (3) the unsolved hit and run death of Nicole Silver, the mother of your youngest child. My guess is that there are some professionals somewhere who are looking into these events and searching for congruencies even as we speak."

"Let them look. There's simply nothing there to find."

∞∞∞

# IX

## August 1991

Simone is worried about their data storage business. It looks as though this could be the second year in a row that MBF Digital Haven & Harbor finishes in the red. Her clientele consists mostly of mid-sized businesses. However the business plan is predicated on having many more accounts in the small business sector. But she and her partners Betty Barrymore and Howard Feldman believe that this is going to be a watershed month in the business world. Tim Berners-Lee, the British IT maven who was working for CERN (European Organization for Nuclear Research) has finally delivered his files and a descriptive paper detailing his vision for the *World Wide Web.*

∞∞∞

Berners-Lee had also published the first electronic address on the web, and referred to it as a "website." Additional information was simultaneously released with the explanation of the World Wide Web project. This material included instructions on how a computer user could contact the website and how users could create their own "web servers" and initiate their own websites and "webpages" within the websites. He also showed how a user could interactively search all of these websites on the newly born World Wide Web. He believed that the web would transform the internet into something that was much more universally usable.

∞∞∞

## August 1991

Simone and her friends had settled their respective interests and contracts with Patel Information Technology Systems and the three friends started MBF Digital Haven & Harbor in December of 1989, with some seed money investments from a half dozen individuals including Simone's ex-husband Frank Babcock. Interestingly the other investors check on their investments monthly as well as at the bi-monthly board meetings for the company. Frank Babcock has yet to personally check on his investment. Instead he allows others to keep the management team on target. The upcoming September board meeting will include third quarter results and the management triumvirate of Betty, Simone and Howard are fretting about the need to secure the third tranche of capital that has been promised by the investors even though their sales results are slightly short of projection and their expenses are running over budget. Regardless they believe that the future will be extremely bright.

∞∞∞

"We'll need to gather all that we can on Berners-Lee's new website vison in order to get the third tranche, because the quarterly results aren't going to be impressive. And our early mover advantage in selection of real estate near the most robust network nodes, may not mean as much over time. AT&T, MCI, Sprint and the other big guys are already building secure data storage into their network facilities. We need to differentiate our offer or we'll get squashed."

"Excellent, focused and personalized service is the only way we can differentiate our company." Betty Barrymore adds. "We need to make things as simple as possible for our clients."

"That and effective pricing." Howard Feldman says. "If we get them to understand that we provide an effective and inexpensive back-up for their data, it will be easier to get them to take the perceived risk of doing things on the internet."

As the CEO of MBF Digital Haven & Harbor, Simone knows that her timeline is tight. As soon as this *World Wide Web* takes off there will be an explosion of new data. Their business could easily go from starving to stuffed in a very short window of time. Management execution is key. They don't want to die of prosperity.

"Do you think we're finally there, Howard? Is this the turning point?"

"Yes. In a word, yes."

"Okay now give us more than a word."

## *Techies, Trials & Technologies*

"I predict that Tim's web will be the biggest breakthrough of the nineties. This is really big stuff."

"Why don't we hear more about it on the news?"

"You know, you see all of these events on the nightly news ... like the Rodney King race riots in LA ... or like Boris Yeltsin becoming the first elected leader of the Soviet Union. People believe that these things are big news. But ... you're right. There has been little said on the network news or in the papers about the *World Wide Web* announcement. But I'm telling you, before long, people will realize that this isn't *only* the most important news of the *month*. It's the most important news of the *year*, and I won't be surprised if it becomes the biggest news of the *decade*."

Simone and Betty are attempting to put Howard's effusive rhetoric in perspective.

"You make it sound like the second coming of Christ. The internet has been around for a long time. Do you really think that this new web concept will have that big an impact on it?"

"Absolutely, and it will happen fast. Think of it this way. Alexander Graham Bell invented the telephone in 1876 and by 1880 there were 50,000 telephones in the United States, and more than 3 million by 1900. And remember all of the infrastructure for the use of the telephone, the switchboards and exchanges and the exchange hierarchy all had to be created from scratch in order for the telephone to take off.

"Now Berners-Lee has created the first webpage. But he already has a lot of the enabling architecture in place. The internet has been around for decades. It's just that very few institutions have been able to use it. It would be like Bell inventing the telephone with telephone wires already laid across the country. I believe that Berners-Lee's *World Wide Web* will spawn additional websites at a much faster pace than Bell's invention created additional telephones."

"I guess this will create a lot more economic opportunity than just data storage."

"Don't go getting crazy-capitalist on us, Betty. We'll make plenty of money just sticking to our plan. First and foremost we'll have to execute the plan. But I think Howard's right. This may be a lot bigger deal than any of us even know."

∞∞∞

## *August 1991*

Betty Barrymore is Simone's longtime friend and business partner. They went to Harvard Law School together in late 60's. However while Betty completed her studies and was admitted to the bar, Simone dropped out. Simone became a political malcontent and at one time relished being referred to as a Hippie. In the mid 70's, Simone begrudgingly joined the business world, but she never abandoned her political awareness. Then, in the late 70's, during her second separation from Frank Babcock, Simone reached out and asked to Betty to come work for her at Easy Mountain Software Solutions. In the early 80's Simone's business career was interrupted by the tragedy of her young daughter's death, and the subsequent sale of her interest in EMSS. Betty continued on in the employ of Patel Information Technology Systems after their acquisition of EMSS. Later the two friends worked together again following Simone's fifteen months in India on a mission of personal discovery.

∞∞∞

Howard Feldman is a native Californian and served as the chief technologist of MBF Digital Haven & Harbor. He hung out in all of the right coffee shops where geeks gathered and he was a regular subscriber to almost every techno magazine that was printed in Silicon Valley and Western Europe. He also had worked with Betty Barrymore and Simone at Easy Mountain as one of two futurists on the EM payroll. He then became one of the three co-founders of MBF.

At 39 Howard Feldman was also the youngest of the three entrepreneurs but he had a much older body. He wore his pants belted high above waist level at the widest part of his protruding stomach. He then tightened his buckle so that part of his fleshy girth bulged out softly beneath his belt, with a counterbalancing slab of lard spilling over the top. The upper half of his torso was short and narrowing toward his thin neck and slight shoulders. His head was quite large and it often appeared to be teetering on top of his tapered neckline in a gyroscopic fashion.

Somewhere in this mass of physical discordance true genius resided. In an unusual personal arrangement, Feldman also lived in Betty Barrymore's Santa Clara home along with Barrymore's live-in significant other Roxanne Santana. This was primarily because the nerdy tech had no social life to speak of, and was fearful of living alone.

∞∞∞

## *Techies, Trials & Technologies*

The conversation among the three MBF executives is taking place in the area near Simone's corner desk. There are no corner *offices* at MBF, only corner *desks* for Simone and Betty. All of the floor space in their Palo Alto office is open. MBF's main data center is located two blocks away and is the heartthrob of their business. Howard Feldman has the only office among the corporate executives and it is located at the data center. There are two conference rooms back at the executive offices but they are only used for potential client visits.

"So let me ask you one other question about the rapid growth of websites, Howard." Simone is trying to hone in on the near term issues. "To date the main users of the Internet have been universities and government agencies. These folks already have a certain amount of interactivity between and among their own local area networks. I gather that the *World Wide Web* is of great interest to these users, but who will be the next group of users that will begin using the Internet as a result of the launching of the *World Wide Web*?"

"That, my friend, is a billion dollar question! I take it back. That, Simone, is probably a *multi*-billion dollar question!"

∞∞∞

Later that evening Simone gets a phone call that she never expected. Frank Babcock calls and asks if they can have dinner together the next time she is in New York.

∞∞∞

Simone hadn't talked to Babcock in nearly two years, even though he is a financial backer of their data storage company. After Babcock recovered from his heart attack in October of 1989, he had become a non-stop globe trotter. He buried himself in his business endeavors like he had never done before. Simone tried to reach him when she learned of the passing of Nicole Silver, but Babcock proved to be unreachable to just about everyone, and her numerous overtures went unanswered. Simone sent a sympathy card and received a formal thank you acknowledgement that contained no other personal notation. She believed that her ex-husband was avoiding her and she felt that it was probably a good thing for both of them, but might not be the best thing for her business.

∞∞∞

## *August 1991*

Now out of the blue Babcock calls her with a dinner invitation. Their phone conversation is brief. Simone is traveling to New York in ten days and she agrees to meet her ex-husband for what she thinks will most likely be a very interesting evening.

∞∞∞

# X

## *August 1991*

Ostensibly the dinner is for Frank Babcock's purposes whatever they might be. Babcock has confirmed that it will be just the two of them at dinner and he says that he has some business issues as well as some personal issues to discuss. Simone is thoroughly intrigued but more than a little wary. She isn't concerned for herself or for her business, she is concerned for her ex-husband. She wonders and she worries. *Why does he want to have a confidential dinner meeting of any sort at this juncture of their lives?* Regardless of her concerns she is certain that the dinner meeting will provide her with some things to think about.

∞∞∞

They arrive nearly simultaneously at a comfortable yet stylish Italian restaurant, just south of Tribeca called Ecco. Although Babcock's townhouse is on the Upper East Side and he works in midtown, he has chosen to have dinner in another neighborhood of Manhattan. Ecco is a small place with an old world warmth and charm. The mahogany paneled dining room is comfortable for Babcock. It is the kind of place where the serving staff makes him feel like he owns his own table – like they are there to meet his every request. The moment she sits down Simone realizes that Ecco is Frank Babcock's kind of place. It is reminiscent of the places they had enjoyed when they first start dating twenty-six years earlier. It is a rare combination of activity with intimacy. Although every table is taken, each table is its own private experience. Babcock has managed to secure a very private table at a rear corner of the dining area. It's a Thursday evening and they are both dressed in business attire for their dinner meeting. Babcock wears a pin

## August 1991

striped navy blue suit and Simone wears a light cream skirt suit and a white lace blouse – business-like, but feminine.

∞∞∞

"You know Simone, immediately after my heart attack I had some time to think about things, and much of my thought process … as well as the issues I considered … changed me in ways I wouldn't have believed possible. Being in a hospital bed can be a very humbling experience for anyone."

"I wouldn't know. Other than for Fox and Maureen's births, I've managed to avoid that experience."

"You're lucky, Simone."

"I realize that."

There's an awkward pause that makes it feel as though neither of them knows where this conversation is headed. Each of them half expects the discussion to be more spontaneous. However neither of them expects it to be overly warm or broadminded. In light of the fact that they had lived with one another for the better part of a decade and had raised two children in their home, they both believe they know the other person quite well. So the awkwardness is surprising. Babcock finally breaks the impasse.

"As I said, the hospitalization changed me. I nearly died so I gave some thought to what others might have thought of me if I had indeed passed on."

"And what did you discover?"

"I had to be honest with myself. I realized that not many people would have truly cared. There might have been some interesting dynamics around my estate, but I believe only a very few people would have missed me *personally*. My business partners would have moved on quickly. I'm not sure if I have any real friends outside of the business world. At the time, my family consisted only of Fox. Now, of course, I also have Jedidiah. Jedd was on his way at the time, but if I had died, he would never have gotten to know me, so it truly would have only been Fox, who missed me."

"Do you want me to tell you that I would have missed you also?"

"I'm not sure. I guess I just want to know the truth about things in life."

"Well we can get over the easy stuff. I would have missed you. One way or another you've been an undeniable influence in my life. For a while I even used your name. I was once a Babcock too. Remember?"

But you have never really loved me?"

In less than a 45 seconds the conversation goes from cautious and casual to intimate if not intimidating. They are instantly in their own world. At first they don't even notice the waiter who descends to within two feet of their table before respectfully retreating after overhearing the spoken question of erstwhile endearment. Then in realization that his services might be required after all, the server offers a delayed interrupting inquiry.

"What can I get you folks to drink?"

"Wine. Bring us a wine list, please."

Babcock immediately answers and then looks at Simone and realizes that he may have usurped her prerogative. "Is that okay with you? Will wine be alright?" Simone merely nods at Babcock and Babcock nods at the waiter, who disappears for an appropriate interlude offering Simone the time to answer her ex-husband's question.

"Frank, I don't know if I can define what love means to me ... even at this moment. I just don't know for sure. But your belief that I didn't *ever* love you may be correct, because my feelings for you never really changed that much." She looks right into his eyes as she says this and tries to continue "I think ..." she hesitates, "you mean well." Then she adds, "And you have told me on many occasions in the past that *you* love *me*. And I can certainly understand how all of that has evolved and changed over the years.

Again Simone slows her response. But it is obvious to both of them that she needs to say more, even at a labored pace. "And I know that in the past I also *told* you that I loved you ... and I think that I wanted that to be true ... but I'm not sure that it ever *was* true. With the exception of one time, I don't think my feelings have ever changed that much for you. And I am extremely grateful for all that you have done for me ... but as I look at things right now, I don't love you. So probably ... I never have loved you. As I said ... I don't even know ... if I know ... what love is."

"That's what I thought." His tone is brusque.

"That's all you can say."

"Yes, that's what I thought." He is still terse.

"I try to look into my soul to give you an authentic answer. And that's all you can say?" Simone's timbre demonstrates that she is startled by Babcock's credibly dismissive response.

The waiter quickly dives in and wordlessly places the wine list in front of Babcock and quickly departs.

## *August 1991*

"Yes, but you have to understand, Simone. I've thought about this much more than you have, so I'm not surprised at the conclusion that you've arrived at. I just thank you for being honest about it." He glances at the wine list quickly and asks his tablemate, "Chardonnay or cabernet? White or red?"

"Just decide, Frank." Simone is annoyed but misty-eyed. She doesn't want to tear-up so she tries not to blink. Frank turns to the wine list and orders a bottle of 1983 Shafer Cabernet Sauvignon. The waiter disappears again.

Babcock returns his gaze to Simone and says, "Unlike your relatively stable feelings towards me, my emotional mindsets ... with respect to *you* ... have been quite volatile. I was blindly in love with you from the day I first met you until the end of our first marriage. I couldn't understand why you wanted to leave me. And it took me a long time to get over the fact that you had cheated on me. But at first I wanted to blame it on others and not on you. I was extremely angry with you but I couldn't control the fact that I still loved you."

Frank Babcock speaks deliberately. Simone can see that he has obviously thought this all through quite recently as he continues his allocution. "Understandably, I think, I grew to hate both Wayne and Mickey Johnson. But I forgave *you*. And I tried to work through things during our second marriage. We also had Fox and Maureen to think about. To me they were the evidence of our love."

Simone's misty-eyed countenance has now given way to big gloppy tears.

"Stop it, Frank. Please stop it. I didn't think we were going ..."

"I'm sorry, Simone. Maybe I should have said something up front, when I asked you to dinner. I do want to hear about you and your business ... and I do have some questions about them as well. However those will have to wait."

Babcock is firm voiced and he knows exactly how he wishes to proceed. "I don't want this to be painful to you ... truly I don't ... but there are simply a few things I want to clear up at this juncture of my life. Who knows how many more opportunities there will be."

"It's okay Frank ... I'm okay ... I'll be okay. I guess I just wasn't expecting this." Simone is annoyed with herself for not exhibiting a more stoic response.

## Techies, Trials & Technologies

"You know, you have kind of hit me by surprise. Just excuse me a second while I go to the ladies' room and freshen up a little." With that she gets up and heads toward the bathroom without another word.

∞∞∞

By the time Simone returns to the table, there is a glass of wine in front of her place as well as a dinner menu. Babcock is already sipping his wine. Simone has taken a full ten minutes to regroup, refresh and retouch her makeup. She has resisted the temptation to simply leave the restaurant and she is now also prepared to handle any conversation, business or personal.

"Sorry I took so long. The upkeep takes a little longer these days." She stares provocatively right into Babcock's eyes and simultaneously sips at the top of her wine glass. She is ready for anything but thinks that she will start by throwing him off his game. Now she has a game plan of her own.

"Well, if I didn't say so before, you look terrific, Simone. But then again you always look great."

"Thank you." The simple acceptance of his compliment threw the ball directly back into Babcock's court. He clears his throat slightly and restarts his earlier dialogue.

"We can order in a second, but I just want to clear some of our personal agenda if you don't mind."

"It's alright Frank. I think I'm ready for it. Go ahead and be as direct as you want to be. I'm prepared to be direct as well."

"So anyway, we were separated for a second time about 15 years ago and then divorced a second time, more than 10 years ago now. I enjoyed the time in between. I enjoyed spending time with you at *Babcock Manor* whenever you came out to see the kids. I knew that I was still in love with you. I didn't want that second divorce any more than I wanted it the first time through. I will tell you this however. My hatred for the Johnsons intensified."

"That's crazy, Frank. I didn't even see either of the Johnsons from the time we remarried until Wayne Johnson's funeral."

Babcock knows this is accurate because he had Simone under surveillance for most of that time. He alters the topic but he plans to return to it shortly.

## August 1991

"Just as an aside here, do you realize that if we had stayed married from our initial wedding day until now, we would have celebrated our twenty-fifth wedding anniversary this past September?"

"But that didn't happen Frank."

"I know."

"So let's not get nostalgic about something that wasn't meant to be."

"I'm just saying ..."

"Look Frank, we have led very different lives ... especially since our second divorce. You have continued to have a super-successful business career. I've had some success myself." She continues to stare into his eyes as she speaks. Simone has a wide mouth and perfectly formed white teeth. The slightest smile is often disarming. She flashes that smile briefly as she adds, "You also married Diane and after Diane, there was poor Nicole. By now, I should qualify as a part of your remote past."

"That's not true. I will never think of you that way. Besides we still have Fox in common."

It is one of the sorest of sores. They both love Fox unconditionally. But he is not *their* son – at least not biologically. However, since Frank Babcock adopted Fox in 1981 the relationship between the two Babcock men continued to be strong throughout Fox's high school and college years. Simone decides that she doesn't want to bring Fox into their discussion just yet, so she returns to a previous topic.

"I told you earlier that my feelings about you haven't changed much over the years with the exception of one period of time."

"When Wayne Johnson died?"

"Yes."

"Well you damn near accused me of killing him myself."

"Truthfully? There was a time when I believed you *did* have something to do with his death."

"And you don't believe that now? So when did you come to the realization that your accusation was off the reservation?"

"I don't know exactly. Maybe it was that following year when everything was in an uproar. When Maureen was sick and I saw the way you took charge of everything, I just changed my thought process. Then when we settled the custody issues, I honestly believed that you were a more capable parent than I was. I couldn't possibly leave my children in the custody of someone evil. So somewhere in that timeframe I came to believe that my suspicions were wrong. And then when Maureen …"

"And then you left for India."

"Yes. We each dealt differently with losing Maureen."

"Maybe so."

"I couldn't have handled the loss without my trip to India. It gave me ample time to reflect on the relativity of the human race as a whole … and my own small place in this world specifically. I feel that I am still in touch with Maureen. I feel her spirit more often now than when she was alive and well."

"So that was the demarcation point for me as well. When you told me that Wayne Johnson was Mickey's biological father, I was devastated. Remember though you told me that after Johnson died. Then later we learn that it's really Mickey Johnson and not Wayne Johnson who is Fox's father. You must realize that all of that is quite humiliating for me. Do you understand why I hate the Johnsons?"

"Should I apologize now? I know that I never did in the past."

"That would probably be helpful."

"Alright then, I'm sorry I caused you such pain."

"Okay. Apology accepted."

"Frank, why are we reopening a lot of old wounds here? Why? Is there a point to all of this?"

"Well I might have something I'm sorry about as well. However I wanted you to realize your own culpability in things before I say anything about my past transgressions."

The waiter reappears and takes their orders. Neither of them has looked at their menu and they both simply choose from the specials that the waiter recites.

"What is it that you want from me, Frank? You have helped me along the way in business as well as in life in general. I am grateful for that. And I also don't want our personal relationship … whatever it may be at this point … to interfere with business concerns going forward. The future of your investment looks very bright by the way."

"Well I'm hoping that I can also be optimistic about the future of my personal life. Money is meaningless at this point. It seems like the more I spend, the more I earn. There is a certain absurdity to all of that. But that's not what I want to talk to you about. Remember a few seconds ago I said that I have some personal transgressions of my own. Well I'm about to tell you something that I've only told one other person."

"Fox?"

"No. Fox doesn't know what I'm about to say."

"It's about Wayne. Isn't it?"

"Yes."

"You *did* have something to do with it. Didn't you?" Simone is slightly more fearful than she is angry. She is not afraid that Frank will hurt her physically. She is afraid that what Frank is about to tell her, would hurt her in so many other ways. She is suddenly glad she had taken her break to the ladies' room when she did. She is now better prepared for what she is about to hear.

"Let me explain. I'll tell you once and then after tonight I never want to talk about it again. I did a few things that I sincerely regret, but I don't hold myself responsible for Wayne Johnson's death."

There is some light Italian mood music playing softly in the background. It functions as an effective acoustical shield for table conversations. They could not be overheard by people at nearby tables. In this situation, the music is surreal. It feels like a musical score for a sad cinematic drama.

"Don't tell me, Frank. I don't want to know." Simone *did* want to know what happened but she is leery of what Frank's version of the events might be. Babcock ignores her request as she knew he would.

"Just before Wayne's death, I ran into the Johnsons at a baseball game at Shenandoah. I was in the stands with Fox. Gil Johnson was pitching for the Skylarks and Wayne and Mickey Johnson were a few rows behind us in the stands. I could hear their voices throughout the game. Wayne and Mickey Johnson were yelling and laughing and carrying on while they rooted for Gil Johnson down on the field. I hated them for all the reasons we talked about earlier. It was the first time I could ever remember that I was rooting *against* the Skylarks or at least *against* one particular Skylark."

"But Gil Johnson had nothing to do with anything that happened. It was a long time before that."

"Regardless he was a Johnson. I hated his father and I hated his brother, so I hated him too."

"What does any of this have to do with the way Wayne died?"

## Techies, Trials & Technologies

"I'll get to that. First I have to tell you that at the end of the game I had a few words with the Johnsons. It was not very public but it involved some name calling and just general anger."

"And Fox was with you?"

"Yes, but he hardly noticed anything. He was too busy eyeing Gil Johnson's girlfriend. As I said this wasn't a big public scene or anything. It was just enough to get me very angry. Also I didn't like the idea of Fox hero-worshipping Gil Johnson. So when the game ended, I had my security guys put a surveillance on Gil Johnson. I wanted to see what this kid was up to."

"Why him? Why not Mickey or Wayne?"

"I already had people watching them." Frank is leaning toward Simone and trying to keep his voice as low as possible. However the sheer memory of these events raises his blood pressure even now. Conveniently those at the closest table have just gotten up to leave.

"But anyway when my people followed Gil Johnson and his girlfriend to the drive-in theatre that night, they saw them using drugs. My security guy tipped off the Nassau County cops and Gil Johnson and his girlfriend were arrested later that night."

"That's a pretty fucked up thing to do, Frank. How could you be such a dick?"

"I said there were some things I wasn't proud of, but I can live with that one. Remember this Gil Johnson kid died several years later while driving under the influence. Maybe I could have helped save him."

"I'm still not getting the connection to how Wayne died."

"Well Wayne Johnson had some connections in the Police Department, and I imagine they don't like seeing family members of cops getting arrested. Somehow or other they let Gil Johnson and his girlfriend off the hook. They were released and there is no record of their arrest. Anyway when Mazzini … my security guy … told me about this, I was pissed off. Why should the Johnson kid get preferential treatment?"

As she listens to Babcock's soliloquy, Simone is amazed that Frank Babcock doesn't realize that his whole life has been one of preferential treatment, but she isn't going to interrupt his flow. Now she wants to hear his story right through to the end. She simply prods him further along.

"So what did you do about it Frank?"

"I told Mazzini that I wanted to teach Wayne Johnson a lesson. I hated him most of all. I simply told Mazzini to do what it took, and to make

## *August 1991*

sure that Wayne Johnson had a good idea of who was getting a measure of revenge without directly implicating me in the punishment."

"Physical punishment?"

"I left that part to his imagination but yes that's what I meant. But I didn't want Johnson to die."

"So then this Mazzini guy *accidentally* beat Wayne to death?"

"No. Mazzini was nowhere near there when Johnson was mugged. In fact for many years Mazzini claimed that he knew nothing about the mugging. He claimed that someone else got to Wayne first and that he would never have had his people beat Johnson so severely."

"And you believed that?"

"I *wanted* to believe it. I didn't want to think of myself as capable of soliciting that kind of violence. So I let my lawyers handle the few inquiries that came my way about my relationship with Johnson."

"But are you telling me that at some time along the way you learned that your security personnel actually *were* involved in Wayne's murder?"

"What I was told about that evening was that Tony Mazzini ... who is now dead by the way ... hired an ex-con by the name of Richie Barone to rough up Wayne Johnson and that Barone then hired Malcolm Johnson, another ex-con to help him with the job. Things got out of hand when Wayne Johnson shot and killed Malcolm Johnson. Barone got spooked and put a deadly beating on Wayne Johnson and then fled the scene of the altercation. So yes, my security personnel indeed initiated the altercation that left Wayne Johnson dead."

"So why are you telling me all of this now, Frank. You have essentially admitted to contracting a murder."

"I never told them to kill Johnson, and neither did Mazzini. Initially Barone didn't intend to kill Johnson either. But somewhere among myself, Tony Mazzini, Richie Barone and Malcolm Johnson there might be some responsibility for his death. Tony Mazzini and Malcolm Johnson are now dead, and Richie Barone is imprisoned at Attica. He should be there for at least another eight years, probably much longer."

"I guess that leaves just you, Frank. What was it you were saying before about certain people getting preferential treatment? And so now that you have told me this, should I be afraid of you also?"

"No, I don't think so. I will say this however. I'm glad I told you. It's a load off my shoulders."

"What's to stop me from running to the police right now and telling them what you just told me?"

"They won't believe you Simone. You are my ex-wife and might have a reason for making such an accusation. Also you have no evidence to back it up. There are no witnesses who can corroborate what I just told you."

"What about Barone?"

"Barone has a pretty long rap sheet and was recently involved in some prison violence. Besides Barone only knew Mazzini. He didn't know Mazzini worked for me. Mazzini took that information with him to the grave."

"What if I told Mickey?"

"Why would you do that, Simone? You'd only hurt the man. He couldn't prove anything either. Besides, it's not like I *wanted* his father to die. However, maybe one day I will tell him myself."

"You realize, Frank, that the courts wouldn't look at this as anything other than pre-meditated murder. You could spend the rest of your life in jail. So if all of this is true, I'm astounded that you are telling me these things. I don't get it."

"As I told you earlier, I've made certain mistakes that I'm sorry about. That doesn't mean I want to spend the rest of my life in prison. I don't see how that would do anybody any good. On the other hand, I do have a certain amount of guilt regarding this whole situation.

"Earlier you said that you told one other person about this ... and that it wasn't Fox."

"Yes, it wasn't Fox. He doesn't know. I told my psychiatrist. He knows. Of course he won't say anything to anyone. And to be totally complete ... there was another person as well. I went to confession when I was in Melbourne, Australia and told a priest about it. But that was a completely anonymous confession. I never saw the priest and he never saw me.

"I didn't realize that you are now suddenly religious, Frank."

"It's not like I'm a religious fanatic or anything but I do find it helpful."

## August 1991

"Other than a few times at Christmas and Easter, I don't remember ever going to church with you, when we were living together. So when did you change?"

"Actually my parents raised me as a church-going Catholic and that continued through my high school years at Shenandoah. Then when I was at Dartmouth my mother died. After that I stopped going. But remember, our first marriage in Newport was in St Mary's. As I recall that was the oldest Catholic Church in the state, and it was you who wanted to get married there."

"You know Frank, if it wasn't for the elephant at the table, this might be a nice trip down memory lane. But for now I want to compartmentalize. I can't deal with all of this any other way. So just answer me this one question if you will. Did your spiritual renewal have anything to do with what happened to Wayne?"

"No, in fact it had more to do with what happened to Maureen."

The waiter arrives with their salad appetizers and quickly sets them in front of Babcock and Simone. He doesn't linger and that allows for a very short interlude in the conversation.

"I can relate to that. I think that drove me towards spiritual introspection as well. You know I was baptized a Catholic but I don't remember having much of a Catholic upbringing myself. And we had both Fox and Maureen baptized but never pushed a church-going agenda with them either.

"Now I'm some sort of a blend between a Christian and a Buddhist. My time in India helped me get a grip on the fact that my spirituality is more important than a selection of any specific denomination. I now think of myself more as a spiritual person than as a religious person. Either way I still know that one person terminating another person's life is still an awful calamity."

"That's an interesting word choice. It doesn't sound as bad as *sin* or *crime*."

"Trust me it's much worse. It enmeshes way more people."

∞∞∞

Later that night after returning to her hotel room, Simone reflects back on one of the oddest evenings of her life. She finds it hard to believe that she has just sat through a dinner with her ex-husband during which he essentially confessed to contracting to kill her ex-lover. It seems unreal, like the plot of a Grade B movie. She is also amazed that throughout the dinner Babcock still refused to discuss his business investment in MBF Digital Haven & Harbor. That part doesn't bother her as much as it fascinates her. The prospect of a business dinner to discuss MBF was apparently a ruse so that Babcock could deliver his confession. She still has a hard time believing it all an hour later. However she has a very explicit reminder. She retrieves her pocketbook and pulls out that reminder.

∞∞∞

When she went to the ladies room near the outset of their dinner, Simone did more than just freshen up. In addition she had turned on her Sony handheld cassette recorder before returning to the table. She had then kept her Sony at the top of her open pocketbook, on the seat next to her throughout the meal. She had wanted to record whatever Frank was going to say, so that she could reflect on it later. What she recorded was beyond her wildest expectations.

∞∞∞

Now back in her hotel room, Simone rewinds the cassette and listens. It isn't the best of recordings, and the soft Italian music in the background sounds much louder on the tape. Still significant snippets of their conversation are audible. The tape runs out just as Babcock is telling her that he hasn't told Fox about Wayne Johnson and that he is thinking that one day he might tell Mickey. How crazy is that! Suddenly she begins to worry a lot, and Simone has no idea what else she should do besides worry.

∞∞∞

# XI

## August 1991

After living in Mill Neck for four years, Mickey and Syd have decided to move back to Garden City. They are taking the two mothers-in-law with them to help with the three Johnson children. The other big change is that Syd has decided to go back to work and Mickey has agreed that it might be a good idea. His only request is that she wait until after the Thanksgiving and Christmas holidays. After some negotiation Syd has accepted a job working for her old boss, John Holt, in the oil and energy futures markets. Her office will be in downtown Manhattan, just a few blocks from Mickey's business. She will start at Gehring Durrenberger Holt the second week in January.

There is plenty of change in store for the Johnson household. The move back to Garden City will be delayed until the summer months. Their new seven bedroom, five bathroom home is being built on a tear down lot and won't be move-in ready until the following June. This works out well with the children's school schedule, so the delay actually helps.

It isn't as if there is anything wrong with their home in Mill Neck. It is simply that Mickey and Syd sense a more community-oriented attitude in Garden City than in the north shore village where they are now residing. Garden City also provides easier rail transportation to Manhattan. And finally Cody and Noah will now be growing up almost in the shadows of Shenandoah, so they will have a feel of what to expect when they are a little older and ready for high school. Jessica will also be closer to Immaculate Mary High School. The Johnsons are building the home they intend to live in for the next thirty years.

## Techies, Trials & Technologies

Mickey arrives home early because they are expecting weekend guests. Fox and Evelyn are going to the wedding of one of Fox's high school buddies. The wedding will take place in nearby Old Westbury, Long Island. They will be enjoying a few days away from their medical residencies in Baltimore and Pittsburgh respectively. It's a Thursday night and Fox has already arrived but Evelyn is not due to arrive until Friday around noon.

By the time Mickey gets home from the city, Fox is already in the kitchen talking to Syd as she's putting dinner on the table for the children. The plan is for Fox, Mickey and Syd to dine out a little later at one of Mickey's favorite restaurants, Steve's Pier 1 in Bayville. The two mothers-in-law are eating at the kitchen table with the young Johnson children.

∞∞∞

"Hey Mickey, how have you been? I'm just catching up on all of the family news from Syd."

"Great, Fox. Things are going well. Market is a little crazy as always but in general business has been good and the family things ... well I guess Syd caught you up on all of that. We're looking forward to the holidays. This should be our last Christmas here in Mill Neck."

Before Mickey and his son could get further into their conversation they are interrupted by Syd's mother.

"Do you see this on TV?" Violet is a news junkie. It's her way of staying on top of everything. She is sitting at the far end of the kitchen table next to a small kitchen TV that is tuned to CBS news. Kathy McDonough is helping Syd plate the children's dinner, so at that moment all of the household residents are in the kitchen.

"Can't see it from here, Mom." Syd is annoyed that her own mother helps out less than Kathy.

"Seems like we ... black people ... can't catch a break lately. Last month they just about lynched poor Clarence Thomas with all of that Anita Hill trash, before finally confirming his Supreme Court nomination. Now it looks like Magic Johnson has AIDS! Wow, I wonder if he's queer. Well he's always kissing that other guy. What's his name? ... Isaiah Thomas, yes that's the guy, Isaiah Thomas. Maybe he's queer too. Whoever is spreading this damn disease ought to be shot."

Everyone stops to pay attention. Certainly this is headline news, but Mickey and Syd hope that Violet won't say anything more controversial.

## August 1991

Violet has apparently forgotten Babcock family history. This is a sore spot for Fox.

"Not everyone who has AIDS is a gay male, Mrs. Spataro." Fox can feel the prejudice. Maybe there is some similarity between racial bias and the bias that people with AIDS feel.

"Maybe having someone like Magic contracting the disease will take some of the stigma away from it and they'll develop a cure faster. It usually takes one of us *Johnsons* getting involved before anything good happens." Mickey Johnson attempts to make light of the topic.

Momentarily there is a bit less tension in the room. However Fox is still fixated on the notion that Violet Spataro has raised about shooting those who spread the disease. It is an eerie reminder of what he did to those who had caused his sister to contract AIDS.

∞∞∞

The nightly news has still another surprise in store for the Johnson family. Buried behind the Magic Johnson revelation is a short ten second teaser that tells the viewers that an arrest has been made in the hit and run death of Nicole Silver.

"Stay tuned." Then the network channel goes for to a couple of minutes of commercials.

"Oh my."

Violet is leery of saying anything more. But her comment is met with breath-catching silence from Fox, Mickey and Syd. Finally Kathy sticks her nose into the news.

"Well it's about time the police got this straight. Maybe now the poor girl's parents can get some closure."

There is no good way for anyone to respond to either of Mickey's mothers-in-law's comments. It is better to simply hear what the news has to say, so they again wait in silence. And then the commercial break ends.

"Police in midtown today announced the arrest of Juan Hernandez, an immigrant from El Salvador, in the hit and run death of Nicole Silver, the fiancé of billionaire industrialist Frank Babcock. Hernandez did not know the Babcock family and apparently left the crash scene because he is in the country illegally and feared deportation.

"NYPD is saying that they received an anonymous tip concerning Hernandez and amazingly he has two prior DWI's on his record during the last three years. Hernandez has been living and working in New York City since 1988."

As the news moved on to the next spot, there was a collective exhaling in the Johnson household, but the sighs of resignation and recognition meant different things to each of them.

∞∞∞

# XII

## November 1991

Frank Babcock arrives home at his townhouse and turns on the television to catch the evening news. The retirement announcement of Magic Johnson is the lead story. Babcock has personally donated more than $2.5 million to AIDS research since the death of his daughter. Others have also contributed large sums but government spending is still somewhat meager and there still isn't a cure.

It's a full 15 minutes after he arrives before Babcock gets to see Jedidiah. His twenty month old son is now walking and talking at a precocious pace. However he is carried down from his fourth floor bedroom by his night nanny, Margot Silver. Silver has settled in as a permanent resident at Babcock's townhouse. Poignantly she has filled in perfectly as the young heir's protector since Nicole Silver has passed on.

∞∞∞

*Early on Frank Babcock had paid little attention to Margot. She was an attractive young woman but definitely more proletarian than her sister. Over time however, Margot's down-to-earth manner had begun to register positive vibes with her employer. He remembered that Hamilton Brophy had asked him about his sexual interest in Margot Silver. Brophy had pointed out that he had been choosing successively younger partners as his sexual conquests. He was now fifty-six years old and Margot was twenty-two, a thirty-four year difference. This theme came up at a session that he had with Brophy in June and then had resurfaced in September after the session at which he told his psychiatrist the details of his dinner with Simone. Brophy had suggested that one of the possible reasons why he was seeking comfort in the arms of younger women was that he was trying to replace the years of lost affection from Simone's youth. When Simone first left him she was still in her mid-twenties. Successive separations, reunifications and divorces all took place while Simone was still a relatively young woman. The fact that Babcock had not had a sexual rendezvous of any sort with Simone for the past thirteen years was something that Babcock was finding difficult to overcome.*

∞∞∞

"Say hello to Daddy, Jedd."

"Daaa." The toddler half runs, half stumbles his way toward his father and then leaps up into the arms of the billionaire. "Daddy, Daddy. Daddy." The young child is effervescent and vibrant as he wraps his arms around his father's neck. However as soon as Babcock puts Jedidiah back on the floor, he runs back over to Margot. The thought goes through Babcock's mind that anyone who observes Jedidiah with Margot can easily believe that she is his mother. There is a strong family resemblance and Margot spends more time with her young nephew than he does. The concern that is raised by Jedidiah's affection for his night nanny is that it more or less ensures that she will be a semi-permanent household fixture. She would have to decide when she wants to move on. Babcock can't fire her without having an adverse impact on his own child. He thinks maybe he should discuss this with Hamilton Brophy.

"Do you want a little private time with Jedd? I can come back down in a half hour and get him ready for bed. Just let me know."

"Yes, that's fine."

"I put some of his toys over in the utility room near the fire escape door. One of his playpens is there also. Should I tell Mrs. Burns to fix you something to eat?"

"I've already had dinner, but yes leave Jedd with me for a while. You can get him around 7:30."

Margot hands Jedidiah to his father and the young boy fusses a little bit before accepting the transfer. Margot then turns around and walks back upstairs to her fourth floor bedroom. Frank Babcock watches her cute little body as she walks away. Nice stuff he thinks – a little less shapely than her sister but a much prettier visage. He wonders what Margot thinks about him. Maybe she isn't too young for him after all.

Babcock then walks toward the back of the second floor holding Jedidiah. He grabs the folded mesh playpen from the utility room and drags it back into the living room area. He opens it and puts his son down inside with a few toddler toys and some stuffed animals.

## November 1991

He sits down again in a chair near the playpen and turns his attention back to the sad Magic Johnson story that is still being reported vigorously. It is a riveting reminder of the last year of his daughter's life.

∞∞∞∞

*Ten years earlier, Maureen Babcock had run away from Babcock Manor & Gardens. Her parents had just gotten divorced for the second time and Maureen had also just learned that her Fox was only her half-brother. Her parents were in the midst of an ugly custody battle.*

*During her five weeks as a runaway on the streets of midtown Manhattan, Maureen (Fox called her "Mo") was repeatedly physically and sexually abused by many people. During this ordeal she contracted an unknown STD (later diagnosed as AIDS.) Maureen's principal tormentors were a pimp by the name of William Beaumont (A/K/A "Billy the Kid") and Beaumont's live-in friend, a transgender whore named Harriett ("Don't call me Harry.") Aristide.*

*Maureen was eventually rescued from the hands of her two low-life oppressors by Tony Mazzini and his operatives. However Babcock's security team was not able to rescue her from the disease that she had contracted. Five months later the badly beaten bodies of Beaumont and Aristide were found floating in brackish waters of Long Island Sound near Little Neck Bay. Nine months later Maureen Babcock became one of the first known female causalities of the AIDS virus.*

∞∞∞∞

Now things are different for Frank Babcock. It's been a little over two years since his heart attack but he has come to view life differently. There is so much complexity in his life. He's not sure if this is a good thing or a bad thing. *Depends upon the day; depends upon the issue; depends upon who else is involved,* he muses. Babcock is a man of enormous wealth and some degree of influence. Yet he is certainly not a man without problems. He gazes over at Jeremiah and notices that his son is gainfully occupied with his playpen full of toys and stuffed animals. Babcock doesn't want to ignore his son. Jedidiah is important to him. But he doesn't engage him while he sifts through his own personal issues.

The hubbub about Nicole Silver's death is now abating as fast as it had inflated earlier in the year. After the police apprehend the limousine driver who ran down Nicole, the media does a 180 degree turn without a hint of an apology. The only lingering negative will be that Babcock has become more recognizable to the general public and his name and business associations now appear more frequently in both business and social news reporting. *What a difference eight months can make!* His aura of privacy has been breached. This concerns him. However he has made a conscious effort to stay out of the spotlight. He recently hired a publicity firm to help him do just that? Their job is to keep his name out of the public eye as much as possible. Now they will try to bury any residual negative effects of Nicole's death.

Aside from the public arena, Babcock has many private issues that are disquieting. Although he has effectively distanced himself from his two former wives, Simone and Diane, his love life is not barren. He has an ongoing – albeit sporadic – sexual entanglement with Masira al-Haddād that has developed throughout the past ten months in spite of the distance between them. Masira has made two trips to the United States during their liaison and she has also met Babcock twice in Marbella, Spain. However Masira has discretely maintained her distance during the time between Nicole's death and the arrest of the limousine driver who had run her down. Babcock doesn't totally understand how Masira keeps their relationship secreted from the eyes and ears of her father's global security staff, but she continuously tells him that it's best if they don't even speak about it. Fortunately, their bedroom relationship is shrouded by their open and visible business dealings. The only downside to all of this is that the Babcock's business dealings have been repositioned on the Arabian side from Abdulrahman al-Haddād to Masira al-Haddād. In fact, Babcock has had no personal contact with Abdulrahman al-Haddād since February. Maybe it's for the better, he muses. But still this makes him uncomfortable, because it is one of the few situations in his life where he is not holding the trump cards.

Babcock has barely cleared these random musings when Margot reappears at 7:30. He hasn't held Jedidiah since he placed him in the playpen a half hour earlier. In fact he hasn't interacted with him at all. He hasn't paid any attention to his young son and Jedidiah hasn't seemed to notice. The toddler is content to play with the various toys in his playpen. But with Margot's arrival, Jedidiah quickly stands up and vigorously shakes the side of the enclosure, smiling broadly as Margot reaches down to pick him up.

∞∞∞

# XIII

## December 1991

Mickey Johnson is having a few beers with Jack Birdsong. In recent years it has become an annual tradition for them to share toddies together at in the *Lion's Lair* sometime between Christmas and New Year's Eve. The small sports pub on Sunrise Highway in Merrick has a large triangular pie-shaped bar. Birdsong has owned the place since the early '80s and it has served as a side commercial interest to his investigative business. It's not particularly close to Mickey's home – about a 30 minute car ride – but Mickey occasionally hangs out there for some buddy time with his Shenandoah pals. Usually he goes there to watch ball games, or as a 19$^{th}$ hole after a round of golf during the warmer months. Mickey has been spending less time at the *Lion's Lair* during the last couple of years. His sons are now getting old enough to have a rooting interest in sports and he is spending more of his leisure time with them. On this occasion, however, the two ex-Marines have just come from a hockey game and Birdsong has some other things he wants to discuss besides the action on the ice.

As they sit next to one another in a familiar corner of the bar, they rapidly recap the Islanders victory and then lapse into an inflated conversation about their own high school athletic careers. This is followed by some light talk about their families and careers.

Although Mickey's hair is turning greyer and Birdsong's hair is thinning rapidly, the two middle aged men share a bond, rooted in youthful comradery and concurrent military service. Finally they get around to the troubling subject matter that they have been debating now for several years – Frank Babcock. But tonight Birdsong has some more specific information that he believes will turn the tide in their debate. He is unaware that Mickey needs no more convincing.

∞∞∞

"So let's go back to the beginning of my concerns about Babcock."

"We could do that. But before we go back over those old accusations, Jack, can we agree that Babcock has been cleared of having anything to do with the death of Nicole Silver?"

"Yes, but the very fact that the cops found the hit and run driver tells you that they spent more time on this accident than they might have spent on it if it involved someone other than Babcock."

"I agree ... makes sense. But when they followed a tip and arrested Juan Hernandez, the first thing they did was try to tie him to Babcock. They just won't give up on trying to nail Babcock for one thing or another." He paused to make sure they were on the same page. "So we agree that Babcock has been cleared of any involvement in Silver's death. Hernandez is simply a livery driver with two DWI's who shouldn't have been behind the wheel. In fact he shouldn't have even been in the country."

"Yeah, if nothing else Hernandez is a hard working stiff. He'd been on the road for 13 hours that day. But I'll concede that Babcock had nothing to do with Silver's death."

"Good, case closed. So tell me about the other stuff. You said on the phone that you had some news about my father's death."

"Remember a number of years ago I told you about some prisoner doing time up in Attica? The guy claimed that there was a third person at the scene of your father's death and more or less indicated that he was that person."

"Sure I remember it. You've only brought it up about ten times since then. The guy's name was Richie Barone. Right?"

"That's right. In the mid-eighties, Barone was telling this story about how your father's death was an accident and that it had been set up by

## December 1991

Babcock's security guy, Tony Mazzini. Barone never did know who Mazzini's end-client was, so he couldn't directly finger Babcock. Mazzini was conveniently dead at the time and there was no one else who might corroborate Barone's story. Anyway Barone never did get an offer for a reduction in his sentence. So therefore he stopped pushing his story. Until recently there has never been a way to put Barone at the site in Queens on the night of your father's murder. That has now changed." Jack Birdsong watched Mickey Johnson's face for acknowledgement.

"Really?"

"Yes. The NYPD never let go of this case. Now with some of the recent developments in DNA technology they've established a breakthrough. Barone's DNA was found on some of the evidence left at the crime scene. Irrefutably he was there!"

"So that supports your theory that Barone was working for Mazzini who in turn was working for Babcock."

"Well the only thing that we know for sure was that Barone *was* there ... just like he swore he was in the past. That's how the DA knew to look for a match with his DNA. So this now lends some credence to his earlier admissions which, of course, he later recanted."

"So if nothing else this could implicate Barone in the murder of my father. They had a half-baked confession six years ago and now they have supporting DNA evidence. Are they going to charge Barone with murder? Is there going to be a trial and everything? No one has approached me about any of this."

"Apparently the DA believes that they would have a hard time convicting him on the DNA evidence alone. This DNA stuff is kind of new. And there's no corroborating evidence for a 'murder for hire' motive. And even if they could somehow connect Barone to Mazzini, Mazzini is now dead. So that still doesn't connect Barone to Babcock. The DA believes that Barone has no idea who Babcock is."

"So couldn't they just come up with a robbery motive like they did when they originally blamed it all on Malcolm Johnson? They could get Barone that way."

"Sure they could try to go down that path. But Barone is already doing some serious time. Apparently he attacked another prisoner with a pipe and inflicted some near fatal injuries. He might have been up for parole before that, but now he's already done a ton of solitary confinement and is regarded as dangerous to others. He isn't about to get out for at least another dozen years. They can go after Barone at any time. But it's Babcock they want. They know that Mazzini was Babcock's security guy at the time. The cops believe that Mazzini was more than capable of intimidating someone ... or as in this case, hiring Barone and the other thug to do of his dirty work for him."

"Why are the cops so insistent about hanging this on Babcock?" Birdsong takes his time answering this question. He doesn't want to get sidetracked from the new revelation. He raises his beer and takes a deep sip and then shakes his head and lets out a slight sigh. He knows he will have to clear this topic before refocusing on the new evidence.

"It's not just the NYPD that is interested in Babcock. It's actually the Feds that have had their concerns about him over the years. They think he's some kind of bad apple. They've always been worried about Babcock's international contacts and liaison's. They were originally concerned about his chumminess with a Russian guy by the name of Kirill Zubkov. They refer to Zubkov as the "Executioner." He used to live in Great Neck about a half mile away from the old Babcock demesne. And for good measure Zubkov had a son by the name of Sergei Zubkov who was apparently Fox's good friend."

"No one is concerned about the Soviet Union these days, Jack. It's coming apart at the seams as we speak. Lithuania, Latvia, and Estonia have already bolted from the Soviet Union. The Kremlin now recognizes them as separate countries. And Gorbachev more or less just abdicated on Christmas Day. The Cold War days are coming to an end, if they aren't over already. Why would the Feds care about some old world spy, like this guy, Kirill Zubkov?"

"You're right. They don't care much about Kirill Zubkov anymore. In fact they believe he's dead. Meanwhile young Sergei Zubkov has abandoned his Russian roots and is living in the UK."

"None of this makes any sense to me, Jack. I remember meeting this Zubkov guy and his son at a high school graduation party for Fox about six ... maybe seven years ago. I also remember some of the weird stories about Zubkov, but I never believed there was anything to them. But it's true that the younger Zubkov and Fox were close friends. They both were interested in computers and high tech stuff. But I haven't heard Fox mention Sergei in a long time."

## December 1991

Mickey pauses for a moment and takes a sip – actually more like a slug – from his beer mug. Then he looks more directly at his buddy who hasn't finished explaining the Feds interest in Babcock.

"However now the Feds are also concerned that Babcock has a lot of friends amongst the Saudis. These ragheads are pretty screwed up people with lots of money. Some of our politicians think that the Saudis are our allies, but there are plenty of people who believe that these rich Saudi families include some pretty dangerous people ... you know religious fanatics ... the whole Arab-Israel thing. At any rate, the federal intelligence agencies are just as interested in Babcock's business dealings with certain Saudis as they were with his involvement with Kirill Zubkov and the Soviets ... or maybe now we should just call them the Russians."

"Even if that's true, none of that would seem to have anything to do with any kind of personal vendetta that Babcock might be waging against my father. It still doesn't explain why they would have an interest in a decade old domestic homicide."

"To tell you the truth our own intelligence agencies don't even talk to each other. The DIA, where I used to work, has little to do with the CIA, George Bush's old organization. And neither of those groups shares its intelligence with the FBI. But someone in one of these organizations must have a hard-on for Frank Babcock, or one of his Saudi clients."

"You know, Jack, I wouldn't give a damn about any of this if it weren't for the fact that Fox grew up as a Babcock. That's why I want to be sure of my ground before I make any accusations. But anyway, going back to your theory about Babcock hiring these guys to attack my father – this is the same theory that you have supported all along. Right?"

"Correct. Only now I have some DNA evidence that supports my theory by putting Barone at the scene of the crime. What about you, Mickey? Do you believe this now?"

"Maybe. This does add some plausibility to your theory."
Mickey has been a believer in the theory for quite some time. He just isn't eager to confirm his feelings.

"When you told me about Barone in the past I thought he might have just made the whole thing up in order to get a reduced sentence. But now that they can show him at the crime scene he becomes more credible. However that's a long way from implicating Babcock."

"Why are you so adamant about this?"

## *Techies, Trials & Technologies*

"Look Jack, over the years I've come to know Frank Babcock pretty well. I can't say I like the man but I don't hate him either. If anything I kind of pity him. He's such a pussy. And, I just don't think he's got the balls to kill anyone." He paused for a second and then said, "You know what kind of guy he is?"

"I've never met him so tell me your impressions."

"Well, like when you were a kid ... you know ... you'd choose up teams to play baseball, basketball, or whatever ... well he was always the last kid chosen ... not because he was the least athletic ... but just because you knew he would suck at crunch time."

"The kind of guy who played right field on your Little League team and bats ninth?"

"Exactly." Mickey halts, thinking, and then adds, "... the kind of kid who had all of the money in the world and no real self-confidence. One time, for the hell of it, I looked up his graduation picture in the 1953 Shenandoah yearbook. You know how they show your picture and then list all of your teams and activities below your mug shot?"

"Yeah."

"Under his name there were no athletic teams listed. They listed only two activities: Chess Club and Christian Sodality. Basically he was a loser. Now he could have changed over time ... you know once he grew into his money ... so to speak ... but the Frank Babcock I know is still a timid loser. Believe me if I thought he truly had anything to do with my father's murder, I'd be all over him like white on rice. I just can't get there."

"But you do believe that Richie Barone was at the crime scene?"

"It certainly sounds that way. But Barone could have just concocted the stuff about Mazzini, and therefore unwittingly about Babcock."

"So then, Mickey, if you believe that Barone was complicit with Malcolm Johnson in the murder of your father, then you have to wonder who hired them and for what reason. If Babcock didn't hire them, who did? And why did he do it? Did your father have other enemies?"

"My father was an imperfect man. But he was a good man. Like everyone else, he made some mistakes and he probably had some enemies. But I think you're making too much of all of this. Maybe Barone and Malcolm Johnson were simply two ex-cons who knew each other and decided to mug some random people. My father was just unlucky ... in the wrong place at the wrong time. Every murder doesn't have to be a conspiracy."

## *December 1991*

Jack thinks about Mickey's characterization of Babcock and once again wonders why he refuses to consider the possibility of a rich "pussy" like Babcock being able to hire someone else to attack his father. Mickey's next few words give Jack an insight that he hadn't thought about as much. "Besides, one positive thing I can say about Frank Babcock is that he did good job raising Fox."

Jack hasn't changed his mind and he is frustrated that Mickey hasn't changed his viewpoint either. Jack decides he won't even mention the "other murders."

∞∞∞

# XIV

## December 1991

Fox is visiting his fiancé during a weekend trip to Pittsburgh. Over the last few months Fox and Evelyn have been wearing the thread on their car tires traveling back and forth between Baltimore and Pittsburgh. Fortunately the 245 mile trip is almost entirely on Interstate Route 70, so they are usually able to make the trip in a little over 3 hours each way if they travel during off-hours.

They are both first year residents in their respective specialties. Evelyn is just starting a four year psychiatry residency at UPMC while Fox is continuing at Johns Hopkins, his medical school alma mater, to fulfill his three year residency requirements for neurology. If he wants to continue on the path of neurosurgery there will likely be another four years of residency to follow.

∞∞∞

The marriage of Fox Babcock to Evelyn Webb had been scheduled to be the social event of the year in Pittsburgh, Pennsylvania. Evelyn Webb's father was a prominent surgeon, affiliated with UPMC, the same hospital where his daughter was now doing her residency. Evelyn's grandfather had also been a physician in the Pittsburgh area. In fact, the family roots in the medical community went back to the late 19$^{th}$ century. The proposed wedding has just been postponed for the third time. Fox and Evelyn were still engaged and they both believed that they very much in love. Others had their doubts. In reality both young physicians were extremely busy and didn't have much time for others. Whenever they weren't at their respective hospitals they were traveling between cities to see one another. And once they got

## December 1991

*together they spent most of their time in bed rather than seeing friends and family or planning for a wedding. So while others worried that the young couple had not yet reset their wedding date, both Fox and Evelyn were content to keep their relationship to themselves. The future would arrive soon enough.*

∞∞∞

With Christmas season approaching they are enjoying their time together in the City of Bridges. Some people still call it the Steel City, but that industry no longer dominates the economy of the western Pennsylvania metropolis. Evelyn's parents live in suburban Murrysville, a little over a half hour east of the city, so the young couple decide to stay in downtown to have more time to themselves. Mark Webb, Evelyn's father owns a two bedroom apartment near the hospital in the Shadyside neighborhood of Pittsburgh. Evelyn and Fox are using it as their weekend sanctuary. They are up early and go for a jog along the Allegheny River and across a few of the numerous bridges that line the waterfront. It is a scenic area of the city where the confluence of the Allegheny and Monongahela Rivers form the Ohio River.

"It's pretty warm for this time of year in Pittsburgh."

"Let's enjoy it while we can. The weather report says that we'll get snow by the middle of next week."

"So you've never told me what you think of my native town? It's not all that bad. Is it?" Evelyn is puffing slightly.

"Actually it's much nicer than I thought it would be when I first came here. In many ways it's a lot more civilized than New York." Fox is less winded. "New York seems to have new groups of people every six months."

They are just about finished with their three mile jog. They stop trotting and are now cooling down as they walk briskly through the wooded bicycle/jogger trail. Their path takes them along the northern shore of the Allegheny River, east of Three Rivers Stadium. The temperature is an unseasonable 54 °F.

"Why are you asking me about it now?" Fox inquires.

"Sooner or later we will be living in one place or another depending upon our jobs. I just wanted to make sure that Pittsburgh is an option."

"I like it more than Baltimore."

"Now there's a ringing endorsement ... kind of like what WC Fields put on his tombstone, 'All things considered, I'd rather be in Philadelphia'."

Fox laughs at Evelyn's comparison but then answers her question more directly.

"We've got some time yet. We can decide this later. But I wouldn't rule out Pittsburgh. We'd certainly consider it. It's your home town and you have family here and for what it's worth you're doing your residency here."

"What about your family, Fox? What about your Long Island roots? What about your residency at Johns Hopkins?"

"Long Island, Manhattan, California, Boston, Baltimore ... I'm not too sure where my roots are exactly."

"But you grew up on Long Island. Right?"

"Yeah, I guess so. I suppose I'm a Long Islander if I'm anything. But my parents have had homes in many places, and recently, so have I. In fact, the one thing I'd like to do when our residencies are completed is travel. I think we should take six months to a year off after we finish our residencies and just take a trip around the world together. I know it would require some coordination with our jobs, but I'd really like to travel. What do you think?"

"In your way of thinking would this be before or after we finally get married?"

"Well we might as well get the married thing out of the way before then. Don't you think? We're a long way from completing our residencies."

"I'm constantly amazed at how romantically you put things, Fox."

"You don't have to be sarcastic. I was romantic enough when we got engaged. Wasn't I?"

On a certain level Fox and Evelyn are sharing a moment of jocularity, but Evelyn worries that Fox might be less excited by the prospects of the wedding and marriage than she is. She knows that Fox loves her and she keeps him busy enough so there is never an opportunity for another romantic interest, even if Fox is so inclined. But Evelyn also knows that the whole wedding ceremony, reception and social hubbub is more for her family than for his. She decides to change the topic to the one doubt about Fox that she has herself. It isn't something that they have talked about since their engagement.

They stop in the middle of the wooded area.

"There's something I want to ask you about, that we discussed a couple of years ago when we were in school together in Baltimore."

"What is it?"

"Remember the time when we did the peyote together?"

## December 1991

"I don't much like to dwell on that event. It isn't one of my favorite memories of days together with you. In fact I try to put it out of mind as an uncomfortable remembrance."

"Alright then ... never mind."

"No. It's okay. I'm pretty sure I know what you want to ask me about?"

"Are you sure?"

"If we're going to get married, we probably shouldn't be afraid to talk about uncomfortable topics with each other." He waits a second or two and then adds, "You want to talk about Sergei and the two street people. Don't you?"

"I'm not sure. I don't want you to tell me anything that you don't want to say, but I worry that this Sergei person may show up again someday. Should I be worried or not? You know we were so tripped out on peyote that time that ..."

"Well we're not wasted now so let's just deal with it."

"Did you kill those people, like you said you did?"

"No, of course not. I couldn't do something like that. But it was a recurring dream that I was having then and still have ... for that matter ... every so often. I hate those people who hurt my sister and I was glad when they turned up dead. They must have had so many people who hated their guts. Sergei and I talked about how we would kill them if we ever got a chance. But it was just talk. The next thing you know they turn up dead. Sometimes I feel a little guilt because of how glad I was that they got what was coming to them. And sometimes I feel bad because I never was able to avenge Mo's molestation in any way. Don't misunderstand. I have never forgiven those creeps and I never will, but I certainly didn't kill them."

Evelyn studies the face of her fiancé as he speaks. She wants to believe his sincerity, but she doesn't. She is now convinced more than ever that Fox committed an abominable act of revenge and had once recounted every lurid detail of the act. She worries about this reality on a number of fronts. How long could Fox continue to hide from the truth and what costs would it exact from him and from their relationship if he continues his denial? Would she truly be able to marry a murderer? Could she possibly spend the rest of her life with a man who refuses to tell her the truth? What else might he be hiding?

∞∞∞

1994

# Techies, Trials & Technologies

# XV

## May 1994

Simone Muirchant is flying in the upper deck of the plane. There are only twenty business class seats in this semi-private section of the plane and it allows for a less crowded feeling for their flight back to the United States. The Boeing 747-400 is moving at nearly 600 MPH. However it hardly seems fast enough for Simone. She is returning from the inaugural *International Conference on the World Wide Web*. It was held in Geneva, Switzerland. Her head is spinning. Howard Feldman who usually owned the *spinning head* in their group at *MBF Digital Haven & Harbor* is sleeping in the window seat next to Simone.

∞∞∞

The conference had been incredible. However the dialog in the surrounding conference rooms, restaurants and coffee shops was what had piqued Simone's interest and attention. In less than three years the Web had grown substantially. The number of universities and scientific institutions that now were connected on the internet via the World Wide Web was growing exponentially. A number of small businesses and even a few major corporations had built their own websites in order to disseminate information about their businesses.

However all of this paled when compared to what the most insightful individuals were now suggesting. The buzz in all of the coffee shops was that the Web would soon become the largest marketplace in the world. It was not something that many had truly envisioned. Now, the earlier perceptions of the Web were vanishing faster than David Copperfield could make the Statue of Liberty disappear.

∞∞∞

Simone's mind is flipping back and forth like a pendulum in a grandfather clock. Her opinions on information technology are swinging from one extreme to another while time simply marches on. Her rapidly moving musings actually cause some minor claustrophobic anxiety even though she is encased in the largest jet in the sky. To Simone it is simply a time capsule that will swallow up the next seven hours of her life.

Once they reach cruising altitude the stewardess comes over to take their drink selections while they peruse the dinner menu. Howard has a sixth sense about a food arrival, so he awakens from his nap.

"And what might I get you to drink this fine evening?" The stewardess has a fairly pronounced British accent.

"I'd like tomato juice." Howard jumps into the conversation the moment he awakens, startling both Simone and the stewardess. Simone is amazed by how Howard went from a deep sleep to a state of full alert. The friendly flight attendant merely smiles and says, "Okay sir." Then she looks right at Simone and asks, "And what can I get *for you*, Ms. Muirchant?"

"I think I'd like something stiffer."

The stewardess glances sidelong at the fleshy girth of Howard Feldman. Then she bent slightly at the waist hovering over Simone like Mary Poppins hovering over the Banks children. She winks and half whispers, "Wouldn't we all now, Ms. Muirchant?" The flight attendant wears a name pin that identifies her as "Tilly."

Simone laughs at the ribald nature of the Tilly's question and warms to the good natured double entendre. She realizes that the woman knows her name by simply reading the passenger manifold.

"For now, I'll settle for a stiff scotch on the rocks, Tilly." Simone smiles back conspiratorially.

The flight attendant moves rapidly back in the direction of her serving station and Simone turns to Howard to further discuss their experience in Geneva.

"I can't get certain things out of my mind, Howard. It was an absolutely fascinating three days."

## May 1994

"Yes it was exciting. Wasn't it? I was happy to hear that the commercial conference for the Web will be held in our neck of the woods in November."

"I was just thinking about that. I heard that the Netscape guy is supposed to be the keynote speaker."

"Yeah, Marc Andreessen ... That's the gent you're talking about ... brilliant marketing mind ... a chap who knows IT as well as anyone. Should be another packed house in San Francisco."

Simone found it interesting how Howard has suddenly adopted a slight British accent of his own. She doesn't know whether he is mocking Tilly or whether it is because of the large number of Brits who were at the conference. Regardless Howard still speaks with his large head gyrating on his spindly neck. He is growing his mid-body paunch and this gives him an even more spherical appearance. *Whatever*, she muses, *Howard is Howard. And thank God he's working with us.*

"I was talking to a couple of young investment banking guys that Jeff knows and they believe that within a year, Wells Fargo is going to offer online retail customer account services on its website."

"Yeah, I've heard that also. But don't think that it's such a big deal. Some banks have been offering internet bank services to their high end clientele for more than 10 years ... long before the Web transformed the Internet. The four big banks in New York: Chemical; Manny Hanny; Chase and Citibank formed some kind of interactive service. Customers could see their balances and actually move money from a checking account to a savings account and vice versa. Chemical had a service that they pumped up called '*Pronto,*' but it turned into a money loser and they dumped it a few years ago."

"So Howard," Simone begins. "I might know the answer to the question I'm about to ask you, but I want to hear *you* answer it. Explanations always sound so much more logical coming from you."

"So what's the big question?"

"Why will the online banking idea succeed this time when it failed so miserably in the '80's?"

Howard Feldman sheds a very disappointed stare at his business colleague as if to say: *Don't you understand any of this? You're our CEO, damn it.* He takes a deep breath and offers up a pedantic explanation of what he thinks is extremely obvious.

## Techies, Trials & Technologies

"All right. Number 1: In the '80's, we had the *Internet* but we didn't have the *Web*. This means that, for the most part, bank services in the '80's were within the confines of a proprietary network, not an open public network like now with the World Wide Web."

Howard lets that much register and then continues, "Number 2: ... this is probably as important as anything ... is improved digital speed. Every year data transmission speed gets cranked up significantly. The banks are now envisioning the ability to interact with their retail customers at lightning fast speeds in the very near future.

"The third important difference is the rapid growth in the number of internet web sites. There are now more than 20,000 new websites every month. Many of these new websites could be transformed into on-line stores. All they need is a payment mechanism.

"The fourth and final reason that I'll offer is the rapid growth of *America On-Line* since Steve Case became the CEO of AOL three years ago and took the company public. Now there are three major Internet Service Providers ..."

"ISP's?"

"Yes, there are three, maybe four ... if you count General Electric's GEnie ... four major ISP's and there are also a few smaller ISPs. But AOL is starting to kick ass by pricing below both CompuServe and Prodigy, the other two big names that cater to the retail market place. After Steve Case sent out all of those free trial diskettes AOL's customer base skyrocketed. AOL claims they now have over a million customers."

"Okay I got all of that, but Jeff says that I might be able to pay my bills online instead of sending a check?"

"Not all of them at first, but over time that's exactly right. The financial services industry will be totally reinvented by online banking. And we won't have to wait long for it to happen. Already people are emailing their credit card information."

"You think that we'll have online banking in five to ten years, maybe?"

"Oh, much sooner than that. I think we're talking more like two to three years. Remember we have parts of this already. Then like everything else there will be a ramp up over time but I think that in 10 years ... by 2004 ... online bill paying will be more commonplace than mailing checks. It might even happen sooner than that."

## May 1994

"Wow, there's so much to think about."

"Remember what I told you a few years back when we started *MBF*. We need to stay abreast of all of this, but at the same time we always need to remember that our business is digital storage. The more data that is created, the more financial institutions and other companies will need secure digital storage and backup capabilities. By the way what other insights has your husband passed along?"

∞∞∞

Jeff Levine was Simone's second husband. She had known him for nearly fifteen years, but they had only been married for fifteen months. It was the first marriage for Levine. It wasn't exactly a marriage of convenience, and it wasn't a marriage that was devoid of romance. More than anything the marriage fit well into the storyline of each of their lives. They were born one month apart in 1942, but managed to get married shortly after both had entered their fifties. They were both now 52 years old but they thought of themselves as much younger and they knew that they looked younger.

Levine had served as the investment banker for Easy Mountain Software Solutions when he was with Salomon Brothers in the late seventies through the mid-eighties. Later he had fulfilled a similar function for Simone once again when she co-founded MBF Digital Haven & Harbor. By this time he had formed his own investment banking advisory group.

Simone's life story was decidedly more complex than that of her new husband. But there were some similarities. Both were transplanted New Yorkers who had once lived on Long Island. Levine was raised as a Jew in the south shore town of Wantagh. Simone was born to Catholic parents but had been raised as a non-denominational Christian in New York City. She had lived on the north shore of Long Island during her second marriage to Frank Babcock.

Simone and Levine also shared a common liberal political viewpoint. They both vigorously supported former California Governor Jerry Brown in the 1992 presidential primaries before eventually supporting Bill Clinton in the general election.

After their marriage, Simone Muirchant simply retained her maiden name rather than go through all of the nominal appellation reorientations that did nothing to change who she was. Levine was fine with that. However Jeff Levine and Simone Muirchant still hid their own secrets.

# Techies, Trials & Technologies

∞∞∞

"Jeff thinks this growth of digital information will soon create more competition for MBF than we can handle. He believes that we should be working our exit strategy real time."

"He's right, of course. But I believe we have a bit more time. We've nearly doubled our customer base over the last year. The market still has plenty of lift left. We have to decide whether to expand or to sell out. If we decide to expand we will have very little choice but to include locations in Europe ... probably London ... and in Hong Kong. Real estate alone in those markets is a pricey proposition."

"I'm not sure Hong Kong is the right place in Asia. Who knows what's going to happen after the British handover. That's only three years away. But I can certainly see the need for space in the London, maybe even in Geneva as well."

"That brings us back to the same old issue of capital."

Howard realizes that he has exposed the elephant on the plane. Raising additional capital would mean dealing with either Simone's current husband or her ex-husband. The latter option is an easier play. Jeff Levine would have to put together some investors to take a secondary position in the company. Going through Frank Babcock meant simply having his hedge fund buy a bigger piece of the company than they now owned, something that they had toyed with in the past."

"I think the facts speak for themselves, Howard. We have grown revenues significantly and profits are near expectations. That should make us a nice acquisition target. You, Betty and I still each own 17 per cent of the company. Collectively we still control the direction of the company. Even though Frank has converted a portion of his bond ownership to equity shares, he still only owns 10 percent of the business."

"Well Babcock doesn't personally own it because he sold his shares to his hedge fund last year."

"Trust me Frank still controls that 10 percent. There isn't anyone at Black Inoculum who is going to tell Frank how they should handle MBF. He gave them a good deal. But I'm not sure how Frank thinks about things these days." Simone and Howard both grow quiet as Tilly returns with their drinks and takes their dinner orders. Meanwhile Simone's thoughts drift to her ex-husband.

## May 1994

∞∞∞

    *Frank Babcock has become quite a conundrum for Simone during the last few years. She never could decide how to deal with Babcock's unburdening at Ecco Restaurant three years earlier. She has kept his taped confession but has chosen not to tell anyone about it. She never understood why he'd told her about it and she is still shackled by her own inability to act on the odd encumbrance of the truth. She sometimes thinks that maybe Babcock knows that. Maybe in some perverted way he is punishing her for her own past transgressions. After all it was Babcock who had engaged in the misconduct that led to her ongoing anguish. It's as though Babcock has rewritten the "Ancient Mariner." The truth may have allowed Frank to feel free but now it is Simone who wears the albatross.*

    *Simone has only seen Frank Babcock once since that night at Ecco. She saw him in Pittsburgh at Fox and Evelyn's wedding. Naturally she didn't invite him to the small private ceremony of her own nuptials with Jeff Levine. And she and Jeff were not invited to the very private wedding between Frank Babcock and Margot Silver either. Since he no longer personally owns any equity in MBF, Simone hasn't heard anything from Babcock about the company either. However, Black Inoculum is capably represented at all of the MBF Board meetings and conference call updates.*

∞∞∞

    Simone takes a hearty swig of her scotch and turns back to Howard Feldman. He is sipping his thick tomato juice through a thin cocktail straw and is apparently processing some thought that he hasn't yet resolved in his mind. Whenever he is in deep thought Howard has a habit of slowing down the normal undulating pace of his gyroscopic movements to a slower more pronounced bidirectional tilting action. It is just this type of movement that Simone now observes. She waits for him to speak rather than interrupt his musings.

    "How did you know that Russian fellow from CERN?"

    Simone smiled brightly. She has a hard time believing that Howard has deliberated for such a long time before asking such a simple question. She wonders if there is more to Howard's inquiry.

    "That young man was once Fox's close friend. Our meeting was totally serendipitous. His name is Sergei Zubkov. And he's not a Russian anymore. He said that he has now applied to become a Brit."

"I saw you talking to him, but I was busy with someone else at the time. I forgot to ask you about him."

"Our conversation was short and it was mostly about Fox. Sergei was very interested in how Fox was doing. Apparently they haven't spoken to each other for quite some time, not even by electronic mail. Sergei works for CERN, but he works out of Oxford University not out of CERN headquarters in Geneva. Truthfully we didn't have much techno talk. I explained what we were doing at MBF but he wasn't very interested ... too blasé I guess. He laughed when I told him that Fox was married to a psychiatrist and was surprised that Fox had foregone that specialty himself."

"That's who I thought he was. I've read a few of Zubkov's papers. He's written a lot ... a very bright guy ... very Web savvy."

"I asked him for a phone number or address that I could give to Fox and he just told me that he now had enough information to find Fox and that he would do so. Then he said to tell Fox quite specifically that he 'has forgotten more about Great Neck then he could possibly ever remember.' I have no idea what he meant by that but he made me repeat it so that I would definitely tell Fox. It's probably some kind of silly childhood code game. They used to do things like that all the time."

Howard stays quiet and lets the conversation about Sergei Zubkov lapse. He stares out the window at the endless blue sky. He enjoys working with Simone and with Betty Barrymore. Yet he realizes that their business venture will not last forever. Nevertheless he thinks there is ample room to grow the business and that all it requires is will power and some near term additional capital.

Simone has finished her first scotch on the rocks and Tilly has returned with a refill as she serves their appetizer course.

"Must have been a busy week. Time to relax now that you're 40,000 feet above it all." She smiles brightly and Simone takes a deep breath. It feels like it's good advice. Simone is not a teetotaler but normally she drinks alcohol sparingly. All the while Howard continues to stare into the blue.

"Well we just came from an internet/web conference. So much is changing in the world that it's hard to fathom how fast it's happening."

Tilly tries to be conversational but she is on a different wavelength. She has no idea what the internet is, much less what the Web is all about.

"Well yes, Americans especially have seen a good deal of change. Just in the past few weeks you've seen both Richard Nixon and Jaqueline

## May 1994

Kennedy pass on. We never thought of her as Onassis ... by the way. Now you have this new fellow, Bill Clinton. Do you fancy him?"

"I think he'll be good for our country. I know the jury is still out though."

"He fancies himself the second coming of JFK. He does like the ole 'slap and tickle' like Kennedy. And that's all hunky dory. We Brits will forgive him for that and for being a bit cheeky. But on the continent we recognize Jack and Jackie as American royalty. And we don't think of Clinton and his mousey Mrs. that way. We think he's a bit blinkered and more of a nancy-boy ..."

"A nancy-boy ... did you say?"

"You know, dressing the part but not the real deal."

Tilly didn't wait around for a rebuttal. She simply turns and goes back to the serving area to fetch trays to serve the next row of passengers. However Simone can't help but snicker. She enjoys this flight attendant but Simone doesn't share Tilly's opinion of Bill Clinton. She likes Clinton a lot. Simone is also intrigued by the new Vice President, Al Gore. She thinks that Gore is imaginative and progressive. She is impressed by the fact that he is one of the few politicians who truly understands where the new information technology revolution is capable of going. She knows a bit about Gore's history as Senator in the 1980's. Gore has provided a friendly political ear to the progress of the Internet and that ultimately he became a key proponent of the Computing and Communications Act which passed in 1991. Simone also is captivated by the new VP's environmental concerns. He speaks eloquently about global warming and preserving the environment.

As she settles back with her second cocktail, Simone also marvels at how people from different countries pay great attention to American politics while most Americans have no idea what's going on politically in other countries. She wonders if that will one day be a major problem for USA citizens.

∞∞∞

Simone falls asleep worrying about worldwide politics. It only requires two stiff scotches for her brain to get out of overdrive and seek the rest it needs. She sleeps through the entrée service. When she wakes up, she realizes that she has been out for a couple hours and the cabin has grown almost completely quiet. She also notices that there's plenty of flight time left. She still feels anxious to get home to begin doing more research on all of the fascinating things that she has heard at the conference.

The main overhead lighting has been dimmed so that passengers who choose to get some sleep can do so. Once awake Simone gets up and walks toward the small upper galley area so that she can stretch her legs without hovering over another passenger.

"So, you've awakened, have you? Might I get you something?" Tilly is still effervescent even several hours into the flight. "You were sound asleep so I didn't leave your entrée. Would you like me to serve it now?"

"Maybe in a little bit, I'm okay for now. Just stretching. I'm just eager to get home."

"Well just let me know when I can fetch something for you to eat or drink."

Simone had enjoyed their earlier conversation. She decides to reengage Tilly as a way of passing time on the flight that she feels will never end.

"So what do you think of the new channel tunnel between England and France? Amazing stuff, isn't it? Just one more thing to make the world smaller."

"Well they've completed the bloody thing. The Queen met Mitterrand on a train halfway through it, but it may be another couple of months before everyone else can get service. A few less flights between London and Paris, I'm afraid. Nothing as exciting as what happens in the US."

"Why do you Brits all care so much about American stuff? Especially about our politics and our government leaders?"

"Well what happens in your country has a profound effect on European policy. There are many Brits who get pretty brassed-off about the US. They believe we should be allowed to vote in your elections. They think we might make better selections for everyone's benefit.

"Also we Brits think that Americans make much too big a deal about personal foibles of your political candidates. We're amused by your media grilling Clinton's arse about all his affairs. You talk more about that than about his economic policies or foreign affairs."

"Americans think that these character issues are quite important."

"Well we Brits could care less about where your Big Willy puts his little willie. We got over that sort of thing twenty-five years ago."

"Yes I certainly remember ... the John Profumo affair. Right?"

## May 1994

"Yup, our bloody prime minister was shagging Christine Keeler. Big whoop. But the world didn't come to an end, and we've moved on. You folks should have gotten over it right after JFK."

They chatted a while longer and finally Simone returns to her seat. Tilly brought her another scotch to go with her entrée and before long Simone is able to fall asleep thinking about the many ways the world is shrinking.

∞∞∞

Simone lands in New York and hopes that she can get Fox on the phone to tell him about running into Sergei. She turns on her new Motorola flip phone and dials his number in Pittsburgh. She doesn't get an answer so she leaves a message.

> "Hello Fox. It's your mother calling. I just got back from a trip to Geneva. It was quite interesting for a number of reasons and I'd love to tell you about it when you get a chance. But what I'm sure you will find most fascinating is that I ran into Sergei Zubkov! He was very interested in how you were doing. Call me when you get a chance. You have my cell phone number. And by the way give my love to Evelyn as well."

He doesn't always call back right away, she thought. But I'm sure the tip about Sergei will get him to call. Next, she calls Betty Barrymore.

"Hello Simone, how was the trip? Betty has been celebrating an anniversary of sorts with her life partner, Roxanne Santana, in Hawaii.

"It was fabulous. I can't wait to give you all of the details. People were calling it the 'Woodstock of the Web.' It was that cool. Everybody who is anybody in tech was these, except you." She is half teasing and half dripping with unbridled enthusiasm.

Simone then gives Betty a brief overview of the Geneva conference and says that she and Howard will both debrief for her when they all get back to California. They both feel excited about that prospect. Then Betty broaches a different topic.

"Hey Simone, I've got an idea I want to run by you."

## Techies, Trials & Technologies

"Shoot."

"Well speaking of Woodstock ... the music festival that is ... they're having a 25$^{th}$ Anniversary festival in upstate New York. They're calling it Woodstock '94. It's going to be held on the second weekend in August, in Saugerties, NY. That's about 75 miles from the original gig. It's going to be on a farm just like Max Yasgur's place and this time even Bob Dylan will show up. What do you think?"

"We're there!" Simone no longer feels like she is in her fifties.

∞∞∞

*May 1994*

# XVI

## *May 1994*

Fox and Evelyn Babcock are spending a rare weekend away from each other. Evelyn has flown to Phoenix for a medical conference and Fox is in West Virginia getting ready to go white water rafting on the Gauley River. It is his fourth such expedition but his first on the Upper Gauley. He enjoys the thrill of the river and being in the outdoors with friends. In fact he enjoys rafting more than skiing, sailing or golf. It's far more exhilarating.

The three friends who accompany Fox on his rafting trip include Joe McCandless and the Burnside brothers, Paul and Eric. McCandless is a friend from Pittsburgh whom Fox met through Evelyn. The Burnside brothers are native Long Islanders, and Shenandoah graduates. Oddly Fox was not super close to either of the Burnside brothers when they were all at Shenandoah together but Eric had also been Fox's classmate when they were both undergraduates at Harvard. Subsequently they became very good friends. Paul Burnside is a year younger than his brother.

∞∞∞

"Did you guys sign the waivers yet? *Y'know* when y'*all* sent in *yer* deposit? *We'd a-wanted ta* get the paperwork *outa the ways* before *y'all* get here. *Y'know*, before we do much else."

"What waivers? We signed them when we did the New River, last year. I thought this was the same company." Joe McCandless is the trip's organizer, even though the other three guys are closer friends. McCandless is the most experienced rafter of the group and he smiles broadly in feint

111

protest at the cute young receptionist with the heavy Appalachian English accent and dialect. Even though he was just recently married, McCandless doesn't hesitate to flirt with the young woman.

Fox and his friends are in a small wooden riverside cabin, which serves as the basecamp for "Swift & Wilde; Whitewater Rafting & River Excursions." The company name is so long it barely fits across the front portico of the cabin. At first glance Fox thinks that they have misspelled "Wilde." Then he notices that the bar/restaurant across the road from the cabin is branded as "Billy Wilde's Place."

"No, we only do the Upper Gauley. It *musta* been some other group. *Don't worry, none*. I got the forms right here. My name is Madison Swift, *by-the-by*, but *ever'one jes* calls me Maddie."

Madison Swift could have just rolled in from central casting to play Daisy Mae in a Li'l Abner movie. She wears tight cutoff jeans that stop at the apex of her thighs and a tight faded pale blue bikini top, over which she sported a well-worn denim-hued shirt. But the fabric is a river nylon not actual denim. The collared shirt is rolled up and tied at the base of her bikini top. This exposes her taut well-tanned midriff. The shirt sleeves are rolled up to her elbows exposing sinewy strong forearms. Maddie had an impossibly thin waist which made her bust line appear larger than it was. She also has broad shoulders and stands soldier-straight as she talks. To complete the effect she wears her hair in two long pigtails and speaks with a genuine hillbilly river queen voice that ripples and flows as naturally as the Gauley itself.

Madison Swift's appearance is a conflict of softness and strength. Her tight hard body is offset by pretty facial features that glow with a natural pink outdoor smile. Her skin is soft enough considering the sun and splash nature of her job, but her forehead is marred by an inch long white scar near her hairline above her left eye. It stands in naked defiance from the rest of her nicely suntanned skin. Maddie is completely unselfconscious about the discernable scar, which Fox immediately attributes to the poorly-executed suture of a rural ER doctor. The final statement of conflicting personal texture is a small tattoo that sits out near her right hip just above her cutoffs. It is a sideways figure eight sign depicting eternity. Just below the infinity symbol are the words: "*Ever to Excel.*"

∞∞∞

## *May 1994*

Maddie hands each of the four would-be rafters a two page form that asks them to acknowledge the fact that over the years there have been numerous fatalities on the river, and that they are undertaking the rafting experience with full knowledge of the risks associated with the trip. When she turns around to get a pen for them to use, the young men all notice a three inch tear in the rear of her cutoffs that exposes an edge to her bikini bottom in matching faded pale blue. After the four men sign the forms, Maddie inspects them quickly and places them in a file drawer behind the counter. She then distributes the pre-rented wet suits, sandals and helmets to her customers.

∞∞∞

"Are we the only rafters you have today?" Fox asks, noting that there is no one else in the small cabin room.

"No, you're *jes* the last customers. We *jes* sent out the other seven of *t'day's* rafts. All *a'em* are on their way to the river now. *Y'all* be the eighth *an'* last of *'em* ... *t'day* anyhow. *'Cept* of course, Billy will be *a-comin'* after *y'all* in the sweeper." She is referring to the fact that her business partner would be manning the "sweep boat" that contains first aid supplies along with emergency rescue gear and some addition food in case one of the forgoing boats has a problem.

Maddie smiles and adds, "Business has been good but we're *a-needin'* more guides. We got three more rafts but we *ain't* got *'nough* river guides. But anyhow ... long as the river keeps *a-runnin'* we'll be *doin' jes* fine."

"Speaking of river guides, when is our guy going to get here? We're ready to go." McCandless is taking charge and is already picking up the life vests that were stacked in the corner for their raft.

"*Ain't gunna* be no guy." Maddie replies in a straightforward manner.

"What do you mean we won't have a guide? I thought that the law in West Virginia required you to have a licensed guide for each raft. I've done the river many times before, but I'm not a licensed guide."

"I didn't say you wasn't *gunna* get a guide. I *jes* said there *ain't gunna* be no *guy* guide."

"What are you talking about? Who's going to be our guide?"

"You're *a-lookin'* at *'er*."

# Techies, Trials & Technologies

∞∞∞

Fox Babcock had come to realize how many years he had spent with his head down working hard and how little time he had spent enjoying himself. Ever since Mo had died, Fox had tried to use every moment to make himself achieve the most that he could possibly achieve. For a while it seemed as though he were trying to accomplish enough for both of them. It was a rare day that went by that he didn't think about her. But time had moved on. It had been twelve years since Mo's death and Fox was now a married man. He had made a point of trying to put Evelyn first in his life.

Fox still occasionally saw Mickey and Syd. And he then accordingly visited with his half-brothers and half-sister, but his contact with his adoptive father Frank Babcock and his father's new young wife, Margot, was sporadic at best. Frank Babcock's other son, Jedidiah, was now four years old but Fox had only seen him a handful of times. He wanted to change that. Fox had tried over the years to bridge the gap between his two fathers, but he had never succeeded in doing so. He also sensed that during the last few years, things were getting worse rather than better between the Babcocks and the Johnsons.

After a lengthy three year engagement Fox Babcock and Evelyn Webb had been married in Evelyn's home town of Pittsburgh on August 22$^{nd}$ 1992. Two hundred and twenty invited guests had been in attendance and had come to the Steel City from 13 different states and five different countries. It was not the kind of small intimate wedding that Fox had envisioned when they initially got engaged, but he and Evelyn had finally given in to Evelyn's father and agreed to a larger event. Fox was simply happy that Evelyn was happy.

Fox had invited all three of his parents and their guests to the wedding, but he didn't believe there was much discourse among them. Complicating matters was the fact that Fox also invited his half-brothers and his half-sister from the Johnson side of his family. To avoid showing favoritism they also invited Frank Babcock's natural son, Jedidiah, who was only two and a half years old at the time. The Johnsons came with their children. Frank Babcock brought Jedidiah and oddly brought Margot Silver also, ostensibly as his son's nanny. Much to everyone's surprise there was much more to that relationship than met the eye and Margot and Frank Babcock were married four months later on New Year's Eve. It was almost

## May 1994

like a chain reaction because shortly thereafter Fox's mother, Simone married Jeff Levine in March of 1993.

After his own wedding Fox returned to Baltimore to continue his neurological residency while his new wife completed her psychiatric residency up in Pittsburgh. They managed to get through another year-long period of a long distance marriage until Fox managed to transfer his neurosurgery residency from John Hopkins to UPMC with the help of Evelyn's father. Now for the last year Fox and Evelyn had been able to live together for the first time ever. And Fox was beginning to understand that the wedding was the easy part of marriage.

∞∞∞

After taking a short ten minute ride in the back of outfitter's truck, with the local restaurateur, Billy Wilde at the wheel, Fox and his friends arrive at the put-in site near Summersville Dam. Wilde drops the paddlers and their gear at the riverside and circles back to base camp.

"*Awright* there are a few things I'll be *a-wantin'* to go over before we *gets* started."

Maddie Swift is facing her four male customers and is about to go through her safety routine. The men watch as she rolls down the sleeves of her nylon shirt as she talks. She also unties the breast level knot and lets the shirttail fall down her torso. Then she re-buttons the shirt from her waist up over chest. When she picks up and dons her flotation vest, it's almost like she's doing a striptease in reverse.

"First we'll be *needin'* to make sure that *yer* personal flotation devices ... *that'll be yer* vests ... fit nice and snug over *yer* bodies. If you go *a-fallin' out'the raft*, we're *gunna hafta* haul *yer* ass back *outa* the water by *holdin' onta yer* vest and *tuggin'* y'*all* back *inta* the raft. If it *ain't* snug *'nough*, the river could tug *yer* PFD over *yer* head *whilst* we're *a-tryin'* to haul *ya* back in."

Maddie is speaking in a loud voice so that she can definitely be heard above the snapping of the river rapids against the large boulders in the water. They are about to put-in at a wide area of the river where the water is much calmer, but it is noisy nonetheless. Their raft is already sitting in about four feet of water but it is snuggled up motionless between two large rocks near an eddy wall.

"Next off, we *wanna* tell y'*all 'bout* the right swimmers' position. Y'*all gots* to be on *yer* back with *yer* feet *facin'* down river *an' yer* head up river. That is, of course, *iffin yer* in the rapids. If you fall in near *one o* the drops ... *thata* be the waterfalls ... then you *gotta* bend *yer* knees up to *yer* chest *an'* squeeze *'em* like crazy. Once *yer o'er* the falls then get back *ta yer* regular swimmers' position *'til* we fish *yer* ass out."

The four men watch captivated as their guide goes through her instructions, with accompanying pantomime. The general instructions are a good five minutes in duration. They include how to hold the paddle over the *t-top* and how and where each of them will be positioned on the raft's pontoons relative to the thwart tubes that cross the bottom of the raft. She also shows them a toss-bag and explains how it might be used. When she is almost finished, Maddie pauses to assess what the men are wearing.

"I see *y'all* got *yer* rubber river sandals. *An'* it looks like *yer* helmets fit good *an'* snug. That's good also. But make sure *yer* sandals *an'* helmets are tightly belted and not loose anywhere. Same goes *fer yer* wet suits, *'emselves*. Strap 'em on good *'an* tight. I already *done tellin'* you 'bout the PFD's. *Jes remem'er, ever'thin'* should be tight as a virgin's pussy." She watches the stunned smirks and light laughs at her surprisingly graphic metaphor.

"Now *we* always *liketa* say that, *so's* we know *we gat yer* attention. *'Cause* this here is *impor'ent* stuff." None of the men say whatever might be on their minds.

"*Jes* remember, tight, tight, tight." She pauses and glares from one to another of the friends and then adds, "Now I ain't crazy about the fit of your wet suits." Only the more experienced Joe McCandless had come wearing his own neoprene wet suit. As the four young men looked self-consciously at their own rubber-covered bodies, Maddie quickly unzips and strips off her own tight denim cutoffs nearly taking her bikini bottom along with them. But she quickly slips into some nylon river pants with ankle ties and a double waist tie and then dons her own river sandals. "But I guess they'll do." She says this as eight riveted eyeballs refocused, watching her dress for the river.

"One last *thin'*. While we're on the river, I'm the boss. We all okay *wit'* that?" No one disputes her power grab.

∞∞∞

What Fox likes most about white water rafting is that it demands his full attention and focus. There is no chance to think about the past or the future. The river requires focus and concentration on the present. And there

## May 1994

is no room for any deliberations about anything going on anywhere else but on the river. In other words there is no room to think about his marriage and his relationship with Evelyn or any other present difficulties. River rafting is literally an in-your-face experience.

However before getting to the river, on the ride south from Pennsylvania, Fox thought a lot about Evelyn. He thought that she seemed happy, but sometimes she seemed to be worried that she wasn't making him happy. Maybe it was some kind of paralysis by analysis that they were both going through because of their respective medical careers. And maybe it had something to do with the psychiatric experiences that Evelyn was embroiled in on a daily basis. Whatever the rationale, in Fox's mind there was a concern that their marriage was losing some of its zest.

∞∞∞

After they put-in just below the Summersville Dam, Maddie gives more specific directions. She says to look for the eddies along the river. These are locations where the circular backflow of water makes for good spots to stage their runs at the more challenging rapids. There are five different Class V rapids on the Upper Gauley. Right as they are pulling toward the center of the river Maddie gives a brief overview of each of these named rapids. She tells them that they will need to watch out for *holes* and where the *holes* are likely to be found. Some are dangerous. Some are not. Some are predictable. Some are not.

They can see two rafts ahead of them and they allow them to get started down past a few less challenging rapids. They watch these rafters pass *Pyramid Rock* heading toward *Collision Creek* and *French Kiss* before they begin to paddle with any enthusiasm. *Insignificant*, the first of the Class V rapids, is more than three miles down the river so they have some time before they will have to show off their skills.

"People *gets* flipped at all spots on the river but we *ain't aimin'* t'have that happen t'us. Remem'er when were a-comin' up on one of them river boulders head on, you got to lean *inta* it rather than *leanin'* back. People *says* it's *anti 'tuitive*, but as the river comes back at *y'all offa* the rock you can't let it swell *unner* the side of *yer* pontoon *'cause* it'll flip the raft. So's that's why we lean *inta* the rocks, not away. Git it?"

"Got it, said Eric Burnside.

"Got it, said Joe McCandless.

## Techies, Trials & Technologies

"We'll be *a-wantin'* to practice that *'long* the way *'afore* we get to Pillow Rock on the second of our Class V rapids. *Afta* that we'll be *makin'* a hard left and we'll be *closin'* in on the halfway mark, that'll be at Hungry Mother."

Fox nods his understanding and smiles at the other crew members as they begin making their way into the earliest rapids appropriately named *Initiation*.

∞∞∞

Meanwhile out in Phoenix, Evelyn Babcock is out to lunch with a number of psychiatric residents from around the country who are attending the conference at the Phoenician Hotel. She is mesmerized by the fact that a group of professionals who are paid to listen to others could talk so much among themselves without listening much at all.

But Evelyn isn't listening much either. She is thinking about her husband. She worries that he isn't happy in Pittsburgh. He has grown up on Long Island in a very different environment. Fox's family life is complicated. She understands that. But Fox hasn't assimilated into the Webb side of their marriage very well. He is always quiet around her father and her uncles. He is very kind to her handicapped brother, Peter, but he is still a bit nervous around him.

Evelyn feels that Fox always carries around an unknown burden. It hasn't always been like that. After they first started dating in med school, Fox became much looser, much more outgoing. He spent an inordinate amount of time studying but when he wasn't working, he was much more gregarious, with a good sense of humor. But that has all begun to change. Fox is growing more distant.

Recently Evelyn noticed that Fox was spending more time with some of his friends from Long Island, particularly the Burnside brothers who are very nice guys. She knows that the Burnside brothers are meeting Fox in West Virginia. She also understands that her good friend Joe McCandless will be on the trip as well. Evelyn has known McCandless since grammar school and had even gone on a few awkward dates with him early in high school. However their friendship had always been entirely platonic. She is reasonably sure that Joe sees it the same way, and in any case, he has just recently married. She is glad that Fox has taken her suggestion to invite Joe on the rafting trip because she believes it will offer an opportunity for them

## May 1994

to become closer friends. She thinks that it will certainly help if Fox develops a close male friend in the Steel City. He is working way too much.

∞∞∞

"We made it through '*Insignificant*' and past '*Pillow Rock*' and now we'll be *a-wantin'* to inch over to river-right here as we *enta inta* '*Lost Paddle.*' And don't let *them* rapids fool *y'all* one bit. They may feel a little slower, but they *liketa be* a lot trickier than people *thinks*."

Maddie is describing the route they have just taken through the first few named rock and rapids formations as well as the rapids ahead. These are the first illustrative directions that Maddie has uttered in the last twenty minutes. Mostly she'd been giving simple river commands like "Forward! Lean In! Backpaddle! Dig! Draw! and Pry!" One time she'd added, "Hole watch on River-left!"

Fox and McCandless are the two bow paddlers whose strokes are most important in setting the paddling pace based on Maddie's commands. All of the paddlers and their guide are thoroughly wet already and they are keenly aware of the fact that the water is colder than they had thought it would be.

"This drops pretty quickly now, doesn't it?" McCandless is endeavoring to demonstrate his prior experience on the Upper Gauley.

"Not as crazy as in *Septem'er* when they go *a-lettin'* the dam loose. Then you're *a-getting'* faster water and a staircase both at the same time. But we've had enough spring rain to make it *in'erestin'*. The water is lower through '*Lost Paddle*' than it is in *Septem'er*, but the gradient is *'bout* the same, even though there's *gunna* be more exposed obstacles and *that'll liketa* be *causin'* more strainers *an'* a few haystacks."

"What's a strainer? And what's a haystack? Eric asks. Eric Burnside is not afraid to show his inexperience and lack of knowledge with respect to 'river speak.' They all know what gradient means but Maddie's other terms are not quite as clear. They are still gliding swiftly along the rapids. Everyone is facing forward so Eric has to shout to be heard over the rushing water

"We're *comin'* up on a strainer straight ahead and we're going to go around to the left *so's* we *ain't goin'* near the haystack on *yer* right. In high water the strainer ain't there. We *jes* shoot over the top *o* it. But right now that strainer is dangerous stuff. *Ain't* much of a haystack *neither*. But we don't want to be pushed toward the strainer"

# Techies, Trials & Technologies

Maddie is referring an area where the lower water level of the late spring has uncovered rocks and tree roots creating an area that is too narrow for rafters to pass between them. However the foamy river still rushes through the ever evolving strainer. During high water, these obstacles are often eight feet deeper in the river and experienced rafters would simply glide over the top. Different seasons present different challenges on the Gauley. In addition to the strainer, the haystack to their right is a standing wave whose height is also relative to seasonal variations. The bottom obstacles help to formulate the size of the wave as it appears to stand still relative to the river bank. The water flows up from the river bottom and causes a stack of white water or an apparent *haystack*.

As Maddie is talking, Eric's brother, Paul, turns his head away from the river to listen just as they hit an unseen river bump, caused by a submerged sleeper. The raft glances off the sleeper and spins quickly to the left before getting caught in heavy water. They are near the second of the four drops that make up *'Lost Paddle,'* and they are about to find out how this section of the river acquired its name.

As Paul turns and the river drops, he loses his balance and falls backward over the front right side of the raft. In trying to catch himself, he digs his paddle deeper into the river rapids and then he loses his grip as he splashes into the surf. His paddle flies upward out of the river as Maddie screams, "Duck." It is not some kind of folksy river command. Everyone knows the meaning of her one word warning. Still the paddle-turned-projectile shoots out of the water and grazes the top of McCandless' helmet before shooting between the crouched heads of Maddie and Fox. Fox immediately realizes how Maddie had earned her forehead scar.

At first Paul looks a little panicky but he hears Maddie yell, "Assume the swimmer's position." Then he quickly realizes he has to get his feet out in front of him, because as he fights to stay afloat, he has fallen about fifteen feet behind the raft, even while his paddle is staying abreast of the vessel and only ten feet or so behind its progress and slightly to the left of the Paul's position. Maddie begins giving the others instructions about the positioning of their paddles to slow the progress of the raft, and as she does so, the lost paddle proceeds down river along – *'Lost Paddle.'*

The other three rafters follow Maddie's instructions precisely even though they seem to be moving left, away from Paul, who is floating directly toward the strainer. As they move left they can feel the water flows shifting

## May 1994

slightly. Then they feel the river surface pull to the left as lower river tides rip in the other direction toward the strainer. They shoot around the tidal split and Maddie directs them past a left bank eddy toward the waters below the strainer.

"Hey, we're getting away from Paul," Eric shouts."

"I'm the boss." Maddie shouts back. "Shift to your brother's spot as we go around the strainer." She knows that the strainer is dangerous and she has quickly broken out a toss-bag but realizes that they just don't have time to use it before they will all hit the strainer.

Fox is the first to notice that the paddle is now entangled by its short T-handle in a bramble section of the strainer. It is just about to pull loose when they arrive twenty feet below and beyond the fast flowing constraints of the narrow passageway. A few seconds later the paddle shakes loose and once again takes aim at those in the raft, only this time it is paddle side first.

"Two strokes and then duck; let me give it a shot." Maddie is instructing the remaining paddlers to pull the boat further right so that the paddle will come at the raft near her rear position. It is on them in a couple of seconds. When it nears the boat, Maddie gets her own paddle under Paul's errant paddle and flips it into the air in a way that slows its velocity.

The paddle lands in the boat after scaling the other paddlers and bouncing off the front of the left pontoon spot that Eric has just vacated. It no sooner lands on the cross thwarts than they look up and see a helmet coming their way head first.

Paul has somehow gotten turned around after holding onto a rock at the strainer for nearly 45 seconds. As soon as he recognizes what his paddle-mates are attempting to accomplish, he allows them to get into place before letting go.

However the water is running so rapidly that he has difficulty fighting to get into the swimmers position. The more he fights the more exhausted he becomes. After they catch the paddle the rafters too are growing weary as they paddle against the flow, trying to stay even. However their raft once again drifts further downstream. They head that way together – the reverse swimmer and the undermanned raft – for about a 150 feet. Maddie finally gets her crew to stabilize and slow the raft so that the helmet gains on them. But the relative motionlessness of the swimmer suddenly strikes her with great alarm. She has seen him struggle but now his body is relatively quiet and she knows that he should realize he is doing the wrong thing by coming head first ... that is if he is conscious. Meanwhile they will soon be at the precipice of the third drop area of *'Lost Paddle'* which will then be followed by a quieter stretch before they hit, *'Tumblehome'* the last of the four drops of the *'Lost Paddle'* group of rapids. Maddie wants to get Paul back in the boat well before then.

"As he gets closer, we're *goin'* to be *a-needin'* some weight on the left pontoon – the downriver side – *so's* we can balance as we pull *'im* in over the right pontoon – this here one that we got 'cross the upriver side." Her commanding voice is loud and clear. Paul is now 75 feet away but fortunately the distance is narrowing.

Maddie takes a look at her crew. She thinks that either Fox Babcock or Joe McCandless is probably the strongest, but McCandless looks heavier so she orders him to switch positions with Fox and she also tells Eric Burnside to return to his original position and tells everyone how to hold the raft as steady as possible as they carefully shift positions. Meanwhile Paul Burnside is bearing down on them – still headfirst. Maddie takes out the toss bag and throws the line to Paul. It is an accurate throw and lands within a foot of the younger Burnside brother. He doesn't see it right away.

"Shit," says Fox.

Then suddenly they all breathe a little easier as they see Paul Burnside break into a frenzy of rolling and kicking as he gathers his strength to get into the swimmers position of feet up and out front. He also manages to grab the life line. However they have traveled a lot further down the river at this point and they are fast approaching the third drop. Maddie has to make a decision as to whether to straighten the boat or attempt to do a haul-in right as the river drops. She decides to stay the course and go for the haul-in.

Paul is now ten feet away and is closing the distance steadily as his brother Eric hauls in the line.

"*Soon's y'all* see us with our hands on *'im an' beginin'* to lift, you folks lean back. Fox, you and me gunna haul-in Paul and try not to overdo it. I *seen* where the raft *liketa'* flip in the past. Let's get *'im* in the middle of the raft *quick-like an' sees* where we're at, from there." Maddie might've spoken her commands in fractured Appalachian English, but her firm tone leaves no doubt whatsoever about who is the Paddle Captain.

As he nears the raft, the others can see that Paul's face is white and blue from fright and the frigid water. And overhead they hear a loud clap of

## May 1994

thunder and see a triple flash of lightning. Big initial drops of rain threaten to add fury to the Gauley River. It is already in an angry mood.

"Okay, let's get *'im*." In one coordinated effort, Fox and Maddie put down their oars and reach down for Paul. Together they haul him out of the water in one long pull. Paul lands waist first on the upriver pontoon and Eric and Joe have to lean almost completely out of the raft to keep it from flipping one way and then have to come forward again as their weight nearly flips the vessel the other way when Fox and Maddie flop their big catch onto the floor of the raft like a beached dolphin. Then the raft catches new speed as they enter the third drop of 'Lost Paddle,' amidst a torrential downpour.

∞∞∞

*White Water rafting was growing in popularity every year, but it was also attracting many adventurous souls who underestimated the power of Mother Nature. The occasional fatality sometimes masked the number of other serious injuries that occurred when casual rafters took on serious rapids. The Upper Gauley River was indeed a serious white water challenge. And yet in recent years there were days when more than 250 paddlers would attempt to run the river. The number of outfitter companies was growing and the number of rafts was also growing.*

*Many of the outfitters would sent out a flotilla with several larger rafts all traveling caravan style down the river. The bigger rafts were generally safer and were always well equipped. The guides very quickly got to know their crews and what they could and could not attempt to do with respect to their paddlers. The smaller rafts were more versatile and agile and could attempt more daring routes through the rapids. Then there were the kayakers who soloed it down the river often tipping or dipping on purpose for the sheer thrill of it all. Many of the guides also undertook these personal voyages from time to time to learn more about the river hazards as these menaces presented themselves at various times of year and at various river heights and gradients. Over time the guides had learned one key law of white water rafting; Respect the River.*

∞∞∞

The raft is spinning slowly but forcefully as they come out of the third drop area. Paul Burnside is lying face up in the center of the raft. The big gloppy raindrops have turned to a more needle-like rainstorm, as a fierce dark raincloud hangs low over the river canyon. Immediately Eric Burnside notices the gash along the front of his brother's right thigh. Some river obstacle has torn through his wet suit and lacerated his leg. The wound to his appendage looks much worse than it actually is, but Paul is shivering and short of breath. Also there is now an inch and a half of water in the bottom of the raft. It has quickly accumulated from the splashing of the river and the downpour of the rain.

"Paul, Paul, are you alright?" Eric hovers over his brother rather than paying attention to the river.

"Yeah, I think … now, I am."

"What happened to your leg?"

"Fucked if I know."

"You're bleeding pretty heavily."

"The *bleedin's* not *s'bad as it looks*," Maddie offers. "Leave *'im* be for a bit and let's get straightened out here. We're *'bout closin'* in on lunch soon *'nough*. We can take a look then. We all *gotta* keep *'least* one eye on the river. You okay there, Paul?" Maddie asks the question in a way that begs a big boy answer.

"Just a scratch, I think. Not too deep." And that's what Maddie gets.

Maddie and the three other paddlers go back to work and manage to find a river-right eddy to pause and stage the run through '*Tumblehome*.' Fox looks down at his friend's thigh as soon as he can safely do so. He agrees with Maddie that the surf and rain is thinning the blood and making it look more widespread than it actually is. Still he assesses that the wound will probably benefit from a pressure bandage of some sort before being stitched.

"About how long before we stop for lunch?"

"Depends."

"Depends on what?

"We could find a portage spot and pull out for a bit. We got a first aid kit in the dry bag. That'd make the trip longer, time wise, *'specially iffin* we plan on *bypassin' anythin'*. However lunch works a lot better *iffin* we make it down past *Sweet's Falls*. That'll be the last Class V and then we only got *'nother* mile *an'* change before we hit the takeout at '*Mason Branch*.' That could be our best bet."

"Why does lunch work better at *Sweet's Falls*?"

"That's where the *beer's* at."

## *May 1994*

"Shouldn't we see if we can bandage up that wound first?" McCandless asks. Even as he says this there's another loud crack of thunder and a quick flash of lightning. As an experienced rafter, McCandless understands that it would be impossible to portage past many of the rapids and that often the weather on the river is quite unpredictable. However because of the low hanging clouds, the river rapids are shrouded in a certain darkness even in the early afternoon.

"*Upta* you guys." It's the first time Maddie has ceded leadership in any way. However she says it in a way that indicates she is clearly a fan of continuing downriver before pulling out for a first aide stop. "I *seen* much worse *'an* that, though."

"Let's keep going." Paul makes the decision. He is feeling a little better but he is still breathing hard from his spill in the white water.

"We *gunna* do *'Tumblehome'* by *goin'* through the slot on river-left. The center slot will look good from behind but the water's a bit low. We can't afford to get pinned there. The left slot's more fun anyhow. *An'* we got to watch out for the river-left holes first, so down the middle we go; then hard left to the left slot. We don't want no swimmers here. The *un'ercut* rocks are *liketa* pin more *'an* one swimmer *o'er* the years. *Nuthin'* fancy now. Let's *jes* play it safe."

∞∞∞∞

The rafters shoot their way through *'Tumblehome'* rather quickly and then paddle away from some river-left hazards and start down towards *'Shipwreck Rock'* and *'Iron Ring.'* They are just short of eight miles into their ten and a half mile trip. They have already been on the river for three and a half hours at that point. The last of the Class V rapids are *'Iron Ring'* and *'Sweet's Falls,'* both of which are nasty all year round, but not quite as challenging as some of the rapids they have already run.

"There's a long rock right down the middle here. We're *goin' t'avoid* river left and take the safety route *paddlin'* down the chute on river right. Got at least one rafter already died on river left *'cause* of the *un'nercut* on the rock."

Fox is growing fatigued at this point. He wants to get past *Sweet's* and off the river, and he is also beginning to worry about Paul Burnside. He is getting a little bit blue lipped. The good news is that he is vocal enough to interact with the other paddlers. But they're managing well enough without having Paul as an active paddler because Maddie is now using the easiest routes through the rapids rather than trying any fancy maneuvers. They also get a break just now. The rain stops as quickly as it began. The cloud moves away from the river and the sun begins shining through once again.

∞∞∞

Forty five minutes later they make it past *'Iron Ring'* and *'Sweets Falls'* and eddy out just below and beyond the falls. There are four other rafts, all larger than theirs, which are moored while the paddlers enjoy lunch. They are quickly joined by another small raft. It is the sweeper manned by Billy Wilde and three of his friends. Altogether there are about 40 people relishing lunch at different points along the shoreline.

Paul Burnside finally gets out of the raft. He has felt good enough to paddle with the rest of the team during the last fifteen minutes of the trip. But he is more than a little wobbly as he gets out and sits on a large flat shoreline rock. Maddie talks to Billy Wilde, who then quickly brings over a large medical box that includes a robust first aid kit and an unused emergency suture kit. The bigger medical box also includes a six pack of commercially bottled quart-sized water bottles. He kneels down near Paul's leg as though he is going to administer first aid."

"Why don't you let Fox do it? He's a doctor."

Fox has already moved over behind Billy and is looking down at Paul's leg.

"You're a doctor?" Maddie asks. "Why didn't you tell us up front?"

"Yeah, you *shoulda* said *sum'tin* when you was *signin'* in." Billy adds.

"Should I have told you if I were an astronaut?"

"You're an astronaut too?" Billy looks perplexed but this makes Maddie burst out laughing.

"Are you guys going to keep farting around or are you going to let Fox take a look at my leg?" Paul begins to shiver once again, even though the sun is now shining brightly. One of Billy's crew buddies comes over with a large dry blanket and drapes it over Paul's shoulders.

Fox begins to tend to his friend's injury and as soon as he cleans it with the bottled water, he notices that the wound is jagged and deeper than he originally believed it to be. He uses a knife and scissors to cut away the remainder of the ripped pants leg of Paul's wet suit exposing his entire leg from his upper thigh to his foot. He cleans the wound and uses the antibiotic ointments from the suture kit. With appropriate pressure and dexterity, he

## May 1994

treats and stitches the gash as best as he can. But he knows that it should be relooked at in a sterile environment at a hospital.

"How much farther from here to the takeout?" Fox asks Maddie.

"We got *'Nemisis,' 'Thumper'* and *'Driftwood'* before we make it to the takeout at *'Mason's Branch.'* None of those is *anthin'* special. We're done with the Class V's. These others all come in about a mile and a half and we could run *'em* in half an hour."

"Alright then, after we get out, how far is the nearest hospital?"

"That'd be Summersville Hospital, *'bout* a 40 minute ride from *Billy Wilde's Place.*"

"Okay, it should be looked at when we finish. You want to run Paul up to Summersville later, Eric?"

"We don't want to miss the dinner, can't it wait until the morning, Fox? You've stopped the bleeding." Paul is the one asking so Fox considers the request and just says, "Let's see when we get off the river."

"Okay, Doc, whatever you say." Paul smiles as he huddles under the blanket.

Maddie watches with interest, from a short distance as all this unfolds. *Not only is he one hunk of good-looking man but he's a dang doctor as well,* she muses.

∞∞∞

The day has been a thrilling but exhausting adventure. Fox and his friends have reservations at a small twelve room motel. The motel is two miles up the road from the Base Camp and *Billy Wilde's Place.* They'll be doing some serious drinking at the pig-roast party after the rafting expedition. So they figure that the less driving they do, the better off they'll be.

The price for the dinner party at *Billy's* is part of the original package they'd purchased. They soon learn that Billy Wilde and Maddie Swift are first cousins and that they are also joint owners of the outrigging company that bears their names.

∞∞∞

*Billy Wilde was formerly in a partnership with his uncle Cullen B. Swift, but Maddie's father had had severe health problems and sold his interest in the business to his daughter for $10 dollars in order to avoid having to liquidate the assets of the business to pay his medical bills. Shortly*

127

## *Techies, Trials & Technologies*

thereafter Cullen B. Swift died from a combination of emphysema, and asthmatic bronchitis. And that was how his daughter, Maddie became partners with his nephew, Billy. That was about a year ago.

∞∞∞

Fox has no idea how old Maddie is but he assumes that she might be about his own age, 28, give or take a year. Billy Wilde appears to be about ten years older than his cousin.

Billy's wife Gwendolyn and two other members of the kitchen staff have been roasting a large pig and preparing all of the sides for the meal while everyone else was out on the river. Most paddlers who are staying nearby change their clothes before returning to the pig roast. The others go straight to Billy's Place. Almost all the Swift & Wilde outfitting customers come back for the dinner and everyone is quite hyped-up.

Dinner is set for forty-three people in total and the group includes about a dozen women. There are some starter snacks on the tables and on the nineteen foot long bar. Billy and Maddie both go behind the bar to help out the bartender while the crowd is filing in. For the most part the revelers are drinking shots and beer chasers, although some of the women are drinking *Wilde Water*, a cheap wine punch that is spiked with 120 proof vodka. A half hour into the drinking everyone is loose. There are five female servers who are passing jello shots, chicken wings and deviled eggs in advance of the main course which includes: scalloped cabbage; baked beans; grilled potato skins and fried okra in addition to the crispy pig.

Joe McCandless is eyeing two of the four women at a table next to where he is seated with his own crewmates. They are younger, and two of them were wearing t-shirts identifying them as students at James Madison University in neighboring Virginia. They are beginning to sing along with the overhead music which is mostly country music with a scattering of popular mainstream billboard hits mixed in. The current airplay is Garth Brooks singing: *Ain't Goin' Down 'Til the Sun Comes Up.*

"Nice piece of ass ... the one with the great tan." McCandless says to Eric Burnside.

"I thought you were engaged." Eric responds.

"Married actually ... but no harm looking," McCandless shrugs.

"I like the little one." Paul Burnside gets in the conversation.

## May 1994

"So what *y'all starin'* at. Why don't *y'all* go over *an'* say hi. They *ain't gunna* bite." Maddie has moved away from the bar once the initial rush has subsided. She arrives over at the table where her fellow paddlers are seated.

"Those two are married men." Paul intones pointing at Fox and McCandless in sequence. Paul has showered and changed into shorts and a collared pullover shirt, similar attire to that of the other crew members. Fox has re-checked the stitched wound and re-bandaged it back at the motel. Paul is feeling a lot better than when he was still on the river.

"That's too bad. But I'm *a-thinkin'* that some bucks *is* more hitched than others." She laughs. "Then again some bucks *is jes* plain unhinged even *iffin they's* hitched. *An'* once *they's* unhinged; they start *actin'* like *they's unhitched*. By the by, there's *offen 'nough* lots a hook-ups among the unhinged."

Maddie says her piece as plainly as if she is describing how people work their way around holes on the Gauley River. She has changed into a pair of low cut jeans. They are what Fox thinks of as "tight, tight, tight," remembering the explicit modest maiden metaphor that Maddie unleashed out on the river.

She also wears a threadbare red and white checkered button-down shirt. The colors look more like a tablecloth at an Italian restaurant in Brooklyn. She doesn't wait to be invited to sit down. She simply pulls over a wooden chair from another table and sits on it backwards so the narrow laddered back of the chair is between her thighs with the top of the back coming up above her chest.

"So Maddie, do you and Billy party like this every day after the rafting?" Fox is curious about a life style that would be in perpetual party mode."

"Tell you what, Doc. The *partyin'* is mostly for the paddlers. As you can see *ever'body* who works here now *'cept* me is *workin' they's* ass off. Too many of us start in with the *partyin' an' nothin'* gets done right. So we *kinda* pick one *'nother* up. She runs her tongue across her lips and adds, "*t'day* ... I'm *goin'* do some *partyin'* ... *t'morrow* it may be Billy or Rick or Gene or Marylou. We *jes* all *kinda* know what's up *so's* we don't take no *'vantage* of one *'nother*.

The four girls from JMU are now standing in a row with their arms around each other trying to sing along to Billy Ray Cyrus' rendition of "*Achy Breaky Heart*" as it is booming through the restaurant sound system.

## *Techies, Trials & Technologies*

Although they do a provocative job of bouncing back and forth as they sing, it is obvious that none of them has a singing voice. The fact that they keep singing anyway is a telltale sign that they are getting quite trashed. A guy from another table begins to clutch at one of the college singers and is summarily seated by one of his pals who yells "Let *'em sing!*"

The buffet table is set up out the side door near where the pig has been roasting all day. The huge hog is now set in the center of the buffet table with one whole side already carved and plated on more than a dozen serving platters that circle the pig carcass. The numerous side dishes are now laid out as well.

When the singing coeds make their way toward the buffet, the Burnside brothers and Joe McCandless are not far behind. Fox wants to wait until the buffet line dies down a bit and remains at the table next to Maddie. Maddie jumps at the opportunity to again take the lead. She put her hand out under the table and high on Fox's thigh. "So, I *never seen no* doctor outside his office nor the hospital. But I guess you docs *gotta* play some too."

"We're human." Fox smiles apprehensively. He is leery but doesn't leer. He also doesn't remove her hand, nor does he acknowledge its placement in any positive way.

Fox decides that if Maddie wants to be so forward he would not stand on protocol. Maddie is a very good looking woman who exudes a certain raw sexuality. However Fox is beginning to reassess his previous estimates of her age. As attractive as she is, there's something almost childlike in her demeanor. "How old are you?" He throws away any discretion that might have constrained such a direct inquiry.

"Nineteen. How *'bout* you, Doc? How *ole er* you?"

Fox thinks for a second before answering. He is amazed. He thought that Maddie might have been a couple years younger, but she is damn close to a decade younger than he is. Apparently life on the river ages people faster than he had thought. Maddie is quite attractive for a woman in her late twenties but looks tatty and frayed for a nineteen year old girl. "Twenty-eight," he finally answers.

"Humph, that's *'xactly* the number I was *thinkin.'* Doc." She'd given up calling him Fox. "*So's* when you agree that docs *is* human *an'* has *t'play* also, does that mean docs *gotta* play on the river or docs *gotta* play *aft'r* the river is run?"

## May 1994

"Not sure. Right now it's time to eat, I think." He gets up and looks down at Maddie and asks, "You eating?"

"Guess so." They get up and join the buffet line.

∞∞∞

Maddie eats her dinner back at the bar. She watches closely as nearly all of the customers eat and drink and grow louder and lewder. One of the JMU girls is asked to flash some flesh and quickly lifts her shirt to the wild whistles and applause of the male and female patrons alike. Tables get pushed aside to make room for dancing and more engaging revelry. Several people are on the makeshift dance floor, including a couple of the waitresses. One of the other JMU coeds is grinding her way through a tight slow dance with a reinvigorated Paul Burnside who has his tongue buried in her mouth at the same time.

One of the paddlers from another table makes a crass comment and before long there is some pushing and shoving. Eric goes to defend his brother and soon there are four or five people in the melee. Paul gets kicked in the thigh right below his river wound and goes down on the floor. Fox and Joe McCandless jump in and try to break things up. Billy Wilde doesn't get overly upset about the fisticuffs. Apparently it isn't a rare occurrence. However he does warn everyone that the next punch thrown would be the last. A couple of the combatants left of their own accord and the Burnside brothers go back to their table and throw back a couple more shots.

"Hey Paul, you're bleeding again. And that bandage is now filthy from rolling on the floor. You need to get up to Summersville Hospital. Let them have a look at it." Fox is worried about possible infection.

"I'll drive him up there if you want," offers McCandless.

"He's my brother. I'm going with you." Eric states emphatically.

They have all been drinking but the Burnsides are wasted. They came down from the motel in two cars with Fox and McCandless acting as the semi-designated drivers, meaning that they would drink less than the other two.

Fox doesn't want to show up at the hospital and risk losing his license. He doesn't want to be seen as a doctor who treated a patient while spending the afternoon boozing it up. He thinks that McCandless is plenty capable of driving – or at least as capable as he is. They all take their time walking to the two cars and even grab some additional bread and pork to eat along the way. Fox's three friends then head up to Summersville Hospital and Fox heads toward the motel.

∞∞∞

After he gets to his room, Fox calls his residence in Pittsburgh to retrieve any messages he has on his home phone's answering machine. He shudders when he hears his mother's message about Sergei. It is a buried memory but it is also like an ongoing horror movie. The call resembles an appendage that is pushing itself through the surface of the grave. He'd only been 15 years old at the time. Sergei had been 18. *At what age are you responsible for your own actions?* He wonders. The question in his mind is not a legal one. He simply continues to conjecture about his own moral compass. He remembers Brother O'Dell back at Shenandoah who often quoted the semi-biblical adage: *There are none so blind as those who will not see.*

He decides to drive back to Billy Wilde's and have another couple of drinks. When he gets there the music is louder than ever and the JMU coeds are still singing off-key. This time it is almost sinful as they attempt to sing along with Whitney Houston's hit *"I Will Always Love You."* He drinks so that he doesn't have to listen. He drinks so he doesn't have to think. He drinks until his moral compass stops pointing north. Later he carries out the second worst transgression of his young life. It is an egregious offense but it is still a distant second.

∞∞∞

The emergency room at Summersville Hospital is packed and none of the three friends who found their way to the waiting room have any desire to sit for very long under the bright lights that make it seem like high noon. But they have no choice. It takes over two hours before Paul Burnside is seen by a doctor and then it takes him another forty-five minutes to be treated. It is a little after midnight by the time they leave the hospital and drive back to the motel. Joe McCandless has totally sobered up and is in a horrible mood. The Burnside brothers sleep most of the way which further irritates McCandless.

He finally pulled up in front of the motel. All twelve rooms are on the ground floor. Paul is assigned to Room 2. Eric is in Room 5. McCandless is in Room 7 and Fox is in Room 11. McCandless parked near his own room and the Burnside brothers got out and walked to the left. As he is ready to enter

## May 1994

his own room, McCandless looks to his right and doesn't see Fox Babcock's BMW. However there is a Chevy pickup parked in front of Room 11. McCandless goes over to have a look at it. He sees that it has West Virginia plates on it. Then he notices the bumper sticker on the pickup. It has a familiar adage below a figure eight infinity symbol. It reads: *"Ever to Excel."*

∞∞∞

# XVII

## *June 1994*

Mickey Johnson is downing another beer on the crowded second floor bar of Keen's Steakhouse just outside of Madison Square Garden. Three longtime friends from Shenandoah have joined him for dinner. They are about to head across the street to *the Garden* to catch a pivotal game of the NBA Championship series. Patrick Ewing and Hakeem Olajuwon are the superstar starting centers for the Knicks and the Rockets respectively. But even though the series is tied at two games apiece, the most talked about athlete at the bar that evening was not Ewing or Olajuwon. It isn't even a basketball player. On Friday, June 17$^{th}$, 1994 everyone is talking about football superstar O.J. Simpson.

"It's kind of hard to believe that *the Juice* could murder his wife. This looks like some kind of frame job. Besides *Juice* was on his way to Chicago when his wife and that Goldman guy were killed." Dr. George "Pudd'nhead" Watson is too big a fan to believe what the news is reporting.

"I'm not so sure of that Chicago alibi. The plane didn't leave until almost midnight. At first I couldn't believe it either. But in today's crazy world, who knows. There are plenty of people who also still think that Hilary Clinton murdered Vince Foster last year. Just because someone is rich or famous doesn't mean they can't be a murderer." Jack Birdsong sounds unconvinced of Simpson's innocence, and he isn't convinced about Clinton's innocence either. But then again the ex-Marine POW has seen many things in life that others might find surprising.

"They're saying that the killer nearly decapitated Nicole with the knife. It has to be someone pretty strong." Kevin "the giraffe" Kislinger is another of Mickey Johnson's Shenandoah buddies. He is the one who managed to score the tickets for the playoff game. Kislinger is a sports radio

## June 1994

personality in the Philadelphia area, after having played his college basketball in Pennsylvania before playing professionally in Europe. And although his high school buddies occasionally still call him *the giraffe*, his radio show fans had morphed that nickname and he was now good-naturedly referred to as *Leaf-Eater*. The sobriquet had begun to take root with his Shenandoah buddies as well. The six foot nine inch, long-necked Kislinger is still almost as thin as he was during his high school playing days.

"So what do you think, Leaf-Eater? Do you think O.J. slit his wife's throat or not?" The question is posed by another guy at the bar who isn't part of Mickey's group. He is a scruffy bearded potbellied individual wearing a Knicks Jersey with Patrick Ewing's number 33 on the back. He's been drinking shots at the bar and is quite inebriated. The Ewing shirted fan obviously recognizes Kislinger, and simply barges into the conversation.

"Frankly I find it hard to believe. I think they'll find out that this is something like the Manson murders back in the sixties. O.J. doesn't fit that profile. What do you think?" Kislinger tries to appease the drunken fan by including him in the conversation but immediately regrets it.

"You never know. This bitch Nicole is a nigger lover. But she dumped O.J. when she finally figured out how stupid he is. Simpson wants to be a white guy and can't pull it off."

"Whoa, whoa, take it easy, buddy." Kislinger tries to cut the guy of – unsuccessfully.

"When his white trash wife decides to dump him for the Jew boy, Simpson acts like the nigger that he is and slits their throats. End of story. They ought to give O.J. about 2000 volts of juice in the electric chair and the world can return to normal."

Kislinger, Birdsong and Pudd'nhead all cringe at the fan's outburst. They might have just sloughed it off as the incoherent babble of a bar drunk if it hadn't been for the fact that they are in the bar with Mickey. They know Syd Johnson has African-American bloodlines. But Mickey grows angry. He is angry more often than not the last couple of years. But this barroom bigot thoroughly annoys him. Mickey reaches over and puts both hands over the man's arms and grabs him by the jersey straps twisting them in his hands and shoving them against the man's clavicle. Mickey towers over the drunk who has clearly misconstrued the attitudes of his audience.

"You know something asshole. It's shitheads like you that cause all kinds of problems in this country. You're wearing a jersey with the name and number of an African-American athlete on its back. Is he your hero? Or is Ewing okay because he scores ..."

"Mickey, cool it, don't kill the little twirp."

Jack grabs Mickey from behind and pulls him off the racist fan, who quickly backs away the moment Mickey lets go of his jersey straps. There are two other young men who have been drinking with the Ewing-shirted man but they make no move to go to his defense. In fact they ease him away from Mickey's group the moment Mickey lets go. Meanwhile Pudd'nhead takes care of the bar bill and the group leaves Keen's before the proprietor asks them to do so. It's nearly game time anyway so they proceed across 7$^{th}$ Avenue and into *the Garden*.

∞∞∞∞

Jack Birdsong is concerned about his buddy. They had been through so much together since their Shenandoah days. But lately Mickey seems to have difficulty controlling his anger. This worries Birdsong.

∞∞∞∞

*Immediately after their Shenandoah graduation, Mickey and Jack enlisted in the Marine Corps. They went through basic training and shipped off to South East Asia together in early 1966. They were both stationed in Khe Sanh during the Tet Offensive. Mickey was wounded by shrapnel inside the edge of the Marine combat base. Meanwhile Jack's unit was patrolling the perimeter of the combat station and took on heavy fire. The continuous bombardment from the North Vietnamese Army caused many casualties and a scattering of the remaining Marines. Jack Birdsong had suffered a debilitating leg wound and was captured by the Viet Cong while trying to play possum among several American casualties. It was a moment in time that he played over in his mind ten thousand times since that day but never spoke about except with Mickey.*

*Birdsong spent five long years in a Vietnamese prison before his release in 1973. When he returned home to the United States he learned that Mickey Johnson was alive. He also learned that despite two separate war wounds Mickey survived without inordinate mental anguish from the war. Birdsong however thought much of life had passed him by. He discovered that Mickey had married his high school sweetheart, Barbara McDonough, but that through some cruel twist of fate Mickey later lost his wife to cancer. Mickey rarely talked about Barbara these days, except with Jack.*

## June 1994

*Over the next twenty years since the war, Mickey and Jack had become as close as ever, maybe even closer than they were in Vietnam. There were so many things that they could talk about only with one another. And many of those issues had their roots in the 1960's. There was no one outside of the family members themselves, who truly understood the odious feud and venomous hatred between the Babcocks and the Johnsons. But if there was anyone who could come close to understanding the feud it was Jack Birdsong.*

*The first time that Jack Birdsong had any inkling about Mickey Johnson's involvement with Simone Muirchant-Babcock was when the two Marines were together in Southeast Asia. A conversation had taken place in January of 1967 right after they were at the USO Christmas show starring Bob Hope. The comedian had a whole cadre of beautiful young women who accompanied him for these shows – including Long Island's own Joey Heatherton. Seeing these dazzling women was what had tripped a typically lascivious conversation between the two young Marines that went back to beautiful Long Island women. Jack and Mickey and all of their high school classmates had harbored craven desires over Simone, who was at the time a gorgeous young assistant to the school principal. Jack remembered that Mickey had been quite friendly with Simone – maybe a little more so than the rest of the class. But that night in Vietnam, Mickey remained vaguely evasive and cool when the conversation got around to Simone. Still, to think that Mickey had scored with Simone was too unbelievable for Jack. Yet he wondered.*

*It wasn't until much later that Jack had learned all of the intrigue that went along with Mickey's father and Simone. Over time the goddess-like aura surrounding Simone, faded into mere mortality in Jack Birdsong's mind. She was merely an older woman and a Babcock, even if she was still beautiful.*

*Jack's law enforcement and intelligence contacts led him to be quite suspicious of Frank Babcock very soon after Wayne Johnson's murder in 1980. However for whatever reason he always had a hard time convincing Mickey that there was more to his suspicions than just a gut feeling. For ten years Mickey had managed to believe that Frank Babcock was too soft to do be responsible for a violent murder and Mickey was somewhat forgiving for lesser transgressions. However Jack believed that in 1991 when he told Mickey about the new DNA evidence that had emerged, he had finally convinced him. He felt responsible. He thought that he had helped change Mickey into a very angry man.*

∞∞∞

As they enter The Garden, the buzz hasn't changed. Basketball fans are still fixated on the emerging story that football player O.J. Simpson is now a fugitive. His attorneys have not brought him in to be charged as they promised and "The Juice" is on the run. This news has morphed the playoffs into a circus atmosphere. Ironically, the Ringling Brothers and Barnum & Bailey Circus performances have just recently been ousted from Madison Square Garden by the Knicks playoff schedule. But now, a full 5 days after the murders took place O.J. is clearly in the center ring of the circus.

"Do you belief it? Everybody here is also talking about Simpson?" Mickey asks the question to put his friends at ease that he is over the racial incident that has just occurred across the street. It is also evident that more fans are crowded around televised news coverage on the interior televisions near the concession stands than are watching warm up drills. But it is getting close to game time. Kislinger has managed to secure some third row midcourt seats so the Long Island friends push past the concession area crowds and make their way courtside.

"Must win for the Knicks, I'd say," Jack opines. "Can't go back to Houston needing two wins on the road."

"I'm confident, Pudd'nhead adds. "Ewing and the Oakley are going to clean up on the boards. We've got this one."

Birdsong is busy procuring four beers from the aisle concessioner and so Mickey moves into his seat as the thickening crowd stands for the singing of the National Anthem. At the opening tipoff the seats are only about 70% occupied even though the game is a sell-out. The duel between the game's big men begins to unfold as promised. Both Patrick Ewing and Hakeem Olajuwon are taking the ball to the hoop and Charles Oakley is fighting fiercely for offensive rebounds. At the end of the first quarter the Knicks are up by a point 22-21. Normally the fans would have been rocking with every lead change but instead there is more of a flat hum over the Garden. There is noise but it isn't very volatile. In fact the seats are still not anywhere near fully occupied. When Mickey comes back to the seats after purchasing the second round of beers, he startles his buddies with the explanation.

"You won't believe what's happening on TV!"

## June 1994

"The O.J. stuff? Did they find him?"

"It's crazy man. People are all lined up near the TV's. They've got the game on in one little corner of the screen, you know like that picture-in-picture format. Well the rest of the screen is covering a police chase of O.J.'s Bronco. Al Cowlings, his linebacker buddy is driving. Supposedly, Juice has a gun to his head."

"Cowlings' head or his own head?"

"Apparently his own head."

The players begin to reconvene out on the floor for the start of the second quarter, but Mickey and his buddies are still standing as he doles out the Budweiser.

"Holy shit. That mother-fucker did it after all." Pudd'nhead fast-forwards to the same conclusion that the others had come to as well. His delivery is nearly as venomous as that of the Ewing fan at Keen's Steakhouse.

"Certainly looks that way." Mickey replies.

"I've got to see this." Kislinger says and starts back up the steps toward the concession area. Mickey, Jack and Pudd'nhead are right behind him.

∞∞∞

The next morning Mickey gets up late. It's a Saturday and Mickey likes to sleep in on Saturdays at his Garden City home. 8:30 AM is late enough, however. By the time he gets to the kitchen table, the whole household is present. Predictably they are talking about O.J. Less predictable is who is on what sides of the fence.

"Good morning, Mickey. How was the game?"

"Knicks won. We're up three games to two. But we don't want to see it go seven."

"Did you see what happened with O.J.?" Violet, Syd's mother takes the lead in bringing Mickey into the household debate.

"Sad situation ... lots of kids who look up to him."

"So you think he's guilty?"

"It looks that way, but that's why we have a judicial system ... to examine all of the evidence. I'll say this though. You don't look innocent, when you sit in the back of a car having already convicted yourself and looking to carry out the sentence with a loaded gun. I just think it's sad. Apparently they have some additional evidence showing he has beaten his wife before."

"See that, Syd. Even your own husband knows he's guilty. The man is an embarrassment to his race and to the human race as a whole. He's a butcher!" Violet is purple with rage.

"He may be guilty, Mom, but for Christ's sake don't convict him over some newspaper report. They enjoy sensationalizing this stuff. Frankly I don't trust the Los Angeles Police Department as far as I can throw them. I think he's innocent. You can believe he's guilty. I believe that he's being framed. And by the way, I didn't hear my husband say that he's guilty. I heard you say to give him his day in court. Didn't you, Mickey?"

"Did O.J. do it, Dad?" Cody looked imploringly at his father for a verdict while younger brother Noah looks on with interest.

"Oh wow. I guess that only leaves two more *jurors* to voice their opinion." He looks over to where Kathy McDonough is busily braiding his six year old daughter, Jessica's hair.

"Guilty." Kathy gave a one word answer.

"Guilty." Jessica echoed her answer.

"So, let's see – by my tally that's three guilty verdicts, one innocent and three undecided votes. I just don't have a firm opinion at this point, but as I said, it doesn't look good for Simpson."

That isn't the slanted viewpoint that Syd wants to hear. She is confused by her own mother's unwillingness to stand up for Simpson's rights. However she is not confused by her husband's jaundiced inclinations. Syd feels that her husband is biased but he doesn't even recognize his own inherent racism. He is frustrating to deal with. She even empathizes with the frustration that Simone Muirchant must have felt many years earlier when she tried to convince Mickey that war is inherently immoral. She is worried that she is facing a similar subliminal value deficit with respect to Mickey's subconscious racism.

"Why jump to any conclusion based solely on media reports?"

"Don't go defending the man just because he's black, Syd? Remember he married a white woman."

"What' that supposed to mean, Mom? You married a *white man!*" Syd finds it absurd that her mother could say something so outlandish. Meanwhile Kathy offers nothing more than her earlier one word reply. It's a mother-daughter debate that she feels uncomfortable joining. There are very few moments like this when Kathy feels uncomfortable being part of the extended family.

## June 1994

"That's exactly right. And I loved Ray until the day he died. We had our differences, especially when it came to your brother, Jermaine. But even if our differences had led to divorce, I could never have savagely murdered him. And that's what Simpson did. He wants to be white. He's not white. Blacks shouldn't claim him either. The man is just a savage ... a depraved human being ... black or white doesn't matter."

"I don't want to discuss this any longer. We'll see what happens." Syd doesn't want the debate to continue in front of her children. She feels that the media is simply engaging in what Justice Clarence Thomas once referred to as a "high-tech lynching for uppity blacks."

Syd turns to her husband and snaps: "Cody has baseball practice at 10:00 o'clock. Are you going to take them or am I?" It's a nasty question because Syd knows that Mickey always goes to his sons' practices and games whenever he's home.

Over the last few years. Mickey has faced the issue of racial unrest in his own Garden City home on several occasions. He knows that racial bias often has more to do with skin-pigmentation than other physiological distinctions to say nothing of other sociological differences or cultural interpretations. If evaluating all of these ethnic variances is an unjust endeavor, denying them is equally disingenuous.

The pigmentation issue in the household is not subtle in all cases. Mickey is clearly white, as is his first mother-in-law, Kathy McDonough. Violet Spataro is clearly black. From there it gets fuzzier. Syd Johnson is a soft-skinned mulatto, who looks more Italian American than African American. Mickey and Syd's sons both have fair skin with black tresses like their mother. Jessica Johnson is now six, soon-to-be seven, years old. With every passing day she begins to look exactly like her mother.

∞∞∞

*Garden City is not a racially diverse village in 1994. All sections of the village reflect an affluence that has transcended more than a century of time. More than ninety percent of the village is white, with about one per cent of the village residents being African-American. Other ethnic groups, including Hispanics, Asians and Native Americans are few in number but collectively comprise the remaining population. Garden City residents are predominantly Catholic and those of Irish-Catholic heritage alone make up nearly half of the residents of the village.*

## Techies, Trials & Technologies

But Garden City is not a remote sleepy Long Island village either. Eighteen miles due-east of Midtown Manhattan, it doesn't hover near either shoreline and its history is not reflective of either a north shore or a south shore legacy. Instead Garden City is centrally located. It enjoys its own rich history and heritage. It was founded in 1869 by entrepreneur, Alexander Turney Stewart. The business mogul also built the Central Railroad of Long Island, as a means of $19^{th}$ Century transportation between New York City and suburban Garden City.

A. T. Stewart was a multi-millionaire Irish immigrant, whose wealth – amassed in the $19^{th}$ century – would have been valued at nearly $55 billion in 1994. He was one of the top ten wealthiest Americans of all time. Stewart made his initial fortune in the dry goods business and is often credited with being the founder of the modern department store that replaced the general stores of an earlier era. His model was then replicated by other $19^{th}$ century retail barons such as John Wanamaker, Rowland Hussey Macy and Marshall Fields among others. Stewart's original department store – sometimes referred to as the Marble Palace – was located at 280 Broadway in NYC and was designated as a national historic landmark in 1965.

Stewart's original concept for the development of Garden City was as a bedroom community for the employees of his company. Because of this vision Stewart has always been considered more of a man of the people. While the colossal fortunes of other $19^{th}$ century industrial barons – the Vanderbilts, Pratts, Roosevelts, Babcocks, Whitneys, Guggenheims, Woolworths and Morgans, amongst others – made their country homes on Long Island's Gold Coast, Alexander Turney Stewart set about creating his own legacy in a more expanded community of well-heeled Americans who settled in Garden City. Unlike the extravagant mystifying mansions of the north shore, the pricey mansions of Garden City were not replete with private roads and gate houses shrouding them from public view. Garden City was a neighborhood community, albeit a very affluent neighborhood community.

The Garden City chronicle over its first 125 years included the contiguous spawning of the adjacent hamlets of Garden City South, Garden City Park and East Garden City. Roosevelt Field in East Garden City was the take off point for Charles Lindbergh's historical transatlantic flight in 1927. Roosevelt Field was later converted into a massive shopping mall that would have made A.T. Stewart proud.

## June 1994

*During its first century of incorporation, Garden City became the home to: Doubleday Publishing Company; Mitchel Air Force Base; Adelphi University and to several prestigious private schools including St Paul's School that was founded by AT Steward's widow Cornelia Stewart in 1879 as an Episcopal boys boarding school and the prominent Jesuit academic institution, Shenandoah High School, that was founded thirty five years later by Father Alexander Skylark, a transplanted Virginian, who usurped the name of his valley homeland to christen Shenandoah as an all-boys school in 1907.*

∞∞∞

Even as the residents of Garden City live out their 20$^{th}$ Century, post IRS, version of the American Dream, the community still has not embraced diversity. If a black woman is seen at a little league game it is assumed that she is a nanny or another member of someone's domestic staff. If a Hispanic man is seen at a landscape nursery it is assumed he is a gardener. A Chinese woman at a grocery store is a cook and so on.

Mickey Johnson's mother-in-law has occasionally been subjected to the same stereotyping when she accompanies her grandchildren around town. Cody and Noah are now in the 5$^{th}$ and 4$^{th}$ grades respectively. Three weeks earlier Cody got into some trouble at school for cold-clocking Danny Dunn on the bus ride home from St. Peter's School in neighboring Mineola. Dunn is a fellow 5$^{th}$ grader who informed Cody that: "your grandmother is a nigger." Cody's response was to clout Danny. When the dust settled Danny Dunn's parents made him march over to the Johnson home and apologize to both Cody and to his grandmother. Things quickly returned to a redefined normal. The school officials were glad that the parents stepped in and settled the dispute without their intervention. The incident was quickly forgotten between the 11 year old boys who were usually best friends.

∞∞∞

Now, three weeks later, Danny and Cody are at baseball practice, and Noah is there with them as well. Mickey is across the field from the boys conversing with a couple of the other parents. They are discussing the same topic that everyone is discussing on June 18$^{th}$, the slow speed car chase in California. While the parents discussion is judicious, most everyone has come to the conclusion that Simpson is guilty. They are shocked by the fact that the whole investigation is being played out moment by moment on TV.

## Techies, Trials & Technologies

"It's not like one of those TV crime shows you see like 'Law and Order.' These are real people. The cops are real. This Marcia Clark woman, the DA, is real. It's not just the news. It's ongoing. It's like … like … some kind of reality show … like 'reality TV.' People are absolutely fascinated by it." This is typical of the bewilderment that the Garden City Little League parents articulate. Similar statements are being made in many other venues as well.

∞∞∞

The conversation among the Little Leaguers is more direct, even if they are simply reflecting opinions that have been offered up by adults in their own homes.

"Man, can you believe O.J. did it?" Danny Dunn is asking his teammates but more or less talking directly to Cody. "My father says that O.J. wants to be a white guy so he married a white lady. Then as soon as she dumps him he slits her throat. He says that you can take the boy out of the ghetto, but you can't take the ghetto out of the boy."

"What's that supposed to mean?" Bruce Carlson jumps into the conversation without removing his catcher's mask."

"It means that O.J. should have married a black lady, and then that white lady would still be alive."

"Well, my grandmother is black. She married a white guy and they didn't kill each other." Cody chimes in.

"That black lady who comes to our games sometimes is *your* *grandmother*?" Carlson takes off his mask this time to ask his question. "Then how come you're not at all black?"

"Cause his father is white, asshole. Look, he's right over there." Danny points to where Cody's father is talking to the other parents.

"I don't know. My Dad says that I'm 75% white and 25% black. So I guess that makes me white, and that's why I look white … because *I am* … mostly."

"Me too," said Noah. "Mostly."

∞∞∞

# XVIII

## July 1994

Frank Babcock is doing something different. After nearly ten years – off and on – of meetings in Doctor Hamilton Brophy's office, Babcock has invited his psychiatrist out to his home in Southampton. Margot Babcock thought that the new home needed a name, just like *Babcock Manor & Gardens* had its name. She named it the *Babcock Sea Breeze Chateau*, most commonly shortening the nomenclature by leaving off the family name and just calling it the *Sea Breeze Chateau*, and occasionally just *Sea Breeze* or even just *The Chateau*.

Dr. Brophy has rejected social invitations from Babcock several times in the past explaining that such encounters are not ethically appropriate. He is acutely aware of several legal and ethical decisions about boundaries.

Boundaries in the practice of psychiatry include what are considered boundary *crossings* and what constitutes more grievous issues of boundary *violations*. Certain behaviors – involving sexual relationships or financial relationships are considered completely verboten and subject to professional discipline, such as medical license revocation or legal malpractice litigation.

However Brophy is also of a mindset that there has to be complete and irrevocable trust between the patient and the therapist. Therefore he believes that upon occasion, a simple boundary crossing, might allow trust and/or understanding to grow. He is also fully cognizant that there is never anything *simple* about a boundary crossing.

With both men fully aware of certain preconditions, Brophy has relented to a social engagement of sorts. He agrees to conduct a multi hour session with Babcock at his summer home on the southeastern fork of Long Island. The verbal agreement between the two men is that Brophy and his wife, Irene will have dinner on Saturday night with the Babcocks at a Southampton restaurant of Frank's choosing but that they will split the bill for dinner. Frank's therapeutic session would be attended only by the two men. Brophy and his wife will not stay overnight at the Babcock residence. It is the first therapy session for Babcock in five months.

∞∞∞

"Have you spent much time in the Hamptons before, Hamilton?"

"Irene and I used to own a place in Bridgehampton. We sold it in the early eighties. As financial decisions go that was *not* one of my better choices. But back then we were spending most of our free time traveling, while real estate values were growing astronomically. I still tripled my initial investment. But of course that's a mere pittance compared to what's happened to real estate out here since then."

"Yes, it's true. I'm not quite sure how I feel about all of the development that's taken place." He thinks quietly and then adds, "but I'm sort of part of all that. I think we own eight residential properties out here, including Sea Breeze and I have long term investments in other properties as well. I'm not sure I understand all of it. It's effectively managed by my personal attorney Irv Walberg and his real estate staff."

"When you said we '*we own, eight properties*,' who were you referring to as part of '*we?*' Does Margot own any part of any of these properties with you?"

"No. Margot signed a prenuptial agreement just like Diane did."

"Then who were you referring to when you said *we*?"

"I wasn't referring to anyone other than myself; maybe I was including my heirs ... my estate ..."

"So that's who was in your mind at the moment when you said '*we own, eight properties*'?"

Babcock thought for a second and then said, "I believe when I said that ... I was thinking about my legal staff and my real estate management team. Those were the images of people in my mind at that moment."

## July 1994

The conversation is typical of a therapy session rather than a social discussion. Brophy is continuously probing for the meaning or motive behind the words and Babcock is continuously evaluating his own vocabulary.

Babcock thinks back over this recent sequence of questions from his psychiatrist and then adds, "Honestly I don't think Margot has any interest whatsoever in these real estate holdings. Her sister ... God rest her soul ... now that woman knew everything about these properties. She asked Walberg and my other lawyers a million questions about them. They all thought of Nicole as just another gold digger. Margot's not like that."

"As I recall from our previous sessions these properties were a bone of contention between you and Diane also."

"Yes, Diane was not particularly happy about my little affair with CC. But all of that is a long time ago. Neither woman is a part of my life any longer. However I will say this much. This house here on Meadow Lane was originally Diane's idea. She never liked living at *Babcock Manor*. I had a much smaller house on this property and Diane wanted me to tear it down and rebuilt something magnificent on the property to replace the old house ... and so I did."

He snickers and then adds, "Of course it wasn't finished until after I divorced Diane. Diane helped design it. She visualized all of the surrounding landscaping features. She was also responsible for the construction delays. She kept changing her mind about everything. I stayed out of it. But fittingly she never got to spend a single night in the finished product."

∞∞∞

*Frank Babcock and his therapist were discussing Babcock's second wife Diane Heath-Babcock. The marriage lasted six and a half years. However by Brophy's way of reckoning the marriage was never an integral part of his client's persona. Brophy also assessed that there was not a lot of intimacy that went along with the marriage. Throughout the duration of that union, Babcock had engaged in a series of affairs with other women. His most prominent affair was with his Southampton real estate agent, Crystal Clungstud-Myer, a Native American member of the Shinnecock tribe who called herself CC.*

*In early 1990, several years after his affair with CC, Babcock divorced Diane. The marriage ended shortly after Babcock suffered a heart-attack in San Francisco and shortly before Nicole Silver gave birth to Jedidiah.*

## *Techies, Trials & Technologies*

*The summer of 1990 was the first summer that Frank Babcock had occupied his new home on Meadow Lane. After settling their divorce according to the premarital contract, Frank Babcock never again heard from Diane Heath. However, as he did with many people in his life, Babcock had his security staff keep tabs on her whereabouts on an intermittent basis to avoid any unpleasant repercussions that might surface at some later date.*

∞∞∞

Babcock and Brophy have been sitting on a short partially sheltered patio at the edge of the rear lawn that sits between Babcock Sea Breeze Chateau and the rim of the beach foliage. The lawn itself is simply a brief 120 feet in depth, and the width is somewhat curtailed by a forty foot long free-form pool that is sunk into a separate pave stone patio. The pool area is separated from the area where they now sit by a pool house and bar area. The entire rear of the living area of the property is fenced off from six feet tall beach grasses. There is also some wild shrubbery between the Babcock lawn and the beach front portion of his property. Just outside a gate in the fence there is a four step lead-on to an arched and elevated private boardwalk that spans the 150 foot wide expanse of beach foliage and lands on the sun-bleached powder of Long Island's south shore.

The Babcock property is on the even-numbered side of the Meadow Lane peninsula. The odd-numbered homes on the north side of the street bordered on Shinnecock Bay and are priced significantly below the even-numbered properties which enjoy ocean front vistas. Much of the magnificence of the individual homes on both sides of the peninsula is hidden from the street by lavish landscaping. However the rear views from upper floors of these homes are stunningly beautiful.

"You have grown to like it out here haven't you, Frank?"

"Somewhat, I guess. I've spent more time out here in Southampton since we sold *Babcock Manor & Gardens*."

"How does *Sea Breeze* compare to your demesne in Great Neck?'

"Well of course *The Manor* no longer exists. The developers tore it down in 1988. But I'd have to say that I do miss it. I lived there for thirteen years, while Fox and Maureen were growing up. And I used to visit my aunts there all the time when I was growing up myself. So my home here doesn't compare to *The Manor* in terms of personal nostalgia. *Babcock Sea Breeze Chateau* is merely a summer home in Southampton. *Babcock Manor* had grandeur and majesty and a sense of history. This place has a sense of

## July 1994

opulence, affluence and novelty. I guess they both have something to offer. They're just very different."

"Does Margot like it?"

"She loves it. She never met Diane and she doesn't associate either of my ex-wives with this place because neither of them ever slept in the master bedroom."

"I'm looking forward to meeting your wife tonight. I think she has had a very profound and positive impact on your outlook on life."

"I couldn't agree more. But one of the defining characteristics of our relationship is that we spend time apart. Our affection for one another is not smothering. But when I'm not traveling, I spend most of my time with Margot and Jedd."

"Doesn't Margot want to travel with you?"

"No. She has no desire to travel to the Middle East, and she doesn't particularly care for many of my Saudi acquaintances. She doesn't understand why the Saudis are such close allies of the United States."

"Honestly neither do I Frank. Other than the fact that we have a military base there, I'm not sure how they qualify as allies. But let's not get political today. Let's concentrate on your personal relationships and your personal growth."

"You and I are both fifty-nine Hamilton. How much room for personal growth do we have? Sooner or later aren't we simply expected to accept that we are who we are?"

Brophy doesn't answer the question. "Okay let's try this a different way. Why do you continue to work?"

Frank takes off his sunglasses and rubs his eyes while he searches for an answer. "I guess so I can build and protect my assets and my estate. Maybe it's simply a game I enjoy."

"And why are you so concerned with your estate? Aren't you simply playing the old game of he who dies with the most toys, wins?"

"No. I just want to make sure that Fox and Jedidiah have all of the same opportunities that were afforded to me."

"From what you tell me Fox is already doing quite well on his own. Jedidiah is only four but if you died tomorrow, he would never have to worry about whatever opportunities financial resources might provide."

Frank realizes how dumb his rationale is. And so he offers up another alternative. "Maybe I just work, because it's what I've always done. That might be vague but ..."

Hamilton Brophy breaks one of his own strict rules and interrupts his patient.

"Now we're getting somewhere. I don't see your answer as vague at all. You're in the fairly unique position of having all of the creature comforts that money can buy. You don't have to work another day in your life. And yet as you said you're working because that's what you've always done."

"But I've changed what work I actually do."

"Alright so explain to me what you mean by that. And remember *work*, to many people means earning an income. You have to recognize that's not a real motivation for you, even if you pretend it is. So tell me about how you think that your career has evolved."

"I'm not sure I like the word, 'career.' It sounds too ..."

"Proletarian?"

"Yes, maybe."

"So tell me how you perceive your *work* has evolved. And put whatever labels on it for whatever reasons you want."

"Should I just start from the beginning?"

"Yes ... well start wherever you want ... we just want to explore how you view this facet of your life ... your work."

"I started working as a lawyer after I graduated from Harvard Law in 1960."

"That was your first job? You didn't work at all while you were in high school or college?"

"No. The first pay check I ever received came after college. And I was both the payer and the payee on that check. It came from Babcock, Gordon, Ellis and Turley." He pauses. "I take that back. We were only Babcock and Ellis at the time."

"Why did you want to become a lawyer, in the first place?"

"I'm not sure, exactly. But when I was growing up there were always lots of lawyers around my father and they seemed important to him."

"We've never talked much about your father in the past. I guess I thought that he was also a lawyer by training and profession. What was his career ... I'm sorry ... his work ...what was his work?"

# July 1994

"I don't know how to label it, but he wasn't a lawyer. I know that much. And he died when he was only 37. But I was just 15. I was a freshman at Shenandoah. My mother spent a ton of time with the family lawyers after my father died. But then she died also when I was an undergraduate at Dartmouth. And then after my mother died I dealt with the lawyers myself as well, because my parents essentially left everything to me.

"But you are unsure about what your father did for a living?"

"He was referred to occasionally as a financier … whatever that means. That's the term my mother and my aunts … my father's sisters … always used to describe his work."

"What did that mean to you?"

"I actually had this discussion at one time with Irv Walberg. I've probably mentioned Irv to you a few times over the years."

"Yes, many times. He heads up your personal legal team. You've mentioned him often in the past … even once earlier today."

"He doesn't head it up anymore. Hell, Irv is now 84 years old, but he did lead the group until about five or six years ago. He's been a family attorney for more than fifty years. And for the record he's still razor sharp, and well respected." The discussion drifts away from Babcock's recall of his financier conversation with Brophy, and settles more on his relationship with Walberg.

"You are very loyal to those who serve you well?" It is a question not a statement.

"Yes, of course. Haven't I been loyal to you Hamilton?"

Brophy isn't quite prepared for the quick flipping of his interrogatory.

"Well … yes … I guess. But I would … I mean … I hope there is more to our professional relationship than just loyalty."

"There is. And there is also more to my professional relationship with Walberg. You are both quite competent in your fields."

"Loyalty is a good thing … most of the time. Yet I believe that it can cause a good deal of pain, whenever the loyalty bond is severed."

"I agree. There have been many times in my life when I've been loyal to various women, and they have not been loyal to me. It's angered me in the past."

"But you're no longer angry with Simone; with Diane; with CC or with Nicole. Isn't that a fair assessment?"

"Very fair ... they're no longer a part of my life."

"Do you believe that you were loyal to these women in the past?"

"Yes until they showed that they were disloyal to me." Babcock asserts this firmly.

"Well we know about Simone's disloyalties, but how exactly do you pin that label on Diane, CC or Nicole."

"They all simply wanted money more than they wanted me."

"And how exactly do you know that?"

"Trust me I knew it when it happened. I could feel it. There's no need for anything more than my own recognition of the truth of their disloyalties. A man can tell. You know?"

"And how about Margot? Has she been disingenuous as well?"

"Not that I know of. Margot is different. She needs little and she demands even less. In fact she demands nothing. I should say ... she asks for nothing. Meanwhile she's given me great comfort with respect to her rapport with Jedd. And yes, I'd say she's been very loyal to me."

"There's that word again. Just how important is loyalty to you, Frank? Is it as important as love? Are you conflating the two concepts?"

"Maybe." He pauses briefly and then confirms his thought.

"Yes. At this stage of my life, loyalty is love." Before his therapist can comment, Babcock offers, "There might be one slight difference however. Remember the Beatles song, Can't Buy Me Love? Well I'd have to say that money definitely can buy me loyalty." He stops suddenly before Brophy can counter and stands up. "Let's go inside for a minute. I'll show you around before the women arrive."

They walk through a rear entrance way that leads to the bi-level recreation area of the house. The eastern half of the ground level facility is a movie and game room. The western half of the recreation area is elevated by three steps. This section is partitioned into a fitness center and weight room on the northern quarter. There are shower, sauna, and steam room facilities on the southern quartile which faces the rear of the house. Between the movie/game room area and the fitness area there's a wide spiral staircase. The stairwell is adjacent to a 6ft by 6ft elevator that can hoist folks through the three floors of the house. It is almost never used.

Due to its proximity to the ocean there is no sub surface level to the Babcock residence. However a sand covered concrete build-up of the front area of the house has created a feeling that the rear entryway and the

## July 1994

recreation facilities are located as a subterranean walkout to a colossal cavern. The faux elevation of the house front is further covered with surface level greenery and lush ocean-oriented landscaping.

"Where does the help reside?" Brophy notices that curiously there doesn't appear to be any place for the staff to live.

"We don't have any live-in help. We our very fortunate to have a one-family, four-person staff that works full-time from May through September. And the Robinsons live in town two miles away from Sea Breeze, at another property."

"One of your properties?"

"Yes, I believe so."

"The young black woman who showed me in when I drove up ... is she one of the Robinsons?"

"Yes. There are two daughters. Julie is the one who showed you in. Marcie is the older girl. She mostly works cleaning the house and helping out in the kitchen. The parents, James and Ella Robinson run the place. They buy all the staples, cook all the meals, change the linens and do the laundry and whatever else has to be done. I have no idea. They just do it. James even does minor repairs around the Chateau."

"So then would you characterize the Robinsons as being loyal to you?"

"Yes. Most definitely. They're fine people ... and very loyal."

"What about you, Frank? Are you as loyal to others as you want them to be towards you?"

"I take care of those who work for me."

"What about Margot? Have you been loyal to her?"

Babcock thinks about that question for a second before he answers. "I've been as loyal as she has expects me to be."

"What about what you expect of yourself?"

"That can be a dangerous question."

"What do you mean by that?"

"I'm assuming you're asking about other women currently in my life besides Margot."

"Well, it's a topic you've avoided so far today. And it has been a center piece topic in the past."

"It's not like I've been keeping a lot from you, Hamilton." Babcock laughs confidently. "And I believe that my relationship with Margot is satisfying to both of us."

"But I gather that there are some things that you haven't told me. Am I correct about that?"

"Yes."

"Do you want to talk about this other woman or women, Frank? Over the years you haven't kept very much from me."

"You're right, Hamilton. There's very little that I haven't discussed with you. But sometimes I need to think about things before I'm able to discuss them – even with you."

"Sex, anger, revenge, frustration, there aren't many things that you haven't been willing to speak about. I know that you don't like to talk much about your business. But you've told me in the past that it's too boring anyway. Do those parameters still hold true?"

"In some ways, yes. And in some ways, no. The difficulty arises because my business and my sex life now have an interwoven element to them."

"This has happened to you before. Didn't you first meet Nicole Silver when she was an associate in your law firm?"

"This is much different, Hamilton. This involves a client ... a very big client ... a dangerous client."

"Why don't you just tell me about it in your terms, Frank? I don't think it's helpful to just talk around the issue. It's a much better idea to address it head on. So let's just begin at the beginning."

"A few years ago I started making many more trips to the Middle East. I had one very large family client that I was doing business with."

"What kind of business? Is this legal business or financial business or some other kind of business?"

"That's just it, Hamilton. This is the kind of stuff that you have no knowledge about. It doesn't matter what business I do with these people. It's the people themselves who are important. It's the people that make a difference to me."

"Is there any one person in particular who makes such a difference for you?"

"Alright, you win. I will tell you a little bit about the al-Haddād family. Abdulrahman al-Haddād is current patriarch of the family. Masira al-

## July 1994

Haddād, is his daughter. I have been having an affair with Masira that dates back to just after the Gulf War in 1991. If Abdulrahman al-Haddād knew about it, I would not only lose his business, I might also lose my life. Certainly Masira would be scorned, shunned or even eliminated. It is a danger that I live with constantly."

"How often do you see this woman, Masira?"

"Every time I go to the Middle East, she serves as my hostess. She helps me execute my itinerary of meetings, dinners and social events. But the nature of that role is not meant to be intimate."

"By intimate, you mean sexual?"

"Yes, of course." Babcock leans back and stands with his shoulders squared. They have been talking as they climb the spiral staircase to the main floor of the house. Now at the top of the landing Babcock wants to stand erect and speak frankly. The disclosure he is making is important to him even though he has vacillated before making it. He is totaling trusting his therapist.

"And this intimacy... this sexual relationship ... predates your marriage to Margot."

"Yes. It began right before her sister Nicole died and it continued right through my marriage to Margot. It's ongoing even now."

"We haven't talked a great deal about sexual things over the last year. Every time I broach the topic, you seem to shy away. But I have to say this isn't what I expected."

"What *did* you expect, Hamilton?"

"I thought that there might be a lingering erectile dysfunction issue that you simply didn't feel comfortable discussing, especially in light of your most recent marriage."

"Quite the opposite, I can assure you. What's interesting is that Masira has helped me cure my sexual problems."

"Do you mean that you no longer have difficulty getting an erection?"

"Yes."

"Well this is certainly a psychological breakthrough."

"Not really, Hamilton. It's actually more of a *physiological* breakthrough."

"What do you mean?"

"Masira has some friends in the UK, who have stumbled across a medication that's not on the market yet."

"An erectile dysfunction medication?"

"I think that it's meant to be a medication for cardiac issues. But it certainly has some amazing side effects."

"Is this medication called sildenafil?"

"Yes, that's right. So you've heard about it?"

"Yes. I've been reading about this recently. It was originally developed to treat pulmonary arterial hypertension. As you can imagine this drug can be quite transformative in the psychiatric field. But it concerns me that you and I haven't discussed previously. How long have you been taking this medication? And how did you get it? It hasn't been approved in the USA yet."

"One of Masira's brothers, Tariq al-Haddād, is a med student in England. He's studying at the Cambridge School of Clinical Medicine. Tariq is surrounded by people in the drug industry who are itching to get financial backing for various medical concoctions. They see Tariq as an access point to the al-Haddād family and its financial backing. I met a few of these people through Tariq, when I was over in the UK a few years back. When I heard about the side effect properties of sildenafil, I managed to get some personal samples. Tariq doesn't know that but Masira certainly does!" It is Babcock's odd attempt at sardonic humor.

"How about your wife?"

"I don't know what she thinks. She has a much different sex drive from her sister."

"Say more."

"There's not a lot more *to* say. Margot seems satisfied. I wouldn't say that our sex life is prolific but Margot doesn't complain. She's a young woman, who knows what she wants."

"With all of this talk earlier about loyalty, I have to ask how you feel about your own sexual infidelity. Or let me say it this way, would you feel betrayed if Margot had a sexual relationship with another man?"

Babcock stops in the middle of the room. There are only the two of them there in the cavernous main room of the house. He lowers his voice anyway and answers. "You probably will think this is strange, but it wouldn't bother me. In a way I half expect it. But I think you used the right word …

## July 1994

infidelity ... to me that's different from loyalty ... or should I say it's different from a *lack* of loyalty."

"Is that why you cheat on Margot, so that you won't feel as angry if you learn that she is cheating on you?"

"Loyalty, cheating, infidelity ... these are all different things."

"You may parse these words differently than most people, but unless you understand why you do so, you will be open to some surprises in how you feel as events unfold."

"You know Hamilton, sometimes I think you shrinks worry more about *feelings* and less about facts."

"Is your generalization of the whole psychiatric profession as *'you shrinks'* an attempt to avoid facing our personal disagreement? Your feelings are important, Frank. They often drive your behavior. And I sincerely believe it's important to understand your feelings ... your emotions. Sometimes the lack of response to your feelings is a reflection of depression."

"I don't believe that I'm depressed ... just disinterested in some things that other people care too much about. This sex thing is a good example. There are some people who use the term 'open marriage' to describe what Margot and I have together."

"So is that what you have then? An open marriage?"

"I said some people ... meaning others ... not Margot and me ... some other people have these 'open marriages.' They grant each other the freedom to have sex with whomever they want."

"Yes and sometimes they even discuss the details of these alternate relationships with each other ... or occasionally even participate in these non-conventional extra-marital sexual connections. Is that what you mean by an open marriage?"

"Yes. But, hear what I'm saying. Margot and I do *not* have an open marriage. In fact, quite the contrary, our prenuptial agreement expressly prohibits Margot from engaging in sexual relations with anyone other than her husband. And I have no desire to participate in any such convoluted sexual liaisons with my wife and others. However as I said before I half expect that Margot might have sex with someone else. And I'm telling you that I'd probably just look the other way. I wouldn't want to know about it ... but I'd understand it."

Brophy finds Babcock's declaration to be quite curious. So many of the personal difficulties that his patient has experienced over the years were rooted in the infidelity of his first wife. But he accepts Babcock's delineation of his relationship with Margot at face value.

"Alright let's change gears a bit. Another theme that you have chosen not to explore lately is your spirituality, your religious beliefs and how they play into your most recent experiences."

"That's fair. We haven't talked about that recently."

"Do you want to spend our time together discussing this?"

"I don't know. Sometimes it feels real important to me and sometimes it doesn't. Don't you think that's odd? As you know, I now consider myself a practicing Catholic. At least that's the framework for my spirituality."

"First off ... I don't think that your partitioning of your spirituality is odd ... at least not in the sense that it abnormal. Most people handle it similarly. As to the business of being a practicing Catholic ... tell me what that means to you."

"It means that I go to church regularly. I almost always go by myself, and I prefer to go during the week rather than on Sundays. I enjoy the peacefulness of a Catholic Church."

"But isn't attendance at Sunday services one of the requirements of being a practicing Catholic?"

"So who are you now, Hamilton? ... The Pope's enforcer?"

"Just trying to follow your thinking, Frank ...that's all."

"Well, I was raised as a Catholic. I received all of the sacraments. I went to Shenandoah High School, a place run by the Jesuits ... and I go to Mass more than most guys that I grew up with ... that's my claim to being a practicing Catholic. I even make a point of going to confession once a year although I try to do that when I travel to some out of the way place."

"Certainly not in Saudi Arabia?"

"Of course not."

"But we do want to return to that topic in our discussion …. Your Saudi Arabian friend ... Don't we? We've been drifting away from this unfinished topic."

Babcock realizes that Hamilton Brophy has simply been allowing the discussion to roam from the subject of his relationship with Masira al-Haddād. This might be simply to put him at ease for a moment or two before returning to a very central driving issue in his life. But he finds a way to avoid it temporarily.

## July 1994

"Maybe we should ... by the way, see this painting over there ...?" Babcock creates a momentary misdirection of his own. "For one odd reason or another it was one of Simone's favorites." He walks over in the direction of the painting. "Unfortunately, she was more interested in some of the Babcock family history than she was in being Mrs. Babcock."

They walk closer to the picture. It hangs off to the side of a large open seating area that could be construed as a living room, a family room, or a giant open den of some sort.

∞∞∞

The layout of the main floor of *Babcock Sea Breeze Chateau* is very open, with the exception of the bedroom areas which are on east and west sides of the floor and the front facing section of the house which has another floor above it, with a small library and a study.

The open space on the main floor runs from the front to the rear of the home separated only by several decorative moveable partition walls that are only seven feet high and no more than eight feet wide. These partition walls are irregularly placed and are sturdy but not structurally weight bearing. The high arched roof safeguards the rear two thirds of the *Sea Breeze Chateau*. A separate roof covers the front library/study area on the top floor. The main arched roof is supported by hidden steel beams that facilitate the open look architecture. The central open area also incorporates a very modern kitchen and dining area. These rooms, in turn, both look out through floor-to-ceiling south facing rear windows over the brush, and across the sand to the ocean tides.

∞∞∞

"Simone liked this painting?"

The painting is quite large and has an ornate antique thick wooden frame. The canvas depicts two uniformed men leaning on long wooden rods in a jaunty manner. The rods appear to be nineteenth century baseball bats. Although the uniformed men are facing each other they appear to be looking skyward. Also superimposed on the canvas is an attractive young mystery woman. She is portrayed in the center of the painting, elevated and slightly muted in the background. Her image appears to be much smaller and completely out of scale and/or perspective with the likeness of the two cadets, as though she is a part of their dream. *(Most art aficionados agreed that her likeness was added to the painting a few years after the original)*

"Yes, one thing Simone and I do have in common is that she is also a baseball fan ... and Yankee fan at that."

They have now walked over right in front of the painting that is obviously quite old.

"So who are these two gentlemen in the picture? Military men ... obviously. And why is that woman where she is? Awkward looking ... I think. And you mentioned baseball. So does this have something to do with that as well? Are those bats that they're leaning on?"

"The painting is more than 150 years old. The two men in the painting are Sam Babcock, who is my great grandfather ... and the other guy is his classmate at West Point, Abner Doubleday."

"He's the guy who invented baseball. Right?" Brophy is now staring intently at the painting which has a bit of an amateurish appeal to it. The painter and the two subjects appear to be enjoying the process whatever it entailed at the time.

"Doubleday is widely credited with inventing baseball but who knows it might have been Sam Babcock. Both of these guys were Civil War veterans fighting on the side of the Union Army. Apparently they were good friends for many years before and after the war. The painting is signed there at the bottom with the initials BS and the date of 1842. However some art experts who've examined the painting in detail differ as to the time of its creation. They also agree that the female figure was added to the painting sometime after its original creation."

Brophy now stares at the female in the picture. "Who did you say she is again?"

"I didn't say. No one seems to know." The woman is shown with a feathered hat and holding a folded umbrella or parasol. Both of her hands are resting on the top of the handle of the sunshade and she is looking demurely at the ground. The young woman has added a good deal of interest to the painting over time but she has never been definitively named. "The painting has come to be known as *The Ball Players and the Parasol Girl*. It has appeared as a curiosity in a few magazines over the years, and I think we got a purchase offer for it a while back."

"I'm assuming that this was on display at *Babcock Manor* before you moved it here. Why did you move it? Do you like the painting as much as your ex-wife liked it?"

## July 1994

"Not really. However it has been in the family forever, and I just thought it would be one thing that I might bring out here to *The Chateau* from *The Manor*. There are many other items ... art and furnishings from *The Manor* ... in storage somewhere, but this is the only art piece from *The Manor* that is on display here in Southampton."

"So, in a way, this beautiful new home of yours, has done a lot to separate your past from your future. But it's good to see that this painting has made its way to the wall out here. In essence it shows that you haven't totally repudiated your past."

"Don't read too much into that Hamilton ... although I realize that it's your job to do so ... I simply like the painting for two reasons. First, it's a conversation piece. That should be quite obvious at this point. And secondly, it has an underlying baseball theme. As you know, I enjoy baseball."

"Alright I won't belabor the point, but when you do your own private reflection on the matter, remember that the painting also brings with it the ties to your ancestry as well as ties to your first wife."

Babcock doesn't offer a rejoinder. They begin walking toward the open kitchen and dining area on the south side of the floor. Frank looks as though he is losing interest in his unconventional therapy session and is now more interested in continuing his cordiality as the tour guide of his home. However Hamilton Brophy cannot disengage from his professional pursuit and after a moment of thought he guides their ongoing discussion on a minor deviation from the path that they had been taking.

"Frank, in light of the fact that we have been discussing one of the artistic links to the Babcock ancestral past, I'm curious as to your views of the future of the Babcock name. A few years back ... before Jedidiah's birth, we once discussed your desire to have a flesh and blood descendant to the Babcock heritage. Now that your youngest son is more than four years old, how do you feel about that topic?"

"I don't think I understand the question."

"Do you feel that both Fox and Jedidiah have equally inherited the mantle of the Babcock surname for years into the future?"

By now they have made their way over to the south facing window of dining room area. Babcock stares out at the ocean in the near-distance. He takes his time and ponders his wording before he replies.

"It's not possible to equate their respective legacies in just that way. Were we only talking about tangible assets, the current plan is for equal inheritance."

Babcock shakes his head as if to clear that preemptive notion. "If we're talking simply about the Babcock name ... well they are both Babcocks. But blood relationships are different. What Jedd will pass along to his offspring is genetically different from what Fox will pass along to his progeny. A hundred years from now there will be two separate strains of Babcock blood ... heck there already are two strains of Babcock blood."

Brophy knows they are treading on an important ... but ultrasensitive topic. He wonders if Babcock's deliberate answer is reflective of the realization that the second strain of Babcock blood is physically Johnson blood as well. He doesn't dare to put the Johnson name in words or interrogatories of any sort. He avoids the train wreck, with a different question and he further softens his query with a generalization of the issue.

"Why do you suppose men feel so strongly about having a male heir who can carry on the surname of their lineage? And in your own case, why is it so important that there be blood associated with the name? Further to the point, wouldn't it be adequate to have a female blood lineage even if the family crest doesn't adorn the letterhead and the latticework on the doorstep?"

"It's important to me. Always has been. Always will be."

"I know that. But, why?"

"I don't know. Maybe it's a sense of posterity."

"Posterity, according to Webster, is not in any way synonymous to eternity, Frank. Are you sure that's what you mean?"

"How the hell would I know, Hamilton? Let's stop playing these ridiculous word games. It's important to me. We both recognize that. Can't we leave it that?"

There isn't much more to say. Brophy is content to allow Babcock to show him around the rest of the house without revisiting the topic. He wants to digest his patient's response to the bloodline issue. He realizes that this is more than a simple matter. Yet he also wants to be better prepared to dive into the issue with Babcock at a later session.

Meanwhile the tour of Frank Babcock's home is also telling Brophy a few things. Regardless of Babcock's display of conceit in the objects that made up his Southampton household, Brophy gets the distinct feeling that

## *July 1994*

Babcock does not really enjoy living there. After all *Babcock Sea Breeze Chateau* was designed by a former wife and more or less furnished and refurnished and named by his current wife. Brophy decides that at another time he will probe Frank's feelings about all of this in greater detail.

∞∞∞

# XIX

## *July 1994*

Margot Babcock feels noticeably younger. She doesn't normally feel this way around her husband, although she will admit to being somewhat submissive to his whims. She has left her step-son, Jedidiah back at their Meadow Lane manse in the care of the Robinsons and has joined her husband with his guests Hamilton and Irene Brophy.

"Do you enjoy all of the action out here in the summer time, Margot?"

"Yes I think I do. You know Irene, the days seem long and full but the summer itself seems to buzz right by. It feels like we just got out here and it's almost August already."

"Thank you for having us out for a visit. It is highly unusual ... actually unheard of ... for Hamilton to socialize with his patients. It sort of makes it difficult for conversation topics, don't you think?"

"Well let's hope not." Margot was trying to be friendly.

"It removes all of the personal social subjects that we girls normally like to gossip about."

"I guess we'll just have to gossip about others."

"Maybe so."

"Hamilton likes the Hamptons. Besides having a few patients who own homes out here, we used to own a house out here ourselves, over in Bridgehampton. We sold it about ten years ago. He wants us to consider getting a place out here once again. I'm not sure, it's a good idea."

Margot realizes that Irene is simply trying to make trivial conversation, but there is something about the way she refers to Frank as

## July 1994

one of her husband's *patients* that bothers her. Yes, that is the nature of their relationship, but the very notion of this makes Margot uneasy. *Is Irene putting herself and her husband above us ...above what she sees as the pitifully disturbed class of individuals who are Hamilton's "patients?" Maybe if Irene simply recognizes that these "patients" are customers, and customers are what will help the Brophys pay for that new house in the Hamptons, she would speak more deferentially.*

"I like it out here in the summer. But there's absolutely nothing going on in the winter. Besides I consider myself more of a city girl."

"But don't you like the beach?"

"I do. But I like our beach house in Bermuda a lot better." It was Margot's way of putting Irene in her place. There is something about the woman that she didn't care for.

"How about Frank? Does he like it better here or in Bermuda?"

"I'm not sure. I guess you'll have to ask him." They both turn slightly toward Frank, who is in serious-minded conversation with Brophy with respect to Middle East policy of President Clinton compared with that of the Bush administration. For the most part Brophy was deferring to Babcock in this conversation because Babcock spent as much time as he did in that part of the world. But both men yielded their discussion topic to engage in the conversation with the women.

"I like both places," Frank opined upon hearing his name mentioned . "But I haven't spent nearly as much time in Bermuda as Margot and Jedd have recently."

"People go about their business in Bermuda without all the catty nonsense that you sometimes find out here on the east end of Long Island." Margot says.

"Do people bother you out here?"

"Not so much. If they don't know us, they don't say anything, but sometimes you can feel the stares. They don't stare at me unless I'm with Frank. Everyone out here seems to know who he is, and it can make us uncomfortable ... at least it can make *me* uncomfortable."

Frank then adds his perspective. "For one reason or another the paparazzi never got the message that Margot's sister's death was an *accident*. When Nicole died, I think I lost most of my privacy. Most of the legitimate press left us alone after they discovered that Nicole's death was a criminal accident, caused by some wetback limo driver ... but the tabloids still think of Margot and me as fair game. Remember their original angle was to intimate that I might have had something to do with Nicole's death."

Brophy listens as the Babcocks tell their tale of woe. He wonders if they would be having the same conversation if he wasn't Frank's therapist. This whole idea of having a social get together is a bit of a psychological experiment on his part. It was Frank's suggestion, but Brophy had willingly acquiesced. He was now coming to believe that it was a bad idea. Most of their conversation was about Frank's issues, and they were no longer on the clock. Once they were out to dinner together, neither Frank nor Margot had asked them about their two college age children. They hadn't asked where they might be going for vacation in the near future. And they hadn't asked if Brophy might be retiring any time soon. Even the brief political discussion that Frank Babcock and Hamilton Brophy had engaged in was more about Babcock's views than about Brophy's opinions.

"So how do you cope with that?" Irene Brophy isn't helping out. Instead she is playing right into the hands of the self-centered Babcocks.

"It's not at all a problem when I travel. In the Middle East in particular, they look at me just like they look at every other American who has been running over there lately."

"How's that?"

"I'm not sure I can capture the essence of it exactly. But it's almost as if they look at us as a vast middle class. It's like the elite few in the Middle East are the chosen people ... as though they somehow usurped that notion from the Jews, whom they despise. Then they have the vast lower class that is comprised of millions and millions of Arabs and Afro-Arabs. To the ruling families of the Middle East, Americans and Europeans are viewed as a vast middle class."

"That's so interesting. I've never heard the relationship between us and them portrayed quite that way." Irene sounds genuinely interested. "I guess I always think of Arabia as primitive."

"Well that's simply not a word I would use to describe my clientele. But I'd agree that your notion is not an unusual one for Americans."

"I think that a lot of Americans are worried about the Arab countries without any understanding whatsoever about the Jewish/Palestinian conflict which is always at the heart of everything and has been for nearly fifty years. But after last year's World Trade Center bombing people are now paying more attention."

# July 1994

"They always do when the conflict hits closer to home, or in this case when the conflict actually hits home."

Margot is tired of this conversation and decides she would now rather talk about the Brophys than the Babcocks.

∞∞∞

"It must be interesting being a psychiatrist's wife. Does Hamilton try to analyze everything?"

"Oh, no, no. I think he leaves those instincts in the office. Don't you Hamilton, dear?"

"Yes, I don't really have much of a choice. Unlike other occupations, psychiatry doesn't leave me the option to talk about my work in detail. My conversations with my patients are confidential."

"But when they do talk about their clients it's awfully interesting. I watched the Menendez brothers' murder trial a few months back and that Dr. Oziel guy certainly was a major factor, even though the brothers didn't get convicted."

"Wasn't that horrible. Those two boys belong in jail for the rest of their lives for what they did to their parents. They butchered them. How dreadful was that!" Irene Brophy is showing her opinionated side. Her husband is a little more concerned where this conversation might lead. Frank Babcock has his misgivings as well.

"I'm not so sure these trials should be televised ... you know ... the Menendez trial made for great TV, and of course now they're going to have the whole OJ Simpson trial on TV as well. It will undoubtedly become a three ring circus."

"I just want to say a thing or two about that Dr. Oziel fellow. To start with he is a psychologist and not a psychiatrist." This distinction sounded as belittling as Brophy intended it to be.

"Secondly this guy's testimony is what caused the trial to be delayed so long in the first place. The lawyers kept debating as to whether Oziel's testimony should be permitted. And then after he did testify, the Defense lawyers tore him apart and in my opinion that's why the separate juries for each brother ended up being unable to reach a verdict. I'm not a lawyer, but in my opinion the Prosecution botched this trial big time and it all had to do with a therapist who shouldn't have been testifying in the first place."

"Why was that?" Frank Babcock is the only one at the table who has paid no attention whatsoever to the Menendez trial.

## *Techies, Trials & Technologies*

"The court found that the physician-patient privilege was voided by the fact that the brothers threatened to kill Oziel. In my opinion that's pretty weak stuff. During my years in practice I have had some threats from patients. It comes with the turf. In no case would I ever dream about testifying against a patient … even if he did kill his parents."

It is a fortuitous time for the entrees to be served. They all look at their plates.

∞∞∞

As the dinner conversation continues to circle around the table each of the four participants wish they were someplace else. Hamilton Brophy is simply tired. He feels as though he has put in a full day's work in a totally new working environment – an experiment of sorts. He realizes it's far too tiring for whatever he has learned about his process.

Frank Babcock has accomplished what he wanted to achieve. He got his therapist to meet his new wife and his wife to meet his therapist. He thinks that could be helpful to him sometime in the future. But surely there could have been a simpler way to accomplish that much. He can't wait for the check to come so that they can call it a night.

Irene Brophy is there supporting her husband. She thought it might be interesting to meet the billionaire and his wife. By the time dessert is served she thinks the Babcocks are nothing special, *just an aimless wealthy bozo and his gold digging young wife. At least she isn't a total nitwit like some of the other young fortune chasing sluts that I've met in the past out here in the Hamptons.*

Margot Babcock feels completely out of place. She is content in her marriage to Frank. She believes that she knew what she was getting into when she married him. There isn't any creature comfort that he has denied her, with the exception of more of his own time. However she tolerates nights like tonight when he drags her out to a dinner where she is the youngest person by more than thirty years. She feels bored to death by the Brophys, whom she considers to be *old farts*.

∞∞∞

An hour later as the two couples leave the restaurant, a photographer from the NYPD homicide sits in a car nearby and snaps a picture through a telescopic lens. He takes two more to be sure he captures a good facial shot of Babcock's guests. He will subsequently add these to the

## *July 1994*

growing file of Babcock's contacts. They will make the identification later back in the city. He's just the guy on the beat. No one is telling him why they want the pictures. But a ride out to the Hamptons is not bad duty.

∞∞∞

## XX

## August 1994

"Well it's certainly been a long time Fox. I hear you're now trying to get into people's heads ... literally." The voice is quite familiar and it gets Fox's attention immediately.

"Wow. Sergei. Is that you? Yes, it's been quite a while." Fox speaks warily into his phone.

"So you're now a married man. I would have come back for the wedding if I had known about it ... not your fault of course ... I've been hard to find, I'm sure."

"I've thought a lot about you over the last ... how long has it been .... Six or seven years? After our last telephone conversation ... what was that in 1987? Yeah, summer of '87, I think it was ... I thought you might have returned to Russia ... or worse."

"No, nothing could be worse than returning to Russia. I try to avoid contact with anyone there who knew my father. Occasionally some Moscow spook finds me and asks some impertinent questions about my work at CERN. I never answer them. I'm now a London resident and I have applied to become a British citizen."

"That's good, I think. Right?"

"Yes, of course. For the moment I'm just a man without a country. But I think that becoming a Brit suits me well. But then again my life is all about alliances and my connections, my friendships, colleagues and business associates are all that I have in life. I don't have family."

## *August 1994*

"No family of any kind?"

"Yes. No family, whatsoever."

"And here I am thinking that I'm the one who suffers from dysfunctional family issues!" He hesitates and then adds, "I guess you only had your father."

Fox feels the conversation is awkward and contrived. He also knows that in the past Sergei has regarded Fox and his sister Mo like family members. He wonders if Sergei might feel any sense of betrayal. After all Fox and Sergei still did share the one deeply entrenched secret that bound them by blood.

"I don't feel good or bad about not having family. It certainly makes life simpler. My father was a complicated man, but for all of his complications he left very few traces. I'm not sure what his contribution to the world was and I'll probably never find out."

"Maybe his contribution was you, Sergei. Maybe *you* are destined to do great things. Certainly you are working at a prestigious institution. My mother recently told me that her business colleagues have read all of your papers and that you are now considered to be one of the foremost thinkers when it comes to possible breakthroughs on the Web."

"I don't know about that. However I have always had an interest in cameras and video productions and those are the areas where my research is concentrated. I think that pictures and videos on the Web will be the most transformative applications in the years to come. Some day we might even have a conversation like this via video phone over the internet. There's a lot brewing. We can talk more about it when we see each other in person."

"That would be great. It'll be great to see you again after all these years. Are you planning on coming to the US any time soon? I don't plan on traveling outside of the country for a while. My residency requirements are pretty demanding on my schedule."

"Can you see the light at the end of the tunnel yet?"

"Not really."

"Well, I'll be traveling to New York to do a presentation to a few financial groups in December. Maybe we could get together then. It would be cool to get back to Long Island again just to see some of the old haunts. Maybe we could meet out there."

## *Techies, Trials & Technologies*

"Sounds like a plan. I just need a little notice because I'm living in Pittsburgh these days. But of course I have family back in New York and we usually visit them sometime over the Christmas holidays."

The two childhood friends talk for another 15 minutes or so but don't dwell on any heavyweight topics. Both young men look forward to their reunion and they don't want to preempt that future event. However when Fox hangs up the phone he has a slight feeling of dread. As much as their friendship was a strong one in the past, it is a completely unknown potency in the present.

Fox had barely mentioned his wife during their conversation and Sergei gave no indication of anyone of social significance who might be currently influential in his own life. There appears to be an underlying assumption that their dark secret remains solely between the two of them and no confidences have been shared with any other person. For the most part this is a correct assumption.

∞∞∞

# XXI

## *August 1994*

Margot Babcock walks through Central Park holding the hand of her step-son Jedidiah. She loves walking with Jedd and is usually accompanied by a member of Frank Babcock's security staff when she does so. However today she is joined by Jedd's brother, Fox Babcock. Normally Margot and Jedidiah would have been out in the Hamptons on a beautiful summer day but they have returned to Manhattan for the day so that Jedd can attend his first major league baseball game with Fox that evening.

Fox is in town to meet with publishers for a medical textbook he is hoping to get circulated. He is staying at the Sherry Netherland Hotel on Fifth Avenue, across from the park. Fox has extended his stay for a day to spend some time with the other male members of the Babcock family. The plans for the three Babcock men to catch a Yankee game have been in place since the beginning of the summer. Although Frank Babcock has earlier promised to go to the game with his two sons, his arrangements have changed and he has left earlier than planned on a business trip to the Middle East.

"Don't you ever want to travel more with Frank?" It's much too awkward for 28 year old Fox to refer to his adoptive-father as *Dad,* when discussing him with the senior Babcock's 25 year old wife.

"Sometimes I feel that way. However I don't want to leave Jedidiah for any extended period of time, and as you know Frank's trips sometimes last ten days or more."

Fox doesn't say anything but simply waits for Margot to continue. "There are some places I would like to go, but the Middle East is not on the top of my list. That's where he's been going a lot the last few years. He thinks it's fascinating. I think it's horrible. I'd have to wear a veil over my face all the time and act like a second class citizen."

She pauses again and then adds, "I'm pretty sure Frank doesn't want me going there with him anyway. Maybe he's worried that I might do something wrong." She looks down to see if Jedidiah is paying any attention whatsoever to the conversation. She knows that young children have a way of being much more perceptive than people give them credit for being, especially a child as precocious as Jedidiah.

When he looks back up, she asks him, "So what do you think Jedd? Should we travel a little more? Do you want to go on an airplane again?"

The younger Babcock heir nods his head with half-hearted enthusiasm. The reality is that Jedidiah often travels within the United States with his step-mother, but he doesn't like long airplane trips because he feels they are boring until you get where you are going. But Margot and her step-son have taken the Babcock jet to Disney World twice and they have flown together to the family's new vacation home in Bermuda several times as well.

"It's too bad that Frank couldn't make the game. And he is headed back to Dubai, tomorrow. Isn't he?"

"Yes. And then he's going to Abu Dhabi and then back to Saudi Arabia for several days and he'll be home in eleven days. For the most part he keeps me posted as to where he will be." She briefly recollects that this was one of her sister's principal gripes about Frank. She never knew exactly where he was.

Fox ambles along with Margot for a few more steps before responding. "I don't hear from him as much as I used to. I think he's satisfied that I've been moving along with my medical career, but every once in a while I feel as though I have somehow let him down. I can't put my finger on it. I just feel that way."

"I think Frank has changed since Nicole was living with him. I try not to think too much about it. I just want Frank to be happy." She slows down and then adds, "Something tells me that Frank and Nicole would never have been happy together. They were very different people."

"Do you think so? Normally I wouldn't say this except for the fact that we have been friends for almost four years now. But I think that Frank and Nicole were alike at one time. They were both very inner-focused people. But I agree with you now. Frank has changed. He is much more

## August 1994

considerate. And he and Nicole would *not* have seen eye-to-eye on a lot of things over time."

"Until she died I never understood how other people felt about Nicole. I took me a while before I realized how poorly she treated Jedd. But the night she died ... well that's a night I'll never forget ... not simply because my sister died. It is a night that took me a while to reflect upon appropriately. I don't know. I guess I was really naive." She hesitates. "Maybe I still am."

Their pace has slowed considerably now, but Fox doesn't interrupt the flow of Margot's story.

"But when I found out that Nicole was just going back to some kind of bacchanal ... leaving me with Jedd ... I was really upset. Of course I missed her at first, but the more I found out, the more I realized that she wasn't always just working. A lot of times she just left me with her son to go out and party. Suffice it to say my memories of Nicole are not what they used to be."

Fox listens carefully to every word Margot says. It's more of an outpouring than anything she's ever said in the past. He wonders if a certain kind of healing is finally setting in.

"What can I tell you, Margot? It certainly has been an interesting few years."

∞∞∞

*Nicole Silver had been dead now for almost three and a half years. The first few months after the accident there were inquiries, negative media coverage and harmful speculation. At first the speculation had been accusatory toward Burke Finnegan and Frank Babcock. Then there was speculation of Finnegan and Babcock being in cahoots with Margot to hurt Nicole. All of that speculation fell by the wayside when the police found out that Juan Hernandez a limousine driver was the actual hit and run driver. Shortly thereafter the police and the media backed off their pursuit of a concocted plot and completely exonerated them from having anything to do with the accident.*

*Still things remained unsettled in the Babcock household. And then one Friday evening in the middle of February, 1992, Frank came home and asked Margot if he could take her out to dinner. Oddly he didn't even seem to know it was Valentine's Day until, they went out. Margot had originally planned on staying home and studying for an upcoming midterm. After dinner when they went home to their common residence, Margot went to Frank's bedroom instead of her own. Babcock was not pushy. In fact he was* kind and gentle at first. Even though he was more than twenty-five years older than any man she had ever made love to before, Margot turned a blind eye to their age difference. She simply matched his neediness with her own need to be needed. Others may have adjudged it an odd symbiosis, but for whatever reason it worked for the two of them. Their affection for each other grew almost as an afterthought.

Margot's parents were not at all happy with the way things began to unfold. In fact they were both younger than Babcock. But they relented when they realized they had no choice in the matter. Still they were saddened that Margot would stay caught up in the murky waters of the Babcock household. Their protestations went unheeded however when Frank Babcock and Margot Silver got married that December right before they rung in New Year of 1993.

∞∞∞

"What about you, Fox? How do you feel about my marriage to your father?" She looks toward Fox but he is unresponsive and keeps looking ahead as they walk.

"You've always been kind towards me, even after I moved from being Jedidiah's nanny to being his step-mother. All of these family relationships can feel pretty awkward at times. Does it bother you at all?"

"Not a bit. Whatever makes my father happy is alright with me. Besides I kind of like my new step-mother." He winks mischievously at Margot in an attempt to lighten her concerns. "Isn't it amazing that my *newest* step-mother could be younger than me?"

"Well, not so new anymore. It'll be two years in December."

"Seems new enough to me. Evelyn and I have been married for a little over two years, ourselves. And it still feels *new*."

They are still ambling toward the center of the park and so Margot takes her time responding.

"And so, how's married life been treating you, if you don't mind my asking?"

Fox changes his demeanor and answers the question authentically.

"We both work an awful lot. We probably see more of our colleagues than we do of each other."

The conversation is interrupted momentarily as two teenage skateboarders zoom by on the pathway narrowly missing the Babcocks. However Central Park being the complex cosmopolitan melting pot that it is,

## August 1994

nothing is mentioned about the close encounter. They simply shoot off into the distance and Margot provides the next few thoughts.

"Well with all of the time constraints that you have it's certainly nice of you to come out to see Jedidiah. When I knew that Frank couldn't make the game, I worried that you might cancel as well." She looked sidelong at Fox before adding, "The other thought that I had was that you might bring Evelyn with you. I'd like to get to know her better."

"Well I happen to like baseball and I also happen to like New York. I don't think that Evelyn cares much about either of those things." He laughs slightly as he says it as though it is the first time the thought has ever occurred to him.

"I'm starting to like baseball, myself. I've gone to a few Yankee games with Frank, but we've never brought Jedd because Frank thinks he's still too young to appreciate it."

"Why don't you come with us then?"

"No, I think you guys had this planned as a male bonding kind of thing. Just take Jedd. It will be great for him, I'm sure."

"I guess I'll have to indoctrinate him in the family rooting rituals. We have to love the Yankees and hate the Red Sox and the Mets."

"I'm glad you're going *today*. The reporters are saying that we might not have much baseball left this season. There may be a strike if the owners and players can't agree on a contract pretty soon."

"It should be a fun game. The Yanks are playing much better than they have in quite a while. They're 10 games ahead of the Orioles and they play the Twins tonight. The Twins are in last place."

Margot squats down on bended knees to speak to Jedidiah at his eye level. "Are you going to have fun with Fox? Are you going to root root root for the Yankees?"

"Can I eat hot dogs and cracker jacks too?" Jedidiah is not normally as animated in his anticipations. But the youngest Babcock is now all smiles.

"I think that maybe you can take a short nap before your brother brings you to the game. OK?"

"OK, Margot." He looks at his step-mother with a sense of resignation but realizes that this is not an arguable proposal. Jedidiah then says, "Can we go home so I can get the nap over? Then I can see the Yankees!"

# Techies, Trials & Technologies

Fox Babcock watches this exchange between Jedidiah and Margot with a passive interest. He shares no blood relationship whatsoever with Jedd. They both have different biological mothers and fathers. If there will ever be any similarities between the "brothers," it will likely evolve from a similar upbringing. The ties will be "nurture" not "nature." Even as he ponders this reality, he wonders how much of an impact he himself will have on the formative years of Jedidiah Babcock. Regardless of the lack of common bloodlines, he still feels a familial affection and responsibility for his "little brother." However the relationship is really more like that of an uncle and a nephew, or maybe even like a father and son in that Fox is 24 years older than Jedd.

Another thought also crosses Fox Babcock's mind: *How will I feel about Jedd if I have a child of my own. It's all Evelyn seems to talk about lately.*

∞∞∞

They are seated along the first base line just beyond the Yankee dugout, and two rows from the field. The seats or similar seats have been in the Babcock family for several decades prior to the refurbishing of the stadium in the early 1970's. Fox can remember sitting in these very seats watching Yankee games with his mother, after his parents had remarried, in the mid-seventies. She was a big Thurman Munson fan.

Fox also remembers watching a game from these same seats with Sergei Zubkov. Sergei was a big Reggie Jackson fan. Fox was 14 at the time. It was the same day that he had earlier watched the Shenandoah Skylarks play in the high school championship.

Fox has several recollections of going to games with his Dad, Frank Babcock, but somehow those memories are less specific. Fox remembers his Dad as a George Steinbrenner fan, saying that Steinbrenner would do anything for a World Series Championship. Tonight's game was originally meant to rekindle some of those old memories with his Dad and start some new ones with Jedidiah. At least part of that goal is being reached.

∞∞∞

It is nearly 11 PM by the time Fox and Jedidiah return to the Babcock townhouse from the Yankee game. It has been an interesting night. Jedidiah is much more talkative than Fox had anticipated. He was interested in many aspects of the game and was thrilled by the large crowd and the size of the stadium. His only complaint was with respect to their seating. He kept looking up at the furthest rows of the stadium and finally asked, "When we come to a game next time, can we sit up there near the top? That'd be so cool!"

∞∞∞

Although he sleeps in the limousine all the way home from Yankee Stadium, Jedidiah manages to walk back into the Babcock townhouse on his own two feet. Fox still has his own keys to the townhouse and he tries to enter quietly with Jedidiah in case Margot has already gone to bed. However as they reach the main living quarters, Margot descends barefooted from her bedroom to greet them. Her hair is down, and she is dressed in an ankle length embroidered Japanese Kimono style robe. The garment is crafted from a lengthy lustrous red silk fabric. It is tied at the waistline with a long silk obi sash.

Almost immediately Jedidiah races past his step-mother and up to his bedroom two floors above them. Margot turns to Fox and says, "I'll be back in a minute. Just give me a second to get Jedd into bed."

"That's okay, Margot. I should get going now anyway. I've got an early flight back to Pittsburgh." His flight out of LaGuardia wasn't until 10:50 AM the following morning, so he wasn't desperately in need of rushing back to his hotel.

"Can you wait just a minute or two, Fox? I'd love to hear how the game went with Jedd."

Margot doesn't wait for an answer. She simply hustles up the rear stairway to the fourth floor, where Jedd's bedroom is located. The master bedroom is on the third floor and Margot has been thinking about moving Jedidiah down to the other bedroom on that floor but has gotten some resistance from Jedd who likes his room right where it is. Fox waits on the second floor and begins to look around. There are some memories.

∞∞∞

*It wasn't that long ago that Fox also occupied a room in this townhouse. Frank Babcock has owned the townhouse for as long as Fox can remember. Fox didn't spend too much time at the townhouse when the main family residence was at Babcock Manor and Gardens in Great Neck. For most that time he was in high school at Shenandoah, and city excursions were limited.*

# Techies, Trials & Technologies

However during his three years at Harvard in the mid-eighties, Fox often stayed at the townhouse when he came back to New York. He didn't like returning to Babcock Manor while Frank Babcock was married to his second wife, Diane Heath-Babcock. Bunking down in the New York townhouse allowed Fox to spend a little more time with his adoptive father. Frank Babcock also frequently stayed there whenever he was working late in the city. Diane rarely went into the city, until they moved there after the sale of Babcock Manor and Gardens in 1987. And then Diane lived there until their divorce. By that time Fox had already graduated from Harvard and had moved to Baltimore to pursue his medical education.

∞∞∞

The brownstone townhouse, which was originally built in 1897 was technically five stories high with four bedrooms and six bathrooms. However the bottom story was a five step walk down that led to an area that was meant to be utilized as the servant's quarters. The upper part of this floor was above sidewalk level, which meant that the second floor and main entrance to the brownstone building was behind a relatively steep eight stair walk up. There had not been any live-in service personnel in the Babcock residence in very many years, but occasionally there were sleepovers for some of the help that worked late into the night for a dinner. The help also used the bottom floor as a daytime resting area, so that they were out of the way until summoned when things were quiet in the household.

The four family residential floors were laid out in a south facing symmetrical stack with each floor having a 1225 square foot layout. A zigzagging staircase led from one floor to the next at the center rear of the house, starting at the bottom level and reaching the third floor. A separate staircase connects the bedroom floors (the 3$^{rd}$ and 4$^{th}$ floors) with the rooftop floor which was partially enclosed and sparsely utilized. The master bedroom suite was located on the third floor at the southwest corner of the house. It had been reconstructed and/or redecorated many times since its original construction, including a major makeover when Frank Babcock and Diane Heath-Babcock made this building their primary residence. It now took up about half of the 3$^{rd}$ floor footprint and contained the only bathroom that was not stacked directly above the bathrooms on the floors below.

Nicole Silver had resided in the master bedroom with Frank Babcock when she lived in the house. At that time Margot Silver, as the part time nanny, maintained a room on the fourth floor, opposite Jedidiah's bedroom.

## August 1994

*Margot didn't move into the master bedroom until two months after her marriage to Frank Babcock and following still another full remodeling. It was now Margot's home.*

∞∞∞

Fox is still reminiscing as Margot makes her way back down to the second floor.

"Can I get you something to drink?" Margot moves quickly in the direction of the liquor cabinet.

"No that's okay. I really can't stay too long." Margot has her back to him so he can't see her disappointment. There's an awkward moment when neither of them knows exactly what to say. Their conversation in the park earlier in the day had been intimate but sheltered by its public venue.

Margot turns around and faces Fox, and says, "So tell me about the ballgame."

Before he hears her question totally, he makes his own attempt to break the suddenly awkward moment of reflection.

"That's a beautiful kimono, Margot. I don't think I've ever seen one that nice."

"Yes I love it. Frank gave it to me as a Christmas gift last year. It was my first Christmas ... so to speak." She turned around slowly to show the whole pattern, front and back, as she moved closer to Fox.

"As I'm sure you know I grew up Jewish. In fact I'm still a Jew, but since I married Frank we celebrate the Christian holidays."

"Exclusively?"

"Well Frank doesn't celebrate any of the Jewish holidays. That's for sure."

"No ... I doubt that he would."

Margot wandered a little closer to Fox as she spoke. She is fingering her silk obi self-consciously and running the wide sash through her hands almost anxiously.

"It's very comfortable. The lining is very soft also. I'm not sure what the lining material is." Fox can feel a freight train bearing down on him. He thinks that he can wait until the last minute to get off the tracks. But now Margot is standing only two feet away from him. "Here feel it."

Margot loosens the obi coupling so that the cross-wrapping top sides of the kimono can be parted ever so slightly, exposing her clavicle and the top of her sternum. She rubs the material between her thumb and the index finger of her right hand. Fox takes the bait and reaches out to feel for himself.

"Nice." His fingers linger. He can't resist the opportunity to part the top of her kimono further. She is not wearing a nagajuban underneath. Her shoulders are now bared and her breasts pop into view. The sash is still loosely in place. Fox doesn't say anything, as Margot now untwists the obi entirely and lets her kimono fall around her feet in a red puddle. The only clothing she is wearing is a pair of red knit panties. She reaches out and pulls Fox toward her. He wraps his arms around her lightly but he is uncertain about what he should do or what will come next. Margot begins to press her body urgently against Fox.

Fox gathers his wits about him. He has cheated once before on his wife. He regrets that incident down along the Gauley River and doesn't want to make a mistake like that again. He doesn't think he can deal with the guilt. He already has way too much guilt in his life. And on top of that, Margot is his father's wife!

Fox gently pushes Margot slightly away from him. However he keeps his hands on her bare shoulders. He looks at her and kisses her quickly on the lips. It is a warm kiss but not a passionate kiss. It is more than a brotherly kiss but less than a lover's caress. It is meant as acceptance but not acquiescence. It is intended as an escape but not as a rejection.

The moment calls for some humor, but wittiness is difficult with Margot standing there a few red knitted stiches from naked, and Fox still fully clothed. He averts his eyes carefully and steps aside but not away. He gives her room to pull her kimono back up around her nakedness and then looks only into her soft moist eyes and with a sparkle to his own eyes, he smiles and softly says, "I thought you wanted to talk about the game."

"What game?" She is slightly chagrined but Fox will not let her be humiliated. He gradually steps off a few more feet of distance.

"We both know it wouldn't be right. We just can't love each other … that way. You are Frank's wife. He's my father. And … oh by the way … I'm also married!"

"I'm sorry, Fox. I just th ………"

"Shusssh. Don't say it, Margot. It's all okay. We can handle it. We know we can. I wanted it as much as you did, but we know it would have been a mistake. Now that she has redressed herself in her kimono, Fox walks back over and hugs her firmly but this time it's a *little bear hug* rather than

## *August 1994*

a *big bare hug.* All the while the ironic reality of a father and son making love to the same woman has not fully dawned on either of them.

"Okay Fox. I understand. That makes me feel better."

"Maybe it's best we talk about the ball game another time?"

"Okay."

A few minutes later Fox walked out on Margot and a few days later the Major League Players Association walked out on its baseball fans. Margot and Fox never did get around to discussing either topic.

∞∞∞

# XXII

## August 1994

"I don't know whether this weekend made me feel younger or older." Simone is curious whether Betty's reaction is similar to her own. There is a nostalgic aura that is more reflective of melancholy than tranquility.

"It wasn't quite the same 25 years after the fact. But there were some definite similarities. Still a lot of rain …. Still a lot of mud and music … Still a lot of drugs. And there was still a lot of sex."

"Speak for yourself, on that last point. I didn't get any then; and I didn't get any now."

Betty laughs but acknowledges what she took to be a self-deprecating remark on the part of her business partner. "See what I mean … a lot of similarities."

"Yeah, but we're now twenty-five years older. Damn, we're in our fifties!"

"So the sex part is a little different. Big deal."

∞∞∞

If the excitement of the original Woodstock was legitimate, the atmosphere in 1994 seemed just a little bit contrived. Unlike 1969, both Betty Barrymore and Simone Muirchant managed to get through the weekend without losing any of their clothing. A quarter of a century earlier Betty and Simone had just begun their life-long friendship. That friendship had been

## *August 1994*

strong prior to their trip to Max Yasgur's farm for the iconic sixties event. The three days of musical intrigue had both strained and tested their friendship in different ways. However that long-ago shared experience became the foundation for their later friendship and working relationship in the business world in the ensuing years. That bond had endured through many twists and turns and was now as strong as ever.

The fifty-two year old friends were political activists at heart. Although their capitalistic success framed their working lives, they both believed there were more important things in life than making a living. They shared an anti-war bias and a belief that most people spend too much time fighting with one another rather than seeing what they might be able to accomplish through cooperative undertakings.

However the friends differed dramatically in their spiritual outlooks. Betty was an avowed atheist. She theorized that everything had a physical or at worst a metaphysical explanation and that most truths will be revealed over time through scientific development. Simone didn't adhere to any strict dogma of an organized religion. However she accepted religious worship as a worthwhile endeavor. She felt that most religious beliefs travel in similar concentric circles or ellipses of some sort. Though neither of them would admit it, their attempt at rebooting their earlier Woodstock experience was in some ways a search for their own magical mystery tour. They were looking for a quasi-spiritual experience like they had on Max Yasgur's farm. And although the music was great at Woodstock '94, the concert lacked the spontaneity and the social consciousness of the 1969 experience. They both knew it had turned out to be empty nostalgia. Yet as they were leaving the concert site they were still searching for that elusive spark.

∞∞∞

"You know what? Maybe we should drive over to the original Woodstock site. I wonder what it looks like now."

"I'm game. Let's go. It's only about an hour or so from here."

The two friends then get into their rented SUV and begin driving in the direction of Bethel, New York, the site of the 1969 Woodstock concert. As they reach the New York Thruway they continue to reminisce about the many things that they did together twenty-five years earlier.

"One thing that was a lot different this time was the amount of personal drug consumption. I remember being wasted the entire time we were at the first Woodstock."

"I also remember that you were screwing everybody regardless of gender." Simone teased Betty.

"Yeah well not this time. But I did manage to score some decent weed over the last few days and I still have a few joints. Should we fire one up for old times' sake?"

"Sure, why not."

As Simone continues driving in the direction of the original Woodstock sight, Betty lights up her joint. "Do you remember when we got pulled over by that cop on the Mass Pike when we were heading to the concert the last time?"

"Yeah what a moron. I still think about that asshole every once in a while."

"You do wonder what happens to people like that."
"Probably propositioned the wrong person somewhere along the way and got canned. I hope he's working in a carwash in Chicopee, Mass."

"Those were great times though ... you know the proverbial good old days. We didn't have any money but we had a lot of fun."

"Speak for yourself. Remember I was married to one of the richest men in the country."

"Yes, but it didn't seem that way then. How was it that the wife of such a rich guy ended up hitchhiking her way back to Massachusetts after the concert?"

∞∞∞

When they arrive at the site of the 1969 Woodstock Festival, it looks nothing like how they remember it, twenty-five years earlier. There is no one around. As Simone and Betty let their eyes roam over the vast open fields their minds conjure up visions of vapor figures of thousands upon thousands of party revelers from that long ago weekend.

They also summon up self-visions of much younger women, maybe even much more attractive women, but definitely more idealistic souls who inhabited this now hallowed ground. They could almost hear the music that was everywhere and they could almost taste the raindrops on their tongues and feel the intense hunger that was not as much a wanting for food as it was wanting for consummate change. The muddy hillside of August 1969 has been replaced by a long sloping grassy knoll. The peaceful emptiness is an odd contradiction to the vitality and joie de vivre that marked the original

## *August 1994*

concert. They walk down the knoll and find a place to sit with their backs against an old oak tree.

∞∞∞

"Some things change and some things remain the same."

"I remember envying you so much back then."

"Really, Betty. What was there to envy? I was pretty messed up. You were about the only person in my life that I felt connected to."

"You've got to be kidding me. You had everything a girl could want. You had men, you had money, and you had moxie. I remember laughing with you about all of the Johnsons you were doing, including your husband's johnson."

"As I recall you were not as interested in men as I was back then, and yet that didn't stop you from a weekend of free sex and lust."

"Lust? What the ... I've never heard you use that word before. Is that a good word or a bad word?"

Simone shrugged. "Just a more inclusive word. As I recall you weren't overly discriminate about who you shared your body with in those days."

"I was probably more into women than men ... even back then. But you're right, sex was sex in those days. There was no real attachment associated with sex and as far as I was concerned no need to make a gender selection."

"So what changed?"

"I'm not sure."

"Did you want to have sex with me, back then?"

"Not so much in the grunt and grind kind of way. I guess I knew that you would have your limits when it came to physical female affection. But yes, I loved you then. For that matter I still love you now. It's just a different kind of love than what I have with Roxanne."

"I've never felt the urge to have sex with another woman ... any woman for that matter."

"Well. I seem to remember a time ... once ... that may not have been the case."

"I think I remember the incident that you're referring to, and that was a long time ago and I remember feeling very squeamish about it. I don't know. I just never felt that liberated, I guess. Even now I choose to have selected memory about that type of thing."

# Techies, Trials & Technologies

"That's okay. There wasn't much to remember anyway. The important thing to me is that you never rejected me as a person, even though you rejected me as a lover."

"I never thought of it as rejecting you as a lover, I thought of it as just being uninterested in having another female touch me in a manner that might arouse her."

"Or you?"

"I wasn't as worried about that."

Betty lit up another joint and took a hit. "So tell me what did you think the original Woodstock was all about anyway?"

"Peace, of course. Peace."

"Do you think it had an impact?"

"On peace?"

"Yes, on peace. Did it have an impact on peace? You know. Everyone made a big deal out of things back then, but war has definitely lingered on."

"You think?"

"Yeah, judging by the state of *peace*, worldwide, I'd have to say Woodstock was an utter failure. But it sure was fun. Unfortunately we were myopic. We were focused on Vietnam. War continues everywhere. Look at Africa. All of the European colonization….. the Brits, the French ….. Belgium, Germany…. The European colonialism has led to mass genocide throughout the continent. Americans aren't the only war mongers now and we certainly weren't back then either."

"Yeah right after we were singing peace and love in 1969, Idi Amin spent the '70's slaughtering people in Uganda. And he was one of the principal leaders in all of Africa."

"Yeah the poor Africans haven't progressed very far. Idi Amin was … the guy was … an actual cannibal. He actually freakin' ate his enemies."

The absurd incongruity of talking about a part of the world that is still utterly barbaric while they are smoking pot in a pristine setting in upstate New York has not registered with either of the two women. But they both are rapidly gaining a mind-numbing buzz.

Betty doesn't get a response from Simone right away about her cannibal comments, and she wonders whether Simone is thinking about the exiled African leader or about something else entirely. After a minute or so she simply says, "I wonder what happened to him. I wonder where he is now."

## August 1994

"Who?"

"Idi Amin."

"We're still talking about that animal?"

"Sort of."

"He's living in Saudi Arabia."

"How do you know that?"

"I forget." Both woman chuckle at Simone's honest but seemingly absurd answer. But Simone's eyes quickly tear up as her thoughts once again returned to Africa.

"Things have gotten so much worse there lately."

"Where?"

"Africa ... especially in Rwanda. It's not blacks fighting whites. It's little black people fighting big black people. The Hutus are fighting the Tutsis. And the littlest black people of all the Twa – the Pygmies that is – they are also starving to death. They're now saying that nearly 820,000 people were killed in that little country just since April."

"That's sickening."

"It's more than 20% of the country's population – gone in less than 5 months!"

"Sick as shit ... we're losing the war on war."

"I can't get my head around those numbers ... that utter carnage. In all of the years we were in Vietnam, we lost a total of 50,000 American soldiers."

"Yeah but more like 2 million Vietnamese people died."

"There's no such thing as home field advantage, when the game is war."

∞∞∞∞

For the first time all day the sun falls behind some low hanging clouds and the open area around Simone and Betty begins to grow a little darker. They are getting ready for some more rain.

"But we were convinced back then that if we didn't do something about it, the world might come to an end." Simone is beginning to feel more comfortable as she shakes off the joint that Betty attempts to pass her. She is already lit, and doesn't want to flame out.

"Well we didn't have all the answers then. And I'd say we still don't have many answers now."

## *Techies, Trials & Technologies*

"So what are we supposed to do ... give up on world peace ... we can't give up on world peace."

The way that Simone blurts this out makes Betty chortle. She hasn't seen Simone state anything so emphatically in quite some time.

"Your right Simone, we'll fight 'til the end for world peace."

"Yep, we'll go to war in order to have world peace."

"World peace is the first step in creating a unified planet."

"And what exactly is a unified planet?"

∞∞∞

The first drops of rain sprinkle down through the mixture of clouds and sunlight. But a light sprinkle is much preferable to the big gloppy raindrops that had made the concert such a mud bath. The two women sit silently for more than a minute simply passing another joint between them as they reminisce about their first trip to this site. Simone breaks the silence.

"So what was so different this time? War was the main thing, last time."

"Huh?"

"The main thing at Woodstock."

"Oh? I thought it was peace."

"Well yeah ... war... peace... however you want to say it... we wanted out... out of Vietnam." Their conversation is now going in circles.
Betty lets that thought hang in the air for a second in an air of harmonious acknowledgement. She finds it difficult to concentrate but is giving it a good effort. Then she adds a different spin.

"It wasn't *all* really about peace and love. And of course the music ...and ...and it was a lot about civil rights also."

"Yes and no. There weren't that many black people at Woodstock, certainly not as many as this weekend. Woodstock '69 had black performers but even the stage acts were predominantly white people. As I recall it, the civil rights stuff was given some lip service but it was mostly about peace."

"Don't forget love. Peace and love ... right?"

"Yes, but the civil rights stuff was secondary by a long shot."

"Women's rights stuff was big though, as I recall wasn't it?"

"I don't know. Sometimes we remember things differently than the way we thought of them at the time. These were all important issues at the time but as I recall it was mostly anti-war."

## *August 1994*

"One thing for sure is that the Woodstock days were a turning point in our own relationship. I remember sitting in our tent in the rain while you finally opened up on all of your personal issues with the Johnsons and the Babcocks."

"I do remember that. I finally got a few things off my chest and I remember being able to laugh at myself. That's never been one of my strong points."

"So what's with you and the Johnsons these days? I already sort of know about you and Babcock."

"I'm glad you think you know about Frank and me because I sure don't."

"You know what I mean. He's backed our business all along ... personally ... and then through Black Inoculum. That shows you something. Doesn't it?"

"Yeah, maybe. But honestly I haven't talked to Frank about anything personal since I saw him at Fox's wedding. Most of what I know about him these days comes from Fox. Of course Fox has probably been the man in the center of all of this from the very day he was conceived."

"Now that's more like it. That's what I want to hear ... the good gossip ... the stuff we talked about at the first Woodstock."

"Well, back then, I was ... well probably to be honest ... I was still somewhat in love with someone that ... well that I wasn't married to. I was, of course, married to Frank. And as you know, after Woodstock I went back to Frank."

Betty lets that thought settle in and then adds. "You say you went back to Frank, but in less than a year you left him again." She pauses again and then offers, "You know this is the first time I ever heard you admit that you were really in love with Mickey Johnson. Of course I always knew that this was the case, but this is the first time I ever heard you say it."

Simone exhales after holding in a hit for several seconds.

"You know, Betty ... I'm not great at talking about myself ... or my relationships."

"But it's me, Simone. If you can't talk to me who can you talk to?"

"Wow, I'm starting to get a decent buzz. I haven't done this in a while."

"You've got to live a little, girl. Lighten up."

## *Techies, Trials & Technologies*

"You know I try not to think too much about the Babcocks and the Johnsons, except of course for Fox."

"Come on Simone. You can tell me. You also think about Mickey Johnson and what might have been. I know you too well. I know you think about him."

"OK. OK. I'll admit that every once in a while I think about the sex. It was the best sex, I ever had in my life."

"Now we're getting somewhere. So tell me what was so great about it?"

"It was ... you know ... a lot more than just physical. I mean the physical was fantastic ... but it was the whole deal ... physical, mental, emotional ... yeah ... very very emotional. I don't know. I can't explain it. It was just great. That's all."

"I take it you don't go there ... or get there ... with Jeffy."

"It's Jeff, Betty. Jeff. Why do you always insist on calling him Jeffy?"

"Sorry Simone. But you still didn't answer my question. It's not the same with Jeff. Right?"

"It's never really the same, Betty. It's just not worth comparing. That's childish."

"Oh ... is it now?"

Simone doesn't answer her friend.

"But tell me the truth, do you ever think about what might have been, if you and Mickey had made a go of it together way back when?"

"That was then. Now is now. Mickey moved on."

"But wasn't it you who moved on, first?"

"What difference does it make? We are where we are."

"You know we used to discuss these things. We talked about all of the tough things. You didn't hide your emotions from me when Maureen died. And I went with you to the funeral when Wayne Johnson died. That was the one and only time I ever saw Mickey Johnson and you didn't even introduce me to him then."

"Sorry Betty, but introducing you to Mickey was not top of mind for me at the time."

"I remember him being a big man, very tall and strong looking."

"Funny you say that. That was the only time that I remember thinking of Mickey as vulnerable."

"But in a very virile way?"

# August 1994

"You might say that. He lost his father and he didn't even know how or why."

"It was a random mugging and murder. That's what the police said. Right?"

"But it wasn't. It was premeditated ... not the murder itself ... but at least the mugging."

"By whom?"

"Frank."

"I've always wondered why things are so weird between you and him. So you think Frank had something to do with Wayne Johnson's murder?"

"I know he did."

This statement shocks Betty, but she's unsure. *Is it just the pot talking?* She decides to take a lighter approach.

"So let's see. What have I missed? Wayne Johnson gets mugged by a young black ex-con, who he manages to shoot and kill, before he himself dies. Are you saying there was as second man? ... And then this other thug gets away and is never identified? Are you saying that this other guy is Frank Babcock?"

"No, what I'm saying is that, Frank somehow hired two guys to rough up Wayne Johnson. Things got out of hand and Wayne was beaten to death, by one or both of those guys."

"You know ... I've always wondered ... whether Babcock might have had something to do with that problem ... but, of course, I never wanted to say something like that to you ... even then ... or should I say even now."

Simone doesn't answer Betty right away. As they continue to share their doobie, Simone attempts to remain focused. But she is unsure how much more she wants to share. The silence lengthens to a more than a minute, before Betty continues her probe.

"What makes you so sure that Frank had any part in Wayne Johnson's murder?"

"He told me."

"Babcock? Frank Babcock *told* you he hired people to *kill* Wayne Johnson!?!"

"More or less, yes."

"Yes ... and 'more or less' ... are two different things ... did he tell you this or didn't he?"

Both women are now trying to think more clearly through their self-induced cannabis fog.

"He told me."

Betty lets Simone take her time with her disclosure. Simultaneously she is thinking about her friend. It's been a while since Simone has seemed truly happy. But that itself is not unusual. For as long as Betty has known her, Simone has been given to prolonged periods of semi-depression. She exhibited those traits after the birth of her two children and throughout her first marriage to Frank Babcock and then she went into a prolonged funk in the early 1980's after Maureen's death.

Then there's the last few years. Betty can't put her finger on the exact time frame but she thinks Simone's most recent malaise has lasted much too long. Betty realizes that in the past whenever Simone exhibited these depressed states, she would at least talk about it with her. And the other thing that she knows is that Simone never lies to her.

"I know it must seem bizarre to you, but Frank actually told me that he hired people to physically harm Wayne."

"So let's take this from the top."

"Is this an inquisition?"

"No. of course not. I'm sorry."

"It's okay. Ask me whatever you want."

"Fair enough. And you can tell me whatever you want to tell me."

"Agreed."

"If I overstep my bounds with a question, just tell me you don't want to answer it. If you want me to stop asking questions entirely I can do that too."

"Okay."

"So how long ago did Frank tell you about his assault on Johnson? ... What's his name again? ... Oh yeah ... Wayne ... Right? Wayne Johnson? Have you known about this since the time of his death?"

"No. I probably suspected it for a long time. But Frank told me about three years ago, August of 1991 to be exact. It was well after we launched MBF."

Betty is slightly affronted by Simone's insinuation that she may be more worried about their business than she is about her business partner. But she doesn't articulate her annoyance. Betty simply waits for Simone to continue.

## *August 1994*

"I'd like to say that I would never have taken any funding from Frank if I knew then what I know now. But the truth of the matter is that I have always had my suspicions. So now I feel guilty about knowing what I know. Does that make any sense to you?"

"Sure, of course."

"It's been weighing on my mind ever since he told me the truth."

"They say that the truth will set you free. But that old adage doesn't say much about what the truth does to others."

"You've got that right."

"So now you've told me about Frank's confession. Who else knows?"

"I haven't told anyone else."

"Do you think Frank told anyone else?"

"Frank is pretty much a jerk, but I do believe it when he tells me that he didn't mean to kill Wayne. He just meant to rough him up, or as Frank put it *teach him a lesson*."

"Does it matter to you?"

"Maybe a little ... I'm not sure."

"But you didn't answer my other question. Did he tell other people?"

"I'm not so sure about that either. Recalling what he told me at the time, he said that he told his psychiatrist and that he told some priest in confession in some foreign country."

"Wow that's bizarre. I don't picture Babcock as the type of person who goes to confession. In fact I don't know *anyone* who goes to confession. I'm not a Catholic so I'm not so sure what that's all about anyway. But even the Catholics I know, never go to confession ... you know ... as far as I know."

Betty tries her hardest not to talk in circles but it is getting more difficult by the moment.

Simone studies Betty's face for a few seconds. They are now staring right into one another's eyes. The pot allows this to be less uncomfortable for a few moments. Simone trusts Betty beyond a doubt. The odd part of their relationship is that they don't often talk about deeply personal matters. It's just that when they do confide in one another, there is no holding back. Nothing is truly off limits and there is no room for deceit or falsehoods. It is not only the basis for a rock solid friendship, it also makes them good business partners.

"One other possibility is that Frank just might have told Fox or even Mickey. I sincerely doubt it but when I listened to the tape ... I remember

## Techies, Trials & Technologies

that near the very end of it ... Frank talks about eventually telling Fox and maybe even Mickey."

Betty is staring and trying to process.

"Yeah ... hard to believe but that's what he said. Now I know that's crazy and I'm sure that hasn't happened yet because I would certainly know the moment that it did, but I ......"

"Woah, Woah, slow down a minute Simone. There's a tape? What *tape* are you talking about?"

∞∞∞

# XXIII

## November 1994

Frank Babcock can't believe that this is actually happening. He is leaving the Criminal Branch of New York State Supreme Court, the trial court in New York State. Babcock has just been arraigned on charges of 1st degree murder as well as a lesser included charge of 2nd degree murder. He has also been charged with conspiracy to commit murder.

This is now more than 14 years after the death of his former nemesis, Wayne Johnson. Babcock's lawyers have assured him that he will be fully acquitted on all charges and that the government doesn't have a leg to stand on. It appears as though the State is basing its case on the testimony of two significant witnesses. The first witness will be a man who has been incarcerated in upstate New York for more than a dozen years. There is some corroborating DNA evidence that will lend credibility to the witness's allegation. The second significant witness they hope to call will be Babcock's ex-wife, Simone Muirchant.

∞∞∞

"Let's go back over what we know through formal and informal channels, Frank. We'll learn a lot more about the Prosecution's case during formal discovery proceedings before we ever get to trial, but we ought to start with what we know now. The Prosecution believes that they can easily establish a motive for murder. They know that Wayne Johnson and your wife had a long standing affair, one that was ongoing before, after and during your first marriage to Simone Muirchant. They also will attempt to show that you believed that your adopted son Fox Babcock was in reality the progeny of the relationship between your ex-wife and the murdered Wayne Babcock. They will contend that a revenge motive is obvious. Are you with me so far?"

∞∞∞

The question is being posed by Phillip Ambrose, the renowned criminal defense lawyer. Ambrose has successfully defended countless wealthy white collar criminal defendants in fraud and embezzlement cases. However he is best known for gaining an acquittal in the "Clue Murders" case wherein his clients the butler and the maid for the wealthy DePietro family had been accused of killing their employers by beating them with a lead pipe in their Connecticut mansion. Some of the same issues of greed, lust and infidelity that had made that case such a national story are now threatening to be exposed in the murder trial that one media outlet has now tabbed as "Babcock and the Bad Cop."

∞∞∞

"I understand what you're saying but some of it isn't true. I never knew that Fox was not my son until after Wayne Johnson was dead. And for that matter as far as I knew Simone's sexual relationship with Wayne Johnson ended more than twenty-five years ago, ... in 1968 to be exact. So technically he was having a sexual relationship with her before and during my first marriage to Simone, but not after we divorced."

"Yes, that's good. But so far that's only your opinion on it. What about Simone? What will she say about her affair with Johnson? And what will she say about how much you knew about it?"

Babcock is somewhat worried on this front. He knows what he told Simone three years earlier but they have never discussed it since that time. He doesn't believe that she has told anyone else either because she knows in the long run it will only hurt Fox. However he hasn't spoken to Simone since a brief conversation at Fox's wedding two years earlier. Periodically he has heard about his ex-wife from Fox, but he has no idea how married life might now have changed her. It is certainly something to think about. He decides he will find out a little more about her current mindset. Regardless he suddenly feels very foolish about what he told Simone in Ecco. He decides that Ambrose doesn't need to know about that dinner conversation, at least not yet.

"Simone won't lie. It's not in her nature to lie. But her version of the truth might not help." He stops immediately and then says, "Damn, this

## November 1994

really is some mess. Does she have to testify? How about Fox? Is he going to get dragged into this too? I could care less about Mickey Johnson. But I imagine that he'll have to testify also. Thank God his brother Gil is dead."

"Frank, we're beyond talking about embarrassment here. We're talking about your life, your freedom. Somehow that hasn't quite dawned upon you yet. Has it?"

∞∞∞

Later that night, Frank Babcock returns to his townhouse on the upper east side of Manhattan. He is free on $3 million bail but has been required to surrender his passport. He has spent the better part of the afternoon speaking with his legal team and he is depleted by the whole experience.

"Frank you must be exhausted. Can I fix you something to drink?"

Margot Babcock looks more than a little drained herself. The slightly built woman is beginning to look older than her years. For almost a week now they have been dealing with the inevitable arrest and arraignment. However during the time it takes for Babcock's personal legal staff to contract with a high profile defense attorney, the media starts digging into every aspect of the indictment. They go back to their previous notes from three years earlier when the big debate was whether or not Frank Babcock had anything to do with the death of his fiancé, Nicole Silver. And it didn't take them long to brush up on the fact that Silver's sister is now Babcock's young wife. The paparazzi are making her life difficult as well.

"Yes, Margot. I could use a scotch on the rocks. And pour yourself a glass of wine or something and sit with me. We have a lot to talk about."

Very quickly Margot goes and gets herself a glass of Chablis and fixes Babcock a single malt scotch. When she returns they sit down together in the second floor living room area.

"As I'm sure you know, I had nothing to do with the murder of Wayne Johnson. I despised the man. But I never said a word to him. I knew who he was and what he had done. But I didn't want to ever dignify his existence by acknowledging his involvement with my first wife. So I never said one single word to him ... not ever!"

Babcock's tone is clipped as though he is expectorating his words. At times like this, his Lattingtown Lockjaw diction sets in more resolutely than usual.

## *Techies, Trials & Technologies*

"I know this is very hard on you, Frank. But we'll get through it together as a family. Jedd is much too young to realize what's going on. And I know that you'll be fully exonerated. I don't care what the media or anyone else thinks. What bothers me is how draining this must be on you."

"It's unfair. We went through something similar to this when your sister was run down. I find it absolutely despicable. The media is circling around the story like a bunch of vultures. But I'm totally in the dark as to who is behind this latest assault on my integrity."

"Whoever it is Frank, they will lose."

"You're right about that. Phil Ambrose assures me that they don't have a smidgen of a chance at getting a conviction. He believes this is all about someone trying to cause me some significant embarrassment. Phil has asked me repeatedly if there's anyone that I can think of that might be behind such a crusade. He asked about Simone. But truthfully I don't believe that she would be up to something like this. I'm pretty sure that she got over it, a decade ago. We've both learned how to deal with our past without driving each other crazy."

"What about Mickey Johnson?"

"That's a possibility. But why now? Why not a dozen years ago? I could understand his involvement. It's no secret that we despise each other. If there's ever been one man who I might've wanted to kill at one point, it's Mickey Johnson. But my issues with Johnson are pretty much in the past, I believe. We've managed to accommodate each other for Fox's sake."

"He actually saved your life in San Francisco. Didn't he?"

Babcock doesn't want to answer this question with a simple affirmative. Although he is grateful to Mickey and Syd Johnson for their role in getting him to the hospital during the 1989 earthquake, he is reluctant to dwell on his own gratitude. It grates on him to think of Mickey in any valiant way, even though it's true that Mickey had acted courageously.

∞∞∞

""It doesn't change the transgressions of the past." He starts to mitigate any depicture of Mickey's heroism but keeps the follow-on thoughts to himself. *Johnson is new money. In reality he's still a peasant, probably descended from the potato farmers in Suffolk County. I could never feel indebted to him.*

"Even if he is involved, Mickey can't make this happen all by himself. Someone else must want to rattle you, Frank."

## November 1994

Babcock gives this some thought before he responds. He wonders if this has anything to do with the al-Haddād family.

"What are you thinking, Frank?"

Babcock doesn't want to answer at first. He knows that he can't discuss the al-Haddād family with Margot. He doesn't want to even consider the possibility that the Saudis have caught on to his affair with Masira. He knows that Abdulrahman al-Haddād is capable of revenge if he knows that an American is having an illicit affair with his daughter. Masira al-Haddād is now engaged to another prominent Saudi citizen. The implications of exposure could be lethal to both Babcock and to Masira.

"I'm simply wondering if this has anything to do with any of my business dealings." He approaches the topic vaguely.

"I understand that some New Yorkers are wary of mid-eastern Muslims, after those terrorists bombed the Trade Center last year. Most people think that those Arabs are just nuts. But some of us think they're dangerous nuts. The tower bombing may not be an isolated incident. Maybe the fact that some of your clients are Arabs makes some people want to give you a hard time."

"Nothing could be further from reality. My Arab clients think just like New Yorkers. They think that those Islamic zealots who bombed the Trade Center are religious fanatics and terrorists."

"Meaning among other things that they hate Jews."

"Oh, I don't know about that. I've never heard any of my clients say anything against Jews."

"Well, they aren't going to say anything like that to you. You're married to a Jew."

There is no venom in Margot's voice as she says this. Her tone is softly sardonic and yet somewhat sympathetic to her husband's plight. "You realize this also. That's why we've never broached the topic of Jedidiah and me traveling with you on one of your trips to the Middle East."

"I don't know exactly what to say. You're right of course. I try not to think too much about the general attitude of Arabs towards Jews. Middle East politics ... well, that's quite a complicated issue. By the way I don't think those religious fundamentalists are too fond of Christians either."

Babcock ignores his wife's point about traveling with him. He knows that could never happen and he's glad she has no desire to travel to the Middle East. However he does have some concern about his clientele. His

201

worries about why the federal authorities just won't go away. *Are they the real reason why the NYPD is charging me? Does this have to do with the federal intelligence community as well as the NYPD? Is this why Ambrose couldn't get the court to allow me to keep my passport? Ambrose better straighten that part out quickly. I'm paying him enough.*

"Do you want to talk about it, Frank? Or should I leave you alone for a while?" Margot is sincere in her question. She speaks very softly but she is still trying to get her husband to share his thoughts more openly, even if that means leaving him alone for a while. She's unsure what's best.

Babcock stands up and straightens his posture. He tries to regain his composure by recalling that Phillip Ambrose was able to get an acquittal in the Clue Murders case … when most people still believe the maid and the butler killed the DePietros. If he free those two he can certainly get a victory in his case as well. But in the end his reputation is important also. Babcock not only wants an acquittal in court, he wants an exoneration in the court of public opinion as well. He knows that he is paying Ambrose an exorbitant fee. Therefore nothing less than total exoneration, vindication and reputation reparation will suffice. In Frank Babcock's mind, guilt is now merely an abstraction. Redemption is the objective.

∞∞∞

# XXIV

## November 1994

Syd Johnson is nearing her third full year working at Gehring Durrenberger Holt (GDH.) She enjoys her professional experience and the rush of daily deal making, but she also enjoys motherhood. Cody, Noah and Jessica are now 10, 9 and 7 years old. Although they are still in their "Wonder Years" every stage of life is important and Syd realizes that she is blessed by the fact that her mother and Kathy McDonough are able to help out with quasi-parental supervision. The challenge of being a working mother is somewhat easier for Syd knowing that she can walk away from her job whenever she wishes. And that may be very well be what she does do when her children reach the more trying teen years.

But for now Syd is invigorated by the dual role of mother and businesswoman. Steeled by this realization she is heading into the office for another day of work following her usual routine of taking the 6:19 train from Garden City into Penn Station and then heading downtown on the 8$^{th}$ Avenue E train to the World Trade Center station. GDH occupies office space on two of the lower floors at 5 World Trade Center, diagonally northeast from Tower 2 also known as the South Tower.

She looks up at the man in the hallway outside the offices of GDH. The man may be an inch over six feet tall but he looks somewhat thinner than she remembered him. Actually he looks a little scrawny. It has now been nearly 15 years since she has last seen her brother, Jermaine Spataro. What has happened to him? He is now suddenly a person of color. His hair is thinning but it is still jet black.

∞∞∞

## *Techies, Trials & Technologies*

Throughout his youth, Jermaine Spaltro had exhibited a dark olive pigmentation to his skin, but his facial features were not characteristically African American. Even his hair had been remarkably thick and straight. It is now wavy. One thing that Syd had in common with Jermaine is their common genes. And as such they each knew that they were 50% African American and 50% Italian American. But at this point in their respective lives they were physically expressing that genetic make-up somewhat differently.

On all of her human resources documents, Syd Johnson had registered as white female. When she agreed to take the job at GDH she told John Holt that she would gladly take the job as long as he wasn't going to hold her up as a token black salesperson. Holt told her that he didn't give a damn whether she thought of herself as black, white, brown or yellow. He just knew that she could be successful at his firm. Then as an afterthought he had said, "We're square on the racial thing, right. When she answered in the affirmative he added, "Just don't do one of those gender-bender deals on me." He didn't mean it to be offensive, so Syd just laughed it off.

∞∞∞

Now as Syd takes in the full measure of the brother in front of her, she sees him only as 100% ethnically black. How strange! It's the primary feeling that envelops her thought process and it creates some discomfort. This discomfort is a composite of several positive and negative emotions that are not at all harmonious.

Positive feelings include the fact that Jermaine looks to be relatively healthy although obviously older than her mental images of him. He still manages a comfortable smile although he doesn't appear to be living comfortably. And he did take the initiative of getting in touch with her, long after she had given up on ever seeing him again.

The negative emotions she feels center around one central question: *What does he want?* She wonders why he has come to see her after all these years. She wonders what he knows about her and what the source of his information may be. These negative emotions become manifest first.

∞∞∞

"What made you decide to come back east after all these years?"
"Curiosity more than anything else, I guess."
"Why didn't you come to Dad's funeral?"

## November 1994

"I don't have a good excuse. I was more than a little messed up then, I guess

"What does that mean? Personal problems? Drugs? 'A little messed up' doesn't tell me much." There is an edge to Syd's timbre that she doesn't mean to expose. In some ways she is talking to Jermaine as if he is a younger brother when in reality Jermaine is nine years older than his sister.

"I don't know, maybe I was a little lost."

"That wasn't your father's fault. Or your mother's fault ... or mine either for that matter. You got lost all by yourself."

"Well I thought ..." Jermaine Spataro stops in mid-sentence, turns quickly and begins to walk away. "This was a mistake ..." he mutters and shakes his head as he quickens his pace. He is almost twenty five feet away, closing in on the elevator when he hears his sister call after him.

"Jermaine, wait."

∞∞∞

There was a lot that Sydney Johnson didn't know about Jermaine Spataro. She didn't know that he was currently living in Missouri, just outside of St Louis. The last she had heard he was living in Chicago. Syd was also unaware that her brother had spent some time in and out of prison for drug offenses or that he was currently employed as a youth social counselor back in Missouri. He had managed to hold down this job for the last three years. He earned two weeks of vacation time each year and he had decided to spend one week of that time this year trying to reestablish a relationship with his sister. While he was in NYC Jermaine was armed with a reference from his work in Missouri for a meeting with a prospective employer in the Manhattan. Syd agreed to meet Jermaine early that evening after the markets closed. Syd suggested a small coffee shop on Cortlandt Street.

∞∞∞

"Let's take it from the top. I get a phone call out of the blue from you, saying that you will be in New York City sometime around Thanksgiving and you'd like to catch up on a lot of what we have missed as brother and sister. Of course, I'm totally flabbergasted. I don't know how you even have my married name much less my telephone number at work. You tell me on the phone that it's a long story, but that you will tell me how you found me once we get together in the city. So now here we are, and I think I'd like to be on the listening end of this conversation for the next half hour or so."

# Techies, Trials & Technologies

"Okay."

But Syd is not quite ready to listen after all. She has one more statement to make.

"You're my own brother and I know just about nothing about you. So go ahead, start anywhere you want. But keep it about you. We can talk about me later ... if I think it's appropriate. Do you even know when the last time we saw each other was?"

"As a matter of fact, I do remember, quite vividly. It was August of 1978. I had just been thrown out of the Army. That's the *true* story, or at least part of the true story. They caught me with another soldier and we had some drugs, pot mostly, that we were selling to other soldiers. This was not a major distribution racket or anything, just sales to our buddies ... enough so that Benny and I could get our stuff for free.

"We could have received a dishonorable discharge. Your father didn't want that disgrace in his family and tried to get things arranged for a general discharge. What he found out was that getting a general discharge for me was even easier then he thought.

"Anyway, if you recall our parents were still living in Paris at the time. He was stationed at the embassy or some such grand nonsense." Syd detects a very negative vibe from Jermaine's use of the pronoun "he" instead of a more affectionate reference to "Dad," or even if he referred to Ray Spataro as "*our* father," instead of "*your* father."

"Well the truth of the matter is that I received an "honorable discharge" or should I say I accepted an 'honorable discharge.' There was no question I had to leave the Army. That was part of the deal, but I'll tell you more about that in a minute.

"You had just started working right here in New York. Your parents were so proud of you. Both of them were. I was proud of you too. I knew that you would make a go of things big time. You were a college graduate, working on Wall Street. It was very cool. I was in the process of returning to Chicago but I came here first. I wanted to tell you the whole story about leaving the Army but I just couldn't do it. Things were going so well for you here and I didn't want be a burden to you. You seemed so excited and happy."

"We had lunch together and that was the last time I saw you until today. Why?"

## November 1994

"It was your father's idea. He didn't want me talking to you. He was embarrassed by me and he didn't want my problems becoming your problems."

"He told you not to see me? Not to call me? Not to talk to me at all?" Syd sounded incredulous.

"Yes, yes and yes."

"And this was all because you got caught with pot in the Army? That doesn't make much sense. And why would you listen to him, anyway?" Syd is very skeptical and it is obvious from her tone.

"Did you talk to him after that? Did you talk to Mom?

"I talked to your father a few times during the next year and only once to your mother. I had stopped thinking about them as my parents." Jermaine felt a little disingenuous by saying he had only talked to Violet Spataro once. It wasn't true.

"They never told me about these conversations."

"For the most part they were still living in Europe then. How much did you see them?"

"Not a lot. But I talked to them at least every six or seven weeks or so. We kept in touch ... even then."

"Did you ask them if they had talked to me?"

"Probably ... but not in so many exact words ... As I recall, even then, if I mentioned your name ... it was met with stone silence. I know it must have been painful to them." She hesitates and then asks, "So what happened after you went back to Chicago?"

"I enrolled in a suburban community college and took a few courses. I wanted to finish my degree ... or at least get an associate's degree. But I made some poor choices about friends and other things."

"What other things?"

"Well I got arrested with two other guys for breaking into a convenience store where one of the other guys worked. It was really stupid. We were totally stoned and were doing it more for the thrill than the money."

"What happened as a result?"

"We got arrested. I got charged with breaking and entry and theft as well as drug possession. I was in jail for a little over nine months. It wasn't pleasant."

## Techies, Trials & Technologies

"I heard some of that from Mom when she was explaining why you weren't coming to my wedding, but she wouldn't tell me much more because she said there wasn't anything that I could do. Maybe I should have pursued it further. But I never got a Christmas Card. I didn't hear from you after I sent birthday cards the first couple of years. All I had was the PO Box that you gave me the last time I saw you. You never wrote back, not even to reply to my wedding invitation. You never gave me a phone number. It was like you fell of the face of the earth or were hiding someplace."

"Well just to set the record straight, I wasn't in jail at the time of your wedding. I was already out. But, believe me I felt like I was "persona non grata" when it came to your wedding. Your father definitely didn't want me there and he told me so directly. He didn't want me anywhere near you or your husband."

"Did you see him?" Syd is astounded by these revelations.

"No. He called me from Paris. For a while he had a phone number for me. And to be brutally honest about it, from time to time he sent me some money."

Syd allows all of this sink in. Jermaine doesn't appear to be in any particular hurry to continue his narrative without prompting so they just stare at each other for a few seconds, each trying to assess the other's thoughts without any real way of doing so.

The small café is half empty and no one is paying any attention to this odd looking couple. To others they may have look vaguely alike even though the male appears to be black and the female appears to be white. But this is quite normal. New York City, after all it is the world's melting pot. What is more dissimilar about the couple is the apparent disparity in social status. The female is wearing a business pants suit. Her tablemate is wearing faded jeans and a worn collared Izod t-shirt. There is a two hundred dollars difference in the price of their footwear.

"So, if I have this straight, the reason we haven't seen each other for 16 years comes down to the fact that you got caught with pot in the Army, and Dad couldn't deal with it."

"No. It's more than that."

"I'm listening."

"Benny and I got caught with the pot, sure. But Benny's father was a general. As far as I know Benny's still in the service."

"So?"

## November 1994

"So Benny and I were lovers."

"You were gay?"

"Still am." They both manage matching wry smiles.

"Jesus."

"Is that a good Jesus, or a bad Jesus?" It is a very relieving disclosure, and Jermaine tries to follow it up with a query. But he is still a little unsure of where things stood. Syd's wry smile has turned into a short giggle before she answers.

"Oh Jermaine. There's no Bad Jesus!" It isn't meant as a religious commentary. Instead it is a statement of understanding. Syd can't help herself and she begins to laugh in her inimitable infectious way. Jermaine hears the rolling reverberating multi pitch laugh that he hasn't heard for the better part of the last two decades. He loves it. He begins to laugh along with his sister, hopefully.

An hour later Syd is on the phone to her husband. "Guess who's coming to dinner?"

∞∞∞

But Jermaine Spataro doesn't come to dinner that night. Instead they make a date for dinner in the city the following night. Jermaine has his job interview and wants to stay in the city so as not to be late for the appointment. This proves to be a good decision because the next day Jermaine is offered a job working for a non-profit drug rehabilitation organization called *Healthy Hours on the Horizon.*

At the ensuing dinner, Mickey takes an odd liking to his long lost brother-in-law and invites him to stay out at his Garden City home for a few days while he decides upon his employment future. Each of the three persons at the dinner realize that this will also entail a reuniting on Jermaine Spataro with his mother Violet Spataro.

Syd is flabbergasted by Mickey's offer to her brother but knows that it will only be for a few days. She hopes that, at the very least, this will be an opportunity for the Spataro family to enjoy an overdue reunion, if not a reunification. She feels confident that her mother will be happy about it. Deep down she wants to be able to laugh about the sores that have been reopened, but she is worried.

Mickey surprises himself with his gracious offer, but realizes that their household is somewhat unusual to begin with. He is also grateful to Syd for her ongoing embrace of Kathy McDonough. He hopes that this can

## Techies, Trials & Technologies

be a small payback in kind. Unlike Syd, Mickey suspects that Jermaine may stay more than a couple of days. But there is something about Jermaine that Mickey finds very genuine. He's not worried.

Jermaine is both surprised and thankful for Mickey's offer. In reality he is quite unsure what lies ahead for him. For many years now, he has been letting fate guide his future, and he is grateful for Mickey's benign spirit. Of the three of them Jermaine is the only one who is aware that it was Violet Spataro who suggested that he come to New York. Intriguingly events played out almost exactly the way that Violet had suggested they would. He wonders what fate will have in store for him now.

∞∞∞

# XXV

## *November 1994*

Fox and Evelyn Babcock are having Thanksgiving Dinner at the home of Evelyn's father, Dr. Mark Webb. Around the table are Evelyn's mother, Chrissy Webb; Evelyn's brother, Peter Webb; and two other couples. The other couples include a young French physician from the hospital who is working on her cardiology fellowship at UPMC. Dr. Désirée Dubois and her husband Philippe are enjoying their first year in the United States. Philippe is working towards an engineering doctorate at Carnegie Mellon University,

Also at the table Joe and Linda McCandless. Linda is six months pregnant. Fox has not seen Joe McCandless since shortly after their summer rafting trip in West Virginia. Mark and Chrissy Webb are friends of Joe McCandless' parents, who are currently traveling on an African safari in Kenya and Tanzania. They have watched Joe McCandless grow up and they treat him almost like a son.

Mark Webb finishes slicing the turkey as Chrissy Webb arrays all the vegetables and side dishes on her formal china across the table and on a nearby sideboard. She is serving a family style dinner. No sooner are they seated when Joe McCandless opens the axiomatic can of worms.

"How are you holding up, Fox? The situation with your father …uh for Frank Babcock must be very difficult for you to deal with. The media is entirely relentless. Have they been bugging you personally as well?"

"Not really, probably because I'm out here in the middle of nowhere. Those paparazzi types only know the coasts …California and New York."
He stops for a second but everyone seems to be waiting for him to say more.

"But they certainly are trying to make life difficult for my father." Fox doesn't appreciate the fact that Joe McCandless shows no trepidation about addressing the awkward subject matter. He certainly doesn't want to go through the entire dinner discussing this topic.

Everyone freezes in uncomfortable silence. The underlying issues are apparent to everyone. First, there is the issue of McCandless's hesitancy in referring to Frank Babcock as Fox Babcock's father. Next is the issue that Fox refers to Pittsburgh as being in the "middle of nowhere." And then finally there is McCandless' direct question about exactly how Fox feels about the recent developments in his family.

In reality only Fox can address each of these issues. After his curt answer the silence is deafening. Clumsily, McCandless leaps to fill the void.

"I don't know how I'd deal with that if I were in your position. They're not giving Frank the benefit of the doubt at all."

"To tell you the truth, Joe, I'd prefer not to speak about it. If you're assuming that this is pretty troublesome to me, you'd be right."

"Sorry Fox, sorry." McCandless exhibits an offended look.

"Ok Joe ... My dad has always tried to treat people without malice. I consider him to be an exemplary good man. For the longest time he cherished his privacy. I know that the most important things in his life are his children and his job."

"Yes, of course, sure." As McCandless speaks, the others look at him skeptically.

"The fact that he's far wealthier than most people, is irrelevant. He works hard at what he does, trying to use his assets to make the world a better place to live. I know that Dad is innocent. I also believe that my deceased grandfather had some friends in the NYPD who have initiated a witch hunt."

Fox's tone is angry. He is angry at himself for allowing McCandless to keep this conversation going, and now he finds himself giving opinions he would rather not have had to give.

"So what is *zis zing* you call *weetch* hunt?" The question is posed innocently enough by Désirée Dubois. She even smiles at Fox to demonstrate her innocuous intent.

"A witch hunt means that the government is trying to malign Frank Babcock without a shred of evidence."

"*Ees* there a *raison* for *deese*?"

Fox suddenly feels as though he himself is on trial.

"Who knows?"

## November 1994

Fox is clearly exasperated. He looks up and around as he gives his two word reply. His glare intimates that he is done discussing the topic. However Joe McCandless is slow on the uptake and fills the short silence with another question.

"So if I've got this straight, they're accusing your adoptive father of killing your grandfather because he thought your grandfather was your father ... or something like that. Is that right?"

"Can we just freaking drop it, Joe? Can't you take a freaking hint? I don't want to discuss this topic with you or anyone else." Fox has cleaned up his modifiers but they sound just like the replaced expletives anyway. His irritation with the subject matter is clear and succinct.

"Fox has been facing this kind of scrutiny at the hospital as well. He doesn't need to hear about it from us." Evelyn chips in. However she comes across as defending Fox where he doesn't feel he needs to be defended. Also by using the pronoun, *"us"* Evelyn appears to separate herself from Fox in an odd alignment with others around the table.

"Let's just move on. Shall we?" Mark Webb never anticipated any of this. He says, "Let's say grace before we eat, because I'm sure we all have many things to be thankful about." Webb then leads the others in a classic Catholic pre-meal family prayer bookended by the sign of the cross.

Throughout dinner much of the conversation remains light as they discuss the Thanksgiving Day football game between the Cowboys and the Packers; the recent mid-term elections and some Webb family trivia.

The discussion of the midterm elections is particularly interesting as Mark and Chrissy Webb are ardent Democrats who are quite concerned about the fact that their party got thoroughly trounced earlier in the month. "We lost 54 damn seats in the House to the Republicans and now they have the majority in that chamber for the first time in over 40 years ... since 1952." Mark Webb offers his assessment.

Linda McCandless grew up in a Republican household and married a right leaning husband. She offers Webb her explanation of the Democrats poor performance. "A big part of your problem is that Bill Clinton let his wife run the task force that was putting together the new health care plan." Linda's opinion is then reinforced by her husband.

"Yea, the healthcare plan was the knockout punch. Why was Hilary Clinton in charge of this in the first place? She wasn't elected to anything.

She's not a Senator or a Congresswoman. And apparently she doesn't know a damn thing about healthcare. So what was that all about?"

"Who knows? But we, Democrats, didn't do well here in Pennsylvania either. We just got two of our incumbents bounced. Now we'll have this Republican guy, Tom Ridge, as our Governor, and Rick Santorum as our new Republican United States Senator. We're going to have to shake things up in the party here in Pennsylvania over the next two years that's for sure."

"Linda and Joe are right about why we lost so much. For the next election cycle we can start by burying the whole Clinton healthcare debacle. Even as a Democrat I wasn't very fond of that." Chrissy Webb then adds, "It was going to cap what doctors and hospitals could charge for certain procedures. And our taxes would go through the roof. That can't be a good thing."

Fox listens to the political discussion without offering any opinion. He didn't vote. He isn't particularly enamored with politics in general and is especially disinterested in Pennsylvania politics. But he is grateful that they have moved on from discussing his father's plight. However when the conversation turns to the ever-interesting details of the upcoming OJ Simpson trial, the parallels with the Frank Babcock trial are too close for comfort.

Evelyn knows that Fox is peeved with the way the dinner conversation has gone. However she doesn't say anything to him as he excuses himself from the table and heads into the family room to watch the fourth quarter of the football game. He is followed into the family room by Philippe Dubois and Joe McCandless. Linda McCandless and Désirée Dubois remain at the dining room table with Evelyn and her parents. Evelyn's brother Peter stands up awkwardly, unsure whether to remain at the table with the women or to go join Fox and the others in the family room. After a half minute of indecision, Peter opts to join the men watching the football game.

∞∞∞

"So how are you feeling, Linda? I remember my first pregnancy, when we were expecting Evelyn, I was absolutely ravenous all the time. And I ate some of the craziest things." Chrissy Webb smiles as she makes her inquiry. She is generally regarded as a very sweet woman. She is pretty in a classical way, with beautiful skin and a slim well-groomed appearance that

## November 1994

never experiences a pimple or a bad-hair day. Other women don't begrudge her beauty, even if they sometimes marvel at her even tempered demeanor. Men regard her as beautiful but not sexy. She exudes a patrician class refinement without a snooty high falutin mien. In general everybody loves Chrissy.

"I'm feeling okay overall. I haven't had any morning sickness like some of my friends, but lately I'm slightly uncomfortable about how much weight I'm gaining." She lowers her hands to her abdomen as she makes this statement with a slightly pained expression, as though she is expected to exhibit some discomfort.

"Well today's Thanksgiving. We're all a bit bloated. You'll be fine after we have a few minutes to digest everything. Besides this is your chance to pamper yourself, don't ignore it. Your baby will arrive soon enough."

Evelyn listens to this exchange between her mother and her friend with a noncommittal attitude. She has her reasons for not commenting, but she doesn't want to broach them as part of this conversation. Meanwhile as the only male left at the dinner table, Mark Webb, decides that he will get up and offer everyone an after dinner cordial. He moves away from the table toward a cabinet just beyond the butler's pantry, where he stows his single malt scotch collection along with a wide assortment of other liqueurs, cordials, brandies, and other after dinner spirits.

"But I'm seeing Dr. Powell on Tuesday and she'll probably tell me what to expect."

Chrissy Webb has her opinions but she doesn't want to upset Linda. She knows Marge Powell through various activities at the hospital. She thinks that Powell is a particularly insensitive physician, who knows very little about her own profession. Chrissy's biases are based more upon personal interactions with Powell than they are on Powell's professional competence. But she is particularly chagrined by Powell's ultra-conservative political viewpoints. She wished that Linda McCandless had chosen a different obstetrician.

The chit chat among the women in the dining room continues after Mark Webb moves into the living room to join the other men. Meanwhile Chrissy Webb is unaware that Linda McCandless's pregnancy is not the most compelling pregnancy that she will be hearing about in the next few weeks.

∞∞∞

"So other than your father's problems, what's new with you, Fox?"

Joe McCandless seems to enjoy the chance to speak to Fox out of the earshot of Evelyn and Linda.

"Nothing terribly interesting. Just working a lot of hours ... both of us have been. Our residencies squeeze a lot of hours out of both of us. It's good to get a holiday off."

McCandless turns toward Philippe Dubois in a conspiratorial tone and says "The last time I saw our friend Fox here was when I went rafting with him on the Gauley River back in May. That was a hell of a good time, even though some of us spent more time in the hospital than the good doctor here. He was tending to the needs of one of the local tour guides."

Philippe's English is not as advanced as his wife's. He is not able to comprehend spoken innuendo. However he is bright enough to perceive a discordance between Fox and McCandless. He makes an effort to change the topic.

"*Eh Amereecan* Football *ees* a smart game. Yes? *Weeth* lots of plans." They watch as the Cowboys huddle up on 3$^{rd}$ down with 9 yards to go.

"These guys aren't as smart as you think, Philippe. The coaches call all of the plays on the sidelines. The huddle is simply a way to tell everyone what play has been signaled in from the bench. Only the quarterback speaks in the huddle to tell the other players what play is called and what the snap signal is. Sometimes the quarterback changes the play at the line of scrimmage however. So there's at least one guy on the field with a brain."

"*Eet ees* very violent sport, though. Yes?"

"It's not as bad as it looks. They all wear a lot of padding. But guys do get injured often enough. I guess it's fair to say it's pretty violent, but it's not like boxing where the object is to knock the other guy senseless." Fox tries to be friendly and somewhat agreeable.

"What are you guys talking about? You both sound like a couple of pussies. Boxing and football are both great sports."

"One thing *ees* good. It *ees* fun to watch. Yes? *Eet* makes you forget other troubles. Yes? In these way it *ees* like what you Americans call soccer and we call football."

Fox is content to watch Philippe derail McCandless's attempt to revisit the summer rafting trip. However he files away the thought that McCandless is just enough of an ass to bring this up again at a less

## November 1994

appropriate moment. He wishes that he had an adequate counterweight to McCandless' compromising data. But he doesn't have the truth on his side.

∞∞∞

*Evelyn Babcock was now in her third month but she hasn't yet made her condition widely known. In fact she had just told Fox about it two weeks earlier. The young couple have had many other issues on their plate during the last couple of months and they wanted to get a better handle on some of those things before making an announcement about their upcoming joy. Of course it would be a lot easier to tell the Webb family or the Johnson family, than it would be to tell Frank Babcock. Part of Evelyn wants to share their joyous news with her family but she defers that joy to a later date even as Linda and Joe McCandless talk abundantly about their own expectant family situation.*

*Oddly enough, and unknown to either Fox or Evelyn, Joe McCandless believes that Fox will soon become a father. However McCandless believes that the mother of Fox's child is six months pregnant, rather than three.*

∞∞∞

The rest of the Thanksgiving dinner proceeds without a major personal flare up as the Webb family and their guests settle in to watch the Cowboys come from behind 24-13 in the third quarter to vanquish the Packers 42-31.

Peter Webb has oddly remained quiet in the family room as he watches the game along with Fox and the others. Peter is normally an engaging personality, but he senses some aggression in the ongoing conversation and so he chooses to stay quiet. Although he was born with Down Syndrome, he hardly considers it an affliction. He believes it is a blessing. He knows that he is different from others but he has grown up with the fawning attention of his parents and his sister. He knows he receives more bountiful love and affection than the average person. He also has an uncorrupted affection for his brother-in-law. Fox is like the brother that Peter doesn't have. He habitually sides with Fox over Evelyn in whatever petty household disagreement might occur whether it's what movie to watch or what to have for lunch. Peter's chromosome disorder usually does not dissuade him from offering his opinions freely. And his ability to express preference without bias makes his opinions that much more compelling. So when the Packers beat the Cowboys and Fox seems to like the outcome, Peter joins him in his celebratory banter.

∞∞∞

Eventually the Thanksgiving dinner gathering begins to wind down. Kisses and handshakes are exchanged as Mark Webb retrieves and redistributes the coats and outer garments that he has previously placed in the front hall closets.

As Fox and Evelyn are nearing the doorway, ready to leave, Joe McCandless gets up from his chair in the living room to say goodbye. He has already had more to drink than what might be prudent. He walks over to Fox and reaches out to shake his hand but in so doing attempts to pull Fox closer to him so that he can semi-whisper in his ear. "Congratulations, rumor has it that you are now an expectant father."

∞∞∞

Back on Long Island, Thanksgiving dinner at the Johnson household in Garden City is a different family affair. Mickey had extended an invitation to his son and daughter-in-law but Fox and Evelyn had already committed to staying in Pittsburgh with Evelyn's family.

But the Johnson family dinner is also a substantial family event. Mickey's other three children are all trying to adjust to the presence of the latest family member/resident, Jermaine Spataro, whom they referred to simply as Uncle Jerry. Jessica and her two older brothers Cody and Noah are in the family room watching the Thanksgiving Day Parade on TV, while simultaneously playing the Dungeons and Dragons video game. They are oblivious to the adult conversations elsewhere in the home.

Mickey's two mothers-in-law have joined Syd in preparing the usual Turkey Day repast complete with two different kinds of stuffing – with and without sausage – and nine different vegetables. These include sweet potatoes and the mashed version of the more conventional edible tuber. The spread also includes corn, creamed onions, green beans, carrots, podded peas, spinach and broccoli. For added culinary diversity, cranberry sauce and a thick turkey gravy pull the plates together.

While the three women work in the kitchen, Mickey and Jermaine are seated in the living room still trying to get to know one another better.

"Have you always lived on Long Island?" Jermaine feels no qualms about being openly inquisitive of his host.

## November 1994

"Yeah. I've lived here all my life except for the war years when I was in Southeast Asia. In fact I've always lived in Nassau County, for the entire time. My father and mother bought a house in Lynbrook when I was 8 years and they lived there until the day my father died. I moved out after I married my first wife Barbara in 1969, but all of my moves since then have been within Nassau County. This is the second time we have lived in Garden City."

"Before this year I had never been to Long Island. In fact, I'd only been to NYC once before and even then I flew in and out through Newark Airport. It's nice out here …. very busy, but in a nice way."

"Interesting way of thinking about it. I just know it as home …. Some good, some bad … but mostly good feelings about Long Island."

Mickey pauses for a second and then says, "Well it's not like you weren't invited to come here before. Sydney really wanted you to come to our wedding." The wedding reminder is not delivered with any malice. They've already collectively talked through most of that. "Of course that was quite a while back. We've been married more than 13 years now. Time certainly flies by."

"You're right about that, Mickey. But some of us have squandered more of that time than others. I'm certainly guilty of that."

"Well it's never too late to make a positive contribution to someone or something or some cause. Maybe your contribution has just been delayed a little bit."

"I hope you're right. But you know I look at you and my sister … and your children and it's hard not to be a little envious."

"I believe we're thankful for what we have." Mickey is at a loss to add any further commentary. There is something about Jermaine's candid assessment of things that reminds him of Syd. It is also true of his mother-in-law, Violet Spataro. They are all very straight forward people who say what's on their minds.

"Do you mind if I ask you about your other son? About Fox?"

"No. What about him?"

"Naturally I've just learned all about these connections for the first time. I knew very little about my sister's family until now. I knew that she had married a guy by the name of Mickey Johnson and that they had a few kids …. That was about it. And of course Johnson is such a common name.

"I read the story about the Billionaire Babcock getting indicted for murder of a guy named Wayne Johnson. It's a big story even out in the

Midwest, but I never could have connected this in any way to my sister and her family. Now Syd has filled me in on some of the details but there's so much I don't know."

"There's not a lot you need to know, Jermaine, but you can ask me about it. I won't take any offense, because I'll assume none is intended."

"I was just curious because this guy Dr. Fox Babcock is your son. Right?"

"Right."

"Well he has also been in the news a little bit whether or not he wants to be, just because he was once thought to be Frank Babcock's son. Right?

"Right again."

"He must be a pretty tough cat to put up with all of the scrutiny and not be affected by it, professionally or otherwise."

"He is. Fox is a remarkable human being. And his wife is a terrific young lady also. They'll be coming east during the holidays. We're hoping that they will spend a couple of days with us. You can meet him then and form your own impression. Of course, my opinion is biased. After all he *is* my son."

The conversation with Jermaine strikes a peculiar strain with Mickey. Although Fox is now 29 years old, it is the first time Mickey has heard his son referred to as "a pretty tough cat." There is something aging about it.

"Wow that will be interesting. I don't want to get in the way or anything, but it would be amazing to meet him."

"Then you will meet him. You are family. Fox is family. Families stick together."

∞∞∞

A couple of hours later as they sit down to the Johnson family dinner, Mickey quickly surveys the table seating arrangements. There are eight people seated at the table, five adults and three children. Mickey is sitting at the head of the table and Sydney occupies the other arm chair at the far end of the table. The two boys Cody and Noah sit on either side of Mickey and his two mothers-in-law, Kathy and Violet sit opposite each other both flanking Syd at her end of the table. The middle seats are occupied by Jermaine Spataro sitting across from his niece, seven year old, Jessica.

When they are all seated, Mickey looks up and addresses Jermaine."

## November 1994

"We have a tradition in the family of rotating the opportunity for leading the family Grace before meals. Sometimes I lead the prayer and others lead it at other times. My only privilege in this tradition is in selecting who will lead us. Now don't worry Jermaine. This is all new to you. So I won't ask you to lead us today; just be ready some time down the road. But maybe tonight could I prevail upon you to lead us, Mom. He nods very specifically to his second Mother-in-law, Violet, because he calls both of his mothers-in-law, "Mom."

"Thank you Mickey. I am honored to do so on a holiday."

Violet wonders if Mickey and Syd realize that she is the primary proponent in getting her children back together. She has been communicating with her son for a little less than a year now, even though she never fully lost touch with him. Her only regret is that she hadn't forged a rapprochement between Jermaine and her husband Ray, before Ray died. Nevertheless she feels an unwavering love for Mickey. Her son-in-law has graciously taken the critical step of inviting her son to be part of his household. Mickey is and always will be *Mickey the Magnificent* in her mind. She knows that Syd is very blessed. However she knows that an open profusion of adoration would simply embarrass Mickey and a heartfelt thanks is more appropriate on this occasion. So she starts their family Grace in the normal family manner and then before making the Christian sign of the cross at the end of their prayer she adds her own words of thanksgiving:

"…. And we would also like to thank you Lord for the many blessings that you have bestowed upon our family. You have united the Spataro, McDonough and Johnson families under a single roof and guided the combined Johnson family in an understanding of breadth of your love. You have brought my son, Jermaine back to us and inspired us all through the unconditional kindness of my loving son-in-law, Mickey and my daughter, Sydney. You have blessed our children with children of their own and both Kathy and I know how wonderful it is to be called 'Grandma' by such beautiful children as Cody, Noah and Jessica. Amen."

It is a simple Grace, but typical of Violet, it gets right to the point. She covers everyone and does her best to show appreciation. She relishes her role as a grandmother and sharing that role with Kathy.

As Kathy listens to Violet say Grace, she warms in the knowledge that everyone accepts her as a blood relative, especially the children.

As Syd listens to her mother, she is inspired to try to be as maternal in her instincts as her mother. She is her true role model in life, even if they occasionally squabble.

As Jermaine listens to his mother, he is grateful for her perseverance. He knows that without her prodding he may never have found his way to New York and Long Island.

As Mickey listens to his mother-in-law, he wonders when he himself will become a grandparent. Fox and Evelyn have expressed the desire to have children, but because of their career responsibilities, Mickey thinks it might be a few years down the road. Little does he know that before the year is out, his daughter-in-law will announce her pregnancy. Mickey would never have imagined that Evelyn's baby will be *his second* grandchild.

As they listen to their grandmother say Grace, Noah, Cody and Jessica just want her to finish praying so they can start eating.

∞∞∞

*November 1994*

# XXVI

## *November 1994*

Thanksgiving in West Virginia is a small low-key event for Maddie Swift. She is the lone guest at the home of her cousin Billy Wilde and Billy's wife Gwendolyn. It's a very slow time of year for the river rafting business, although there are still some crazy adventurers, who eagerly brave the colder water and the less predictable weather of the late fall.

Maddie has not worked on the river since Labor Day right after the end of the first trimester of her pregnancy. But she has now found a new job as a receptionist for Dr. Marie Dorsett who also happens to be her personal obstetrician/gynecologist. Normally it would be somewhat less exciting work than paddling on the river, but given her personal circumstances Maddie is quite grateful that she has secured the opportunity to work for Dr. Dorsett.

"Your boss is such a nice lady and so smart. Makes me wish *I'da dun* better in school myself. *Bein'* a lady doctor is pretty cool stuff." Gwendolyn is anything but an academic wonder. She had dropped out of high school before starting her senior year. However her comments to Maddie seem to drip with genuine regret. She believes that just a little more effort might have changed the course of her life. Both Maddie and Billy are high school graduates and feel a slight sense of social superiority although neither of them wants to exhibit this to Gwendolyn.

"Well I *ain't never* wanted to be *no* doctor, myself. But I sure as heck am happy working for Marie. I'm *gettin'* to meet all kinds of nice people who are *'spectin'* to have kids soon.

Billy Wilde is busy whittling the small turkey that Gwendolyn cooked for dinner. He is talented with the carving knife. Although the turkey is small Billy is maximizing the yield of both dark meat and white slices so that there will be plenty for their three person dinner with leftovers for the following day.

"So does *all o' them* patients that you see *comin'* through the office ... does they ask y'all much *'bout* your own baby that's *a comin'*?

"Not really. Most *o 'em* don't know. *'Til* this past month I wasn't *showin'* much yet."

"How *'bout* your doctor friend?"

"Yes, she knows of course. She's my doctor."

"No. I'm *a-talkin'* 'bout *yer* other doctor friend ... the Daddy doctor."

"I *ain't* told him yet. I *ain't* even seen him since that fateful night. But I *kinda* half told his friend, when he called up to make a reservation for *raftin'* last month. That's about it."

"How do *y'all* half-tell *somethin'* like that."

"I told *'im* I was pregnant and he dun asked me *outa da blue iffin* it was someone he knew."

"*Whatya* say to that."

"I said 'maybe' and that I wasn't *answerin' no* more questions *'bout* my personal life."

"Sounds to me like you gave *'im all the answerin'* he needs. Wonder if you'll be *hearin'* from your doctor friend any time soon."

"We'll see now. Won't we? We'll just see."

∞∞∞

# XXVII

## December 1994

Simone has persistently resisted the notion of destroying her tape on several occasions in the past. She has played it to herself a handful of times over the last few years. She also played it for Betty when they returned to San Francisco after the Woodstock '94 Concert. But Simone never mentioned it to the police.

Although the sound quality is pretty poor, Simone remembers each and every word that Frank Babcock uttered that evening at Ecco in 1991. She can almost see his face as he confesses to participating in Wayne Johnson's demise. And now he is being charged with murder in New York. She wonders if she herself is now guilty of a crime. She has been questioned thoroughly by the NYPD investigators who traveled to San Francisco for the interview. She'd hired an attorney to accompany her for those interviews. She told her attorney about Frank's confession but she didn't tell him that she had taped her husband. Regardless her attorney advised her that she couldn't invoke marital privilege because she hadn't been married to Frank Babcock for quite some time and the NYPD wanted to ask her about things that happened outside of the time of her marriage anyway. Such a ploy would only delay the inevitable subpoena. She would have to testify sooner or later unless she invoked her Fifth Amendment rights. While there might be some basis for that, it just didn't seem like the smartest thing to do.

The NYPD investigators questioned Simone about her relationship with Babcock and she answered most inquiries vaguely. She wanted to hear what they asked. She wanted to know what they thought ... what they knew if anything about Babcock's involvement in the death of Wayne Johnson. But she was purposely reluctant to share what she knew ... at least at first.

∞∞∞

Oddly for Simone, she is apparently a person of interest in two separate investigations regarding her ex-husband. Concurrent to the murder charges, the FBI is conducting its own investigation of Frank Babcock. She is not sure why. They said something about potential money laundering allegations but Simone believed this was a mere ruse.

Her interviews with the FBI cover three major themes: what she knows about Frank Babcock's dealings with his Arab clients; what she knows about Frank and Fox Babcock's connections to Sergei and Kirill Zubkov; and what involvement Frank Babcock has with her current business, MBF Digital Haven & Harbor. Simone tells her lawyer that the FBI's inquiry is a total fishing expedition and that she is particularly surprised to hear their inquiries about the Zubkovs.

Clearly the FBI is not directly concerned about the murder of Wayne Johnson. That is not a federal issue anyway. Besides there is no way the Zubkovs could possibly have had anything to do with Wayne Johnson's murder. Wayne Johnson never even knew the Zubkovs. Simone does allow that she saw Sergei Zubkov when she was at the International Conference on the World Wide Web, in Geneva earlier in May. The federal agents seem to be already aware of this fact. So the mystery of what the FBI is fishing for, remains quite unclear to Simone.

What annoys Simone most about the line of questioning that the FBI pursues is that some of it harkens back to her relationships with Wayne and Mickey Johnson. If the FBI isn't investigating the murder of Wayne Johnson, what possible interest could they have in those details? Maybe they are testing her temperament with regard to her ex-husband. Maybe they believe that she knows more than she says about Babcock's other business interests and are looking to create an incentive for her to tell them more about these business interests. However the reality is that other than the fact that Frank Babcock has provided financial backing for MBF Digital Haven & Harbor, she knows very little about Frank Babcock's business interests.

But right now Simone is not as concerned about the ongoing FBI investigation of Frank Babcock's business as she is about the NYPD's investigation of Babcock's complicity in the murder of Wayne Johnson.

## December 1994

Simone knows that if she gives the tape to the authorities a conviction becomes almost certain. However she also realizes that she would have to testify in court as to how she managed to get this taped confession of sorts and why she did nothing with it for such a long time. She doesn't relish the idea of courtroom drama. She's also not certain that she wants to see Frank Babcock convicted of any crime that could result in the lifelong incarceration of her former spouse. The truth is that Simone doesn't know what she wants. And oddly enough she experiences a feeling of personal guilt about everything to the point that she has to keep reminding herself that she hasn't committed any crime ... at least not yet.

∞∞∞

Fox and Evelyn Babcock are back in New York for short visits with his two sets of relatives.

This Christmas season the visits are different from past holiday visits. The young couple's first stop is dinner in the city with Frank and Margot Babcock. Thankfully they agree not to dwell on a deep discussion of Babcock's indictment. They share the news of Evelyn's pregnancy and talk about their respective medical careers. Frank talks fuzzily about his travels through the Middle East. But he skirts the fact that these travels are now on hold pending the outcome of his legal predicament.

∞∞∞

Evelyn's relationship with Frank Babcock is interesting to say the least. She doesn't know what to think about the charges that have been leveled against him. She believes it's best to follow Fox's instincts regarding his adoptive father. However the complexities of the situation ensue when Evelyn thinks about the Johnson side of Fox's family. She has seen more of Mickey and Syd Johnson and their children then she has seen of Frank Babcock. She also enjoys their company whereas she is mostly ill-at-ease around Frank Babcock ... now an accused murderer.

Evelyn knows that it's a very difficult situation that Fox now finds himself in. On the one hand Fox grew up in Babcock Manor with his adoptive father Frank Babcock. On the other hand in recent years Fox has become quite close to his natural father Mickey Johnson. A decision as to which side of the upcoming trial Fox would favor is almost as difficult as the decision that King Solomon faced when he resolved to split the baby. Evelyn realizes that sooner or later that day of reckoning will come, but she is entirely unaware of the position that Fox will take.

Evelyn also worries that the circumstances surrounding the trial for the murder of Wayne Johnson might bleed into some discovery concerning the murders of William Beaumont and Harriett Aristide. Evelyn is already aware that Frank Babcock had nothing to do with those murders. Consequently, she bears her own Babcock surname with a certain degree of apprehension

∞∞∞

Margot Babcock is predictably quiet throughout the evening in spite of efforts by both Fox and Evelyn to bring her out of her shell. Fox realizes that Margot is feeling somewhat embarrassed about the events following the baseball game in August, so he purposely makes a point of being buoyant and outgoing and asking several questions about Jedidiah. It is his way of letting her know that the August encounter is now buried in the past. This is best for both of them. The evening is bizarre in that none of them ventures beyond the perfunctory Christmas niceties to deal with anything of substance besides the discussion of Evelyn's pregnancy. Everyone makes an effort to be civil with one another because everyone feels the need to do so.

∞∞∞

Stop two of Fox and Evelyn's holiday travels takes them out to Long Island and Fox's other family. The young physicians are staying at the Johnson busy home. There is less tension in Garden City than in the Babcock's Manhattan townhouse. It's not like the murder trial of Frank Babcock is not a big deal in the Johnson family. It certainly is a big part of things past and things yet to come for the Johnsons. It's just that there is a much more going on in the Johnsons household. And even something as compelling as the murder trial of Frank Babcock cannot overwhelm the daily pursuits of the Johnson family.

Fox and Evelyn had toyed with the idea of staying at The Garden City Hotel but Mickey was insistent that they stay with him at his home. Fox and Evelyn soon recognize that whereas the mood at the Babcock home was anxious, the Johnson domain is very animated.

Besides his half brothers and sister, and in addition to Mickey's two mothers-in-law, Fox finds that there is a new extended family member temporarily residing in the Johnson home. Jermaine Spataro is Sydney

## December 1994

Johnson's brother but Fox never even knew Syd had a brother until just this week. A long time back ... around the time of Mickey and Syd's wedding, Syd had made a vague reference to a brother, but Fox had erroneously assumed that Syd's brother had passed away long before the wedding.

∞∞∞

Jermaine is an interesting addition. His presence causes Fox to wonder what other assumptions he has made about the Johnson household that might be amiss. Ever since he first met Mickey in June of 1981, he viewed the man as the living embodiment of the American dream ... a beautiful wife ... beautiful children ... a great job ... and tons of friends with similar backgrounds. He viewed Mickey as the prototypical Shenandoah alumnus. And early on he believed that Mickey was his brother. But as he soon learned everything in life was not always the way it was presented. He has thought about Mickey and his background a great deal over the ensuing years.

However Fox never thought much about Syd's ethnic heritage although it was somewhat apparent when he met her mother, Violet Spataro. But mainly Fox thought of Syd as a wonderful mother for his two half-brothers and his one half-sister. And whereas Violet was black skinned, Fox didn't think of Syd as being black at all. However, he now sees that Jermaine embraces his ethnicity in a more overt manner. He speaks of many black cultural issues and encourages his two young nephews in their appreciation of rap music. But Fox keeps most of his thoughts on the matter to himself.

∞∞∞

On their first night visiting with the Johnsons, Evelyn and Fox enjoy a spirited discussion over dinner with all of the members of the household on a large range of topics. However before long the younger Johnsons retire to other parts of the house and Mickey and Fox enter the kitchen and continue conversing with Syd. This leaves Evelyn alone with Jermaine in the dining room.

"So it must be nice for you to have a reconciliation with your sister after so many years of being apart." Evelyn is not afraid to surface the family issue that Fox has been reluctant to probe with Jermaine.

"Yes, it *has* been nice. But I have to tell you things happen at a much different pace here on the east coast than they do in the Midwest."

"Where was it that you were living again ... St Louis?"

"Berkeley, Missouri. It's a suburban area near St Louis. People know Berkeley because of Lambert Field the airport for St Louis. The airport is technically in Berkeley and Boeing also has a plant there."

"So Missouri's a lot different from New York?"

"Oh yeah. Absolutely. People used to kid about Missouri being the 'Show me State' and New York being the 'Shove me State.' That might be a little harsh but people tend to believe those stereotypes. Many people in Missouri grew up there and never want to leave. Berkeley is a little different. It's predominantly black families that live there and they tend to want to get up and get out of the area. A lot of people live in poverty there."

"How did *you* feel about Berkeley?"

"Well I've been a nomad for most of my life, so maybe my opinion doesn't carry as much weight."

On the contrary, by moving around a bit you have the ability to compare, just like we're doing now ... comparing Long Island to Missouri."

"Believe me there is absolutely no comparison possible between Garden City, Long Island and Berkeley, Missouri. For that matter the only way you can compare St. Louis and New York is by their sports teams."

"I know how you feel. I grew up in Pittsburgh and Fox and I live there now. It's a fabulous city, but I think that it's been hard for my husband to adjust. He's used to the adrenaline rush of Long Island and New York City."

"How's is he handling all of the hubbub around the upcoming trial?"

"Well to start with he is totaling ignoring the media as am I. Secondly, there's not much about that topic that either Fox or I care to discuss. I'm sure you can understand why."

"Sure I can understand the difficult position you and Fox are in. Your husband must have some allegiance to both of his fathers. It's the biggest question anyone can have about the whole deal. What does Fox Babcock think?"

Although Evelyn started the whole conversation with a personal inquiry about Jermaine's family history, she is none too pleased to see how quickly the conversation turns to the Babcock/Johnson feud. She makes a mental note not to fall into this self-set trap again. She decides to simply ignore the continuing inquisitiveness of Mickey's new-found brother-in-law. She fully realizes that Mickey is tangled up in this tortuous web as well. *Weren't they all; to some degree?* It is the last thought she allows herself on

*December 1994*

the topic for the evening. Besides the following afternoon she is scheduled to accompany Fox to lunch with someone she is interested in meeting, even if she is somewhat fearful about the encounter.

∞∞∞

# XXVIII

## December 1994

Fox wants to reunite with Sergei alone. However Evelyn uncharacteristically insists on tagging along with her husband when he meets his childhood friend. Although Sergei is staying at a hotel in Manhattan, he says that he wants to return to Long Island for old time's sake. They agree to meet at a place that Sergei and Fox both remember from times past ... from the summer of 1985 to be exact. It's been more than 9 years since they've seen each other and more than 13 years since their summer of vengeance. The two men were mere teenagers when they committed an act of retribution that Fox has been unable to purge from his memory since.

Fox and Evelyn are waiting for Sergei in Patrick's Pub, a popular Irish watering hole that happens to make the best Irish Coffee west of Dublin. When Sergei arrives Fox immediately notices a physical difference in his childhood friend. Sergei has lost almost 30 pounds of excess weight that he had previously carried. He seems to be in excellent shape. Now in his early thirties, Sergei is a smart-looking young man. He appears comfortable in his own skin, even carrying himself with a slight bit of a swagger. Sergei has always been a self-confident person but his demeanor is sometimes confusing to others who might have regarded a younger Sergei as a quirky teenager.

∞∞∞

"So you must be Evelyn Babcock, I assume. Did you know what you were getting into when you married my friend, Fox?" Anyone who witnessed this self-introduction on the part of the Anglo-Russian might have perceived

*December 1994*

the question as an affable overture. However his tone almost allowed a literal implication of the question.

"Surprisingly, I did know what I was getting into." Evelyn delivers her answer with only a slight smile and without wavering her steely-eyed contact. Sergei blinks first. However his rejoinder digs the significance of the introductory remarks that much deeper.

"So then there are no secrets among us?"

"I wouldn't go that far." Fox tries to smile his way through these initial greetings. "But it's probably safe to say that you two know me better than anyone else in the world knows me. I'm glad we all have this time to get together." Fox immediately regrets that he allowed Evelyn to come along.

Fox knows it's impossible to keep things impersonal, nor does he really care to do so. He is curious about what Sergei has been doing over the past nine years. He has read some of Sergei's articles about the *World Wide Web* and wants to know more.

They are all served a cream-headed Irish Coffee as Fox sets the stage for at least part of the conversation. "My mother has sent me copies of your writings as though I would not look to find them myself. But I have to tell you, I never thought that you had such an optimistic spirit."

"So you thought of me as a skeptic like yourself?"

"Maybe ... well yes ... where do you think I learned to think that way?"

"Wow. You have changed Fox. I was kidding. I agree that I was at one time a much more skeptical person. But I recall that you were always the one who was buoyant and hopeful about the future. I remember hearing that exuberance in your valedictorian speech at your graduation from Shenandoah."

"Yeah, well that was ten years ago. Things are happening much faster than we predicted."

"That's for sure. And the breakthroughs are everywhere, not just in the United States and Europe. That's the true beauty of the *Word Wide Web*. After CERN announced 18 months ago that The Web would be free, the information explosion has been nothing short of mind-blowing. Because there's no financial barrier to entry, the whole world is jumping into the fray. It's impossible for any one person or company to keep track of all of the innovation. In fact, it's not *short* of mind blowing ... it *is* mind blowing. That

## Techies, Trials & Technologies

one decision ... a free WEB ... will dramatically change the world! It may prove to be the most important decision ever! Everyone will have access to all kinds of information."

"Isn't that what all these new things .... these search sites ... I think some people call them search engines ... are trying to do?" Fox is joining in Sergei's enthusiasm and it's starting to feel like the good old days when they first started dabbling into computers together as teenagers in Great Neck.

"Yeah, but no one has it down pat yet. And all of this free information – we just don't know yet whether that will be a good thing or a bad thing."

"You two guys seem to be pretty excited about IT in the future. Do you think many more people will make careers in this field? They're not yet teaching this new technology in our high schools and colleges."

"Sergei, you have to understand one of the underlying reasons for Evelyn's question. She is looking out for career opportunities downstream for our son or daughter. Evelyn and I are expecting our first baby in May."

"Well congratulations. I guess more things have changed in your world than I thought. Wow, a doctor; a married man ... soon to be a father. That's a lot to process."

"Well maybe we've both changed a little." Fox still speaks more tentatively than Sergei.

"It's great that you guys still have a common interest in computers and IT. You may have gone different ways but you still have some things in common."

"Fox and I may have more in common than you think, Evelyn." Sergei offers an empty-eyed chortle.

Evelyn puts her hand to her womb in an inadvertent protective gesture.

∞∞∞

It is Friday December 30th. There is one more night left before New Year's Eve, 1994 and Fox Babcock and Mickey Johnson are sitting in the wine cellar of the Mickey's home. Syd and Evelyn and the rest of the household have all already retired to bed. Mickey can sense that Fox is carrying around a bigger burden than impending first time fatherhood.

Over the last dozen years Fox and his natural father have become very close and it is a relationship that neither man wants to jeopardize. The rapport building has not come easily. But somehow Mickey has succeeded.

## December 1994

He has gained Fox' trust by never criticizing Frank Babcock and never exposing the deep seated hatred that he feels toward the man. Over time Fox has grown comfortable sharing his own misgivings about Babcock.

"I like the intimate feeling of this room, Mickey. Do you come down here often?"

"Not that often. Occasionally Syd and I will come down here for a nightcap. When I had it built, I didn't want any advanced electronics installed. Naturally I can't allow other features to impact the lighting or temperature. Some of the older wines can be temperamental."

The wine cellar is not very large. However it is warmly decorated, and holds about 1400 bottles. The walls are oak paneled as is the racking. In addition there is a small table that could possibly fit six chairs but there are only four cushioned high back chairs in the room.

"You seem distracted, Fox. Is everything OK?"

"Most things, but not everything."

"Everything is fine with you and Evelyn and the baby?"

"All of that is ..." He starts to answer but stops, not really knowing what to say.

"So am I going to have to keep clawing at what's getting to you or will you just confide in me? Your choice. I just want you to understand that I'm here for you. That's all. No matter what. You're my son."

"Thanks, Mickey. I appreciate that. I really do. For the most part, things are OK. But Evelyn is not too thrilled by all the attention that is coming to the family because of ... you know ... the arrest ... the potential upcoming trial and whatnot."

"We don't have to talk about that ... if you'd rather not."

"That's the approach that Evelyn and I took when we had dinner with Dad ... with Frank ... and Margot ... the other night. We mostly just avoided the topic. Truthfully, that just made it more awkward than it might have been. Face it, my adoptive father is accused of killing my grandfather ... your father."

Mickey gets up out of his chair and takes two steps over to a small oak cabinet that is on the opposite side of the wine cellar. He takes out a bottle of 20 year old Macallan single malt scotch. He doesn't respond to his son's statement but simply pours two double shots of the scotch and hands one to Fox. Fox accepts the glass and takes a sip that is more like a swig. He decides to let his statement stand until his father responds. It takes nearly a full minute.

"I don't know for sure what happened that night, but you should know that in my mind, I haven't ruled out the possibility of Frank having had something to do with it."

"He's not a violent man, Mickey."

Again there is a thoughtful pause, and Mickey gathers his wits. He can't display any of the anger and rage that he feels towards Frank Babcock. Yet he also doesn't want to lie to his son. It's a difficult needle to thread.

"You know Fox, I've come to believe that every man has a capacity for violence. No matter how we try to control it, there is always a danger that it can spill over. Maybe every man has a boiling point."

Fox takes another swig of his scotch. Mickey's comment takes him by surprise. *What does he mean?* Fox realizes that as a young man … a teenage boy actually … he himself was overcome by a violent rage. Could Frank Babcock have been similarly provoked? Fox wonders if Mickey has ever been moved to an act of fury. Surely his years in Vietnam must have unleashed some of that ferocity.

The dilemma confronting Fox is unique. He has two men he considers fathers. He loves them both. They have both been instrumental in his personal development … Frank Babcock, during his school years and Mickey Johnson, during Fox's early adulthood.

Fox sometimes treats Mickey more like a protective older brother, but he knows that there is mostly animus between the two men, who each think of him as their son. There is no rational way that they can act constructively as one family.

Nevertheless Fox trusts Mickey more than any other person in the world. It is a trust that Mickey has earned over more than a dozen years since father and son were first introduced as brothers at a meeting at Shenandoah High in 1981. The relationship has been carefully cultivated by Mickey who has allowed Fox whatever emotional freedom he has needed to work his way through the issue of his ancestral ambiguity.

∞∞∞

"So then … you believe Frank killed your father?"

"I think he was involved in some way, yes."

It was a major admission, one that Mickey worries might distance himself from his son.

## December 1994

"At least you're honest about it."

"What do you think, Fox? Do you think that Frank had nothing whatsoever to do with the death of your ... your grandfather?"

Fox's response sounds tentative. "I don't think he killed him or that he conspired to kill him."

"But?"

"But my mother thinks he did."

"I know."

"And now I know you think he did it, right?"

"Yes."

"That's a lot for me to process."

"I know it is, Fox. And I know how you think about Frank. Truly I do. But those feelings don't have to change even if you did believe that Frank was involved somehow."

"Everything about this makes me angry. And it's been that way my whole life."

"I know."

"I'd say that, basically, it's all my mother's fault. If she hadn't been doing what she was doing way back when, we wouldn't all be so ...well, so screwed up." His irony is deadened by his anger.

"We all bear some degree of fault, Fox. ... Frank; myself; my father; your mother - everyone but you, Fox. The trouble with our fault and our anger is that it didn't have to be resolved violently. That's where I believe that Frank bears more of the blame than any of the rest of us."

"You know, Mickey, I just don't want to believe that Frank had anything to do with the murder of Wayne Johnson ... someone I never met, even though he thought he was my father ... even on the day he died. It's all so crazy. And bizarre as anything is the fact that in other circumstances, I might not even have been born. Try living with that reality."

"That must make things harder to digest."

"It's incomprehensible, Mickey. In fact, if you want to know the truth, that's probably the main reason I decided against psychiatry. I knew that I couldn't even heal myself. The physical and neurological aspects of the brain are much easier for me to deal with than the neuroses and psychoses that I would otherwise be dealing with."

"Can we still have *our* relationship remain the way it has been?"

"What do you mean?"

## Techies, Trials & Technologies

"Can you and I still respect each other regardless of Frank's fate?"

"Yes ... as long as you do what you're doing now ... You have to stay perfectly honest with me."

"That works both ways, right?"

"Right." Fox knows that he is being ironically disingenuous with his father. He doesn't lie to him, but neither is he fully forthcoming with other troubling aspects of his young life. There is no mention of the murders of William "Billy the Kid" Beaumont and Harriett (*"Don't call me Harry,"*) Aristide. And Fox also avoids the disclosure that he is now the expectant father of *two* separate children. That much he hasn't yet told Evelyn either.

There's a long silence as Fox drops off into his own reverie. Mickey doesn't push the conversation either. Fox wonders about something he had once probed in his psychiatry studies. One psychiatric writer had twisted the words of the British poet William Wordsworth: *"The child is the father of the man."* The psychiatric reinterpretation of Wordsworth posed the theory that in many cases a child is destined to recommit the sins of the father. Fox thinks that it is staggeringly tragic that he has somehow recommitted the sins of *both* his fathers.

∞∞∞

*1995*

# XXIX

## February 1995

Fox Babcock has not been to his mother's home since shortly before he and Evelyn were married. His trip to San Francisco has a certain bit of nostalgia blended with the many other emotions of the moment. Jeff Levine is in Arizona for the weekend so it will be just the two of them to share time with one another. It's the first time that Fox has spoken to his mother since he and Evelyn told Simone that she would soon be a grandmother. However Fox didn't bother telling her that she might cross that milestone a few months before the birth of Evelyn's child. Actually, Maddie Swift's baby could arrive any day now.

In fact it was only one month earlier that Fox even made that disclosure to his wife. He was astounded that Evelyn wasn't devastated by the news. Sure she was upset, but she didn't break down and skewer him with hatred. In fact, she was understanding in a way that he knew he himself never could have been. He knew his wife was an open-minded liberal ... very much like his mother ... but he never envisioned that Evelyn would be so tolerant of his potentially life altering transgression.

∞∞∞

*The discussion between Fox and Evelyn about Maddie and her baby had been a fascinating one. Evelyn's reaction was not at all what Fox had expected. There weren't recriminations or vindictive responses. It was almost as if Evelyn already knew what Fox had done. But if she harbored any ill will toward her husband or her husband's other child, she was effective at sheltering these feelings.*

∞∞∞

"How is Evelyn doing? I'm sorry that she wasn't able to make the trip with you."

"Ev is doing just great. She's had a little morning sickness and she's had to reschedule a few appointments at the hospital but generally she is doing just fine. How do *you* feel about being a grandmother?"

"It'll be different from being a mother, I'm sure. I hope to do a better job at grand-parenting. But I'm certain that you and Evelyn will be terrific parents."

"I hope you're right."

Neither Fox nor his mother pursued the baby topic any further. Simone doesn't ask Fox if either he or Evelyn plan on taking time off to care for the infant when the baby arrives. She doesn't ask how Evelyn's parents have reacted. Simone doesn't ask whether Fox is hoping for a boy or a girl. There is simply another topic that is weighing on both their minds. But Fox doesn't go there right away. Instead he enquires about his mother's new job.

"Are you going to commute from here or are you going to get an apartment over near the university?"

"I'll just continue to commute. Most days it's only about a forty-five minute drive."

Simone has made an important decision recently. She has already started her new job as a professor at Berkeley University. Her good friend Dean Barrow has been asking her to teach a course at the school for several years. But once she decided to sever her business ties with Betty Barrymore the change came quickly. Simone wants to turn a corner and this opportunity has been waiting for her for some time. It's one course at night for starters but it gets her foot in the door of academia. Besides she knows she will have other issues on her plate in the imminent future.

"I imagine your professorship will be a slower pace than the rush of running an IT business."

"I just need to get my mind off the upcoming trial. I'm still hurt and angry that Betty betrayed my confidence and so I can't work with her any longer. I'll say this much, however. Betty, Howard and I have been able to work out a very amicable severance agreement although there are several MBF equity issues that are still in the works."

"So Mom, are you at least talking to Betty and the other guy ... Howard? You've known them for quite a while, especially Betty."

## February 1995

"I confided in Betty and she betrayed my confidence," Simone repeated.

"What did she do that was so unfaithful ...if you don't mind my asking?"

"I thought you'd ask me that. And I've thought about how I'd respond when you did. I told Betty something that I have never shared with anyone ... not even you, Fox. Maybe I should say ... *especially not with you*. It's a secret that I've guarded for a long time, but it's also something that'll now be exposed in Frank's upcoming trial."

"What on earth could that be?"

"Trust me. I've given some thought about how to answer your questions, and I hope you will allow me to answer them my way. Just wait here for a second."

Simone turns and walks into her bedroom. She returns with her tape recorder which was loaded with the Ecco dinner tape. She hands it to Fox.

"This is a recording of a conversation between Frank and me that took place more than three years ago. I'm not going to play it for you because I want to be able to honestly deny that I did so."

"So what do you want me to do? Should I take it home with me?"

"No. I want to keep it. I haven't made copies and I don't intend to do so. The content is self-explanatory. In a few minutes I'm going out for a short walk. I want to pick up a couple of nice bottles of wine. I'll also arrange for dinner to be brought in when we're ready. You can play the tape ... if you want to ... while I'm out. I'll give you about forty-five minutes or so."

"Geez Mom, this all seems so contrived."

"It *is* contrived Fox. But I don't want you to be surprised by anything once the trial begins."

Within minutes Simone was down the steps and out the door. Fox picked up the tape recorder and popped the tape out of the machine. It was marked: Ecco Restaurant - August 1991. He snapped the tape back into place inside the machine and hit the play button.

∞∞∞

Back in Pittsburgh it is almost 10 PM. Chrissy Webb is helping her daughter clean up after dinner. Evelyn Babcock's home is less than eight miles away from her parents place. Chrissy Webb went over for dinner with her daughter alone, because her husband is working late again at the hospital. Her son, Peter, wanted to stay at home and play *Donkey Kong*

## Techies, Trials & Terrorists

*Country* on his Super Nintendo Entertainment System. Sometimes, Chrissy has a hard time understanding the priorities of the men who live with her. The fact that the new Nintendo system features new 3D graphics and introduces *Diddy Kong* and *King K. Roo,* means absolutely nothing to her.

Unlike the discussion that Fox is having with Simone in California, Evelyn's discussion with her mother is *all about the coming baby.* Chrissy is thrilled that she is going to be a grandmother. There is something stabilizing and reaffirming about that role in her life. In some ways it further cements her role as Mark Webb's wife, even though they have already been married for 35 years. Chrissy has dealt with insecurity in her marriage. But she never discusses it with her daughter. Chrissy knows that her husband has cheated on her throughout their marriage and she thinks that her daughter is probably aware of that fact. She has coped with the problem by recognizing that Mark would never leave her for one of the tarts that he has an occasional fling with. It would destroy his reputation as a family man and a pillar of the Catholic Church in Pittsburgh. So by extension, in Chrissy's mind, her role as grandmother represents an even deeper matriarchal role channeling. She also sees the baby as a reaffirming rooting for Evelyn as Fox Babcock's wife, just in case Fox has similar shortcomings to those of his father-in-law.

Evelyn has a different agenda in mind as they clean up the dishes.

"So Mom, I have something else that I want to tell you and now is probably as good a time as any."

Chrissy's antenna are up. This doesn't sound like the preamble of good news.

"Yes, dear?"

"As we have been discussing, Fox and I are thrilled to be expecting a baby, but there is a slight complication to our joy."

"Oh? What is it, Evvie, dear? What is it?" Having had a child that was born with Down Syndrome, Chrissy is immediately concerned about the health of her future grandchild. But she also realizes that it is still early in the pregnancy, so this is probably not the "complication," that her daughter is referencing.

"Our baby is fine and healthy so don't worry about that."

"Thank God for that. Then what is it, Evelyn?"

"There is another fine and healthy baby who is on the way also. Fox will be the father of two children very shortly."

## February 1995

"You're having twins?"

"*No*, Mom. I wouldn't have referred to that as a *complication*."

Chrissy cringes as she immediately understands the dilemma. "So it isn't a *complication* after all. It's a *curse*. Isn't it."

"No Mom. It's not a curse at all. I have always known you to be a good Catholic woman. How can you refer to any child as a curse? I know you didn't mean that."

"So who is this other mother-to-be? And when is her child do to be born?

"Very shortly, actually." As fortune would have it Evelyn answers the second question first and it throws Chrissy off guard.

"Oh my God, no. Tell me it's not Linda McCandless's child."

Evelyn smiles at a time that she normally wouldn't smile but she can't help think about the way her mother reasons. "No Mom. Joe and Linda's baby is Joe and Linda's baby. Fox and me ... we have our own baby also. But Fox has another baby on the way with another woman.

"Do I know her?"

"No you've never met her. In fact, I've never met her either. Fox foolishly impregnated this woman while he was on that white water rafting trip with Joe and Fox's Long Island friends."

"Is that what these men do on those trips? I thought it was just high adventure and all that ... well maybe it's a different kind of high adventure than I thought."

"Well ... so now you know."

"You poor dear ... how do you put up with this kind of thing, anyway? Does everyone else have to know? I can't fathom how angry you must feel toward Fox. But remember, he's the father of your baby also. You can't just ... oh ... I don't know."

"Look Mom, I didn't want to upset you. I just thought it might be better if you heard it from me and not from someone else."

"Well in God's name, who else might I hear it from?"

"I don't know Mom. I just thought I'd tell you. That's all."

"How does this affect you and Fox ... your marriage?"

"I certainly wasn't happy to hear it. As I said it is a complication. I've thought about it ... a lot actually. I know that anger isn't helpful. For now, I have chosen to forgive him. Fox was a fool to do what he did, but I know that he still loves me. I think I still love him too. It's hard to say what the longer range impact might be."

"But he cheated on you ... doesn't that make you angry? Sometimes I think that Lorena Bobbitt had the right idea." Chrissy Webb shows a rare belligerence. She is referring to the news story that made the headlines 18 months earlier.

"Yes. It made me angry at first ... but not *that* angry. I'd rather prefer that the father of my son was not a eunuch."

"I'm not advocating castration. Besides that Bobbitt guy somehow retrieved his private part and got it reattached. They should have left it for the vultures."

"Mom? I've never heard you talk like this."

"I'm just saying that sometimes men have to be reminded to clean up their own mess."

"Are you saying Fox should ask her to get an abortion?"

"No, of course not. But he needs to make sure that this is not an issue that lingers over your marriage forever. Of all people ... he should understand that."

"I am still not sure if the anger will return or linger ... I know that I am less angry now than when Fox first told me."

"It's not something you will get over easily, Evelyn. Trust me. And for you it's even harder ... there's that other child that will always be there to remind you."

"Fox is not the first man ever to break his marriage vows. But he is still a good man. As I said, for now, I have chosen to forgive him. I hope my choice will last."

"Is this all part of what you learn about in your psychiatric residency? What do they call it? Anger management?"

"I don't readily think of it that way. This is much more personal than something I might learn professionally. But I do believe my educational experience ... it has helped me cope."

"I'm not sure that I could have been as benevolent about it if your father had put me in your position."

"Let's not go there, Mom. No one else has to know about Fox's other child. In fact, I thought a lot about it before I decided to tell you. But I wanted to share with someone else besides Fox and you were ... you are ... the only choice that I felt comfortable with ... okay?"

## February 1995

Chrissy moves over and wraps her arms around her daughter. "Yes, okay, of course it's okay, Evvie. You are my daughter and I love you. All I want is what's best for you."

∞∞∞

Later, after her mother has gone home Evelyn turns on the TV in her bedroom. As she is putting on her nightgown and getting ready for bed. A cable news show is on the screen. There are two opposing commentators debating the ethics of President Clinton. *I'm not sure what I think of him*, Evelyn muses. She recalls all of the news coverage of the many affairs that he supposedly had while he was Governor of Arkansas. She wonders whether or not Hilary has truly forgiven Bill or if it is merely expedient for both of them to pretend to like each other. She knows that her mother thinks that Hilary Clinton is a wonderful person, but she also realizes that her mother and Hilary have something in common.

Evelyn wonders why people are more apt to forgive men than women for infidelity. Bill Clinton is certainly not the first US President to have extra-marital affairs. Jack Kennedy was a renowned womanizer and Ronald Reagan was thought to have bedded half of Hollywood during the rise of his political career. His conquests reportedly included: Lana Turner, Ava Gardner, Doris Day and Betty Grable. Marilyn Monroe was also reported to be a Reagan conquest.

That last name is an interesting one to Evelyn. She wonders: If Marilyn Monroe had sexual relationships with at least two Presidents – Kennedy and Reagan – to say nothing of baseball star Joe DiMaggio and actors Frank Sinatra, Marlon Brando and Tony Curtis, then why weren't these men considered her conquests? Monroe even had a long standing affair with gangster Sam Giancana. And yet in spite of all of these relationships, Monroe was always regarded as the "dumb blonde," the quarry, in a way. She was regarded as the prey for these men and not the other way around. *Maybe I should rethink my attitude.*

As the news continues there is another story on Ronald Reagan, and she starts to think of the man differently. Just this past November, the former President had announced that he has Alzheimer's disease. The story seems to be probing the idea that Reagan may have been suffering from the disease well before the announcement, even back to the second term of his presidency. *I wonder what Nancy Reagan thinks about him now.*

# Techies, Trials & Terrorists

Evelyn listens to one last news story before she goes to bed. It is an update on the O.J. Simpson trial and the latest testimony about the possibility of evidence tampering on the part of the LAPD. Evelyn has always thought of this as being a slam dunk conviction case for the Prosecution. She is now beginning to wonder what role money and celebrity can play in the attainment of justice. She can't ignore the implications in the Simpson trial and can't help but wonder what the impact of these factors may be in the trial of Frank Babcock.

∞∞∞

# XXX

## *August, 1995*

Frank Babcock has lost about 15 pounds and the hair in his inordinately thick mane has begun to thin out slightly, even though his hair stylist makes a good effort at keeping the encroachment of gray hair at bay. The weight loss does not go unnoticed by Dr. J. Hamilton Brophy. In fact Babcock has become a near full time preoccupation for Brophy. The psychiatrist wants things to change.

"You know Frank, you and I have been working on your emotional strength for almost exactly ten years. That's how long we have maintained our therapeutic relationship. When I reviewed my files I noted that there have been gaps of more than a year along the way, but it has still amounted to a very long term connection. And I recognize that somewhere along the way it has become a friendship. But I want you to know that both the length and the depth of this relationship are unique to me in my professional career. Actually they are highly unusual for almost any therapeutic relationships."

"That's interesting. Are you telling me that I've taken more time to get my head on straight than any of your other patients?"

"If I accept your terminology," Brophy speaks deliberatively. "You will have to accept all the vagaries of my one word answer: 'yes'. Are we square with that?"

"Yes."

"So the reason I bring this up at this stage is to tell you that my professional instincts tell me that you may be better served by being treated by another psychiatrist."

"We've had this conversation in the past and we've moved on. Why are we revisiting this issue right here and now ... right when I may need your help more than I have in the past?"

"Fair question ... and one that I have already asked myself many times."

"So?"

"So let's just talk through where we find ourselves right now. We have a private ... intimate doctor-patient relationship that is geared toward resolving several emotional burdens that you have been finding cumbersome to handle all alone. Is that fair?"

"Fair enough."

"And I think that we have alleviated some of those burdens and redirected some others during the course of your therapy. Is that also a fair assessment?"

"Yes, I think that's fair."

"And to be perfectly candid, as a physician and therapist, I have learned from our sessions and have probably made professional progress as a result of treating you."

"So tell me again, why I am getting the bills? And why am I paying you instead of you paying me for this elaborate education that you're getting?"

"If I acknowledge that there is some unusual justification for your question will you at least allow me to put some other pertinent information on the table for us to ponder?"

"Go ahead."

"Let's start with the fact that you still have a murder trial in front of you. There is no way ever that the doctor-patient privilege will be compromised. But of course I am well aware of the facts – as you have told them to me – in your case."

"Should I expect anything less?"

"No. Of course not."

"So is my upcoming trial wearing on you, Hamilton?"

"Not personally, but it does concern me that it is such an all-encompassing topic between us that I might not be serving your other needs very well."

"What other needs are there, at this point?"

## *August 1995*

"Your relationship with Fox, his wife, your grandson, Mickey ... don't these relationships mean more to you than you say? We have not spoken about them very much of late. It seems like we have been endlessly discussing the events of the distant past ...those events that have led up to your trial ...whenever that will be."

"First of all, my grandson's name is Mikey, not Mickey. It's pronounced like the kid in those 1970's cereal commercials ... *MIKE EE*."

"Yea, I remember those spots. The 'Mikey likes it' commercials. They were very effective, I think. ... so okay then your grandson's name is Mikey."

"In fact I just call him Michael or Mike. I'm sure that's what he'll be called once he outgrows these infantile ... childish names."

"Does it bother you that his nickname is so similar to the name of Mickey Johnson?"

"That's a dumb question, Hamilton. Of course it bothers me ... at least a little bit."

"Good to see we're still being honest with one another."

"We've only established that I am being honest with you."

"What's that supposed to mean?"

"Just what it sounds like Hamilton. You want out of our professional relationship but you keep hinting that I'm the one who should ask for it. You can't handle the drumbeat of my legal problems and put them in perspective for your psychiatric practice. In other words, I'm a patient that you can't ... or won't treat."

"No Frank, that's not true. I can certainly continue to work with you. But you must remember that I am your therapist ... not your lawyer. My problem has been that whenever I try to get you to see how the others involved in your trial might see things, you clam up. You act as though I am taking their side in the legal proceedings. This is not my intention at all. But on the multiple occasions that I have tried to get you to see things through others' eyes, I have only succeeded in making you angry. That's exactly what I want to avoid and I have been unsuccessful in doing so."

"Well these goddamned charges are taking so long to get to trial that it's almost like I have served my sentence already."

"Well the Simpson trial is still not over and it's been well over a year since he was arrested."

"This is much different Hamilton. Simpson is a butcher. The trial is just a formality. The evidence is overwhelming. No doubt about it. He'll probably be in jail for the rest of his life." Hamilton Brophy is intrigued by the indignation in his client's voice.

∞∞∞

*The truth of the matter is that a year earlier Brophy had exercised bad judgement with Babcock when he had visited Babcock at his home in the Hamptons. The NYPD had seen Brophy and his wife out at dinner with the Babcocks, leading them to infer that Babcock/Brophy association was a personal friendship rather than a professional doctor-patient relationship. This threatened to open Brophy to subpoena from the Prosecution. This was an absurd claim but it was enough to file motions thereby causing further delay. These additional delays were burdensome to the defendant. This was merely one of many prolonging tactics on the part of the Prosecution, while it attempted to piece together its thin case for murder. The most recent delay was caused by the hospitalization of the trial judge. At the moment they were uncertain as to the seriousness of Judge Robert Rittershaus' cardiac condition or the potential length of his convalescence.*

∞∞∞

"There are plenty of others besides yourself, Frank, who want the trial to finally begin."

"But none of you risks going to jail for the rest of your life if things don't go well."

"You're being charged with murder, Frank. And the things that you've told me in confidence would amount to a confession to the crimes that you been charged with. They would in fact be murder in the eyes of the law. But confidentiality is a bedrock principal of our relationship. It will never be breached."

"I sometimes worry that you remind me of that too frequently."

"Don't."

"Don't what?"

"Don't worry. You said that sometimes you worry that I ..."

"Enough of this nonsense. I trust you. Let's move on."

"Good idea."

"I know that they think I could have told you something about that evening in 1980."

"They can think whatever they want."

## August 1995

"But it's still unprofessional police work. They shouldn't try to convince you to say that I am intimidating you and that you feel threatened, so that you can testify."

"This whole tactic has been inspired by the Menendez trial in California. But the Menendez brothers are being retried now anyway. And that's a whole different situation. For that matter this is a whole different state. Anyway it doesn't matter."

"You would never say anything even if you *were* afraid of me?"

"Of course not. And for the record I'm not afraid *of* you Frank. But I am afraid *for* you."

"But they still have approached you and have attempted to get you to testify? Is that right?"

"Well I'm actually not so sure what they want, but whatever it is I'm simply not going to talk about one of my clients. What surprises me a little bit is how much they are invested in getting a conviction against you. Also they seem to be coordinating some of their efforts with the FBI. What do you think that is all about? The FBI would have no jurisdiction in your murder trial."

"I agree. There are so many other crimes that you'd think they would be chasing after. The Oklahoma City bombing for one. Those crazies killed 168 people including 19 children. That's what people now call terrorism. That's who they should be chasing down ... terrorists here and abroad."

"I'd have to say they're doing a decent job on that front. They nabbed Timothy McVeigh and that Nichols guy pretty quickly."

"But there may be more of these crazies out there. That's what the FBI should be looking for, not trying to harass tax paying citizens like me."

"There's been no indication that McVeigh or Nichols didn't pay their taxes."

"Come on, Hamilton. You know what I mean."

"Well, I guess I do. They are trying the people who bombed the World Trade Center garage right now. These guys are from the same stretch of sand as some of your clients. Maybe they want to make sure you don't have any anti-American biases of your own."

"That's patently absurd."

"You have some interesting Arabian clientele. Do you not?"

"Yes, but they're not involved in any of these crazy terrorist attacks. And even if they were, what would that have to do with me?"

"You're still handling some significant financial transactions for them. You told me that yourself. The Feds are probably interested in how the money moves to fund these violent acts. Maybe they think you know something about that."

"You know what, Hamilton ... I think you're reading too many mystery novels or watching too many espionage movies or ... or ... or whatever. My clients have nothing whatsoever to do with terrorists. They're too busy making money off their oil investments."

"How are you handling these folks now that you are no longer allowed to travel outside the country? Oh ... and by the way ... how are you handling your relationship with Masira al-Haddād?"

"I haven't seen Masira ... or any of her family for that matter ... since I was arrested."

"So you are no longer doing business with Abdulrahman al-Haddād?"

"I didn't say that. We still handle some business for the family but mostly through the son, Tariq, who is a medical doctor. Tariq is now working in New York."

"Last November you told me that Masira was getting married. Did she go through with her plans?"

"Yes, I believe she did."

"You *believe* she did or you *know* she did?"

"She got married. No doubt about it."

For a few seconds Frank Babcock says nothing else. His mind seems to be wandering. He is growing increasingly irritable. Finally he says, "Let's not talk about my Saudi clients. Who knows how much longer I will have any of their business anyway."

"Alright but one last question if I may. You refer to the al-Haddād family as your clients and yet you are close to them in some ways ... some, somewhat complicated ways maybe ... would you say they are your friends or just clients?"

"That's another one of your dumb questions, Hamilton. What difference does it make? Are you my therapist or my friend? Is Masira my client or my girlfriend ... or ex-girlfriend? I don't know how to answer these questions. What do you want me to say? What labels do you want me to use?"

## August 1995

"I don't want you to say anything Frank. I simply want you to think about these relationships. Do you know how you yourself, determine friendships?"

"I don't want to talk about any of this anymore. I think that this has been a rather unproductive session for me, and I want to leave now. You can bill me for the whole hour. I don't care."

"Oh so now you *are* defining *our* relationship after all."

"Enough Hamilton! That's enough! We're done here." With that Frank Babcock got up and abruptly left the office of his therapist.

This isn't the way Hamilton Brophy wanted their therapeutic relationship to end.

∞∞∞

*Techies, Trials & Terrorists*

1996

*Techies, Trials & Terrorists*

# XXXI

## March, 1996

Simone is ready to terminate her professorship at Berkley when the semester ends in June. But she realizes that she may be compelled to end her academic work even earlier. She's been teaching an elective undergraduate course in female entrepreneurship. She is now in the third semester of her short teaching career. However her reputation as a professor has recently been overshadowed by infamy. Many members of the media have hinted at her being a star witness for the Prosecution in the Long Island murder trial of her ex-husband, Frank Babcock. The delays in the trial have been extraordinary, and Simone has suffered with each delay. Speculation has run rampant as to what Simone might say.

The trial is now scheduled to begin before the academic semester is over. It has already been significantly delayed twice. The most recent delay actually ended in a mistrial after the trial judge suffered a heart attack right as the trial was beginning in November of 1995. The delay led to a mistrial as the judge subsequently succumbed to his health issues and died three days before Christmas. Earlier delays had followed numerous motions to dismiss, based upon the nature of the evidence that the Prosecution was finding difficult to substantiate. The Defense had sought appeals of certain decisions based upon their client's right to a speedy trial ... all to no avail ... and ironically further delaying the trial. But Frank Babcock and his attorneys had come to realize that this was a murder case that the government definitely wanted to see through to a conviction. Babcock himself was growing frustrated with his legal team over all of the delays and the ongoing restrictions on his travel and business dealings.

∞∞∞

The last year and a half has been brutal for Simone. In some ways her efforts at Berkeley have allowed her to relive some of the activism from her own college years at Columbia. She enjoys working with the students on many fronts but she is discouraged that matriculation to her classes has been ninety percent female. On the other hand, she likes teaching a night course. She thinks that it attracts more industrious students.

Simone is also surprised that some her students have criticized her for twice selling out too soon on her own entrepreneurial endeavors. Apparently she has not been able to impress upon her students the significance of other values besides financial return. As she stands in front of her classroom, she also comprehends that some of her students can't relate to her. They're aware that she has occasionally received funding for her entrepreneurial efforts from her billionaire ex-husband. This is the same man whose murder trial she will soon testify in.

Her current class consists of nineteen undergraduate students. They are ethnically diverse but 16 of the 19 are female. Given the course topic the class mix should have been anticipated, but Simone had clearly hoped for more male participation. Her evening lecture is nearing the ending time of 9:00 PM as she describes the homework assignment.

∞∞∞

"How do you explain the significant under-representation of women in the emerging IT industry? I'd like you be concise in your opinions. Limit your written responses to under 2500 words, but be sure to corroborate your viewpoints with the specific documented opinions from worthy sources. Remember also to focus specifically on information technology. I know that there is ample material on other industries included in our course bibliography. You can certainly use these other industries to compare and contrast. I have provided you with a copies of several recent articles germane to the topic. Naturally I encourage your own research and very much value your own considered opinions on the topic."

As Simone speaks she looks around the classroom at the faces of her students. Many students have averted their eye contact as they pack up their books and get ready to leave. However one face that looks directly at Simone

## March 1996

is that of a young black woman who has repeatedly argued in her previous assignments that being a woman entrepreneur is not nearly as challenging as being an African American entrepreneur of either gender. As most of the class ambles out the door, this young woman approaches Simone.

"I just wanted to tell you how much I respect you for teaching when obviously you could be resting on your business laurels instead of putting in the time as a professor."

"Thank you, Lynette. Sometimes I wonder why I do this myself ... especially when my personal life gets cloudy."

"I think that some of my classmates talk too much about what they think your personal life is about and not enough about what you've accomplished in the business world."

"Well thank you again ... Lynette ... for saying that. I'm not immune to what gets said about me, but I do wonder why students in their twenties would be at all interested in the personal life of someone in her fifties. I can tell you that wasn't the way it was when I was in college. Anyone over 50 was just plain old."

"It's just that they read what's in the tabloids. Then they think they know everything. Realistically most of us aren't able to put ourselves into your shoes. But honestly I look at you as a role model. It must be just awful to have people crawling all over private issues. I know I wouldn't like it. That's all I wanted to say. Just thanks for being you. I'm getting a lot out of your class." Lynette looks up at her without a smile and turns around to leave.

Simone has seen too much in life to be influenced by false flattery and she knows it when she hears it, but there is something about Lynette's mien that leads her to believe that the student is sincere. Simone almost wishes that the young woman would stay longer and talk some more. She knows that in addition to her interest in female entrepreneurship, Lynette also has a keen interest in IT. But more than anything else, Simone has been missing friendly female companionship since her fallout with Betty over the Babcock tape. Simone still hurts from her belief that Betty betrayed her confidence. She should never have played the tape for her.

∞∞∞

# XXXII

## April, 1996

The annual Shenandoah Golf Classic attracts nearly 400 golfers for the biggest fundraising event of the year for the high school. The tournament utilizes the links of two separate golf clubs and has a shotgun tee off on seventy-two different holes on four different area courses. The class of 1965 is well represented at the 1996 tournament with 22 class members playing in the event. Mickey Johnson's foursome includes: Kevin "Leaf-eater" Kislinger; Jack Birdsong and Dr. George "Pudd'nhead" Watson.

All four men are successful in their own fields. Birdsong's security business has recently blossomed into an international operation with an office in London and another in Israel. Pudd'nhead's pediatric practice in Manhattan has also expanded. He has two physician partners, whom he has been practicing with for many years. The partnership has lasted longer than any of his marriages, and the group also currently employs thirteen associate physicians and numerous physician assistants and nurses. Their clientele includes the children of many prominent Manhattan socialites and captains of industry.

Leaf-Eater has broadened the scope of his radio presence. He has morphed his sports show into a political commentary show and is now working for a group broadcasting out of New York while he is living in New Jersey. He now loves to talk politics even more than he likes to talk basketball.

They are nearing the tee for their 17$^{th}$ hole, a deceptive 218 yard Par 3. There are two small bunkers on either side of the green that don't seem like a big concern. However the green itself is smaller and steeper than an

## April 1996

average green. It is rated as the 3rd hardest Par on the course. The hole is best played to err left or right on the green rather than long or short. Coming up short is problematic as the green slopes downward and tends to dump short shots back toward the small bunkers. Long on the green makes for difficult uneven downhill puts. Left or right and close to pin high are the best placements other than in the hole. All four Skylarks have played this hole at least a dozen times over the years.

Each hole on the course has two foursomes playing it right from the shotgun outset. The foursome in front of the '65 Skylarks includes four duffers from the class of '61. So Mickey's foursome has to wait near the seventeenth hole while the others tee off. As they approach the tee box, Pudd'nhead opens Pandora's Box.

"How are you and Syd and the kids holding up with the circus surrounding the Babcock trial? And your son Fox ... how is he holding up?"

Pudd'nhead has been married and divorced three times. He is not very popular with the wives of his Shenandoah buddies, Syd Johnson included. But Pudd'nhead still gets along well with his fellow Skylarks. He knows he is touching upon a subject that Mickey has not discussed openly. Mickey has conversed about it with Jack Birdsong, but that is to be expected. The other members of the 1965 Skylarks simply respected Mickey's privacy and didn't bring it up. But everyone is aware that the trial is scheduled to begin in ten weeks.

"You've been wrestling with the Babcock trial for so long ... it's amazing you still have your sense of humor, Mickey." Pudd'nhead follows up nervously before allowing Mickey to answer his question.

"About some things, I guess. But if I didn't have a sense of humor about my golf game, the other stuff would just drive me totally nuts."

In reality, Mickey plays a decent game of golf. It is somewhat remarkable because he has not been able to raise his right arm much above his right shoulder since he returned from Vietnam in 1969 with a serious upper arm injury. Over time he taught himself to hit a golf ball, as well as a baseball, left handed. Although he still can't quite manage a full swing, he is able to generate sufficient power and accuracy to be quite competitive. Even his close friends often forget about his injury when they play.

"At least you still drive the ball a good distance ... and straight most of the time. So your game *looks* good, even though you suck."

## Techies, Trials & Terrorists

"Thanks, Pudd'n, I appreciate the encouragement. The only reason your game is any better than the rest of us is that you get a lot of practice when your wives keep throwing you out of the house."

"Touché."

"But you're right, I'll be glad when this trial is over. At least I think I'll be."

"Well, we all hope it works out the way you want."

Therein lay the difficulty. Mickey hates Frank Babcock, but he knows that his own son Fox Babcock would be gravely impacted by a guilty verdict in the upcoming trial. This is precisely why a round of golf is such an effective tonic. It let him worry about other stupid little things, like his short game.

Mickey is glad to have this time with his friends for another reason. He knows he has their support regardless of the outcome of the trial.

"Is Fox playing in the tournament today, Mickey? I know he missed the tournament last year but he and his group have played in the past. Those younger guys usually party big time at the dinner."

Pudd'nhead is now standing above his teed-up ball waiting for the previous foursome to finally clear the green in front of them. He has recently put on about twenty pounds. He looks less healthy than might be expected of a prominent physician.

"No." He waits as Pudd'nhead disregards his answer and sends a 5-Wood drive up onto the green but 11 feet short of the hole and 7 feet to the left. The medical man disregards the soft congratulations from the other golfers and turns toward Mickey waiting for him to complete his answer.

"I talked to Fox last week. He's pretty tied up with his neurosurgery residency. I'm sure you know how those things can be. So he didn't make the trip out from Pittsburgh this year."

Mickey hits his shot short and it spins off the green and back into the bunker.

"Damn." He retakes his swing this time at the thin air as though this phantom second drive might have been better. He simply shakes his head and walks away from the tee box as Jack Birdsong prepares for his own tee shot. Birdsong realizes that the others are listening carefully to the exchange between Pudd'nhead and Mickey. They are all supportive of their friend but none of them wants to broach the topic of the upcoming trial. So far they have played most of the round without airing out the dilemma. None of them really knows how Fox Babcock feels about the murder prosecution of

## April 1996

his adoptive father. They are all also unsure if Mickey knows how Fox feels about it.

After three of the four golfers get bogies on the hole with Pudd'nhead carding the only par, the golfers move on. Jack and Mickey ride in the same cart and as they head toward the final hole of the afternoon, Mickey opens up to his closest friend.

"I appreciate the fact that you guys have avoided asking me about the trial."

"Don't mind Pudd'n. He's not trying to pry. Like the rest of us, he wants you to know that regardless of what happens, we all have your back."

"No. I know that. I'm cool with that. It's just good to be away from it for an afternoon. It's a thick fog hanging over just about everything else."

"If you don't want to discuss it, I'll tell Pudd'n to just keep his mouth shut."

"No, don't do that. Pudd'n means well. But I don't have many answers for myself let alone for others."

"Got it. End of topic. Let's see if we can knock out a couple of pars on this last hole."

"Yeah good idea. I should have just let the bastard die back in San Francisco." Mickey's tag on remark answers all the questions that Jack might have had anyway.

∞∞∞

# XXXIII

## July 1996

After nearly twenty-one months of ups and downs, the district attorney's office is about to make its opening statement in the murder trial of Frank Babcock. Prosecutor Máire Higney steps up to the podium looking much younger than her true age of 44. She has a spray of freckles that spread cross her slightly upturned Irish nose and under both of her watery blue eyes. She is a few pounds overweight, but not noticeably so. She is reasonably attractive but her hair is chopped and not at all stylish. She looks impeccably honest. She also appears slightly innocent. In reality she has delivered numerous guilty verdicts during her thirteen year career as a prosecutor. Juries like her. Juries trust her.

However Higney realizes that the Prosecution has an uphill battle. They have no first hand witness to either the murder itself or to any plot or conspiracy to commit any act of violence on the part of Frank Babcock. They are long on motive and short on evidence. Higney and her team know that the trial outcome will depend significantly upon what evidence will be allowed by Judge Black. And for the last several months there have been numerous motions and countermotions with respect to admissibility of testimony concerning a missing tape. But at least now during her opening statement, Higney grasps that Black will grant her some latitude with respect to how she depicts the murder of Wayne Johnson that took place nearly sixteen years ago. After addressing the judge and the jury in some polite initial remarks, Máire Higney gathers herself for about ten seconds before embarking on her opening statement.

## July 1996

"… So we find ourselves here in this courtroom many years after the homicide death of New York City Police Officer Wayne Johnson. Officer Johnson was not just a law enforcement officer for the city of New York, he was also a husband, a father, a neighbor, a friend and a United States citizen, whose life and liberty were taken away by several men who ruthlessly plotted to end his life and very unfortunately succeeded in doing so.

"During the course of this trial we will expose some aspects of Officer Johnson's life that will show him as humanly flawed. We will not endeavor to paint Wayne Johnson as the perfect husband or the perfect father. He had his weaknesses, just like you and me. And over the coming days you will see some of those shortcomings because they help to establish the crystal clear motive for his murder. However as you learn of these personal failings on the part of the decedent, don't ever lose sight of the fact as an American citizen he was endowed by his creator with the inalienable right to life, liberty and the pursuit of happiness.

"You will learn shortly how an arrogant billionaire – the defendant, Frank Babcock – cowardly conspired to deprive Officer Johnson, of his most basic right, the right to life. We will prove beyond a reasonable doubt that the defendant – in the final act of a pent-up jealous rage – commissioned the murder of an innocent citizen of New York State and the United States of America. The State is confident that you as jurors will exercise your own civic responsibility – and after appropriate evaluation of all the facts in this trial – that you will render the correct verdict of murder in the first degree. Then justice can be served."

Another lengthy pause ensues as Higney appears to be reevaluating her own remarks. She is well aware that she has summarized her case without yet telling the jury what evidence she intends to put forward. It is not an unusual tactic, and it is one that has been measured in advance. Realizing that her evidence might be weak, Higney wants the jury to leap forward to the conviction immediately and then she will simply provide an outline of the evidence that will support that verdict. Regardless she wants them to see the result first in the hope that they will appropriately line up the evidence themselves in support of the desired verdict. Then if she looks a little awkward it's alright. She may garner empathy from a jury that already is thinking: "guilty."

As Higney continues her opening statement and begins outlining her evidence against Babcock, there is significant interest among the courtroom press about the other trial attendees, particularly family members.

For months the media has depicted the trial as a love quadrangle that has many antagonists both in the Johnson family and among the Babcocks. Behind the rail on the Prosecution side of the courtroom gallery, Mickey and Sydney Johnson sit listening closely as Higney speaks to the jury. Mickey appears stoic. Syd is more edgy. Neither has answered any media inquiries leading up to the trial. Mickey's buddy, Jack Birdsong is sitting next to him. Most people have no idea who he is.

On the opposite side of the courtroom, Margot Silver-Babcock is sitting with her mother directly behind the rail that separates the defendant's table from the main body of the courtroom. In substance Margot sits about four or five feet directly behind her husband. But the defendant has not turned around even once to acknowledge her presence since the judge entered the courtroom.

Seated behind most of the gallery of spectators near the center-rear of the courtroom, Simone Muirchant waits with her husband, Jeff Levine. They have purposely chosen their seats so that spectators would be forced to turn around in their seats if they choose to gawk at the Prosecution's most substantive witness. Outwardly the defendant's ex-wife appears to be relaxed. However she is merely guising a stomach in turmoil, a headache that is pounding and a heart that is confused. For the last few years she has also been dealing with severe temperature changes – as well as mood changes – related to the late onslaught of menopause. She is determined to testify truthfully, when her time comes to appear on the witness stand. The trouble is that she is uncertain what the truth encompasses. Simone also knows that

## July 1996

she will not testify until the latter stages of the Prosecution's case. She does not know all of the details that other witnesses may provide.

Also in the courtroom, seated by herself near the rear of the gallery is Kathy McDonough. None of the media, and only a couple of the other spectators know who this woman is. However Mickey is appreciative of her show of support. He also appreciates the support that is being provided by Violet Spataro who is managing the Garden City household and his children's activities during the trial. Kathy has her own reasons for loathing Simone Muirchant. Not only was Wayne Johnson the father-in-law of Barbara Johnson (nee McDonough) but Wayne had also been Kathy's friend. Kathy and her husband Don had also suffered a loss when Wayne Johnson was murdered. But Kathy keeps these thoughts to herself. No one is talking to her anyway.

∞∞∞

In truth, the McDonoughs had not always been close to the Johnsons. In the 1960's the Johnsons lived in working class Lynbrook while the McDonoughs lived in the more upscale neighboring town of Rockville Centre. Kathy had originally hoped for her daughter to be attracted to a college man rather than a soldier. But as their daughter Barbara grew closer and closer to Mickey, Don and Kathy also grew closer to their future son-in-law. And when Mickey was in Vietnam, Barbara frequently visited with her future in-laws and everyone seemed to be happy enough with the arrangement. Barbara even served as a surrogate older sister to Mickey's much younger brother, Gilly.

Now at 71 years of age Kathy replays the sequences in her mind since her daughter first met Mickey: the good ones and the bad ones ... the unpredictable see-saw of life. First she remembers the toughest moments:

> Barbara waiting for Mickey to come home from Vietnam
> Mickey's Mom, Maria Johnson, getting breast cancer
> Barbara being diagnosed with melanoma
> Maria Johnson passing away with Wayne at her bedside
> Barbara dying with Mickey at her bedside
> Incessant arguments with Don after Barbara's death
> Heavy drinking binges that accompanied their quarrels
> The murder of Wayne Johnson
> The car accident that killed Gilly Johnson
> The death of her husband, Don

# Techies, Trials & Terrorists

But there were good times also:

> Barbara's college graduation
> Mickey's homecoming from Vietnam
> Barbara and Mickey's engagement and subsequent wedding
> Shared holiday celebrations with the Johnsons
> Her collaborative recovery with Don from alcohol abuse
> Mickey and Syd's engagement and marriage
> Being received as family by Mickey and Syd
> Invitations to the Johnson children's christenings
> Shared holidays with the new generation of the Johnson family
> Mickey and Syd inviting her into their home after Don's passing
> Watching her surrogate grandchildren grow and thrive

Throughout all of these years, Kathy had never met Simone Muirchant or Frank Babcock. She acknowledged their consequence in Mickey's life but she had never laid eyes on either person. Neither person attended Gilly Johnson's wake or funeral. And although Simone was apparently at Wayne Johnson's funeral, Kathy had no idea who she was at the time. Kathy doesn't remember seeing her and she knows that they weren't introduced. Kathy only knew Simone was there because Mickey had once told her that.

Over the ensuing years as her son-in-law became more like the son she never had, Kathy became much more vigilant of any residual pain that Mickey felt because of his involvement with Frank Babcock and Simone Muirchant. Because of this she began to loathe both of them.

Syd Johnson had once told Kathy that Simone was a far left thinking liberal who opposed all war and violence throughout the world. Kathy was scornful. Here was a woman who never wanted anyone to lift a gun in anger and yet she was able to start a decades-long war between the Babcocks and the Johnsons simply by dropping her drawers. This hypocrisy triggers Kathy's loathing of Simone.

∞∞∞

The personalities in the gallery are enough to fill any newspaper's thirst for intrigue. However the media and the public at large are waiting to see if there will be an appearance in the courtroom by Doctor Fox Babcock.

# July 1996

No one has been able to get a soundbite from the human being who has long been at the nuclear center of the controversy. And there is no legal reason why Fox would be compelled to make an appearance at the trial. Although both the Prosecution and the Defense have listed Fox as a potential witness, neither side actually intends to call him and he has not been subpoenaed for an appearance. As a witness he might be able to provide background for motive or he could possibly dispel that motive. His testimony would certainly be a wild card. From the very instant that he was conceived in 1965, the young doctor has been the focal point of the animosity between the Babcocks and the Johnsons. Yet to this very day, no one seems to know whether Fox considers himself more of a Babcock or more of a Johnson. That enigmatic reality has much to do with why both sides are hesitant to call him as a witness.

∞∞∞

Meanwhile Máire Higney continues on with her opening remarks. She tells the jury how she is prepared to present witnesses and evidence to demonstrate that the murder of Wayne Johnson was carried out by more than one man. She emphasizes that the murder was "anything but a robbery/mugging gone awry."

Higney wants the jury to be able to follow her story line. She says that she will show that the murder of Wayne Johnson was pre-meditated and pre-plotted by mercenary killers commissioned by Frank Babcock. Even as she speaks Higney realizes that the Prosecution bears the burden of proof. Her evidence will have to overcome reasonable doubt. That doubt might arise as jurors wonder why the NYPD took so long to bring the case to trial and why they had officially declared it a random mugging/murder, fourteen years earlier.

Higney also tells the jury that the Prosecution will present evidence demonstrating a bizarre love-quadrangle, wherein both the victim and the victim's son had sexual relationships with the defendant's wife and that one of these relationships resulted in the birth of Fox Babcock. Higney asserts that testimony will show that Fox Babcock is legally Frank Babcock's son and genetically Mickey Johnson's son. Higney tells the jury that the defendant had long believed that Fox Babcock was his own flesh and blood, but that at the time of the murder Frank Babcock knew that he had been cuckolded and he suspected that Wayne Johnson was the father of Fox Babcock. She contends that seeking retribution, "Frank Babcock commissioned a cold blooded murder."

∞∞∞

When it comes time for the Defense to make its opening remarks, the difference in opposing lawyers is pronounced. Phillip Ambrose, is joined at the Defense table by two other attorneys. Lincoln Pierce, is a tall middle aged black attorney with a charismatic smile and a name comprised of the surnames of two nineteenth century presidents. He served as Phil Ambrose's second chair during the "Clue Murders" case and is respected not only by Ambrose but by many other members of the legal profession as well as by the media and the general public. Phil Ambrose has deferred to Pierce to make the Defense's opening statement in the Babcock trial.

The third attorney seated at the Defense table is Helen Vereen, a saucy raven-haired eye-turner. She appears to go out of her way to be distracting to the two young male attorneys sitting at the Prosecution desk with Máire Higney. But the five male members of the jury are her primary target.

Vereen is relatively new to the Ambrose legal team. Wearing a tightly pleated navy blue skirt and a similarly close-fitting white silk top, Vereen is a formidable physical presence. However what most of the male observers don't know is that Vereen is a talented professional kinesics reader. She has been one of the principle contributors to the Defense's vetting of the jury during the earlier voir dire.

Not only can Helen Vereen read body language but she can *speak* it as well. In many very delicate ways her subtle physical reactions to the court proceedings speak in a convincing manner to the men in her audience. She will let them know what is important and what is sketchy. She never has to utter a single word to accomplish her communication.

So, earlier as Higney is telling the jurors that Frank Babcock suspected Wayne Johnson of being Fox Babcock's father, Vereen is subtly creating a facial expression of disbelief. It is not an extremely overt expression but it is compelling nonetheless to the Vereen watchers. Her chin lifts attentively. Her eyes narrow slightly in disbelief. Her wordless lips part marginally in feigned objection. The rest of her body language works in concert. She repositions her crossed ankles and tightens her long legs in an expression of rejection. She has also stiffened her back, squared her shoulders and thrust out her slight chest in a posture of protest.

# July 1996

After the Prosecution's lengthy opening statement that has taken nearly an hour and twenty minutes, the judge declares a fifteen minute hygiene break to allow the jury some comfort before what is expected to be an equally lengthy opening statement by the Defense.

∞∞∞

While the trial is beginning back in Queens County in New York City, Dr. Fox Babcock is taking a rare day off from his neurosurgery residency. He is spending time with his 13 month old son, Michael Francis Babcock. Fox enjoys playing with Mikey more than anything else in life these days. In his first 30 years of life Fox has already experienced much more family drama than most people will experience in 10 lifetimes. Still he also wishes that he could spend some time with his other child, his daughter in West Virginia. But that complexity is quite fluid in nature and Fox is uncertain how it will eventually unfold. His immediate concern however is his father's trial on Long Island.

∞∞∞

Fox knows what really happened in Jamaica, New York in June of 1980. When Frank Babcock was charged with murder twenty-one months earlier, Fox had had his own doubts. But after hearing his mother's tape, Fox knew the basics about his grandfather's death. However at the time he also had his own problems. He was expecting two children by two different women. He was worried about his marriage. As if this weren't enough trauma, Fox was also concerned that his childhood friend might reenter his life in a very negative way.

Fox had worried briefly about the rekindling of his friendship with Sergei Zubkov. However, the most worrisome topic has not resurfaced since their short reunion at the end of 1994. Zubkov has returned to his work in London and the two men have conducted an intermittent electronic mail correspondence since that time. Their "email" conversation centers on their common interest in information technology. They never mention the demise of Maureen's tormentors. Fox has come to believe that Sergei is probably equally concerned about the possibility of an unwanted disclosure. After all Sergei had planned the meeting with Fox that one time at Patrick's Pub. He probably wanted to ensure that they were each maintaining their own confidence. Since that time Fox has felt secure with the secret but no less guilty about the crime.

# Techies, Trials & Terrorists

∞∞∞

However Fox has the other reason for anxiety. His relationship with Evelyn had been challenged by the birth of his other child. Originally he was uncertain about the paternity of his daughter because he had only had intercourse with Madison Swift on one occasion. But because his own bloodlines had been mired in uncertainty in the past, Fox was quick to allow paternity tests which definitely proved Maddie's claim that the young doctor had fathered her child.

Fox had returned to West Virginia and had spoken to Maddie Swift in January of 1995. He had dreaded the trip down to see her but was well received by Maddie when he showed up. She was fully eight months pregnant when he arrived. Maddie let him know right away that she intended to keep her baby and that she didn't expect anything from him by way of emotional, physical or financial help. She had ruled out abortion months earlier. It wasn't an option for her. And she had no plans to put her baby up for adoption after the birth. There was no other man in Maddie's life at the time and she was now living with her cousin Billy Wilde, and Wilde's wife, Gwendolyn.

Fox had been surprised that this trip hadn't felt as awful as he thought it might. But it certainly had produced a new emotional burden. He wasn't sure how he would feel about this over time. At the outset his first instinct had been to ensure that Maddie received appropriate prenatal care, so that she and the baby would go through the pregnancy and birth without complications. He arranged for all of the medical bills to be sent to his attorney, so that he could arrange for payment, and he told Maddie that he would fully support the baby after the birth. When he arrived in town, she thanked him for this consideration.

With Evelyn's blessing, Fox returned to West Virginia in February of 1995 for the birth of his daughter. Maddie didn't give him much say in selecting the baby's name, as she had already decided on calling her, Dolly. There wasn't much discussion about the surname either. Maddie wanted her daughter's name to be Dolly Swift. Fox had not objected.

∞∞∞

# XXXIV

## July 1996

Back in Queens County in New York, Lincoln Pierce begins his opening statement. Pierce is handsome and refined with a deep resonant voice that is pleasant and radiates warmth. The jury thinks it's hearing a younger version of James Earl Jones. Pierce tells his audience that his opening comments will not be long on rhetoric. He infers that the Babcock defense strategy is to demonstrate that the Prosecution has not proven its case. The Defense believes that they stand a chance of gaining a directed verdict from the bench if they do a good enough job dismissing the testimony of the government's witnesses.

The backup defense strategy will be the same one that was employed in the recent OJ Simpson trial. Nine months earlier, Simpson was acquitted of murdering his wife, Nicole Brown Simpson (as well as her friend, Ronald Lyle Goldman.) In the Simpson trial, the defense strategy revolved around the suggestion of police negligence, incompetence and/or corruption. Babcock's Defense team believes they can demonstrate some of these same attributes in their client's case, if it proves necessary to do so. But they don't truly believe it will get that far, because unlike the Simpson case, Babcock's lawyers do not have a mountain of physical evidence that they need to discredit. In fact there is very little forensic evidence and no eye witness testimony whatsoever that ties their client to the murder scene.

"... and so ladies and gentlemen you will soon see that the State has brought this case before you with questionable motivation. You can speculate as to what that motivation may be, but in essence it's not necessary. Whatever the Prosecution's motivation may be, they do not have any credible evidence to back up their charges against an innocent man, who has already endured the humiliation of betrayal by a faithless wife. You will see that this same faithless wife has a moral compass moving north and south; east and west so fast as to be rendered useless as a measurement instrument. We believe that you will come to know the Prosecution's chief witness as both an unfaithful wife and also as an unfit mother. You will see that she has often chosen a culture of drugs and wanton self-indulgence over the responsibilities of marriage and family.

"Now it is fair to say that Ms. Muirchant has achieved some degree of business and financial success over the past 15 years, and we certainly won't deny the fact that she has garnered the respect of some members of the business community in so doing. But there will be two facts worth noting in assessing the worthiness of the success that she has achieved. Fact number one is that long before she achieved any business success whatsoever, she had married one of the richest men in the world ... a man she now accuses of contracting the murder of one of her lovers. Fact number two is that much of her most recent success has been funded by this same man who was once her husband and who has more recently provided angel funding to her business endeavors."

Ambrose, Pierce and the rest of the Babcock Defense want to get out in front of the fact that their client has funded the Prosecution witness's business. They don't want the Prosecution to hint at any ulterior motive for that funding. But they also want to show that Babcock is not a vindictive person. He obviously doesn't despise his ex-wife after she twice walked out on him.

## July 1996

> "But now these are mere background facts. The *'relevant'* facts of this case revolve around activities that occurred in the 1970's leading up to Wayne Johnson's untimely death in June of 1980. I call your attention to these *'relevant'* facts, precisely because they are *'irrelevant'* in the case that is before you today. The Prosecution will attempt to build up a backdrop of marital infidelity as a motive for murder. But don't be fooled, these facts only impugn the character of the *witness*. They do not indicate a motive for murder on the part of the defendant."

As he is speaking the words "relevant" and "irrelevant," Pierce highlights the difference by raising two fingers on each of his hands to emulate quotation marks. He thereby emphasizes and distinguishes the difference in meaning of each word. As he pauses to allow his point to sink in, he also shrugs in dismissal before speaking words that are also dismissive.

> "Now really... Do we really don't need to go down this path of *possible* motive in the first place? The facts stand on their own. You can undoubtedly see this murder in the same way that the New York Police Department saw it for so many years. It was a random murder committed by a single assailant, who died in the process of committing his crime. And in the remote possibility that there was a second assailant at the crime scene, there is no evidence whatsoever implicating my client in the actions of that assailant. The Prosecution will fail dramatically in their fruitless attempt to present a story concocted and pieced together by overzealous law enforcement officials.
>
> "But there is no need for us to go down this path right here, right now, in our opening comments. In fact there may not be any reason for us to tackle some of these issues *at all* during the coming days, because as you will see shortly, the Prosecution does *not* have

a weak case … they have *no case* at all. There will be *no credible evidence* linking our client to this murder in any way. Without *hard* evidence, any suggestion of motive is entirely irrelevant. However as you will soon see the Prosecution will have great difficulty providing substantiation for motive as well. So that's it in a nutshell: *No evidence; No motive; No case….* No, no, no."

As he is articulating the last nine words of his incredibly brief opening statement, Lincoln Pierce speaks very deliberately. He stresses each word while shaking his head from side to side for emphasis. His deep resonant voice is warm and friendly. It is an effective tool. Meanwhile back at the Defense bench, Helen Vereen meekly moves her head from side to side in unison with her colleague. Her kinesics are more subtle. She also parts her hands which were previously clasped in front of her with her fingers intersecting. She moves her hands about six inches apart and turns her palms up in a signal of bewildered acceptance of an obvious truth. Many members of her compliant audience watch in silent agreement. They are tilting before a single witness has been called.

∞∞∞

Even though the opening statement by the Defense is brief, it still brings the trial to a logical break point for the day. Because a number of pre-statement procedural motions were debated at the outset of the trial, the jury wasn't able to hear either opening statement until after lunch. The judge adjourns the court room at 4:30 PM rather than begin the presentation of witnesses and evidence later that day.

∞∞∞

That night in Pittsburgh, Fox and Evelyn Babcock watch as the national news mentions that the Babcock murder trial has begun back in New York City. The coverage lasts less than 30 seconds on the screen but Fox sees camera shots of both his father and his adoptive father entering the courthouse. There isn't much more to the coverage than that.

"Do you think you might get a call from either of them?"

"I seriously doubt it. At this point, I don't want any calls either. What would I say, anyway?"

## July 1996

There is no good answer to Fox's question, so Evelyn doesn't offer one.

"Maybe we should just watch something besides the news, Fox. The news is so negatively focused all of the time these days. I don't remember it being like this when we were growing up."

"So then, what's your professional psychiatric assessment with what's wrong with the world in general, that we have all of this negative news?"

"I'm not so sure that there's anything *new* that's wrong with the world. I think that we just hear more about negative things these days. We simply assume that the world is getting more criminal."

"I don't agree. There is a negative trend and it is swelling. Just look at the last few years. You have the bombing in the garage at the Trade Center... utter madness... terrorism they call it. Then you have the Oklahoma City bombing. You also have the Japanese cult that released Sarin Gas on 5 subway trains in Tokyo. Worse yet, it seems like every day there is a new suicide bomber blowing himself up in the name of Allah on some bus or street corner in Israel. These are all crimes that are not directed against individuals but against ideas and cultures. It's sick, probably muck sicker than some of the people you see in your residency on a daily basis."

"Well what do you think should be done about it?"

"If I knew the answer to that maybe I would have stayed in psychiatry, like you."

"Don't get so upset, Fox." She moves over closer to him on the couch that they are sharing. "You are a good man and I love you."

∞∞∞

# XXXV

## *July 1996*

It is now day three of the trial and the Prosecution is already putting on its sixth witness. The previous witnesses were law enforcement officers who have been slowly resetting the crime scene as they uncovered it in 1980. Ballistics witnesses have testified that the gun that shot Malcolm Johnson was indeed fired by Wayne Johnson. Yet there is no conclusive evidence indicating how the gun arrived at the scene in the first place. There has also been testimony as to the nature of the wounds that were suffered by Wayne Johnson before he died. Most of the testimony indicates that there was more than one assailant at the scene when Wayne Johnson was beaten to death. However this testimony conflicts dramatically with the original findings of the investigation which had indicated that Malcolm Johnson was likely the lone killer in the assault. The Prosecution tries to show this earlier theory thoroughly flawed by an exhaustive airing of newly interpreted physical evidence.

During the cross examination of the law enforcement witnesses, the Defense doesn't try to directly rebut the idea of a second killer being at the scene of the crime. Rather it simply continues to peck away at the fact that the NYPD and the Prosecutors Office had drawn very different conclusions 16 years earlier. In 1980, they deemed the attack on Wayne Johnson to be a random murder/robbery perpetrated by a single assailant. These continual

## July 1996

reminders to the jury, let them know that the Defense believes that the Prosecution is manufacturing its case out of falsehoods, half-truths and sensationalism. And so cross examination by Phillip Ambrose and Lincoln Pierce has aimed at creating an aura of duplicity around the testimony of each witness. They claw back at every piece of evidence trying to give a different interpretation of the findings. Meanwhile Helen Vereen has been carefully studying the jury while some jury members occasionally study her. Her reactions remain delicate and subtle but she is simultaneously sending subconscious signals to the jurors about who to believe and who not to believe.

∞∞∞

"The State calls Myles Cooper."

The government's witness is sworn in and the Prosecution immediately asks a number of questions that help establish Mr. Cooper's bona fides as a forensic expert specializing in DNA evidence. The supporting DNA testimony is unusual in one sense. The DNA samples in question are not from the defendant or the victim, but rather the DNA samples were those of a witness who would testify to being a co-conspirator and a co-perpetrator of the alleged murder of Wayne Johnson.

The whole arena of DNA testing has already been argued and reargued in pre-trial motions from both sides in the case. Several years earlier the Prosecution had been able to substantiate the claim of Richie Barone that he had been at the murder scene and participated in the murder of Wayne Johnson. However Barone's version of how the murder actually occurred kept changing and so they were reluctant to try the defendant on DNA linked testimony of a convicted felon. The public was still skeptical of DNA evidence, but that was changing. The last few years had seen a surprising number of felony criminal cases wherein DNA evidence was used to convict or to exonerate various defendants. The most recent acquittal of OJ Simpson however threw some cold water on DNA evidence and testimony, but the Prosecution decided to push with DNA evidence anyway.

Higney takes her witness through a number of questions about how DNA identifications are made and the facts around the certainty of the identification and then pushes for his conclusion.

"Based upon your examination of the DNA samples from the June 1980 crime scene in, have you been able to reach a conclusive determination?"

"Yes we have a definitive result. The crime scene DNA matches the DNA that was labeled as being from a Mr. Richard Barone."

"And how certain can you be that the samples are a flawless match?"

"Fortunately in this case we have previously unidentified blood and skin samples taken from the victims clothing. We also have blood samples taken from areas in and around the victim's mouth and on a tooth of the victim. The chance that the DNA came from someone other than Mr. Barone is less than 1 in 6,780,312."

∞∞∞

When the Defense cross examines Cooper, the witness is asked many detailed questions about interim testing reports, computer outputs, the validity of the skin samples versus the blood samples, hand written lab notes, the chain of custody of the DNA samples, and the number of times Cooper has testified in a court room. This is the only witness who will be interrogated by Helen Vereen.

The questions come rapid fire and Cooper is sometimes slow to respond. Obviously he can only answer chain of custody questions about the time that the samples were in his lab. However in order to lend credence to his testimony he inadvertently extrapolates his answer to be inclusive of the time when the evidence is either in the hands of the police or the courts. Vereen raises her eyebrows in disbelief when he does so, but chooses to keep firing different questions rather than go after the obvious overreach. She thinks the jury will interpret her own reaction as an appropriate dismissal of his credibility.

Cooper tries to answer each question as honestly as he can but the pace of the questions make his answers appear disjointed. Some of the jury members appear to be following along closely, while others appear more interested in the Defense attorney conducting the cross examination.

By the time Vereen finishes her cross examination, the jury is more confused than convinced by the DNA testimony. They have yet to hear from Richard Barone, so they are not yet certain why this is important anyway.

∞∞∞

"The State calls Mr. Richard Barone."

The witness is sworn in. A question or two is asked to verify the identity of the witness as being more commonly known as "Richie" Barone.

## July 1996

Then the Prosecution begins by establishing the already disclosed fact that the witness has a checkered past.

"Mr. Barone, you currently reside at Attica State Correctional Facility. Is that correct?" Máire Higney begins by letting the jury know that the State's witness is not being held up as a model citizen and that his credibility will have to withstand their disdain for some of the many crimes that he has committed over the course of his lifetime. She knows that he is about to confess to a crime that he has not yet been convicted of committing.

"Dats right."

"And how long have you been housed at Attica?"

"Been at Attica *mosta* my life, I guess."

Higney asks a few additional questions that clarify the fact that Barone has spent a significant portion of his life in prison. In an odd way his truthfulness about his incarceration lends a tentative sense of credibility as he answers each question directly and without hesitation. Then Higney begins to bore in on his association with Babcock's security agent.

"Mr. Barone, Did you know a man … now deceased … by the name of Tony Mazzini?"

"Yeah, I *knowed* Mazzini. I *knowed* him since just *bafaw* the Johnson job."

"How did you first meet Detective Mazzini?"

"I met him right *bafaw* I got *outta* the jug in 1980. He met me up in Attica. Seemed to know a little about me … We grew up *inna* same section of Brooklyn. But of course I *di'nt* know him when we *wuz* kids …you know … in da *neighbahood*. But later we found out *dat* we both knew *sum'uda* same guys."

"And that neighborhood was where exactly?"

"Flatbush."

"So can you tell the jury what occasioned that first meeting between you and Tony Mazzini?

"No. There *wasn't no* occasion *'bout* it at all. Not like it was Christmas or *nuthin'*. He was an ex-cop and he had some connections. He asked to see me because he had a tip that I might know somethin' *'bout* somebody else's mischief. I *rememba* that I knew *nuthin' 'bout* the people he wanted to talk about. But they *was* Italians so I *wouldn't a* told him squat even if I did know *somethin'*. Then later after the Johnson job, I figured he *jus'* made up the other bs ... you know... *jus' so's* he could size me up ... *bein'* that I was about to get out."

"Are you saying that Mazzini was checking you out to see if you might be the man he wanted to hire to attack Wayne Johnson?"

"Objection, your Honor ... leading the witness."

"Sustained. The jury should ignore the question. Ms. Higney, you know better."

Higney moves her freckled face closer to the witness and rephrases her inquiry. The mild reprimand was worth the seed she had planted.

"Mr. Barone could you tell us what you meant by saying that Tony Mazzini was 'sizing you up?' What was he sizing you up for?"

"For what you *jus'* said *bafaw.*"

Judge Black stares at the witness wondering whether or not Barone is playing games or if he is actually as simple-minded as he is making himself out to be. But Black says nothing and waits for Higney to ask for clarification. For her part Higney would rather that Barone's response just linger. If it lends credence there's no need to ask for further clarification.

"In your own words please, Mr. Barone, why did you believe Mazzini was sizing you up?'

"To go work for him."

"In what capacity?"

"Huh?"

"What kind of work did you believe Mazzini wanted you to do?"

"As I *says bafaw* ...the Johnson job."

Prosecutor Máire Higney lets Barone's answer sink in. She nods her understanding. After a short pause Higney then begins to question Richie Barone in great detail about two meetings that Barone had with Mazzini between Barone's release from prison and the time of the attack on Wayne Johnson. She is careful to focus on the clear testimony surrounding Mazzini's commissioning of Barone to attack Johnson, but she treads lightly on the topic of Mazzini implicating Babcock in the plot, because she knows that the evidence is very thin. However after establishing the fact that there was indeed a conspiracy to harm Wayne Johnson, she bores in with her questions for Barone.

"So it was clear to you that Mazzini was the middle man for another person who wanted to harm Wayne Johnson. Did you inquire about the identity of that person?"

## July 1996

"Not at first. We *jus'* called him *da* 'Mystery Man.' Mazzini thought it was best that I *di'nt* know his name. But one time Mazzini slipped up and instead of calling him *da* 'Mystery Man,' he called him 'Babcock.' I *di'nt* make much of it. I *jus'* had a job to do and I got paid in advance. I *di'nt* want to know *'bout* Babcock *no* more than he wanted to know *'bout* me."

"And did you subsequently discover the name of the man who had hired Mazzini to hire you."

"Objection, your Honor."

"I did ... that man over there." He points at Frank Babcock before Judge Black can rule on the admissibility of the question or the answer. Babcock recoils reflexively from the pointed finger, but maintains a reserved facial expression. Phillip Ambrose is immediately on his feet making his case, moving toward the bench, so that his theatrics will take the jurors eyes off his client's demeanor.

"Objection your honor, the witness has never met our client. He has never spoken a single word to our client. In fact he has never been in the same room as our client until the start of this trial. To insinuate that he can point and visually identify our client as his co-conspirator is utterly prejudicial nonsense."

"The court will be in a very brief recess, while the Defense and the State meet immediately in my chambers."

When they arrive in his chambers, Judge Black appears to be annoyed. He wants to have this discreet conversation in his chambers rather than at the bench so that the jurors can draw no inference from the heat of the conversation. He turns first to the Defense attorney and says "Your objection is duly noted, counselor. And you will have your opportunity to cross-examine the witness."

Then Black turns toward Higney and asks: "Where are you headed with this testimony? The State has already stipulated that this witness has never met the defendant. The jury has been so informed by the Defense in their opening statement, and just now in open court. We have also ruled after pre-trial motions were filed about the admissibility of unproven third party prison balderdash. It will certainly not be allowed or alluded to if that is your intent. Do I make myself clear?"

"Very clear, Your Honor."

"Is your witness prepared to testify that he heard that the accused was identified at a later date by Mr. Mazzini, the reputed co-conspirator? If so why has the court not been apprised of this testimony before now?

"Your Honor, the witness has been vague with the State about this in the past. Sometimes he has said that he heard from Mazzini that Mr. Babcock was behind the plot. At other times, and for whatever reasons, Barone has been more tenuous. The State simply wants the witness to tell everything he knows right here and now under oath in this courtroom."

"The witness has already testified that he once heard the name Babcock. We know that he only met with Mazzini one additional time shortly after Wayne Johnson's death and that he never met with him again right through the time of Mazzini's passing. I am going to sustain the objection and strike the question as well as the testimony. Let's go back inside."

∞∞∞

"Ladies and gentlemen of the jury, you will ignore both the question and the answer to the previous line of inquiry right before the recess. Specifically overlook the Prosecution's question to the witness regarding a *'discovery'* about a potential hiring of Mr. Mazzini by an unknown third party. And you will also specifically disregard the witness's verbal and nonverbal response to the expunged question."

The Prosecution now takes Barone through the specific details of the crime, some of which the jury has heard during previous testimony from forensic experts or through the opening statements by the Prosecution and by the Defense.

The jury however sits on the edge of their seats as they hear the first hand recitation of Barone's account of how he and Malcolm Johnson accosted Wayne Johnson in an alleyway near the Jamaica, Queens subway station and how they then proceeded to beat him "to teach him a lesson" for the mystery man. They sit transfixed as they hear Barone testify that Malcolm Johnson "monkey punched" the victim in the back of the neck and how he himself then proceeded to kick Wayne Johnson in the ribs after he had fallen. The jury watches Barone's lips as he retells the story of disarming Wayne Johnson and punching him in the face multiple times with a brass-knuckled glove, while Malcolm Johnson plays lookout for the police or any other passers-by.

Richie Barone's voice is raspy but the jury has no trouble comprehending what he is saying. Barone then testifies how *Wayne* Johnson

## July 1996

had a concealed second gun, which he used to shoot and kill *Malcolm* Johnson, whom Barone repeatedly refers to as "MJ." Barone then recaps the story of how he re-attacked Wayne Johnson and disarmed the beaten and bleeding victim a second time.

"And at that time did you think that *Malcolm* Johnson was dead?"

"I *knowed* he was dead. The cop fired three ... maybe more ... shots *an'* least two *a'dem hits* MJ right smack in *da* forehead. He *di'nt* move an inch *afta dat an'* there's blood everywhere."

"How about *Wayne* Johnson did you think that he was dead also?"

"Well, at first, I wasn't *intendin'* to kill *da* copper... *that* Johnson, but I beat him as best I could ... and he wasn't moving much ... if at all ... so I thought he *could* be dead, but I wasn't sure. *Den* once I heard the sirens, I wasn't *gunna* stay *'round* to find out."

∞∞∞

Barone's testimony about the night of the murder is absolutely riveting. Regardless of his creditability with respect to other aspects of the plot, his recitation of the actual events of that night in June of 1980 is quite convincing. There is little doubt in anyone's mind that Richie Barone attacked Wayne Johnson exactly as he said he did. The Prosecution believes him and the Defense believes him as well. More importantly the jury most likely also believes this part of his testimony. The previous DNA testimony now looks even more convincing in retrospect.

Sitting in the gallery, Mickey Johnson also believes Richie Barone. Hearing his testimony he concludes that not only did Barone kill his father, but that he was hired to do so. He also realizes that Barone's attempt to connect Frank Babcock as the person who paid for the attack on Wayne Johnson sounds much less credible. But Mickey himself has no trouble believing it.

Sitting to Mickey's left, Syd can read his mind without even facing him. She feels his rage. She's worried. Sitting to Mickey's right, Jack Birdsong is empathizing with his friend. He too has no trouble believing Babcock hired Barone to kill Wayne Johnson. Mickey's stoic face has reddened considerably during Barone's testimony, but until now he has been stone silent. Finally, Mickey leans toward Syd and whispers urgently, "Dammit, Fox should be here."

Syd is somewhat surprised that this was Mickey's only response to the proceeding so far, but the judge has demanded that the gallery stay absolutely quiet, so even the one lapse is unexpected. However, Syd understands her husband. As much as he loathes Frank Babcock, he loves his own son Fox Babcock. And Mickey wants Fox to know the truth. Yet he doesn't want to be the one who tells him.

∞∞∞

Máire Higney continues examining her witness "So, Mr. Barone, let's move along once again to what happened *after* the evening of Wayne Johnson's murder. Did you speak to Tony Mazzini?"

"Not immediately. Like I said *bafaw*, I already got paid so I figured there's no use adding any more dots that someone might connect later on. Besides, I *knowed* that Mazzini would get to me to find out how things got so fuc... so out of hand. And I was right, he found me about three days later, and I told him what went down."

"How did Mazzini react?'

He wasn't a happy camper. But he just told me to lay low for a while."

"And when did you next see Mazzini?"

"I *di'nt* see him again."

"And why was that?"

"I got in some hot water over another thing."

"By 'hot water' do you mean that you got arrested for committing another crime?"

"*Dat's* what I'm *sayin'* yeah."

"And when was this crime committed?"

"I'd say, *'bout* six months *afta* the Johnson thing."

"Mr. Barone, were you, in fact, arrested in December of 1980 for armed robbery and assault on a police officer?"

"Yes."

"And were you convicted and incarcerated once again in April of 1981 for these crimes?

"Yes."

"And our records also show that you have been imprisoned at Attica for the past fifteen years. Are these records accurate and factual?"

"Sounds about right to me."

"So when - during your incarceration at Attica - did it occur to you that it might be the right time to tell the authorities about your actions on the night of Wayne Johnson's murder?"

## July 1996

"Well I always knew that I *done* what I *done*, but I *di'nt* want any more time in the jug so I kept my mouth shut. Then I started thinking about all the things I did that I wasn't too happy about and I figured that maybe I could do something to fix one of the things that I screwed up."

"And when was it when you had these thoughts?"

"A long time ago. It was right about when Mazzini died, whenever that was."

"The records show that Tony Mazzini died in September of 1984, so that would be about 12 years ago. Would that approximate the time frame for your change of heart about confessing to this murder conspiracy?"

"Objection."

"Sustained. The Defense may rephrase the question."

"Was it more than a decade ago that you first told the government about your involvement in the murder of Wayne Johnson?"

"I'd say that's about right. But at first … I *jus'* told them I *knowed* who *done* it … not that I *done* it myself."

"And what happened at that time."

"Not much. At first they acted like they *di'nt* believe me. But I wasn't *gunna* give it up for *nuthin'*."

"So when did things begin to change?"

"I ain't exactly sure *'bout* that. But it was a few years later … maybe it was a lot later."

"Well we have heard testimony from the NYPD earlier in this trial that they were first able to identify your DNA as being at the crime scene, in 1991. Would that be about the time they showed more interest in your story?"

"Objection, your honor. The Prosecution is once again leading their witness."

Judge Black looks up from his apparent reverie, and appears to replay the question in his mind, and then frowns as though he regards the objection as trivial."

"Overruled. I'll allow it." He looks like he wants to say more but simply pauses and then nods toward Máire Higney as an indication that she may continue.

Higney then asks Barone a number of questions pertinent to the time frame between 1991 and the present day. The questions simply lay out an ongoing but intermittent dialogue between the State and its witness, while the witness remained incarcerated at Attica over the intervening five years. The implication of all of these questions is simply to demonstrate that Barone never changed his story throughout this period of time. Before finishing with her witness, Higney touches on the motivation for his testimony.

"Mr. Barone, we have already noted that you cooperated fully with the Prosecution over many years as it pressed to get this indictment to trial. Have you been offered any *specific* incentives for your cooperation?"

"No ...not yet."

∞∞∞

Mickey watches the testimony of Richie Barone with restrained hatred. He doesn't know what part of Barone's testimony is true and what has been concocted. But at this point in the trial Mickey is certain of two facts: Richie Barone: he is an evil human being, and somehow his DNA has been found at the sight of Wayne Johnson's murder. Mickey represses the urge to jump out of his seat and physically strangle Barone. He is astounded about how emotionally charged he is feeling. He has never personally experienced such rage before.

Sitting by her husband's side Syd Johnson shares her husband's enmity towards the State's witness. She has been holding his hand through much of the testimony and has felt his right hand clench into a fist with an uncharacteristic strength. In recent months Mickey has had some renewed problems with the strength of his right arm. The war injury weakness had radiated down to his right wrist and hand. But now Syd is experiencing a rekindled digital strength from her husband. It actually scares her.

Sitting on Mickey's left is Jack Birdsong. Jack has been at Mickey's side for most of the trial just as he had been at Mickey's side for much of the Vietnam War. Jack is letting others run his business while he stays with Mickey. He is trying to digest everything. Like Mickey he doesn't believe everything that Barone says is truthful, but rather that the gist of his testimony is accurate. He is certain that Babcock played a role in the death of Wayne Johnson. What bothers Jack the most is that justice has been delayed so long. Babcock should've been behind bars years ago, and yet for now he is still a relatively free man. Jack is angry... justice delayed is justice denied. Frank Babcock has yet to spend a single night in jail.

∞∞∞

## July 1996

At the Defense table, Frank Babcock sits stoically satisfied and accepting the premise that his Defense team is effectively sowing the seeds of doubt amongst the jurors. He is certainly nervous but he is also determined to appear confident. He is making a decent show of it. But unlike other onlookers Babcock is not fixated on the actual testimony. Instead he is fixated on what the outcome will mean. He is thinking about what he will do with his freedom once the trial is over and he is once again able to travel freely.

Oddly enough Babcock has little concern about Simone's upcoming testimony. He believes that she will come across as someone who is honest but gullible and fickle; intelligent but unwise and inconsistent; attractive but flighty and whimsical; coherent but confused and capricious. He is glad she won't have her stupid tape to back up her testimony. That will allow the jurors to believe that she misinterpreted everything she was told at the Ecco dinner. He is also glad that he won't have to testify personally. Even though he never intended to kill Wayne Johnson, Frank Babcock knows that he is now attempting to get away with murder.

∞∞∞

Seated behind the Defense table, Margot Babcock is feeling lonely. Her mother isn't much help as she keeps making barely perceptible gasps at every new twist and revelation of the trial. It seems to Margot that her mother is saying, *'I told you that you should never have married this man.'* Hadassah Silver's whisper-gasps are probably audible only to Margot but they are aggravating nonetheless. While Margot eventually manages to block out her mother's whisper-gasps, she can't help wondering what life might be like without her husband. How will she care for Jedidiah, emotionally?

Undoubtedly she will still have the financial security and wherewithal to do just about anything she wants to do. The trouble is that Margot is not an ambitious person. She has no idea what she might want to do. But she understands that if Frank is convicted she will have to find another man to assist her in doing whatever she chooses to do. Meanwhile Hadassah Silver is secretly hoping that she will be able to help her daughter with that search.

∞∞∞

## *Techies, Trials & Terrorists*

At the rear of the courtroom, Simone Muirchant waits for her turn to testify. She waits with her husband and with her attorney. Her attorney has informed her that either the Prosecution or the Defense may make a motion for her to be excluded from the courtroom when others testify, but no such motion has been made by either side. He has also told her that she has no reason to worry about any personal legal liability as long as she tells the truth the way she has told it to him. But this is not what worries her most. What worries Simone is that she does not know what she wants the outcome of the trial to be. In a perverse kind of way, Simone wants Frank to be found guilty but she doesn't want him to be incarcerated. However she knows this is not a likely or even a possible outcome of the trial. If he is convicted he will be punished.

∞∞∞

Kathy McDonough also sits in anguish. She is distressed by two people. She now has come to realize that Simone is the woman seated just a few seats away in the row in front of her. She still despises Simone but now she can loathe the sight of her as well as the mere specter of the woman. She also detests Frank Babcock and everything he stands for. If he had been more of a man, maybe Simone would never have cheated on him in the first place. *Those two deserve each other*, she thinks.

∞∞∞

# XXXVI

## July 1996

When it comes time for the cross examination of Richie Barone, Lincoln Pierce and Helen Vereen return to the Defense table in deference to the lead counsel for the Defense, Phillip Ambrose. Ambrose is a commanding figure. Although he is short and stocky, he moves quickly and speaks decisively. He is well groomed and wears a custom made black suit with a narrow pin striping that somehow makes his physique appear more powerful than portly. His styled dark hair allows him to appear much younger than his true age of fifty-seven.

"Mr. Barone, you testified that you have spent a good deal of your adult life at the maximum security New York State prison in the town of Attica, New York, also known as a supermax facility. Is that correct?"

"If you say so."

"Is that a yes or a no, Mr. Barone? Your answer … not mine … or anyone else's answer for that matter. So what is it? Yes or no?

"Yes."

Ambrose is satisfied.

"In fact, you have been sentenced to reside in this prison after four separate convictions. Ambrose pauses. "…. including crimes committed while you were residing in this prison. Isn't that correct?"

The prosecutor leaps to her feet. Ambrose is waiting for an answer.

"Objection, your Honor. This line of questioning is irrelevant in light of the fact that the State has already acknowledged the witness's incarceration in its pre-trial stipulation. Furthermore, the State made mention of this fact in its opening statement saying that we will be calling a witness to be heard who is currently confined to a prison cell in Attica. Additionally the witness has already testified to the fact that he is currently incarcerated at Attica. And finally ... both the witness and the jury are aware that Mr. Barone has *not* been offered a plea bargain in exchange for his testimony. What possible relevance could there be in rehashing the witness' current and ongoing rehabilitation at the state prison except to unlawfully further prejudice the jury against the defense witness?"

"It goes to motivation, your honor. The witness ..."

Before Defense counsel can deliver his rationale Judge Black bellows: "Counselors please approach the bench."

"I'll get right to the point, so that at least *someone else* will do so. What *is* your point, Mr. Ambrose?" Black was speaking in a very soft voice but the jurors could at least see and sense that the Judge was directing his ire at the counsel for the Defense.

"Your honor, the Defense believes that the true motivation behind the witness's willingness to testify, goes well beyond any potential plea bargain promise. We believe that the witness is looking for his own 15 minutes of fame. We aren't wandering into any uncharted waters, your Honor. As the Prosecution duly noted, the jury is conscious of the witness's past criminal history and his current incarceration. However the experience of the State's counsel would surely lead them to believe, as we do, that an additional sentence on top of the time he has yet to serve would be somewhat non-impactful to the witness. In order for the jury to properly consider whether or not the witness is lying or embellishing his testimony in any way, we deem it critical for the jurors to see the entire motivation for what we believe to be false testimony."

Higney didn't wait for the judge to respond but rather whispered, "And what part of the witness's testimony would you like to impugn at this point?"

"Really Counselor? Do you really have to wait for our cross examination to continue in order to discern that much?"

Judge Black jumped in and halted the whispering spat. "Yes, we do have a jury trial proceeding here. Let's not try it at the bench."

Black looked from one lawyer to the next, ensuring that he was being heard. "I'm inclined to allow the line of questioning to continue. However

## July 1996

fair warning, counselor, if you don't narrow in on this 'additional motivation' quickly, I will cut it off and potentially strike some of the foregoing testimony from the record."

Back in front of the witness and jury, Phillip Ambrose risks further alienation from Judge Black.

"During your lengthy stay at Attica, did you have the opportunity to meet any of the more notorious prisoners, who also called this institution home?"

"You mean famous prisoners? Yeah we had a lot of them."

"Objection your honor."

"Overruled! However, Mr. Ambrose, you are running out of runway. The witness will answer the question."

"Sure Attica is famous for lots of guys, *goin'* way back to the great bank robber Willie Sutton..."

"Your Honor, *pullleeese!*" Higney is once again on her feet.

"The witness shall continue his testimony."

"Of course I *di'nt never* meet Sutton, but I did meet the crazy 'Son of Sam' ... David Berkowitz ... He's been *doin'* time at Attica since the late 70's."

"And there was David Chapman. He smoked the Beatle ... you know ... John Lennon. Chapman's been at Attica ever since ... a real whack job. More recently we got ourselves one Colin Ferguson, the guy who shot up the Long Island Railroad *jus'* for the fun of it. He's *doin'* time for six homicides and he shot couple *a* dozen more. Crazy son of a bitch ..." Barone's face lights up. Then he adds: "Ferguson looks a lot like him. Those guys could be twins." He points at Lincoln Pierce as he speaks. Pierce freezes. He doesn't want to interrupt the flow of his colleague's cross examination.

"These guys are *nutjobs*. *Dat's* why *der* famous. Most of the guys who are in *da* place ... you know why they *done* what they *done*. They ain't famous but they're still dangerous. You *gotta* watch *yer* back."

"Objection, your honor, a little latitude with regard to motive is one thing. An irrelevant treatise on the history of Attica is something else altogether. I'm sure the jury is more eager to hear whatever cross examination of the *facts* of *this case* the Defense wishes to offer. I move to strike the irrelevant history or should I say histrionics."

"Your motion is sustained. Strike all of the testimony about the witness's fellow inmates. The jury should disregard the questions and answers with respect to any and all other prisoners at Attica."

Judge Black then turns toward the Defense counselor and warns him. "However ... as to motive ... one more question, Mr. Ambrose. Make the most of it."

Ambrose has let the witness get away from him ... on purpose. He wanted to show that in a bizarre way the witness is somehow proud of his detention at Attica. However Ambrose isn't particularly happy that his fishing expedition has led Barone to indicate that Ambrose's co-counsel and colleague is a look alike for a mass murderer. The instruction from the bench leaves him no other choice than to throw a Hail Mary pass and hope for a touchdown. He lets it fly.

"So Mr. Barone, please tell us exactly *why* have you chosen to come here voluntarily to admit your guilt in attacking Wayne Johnson and to testify against Mr. Babcock. *Why*?" Ambrose snarls as he poses the question. He wants to do whatever he can to aggravate Barone and allow the jury to see the kind of dangerous and disingenuous character the Prosecution has chosen as its witness.

"The reason I'm here is to see vermin like Babcock get their due. He knows damn well that he's guilty as hell. He *jus'* hires people like us ... me and Mazzini ... to do his dirty work. He should be in Attica with the rest of us. He's no different than Chapman or Berkowitz. He's a killer."

"Do you hate Mr. Babcock?"

"Yes. He's scum."

"Mr. Barone, have you ever met Frank Babcock?"

"No."

"Did Tony Mazzini ever tell you that Frank Babcock hired him to hire you?"

"No, not exactly ... other than that one time he slipped up. I *tole* you dat.

"Mr. Barone, did Tony Mazzini ever tell you explicitly to kill Wayne Johnson?"

"No."

"So then, Mr. Barone is it your testimony that neither Tony Mazzini nor Frank Babcock ever told you directly to kill Wayne Johnson."

Barone looked a little puzzled at the fact that he was somehow now denying that he was directly instructed to commit the murder. "Yes, I think that's right. I was just *'sposed* to rough him up. I think that was the plan. If I killed him ... so what."

## July 1996

"Mr. Barone, did Tony Mazzini recruit Malcom Johnson to work with you in your assault on Wayne Johnson?"

"No, I got MJ myself."

"To the best of your knowledge did Malcolm Johnson ... I believe you are referring to him as MJ ... did MJ ever meet Tony Mazzini?"

"No, he never met Tony."

"Can we assume then that Malcolm Johnson ... MJ ... never met Frank Babcock?"

"You can assume whatever you want to assume."

"Let me rephrase my question. To the best of your knowledge did Malcom Johnson ever meet Frank Babcock?"

"No, that didn't happen."

"Can you therefore state that Frank Babcock never instructed *Malcolm* Johnson to kill or harm *Wayne* Johnson in any way?"

"Objection your honor. Counsel is merely badgering the witness to assert something he could not possibly know. The witness has already testified that he believes that Malcolm Johnson never met Frank Babcock."

"Withdraw the question, your Honor."

Judge Black appears to be somewhat disinterested or distracted. Without commenting on the objection, he simply instructs the jury to ignore the Defense's last question to this witness. Of course everyone involved realizes that the jury doesn't truly *unhear* things that have been said. To give this a little more time to sink in, Ambrose shuffles his paperwork as though he is searching for something that he needs to proceed with his cross examination. After about 30 to 45 seconds, he looks up from his papers and then readdresses the witness.

"Now then Mr. Barone, let's turn to your testimony about your altercation with the deceased Mr. Wayne Johnson. It is your contention that you knew that Wayne Johnson was not dead when you escaped from the crime scene. Is that correct?"

"Yes ... well I wasn't sure. But I thought he was probably still alive."

"And you have also testified that it was never your intention to kill Wayne Johnson in the first place. Is that also correct."

"Yes."

"And that you personally were never given instructions by Mr. Mazzini to kill Mr. Johnson ... correct?

"Yes, right."

"You testified earlier that you only learned of the death of Wayne Johnson when you heard about it on a radio news report. Is that correct?"

"I already said *dat*."

"At that time were you worried about what the police might find at the murder scene? Were you worried about what they might find out in one manner or another?"

"I was glad he was dead. Dead men don't talk. Same with MJ. I knew that if he was dead, he couldn't say *nuthin'*. But yeah, I was a little worried at least for the first couple of days ... ah maybe a week or so. But when I never heard *nuthin'* from the police after a couple of weeks, I figured, I was in the clear."

Ambrose begins to shuffle his notes again, giving the jury time to digest the testimony they have just heard. He doesn't want to rush their thought processes.

"You also testified that you had very little contact with Tony Mazzini immediately after Wayne Johnson's death. Correct?

"Yes."

"Who initiated this first contact after the incident?"

"Mazzini."

"Why?"

"I *di'nt* know why he wanted to talk to me, but I *di'nt* want to talk to him for *no* reason. He paid me in full and in advance for roughing up Johnson. I was pretty sure he wasn't *goin'* to pay me any extra *jus' 'cause* I killed *'im*."

"How about Malcolm Johnson? Did you pay him his share in advance?"

"MJ *di'nt* have *no* share."

"What do you mean by that?"

"Well, I *jus'* face-tempted his manhood to *he'p* me out *wit'* roughing up Johnson. I never promised MJ *no* specific payment for his help. He *jus'* knew that if he *he'ped* me out, that I'd take care *o* him. Besides I *jus'* met MJ during the last year that I was in Attica ... the first time that is ..."

"You are referring to your first period of incarceration at Attica?"

"Yes."

Ambrose proceeds to then take Barone through a number of questions about how he met with Tony Mazzini and how they plotted the attack on Wayne Johnson. He said it all came about in less than three days. He knew that Mazzini was an ex-cop who ran some kind of security business.

## July 1996

It was Barone's contention that Mazzini had been grooming him to help out and he had no idea how long Mazzini had been planning the attack.

Most of this questioning was merely meant to reinforce the fact that things happened very fast for Barone after he was originally released from prison, and there was no time for an extended plot or conspiracy to have taken place. The interrogatories also continue to underline that Barone was supposed to intimidate Wayne Johnson but not to kill him. Then just as the questioning seems to be getting overly repetitive and almost monotonous, Ambrose attempts to lead the witness into a quick repudiation of the conspiracy charge.

"So then, Mr. Barone would it be accurate to say that Mazzini never paid you to *kill* Wayne Johnson?"

"Objection, your Honor, the felony murder doctrine specifically states that even an unintentional death occurring in the commission of a felony is still regarded as murder."

"Overruled. The State should recognize that these points of law will be addressed when the bench charges the jury. Right now we are simply looking to discern the factual evidence of the case on hand. I'll allow the question.

Barone waits for Ambrose to re-ask the question.

"Yes or no, Mr. Barone. Did Tony Mazzini pay you *to kill* Wayne Johnson?" He stresses the infinitive.

"No."

Higney is very satisfied with the judicial temperament of Judge Black. Even though Black properly overruled the prosecutor's objection, she was able to infer that the Defense might be conceding the fact that Mazzini did attack Wayne Johnson. The other satisfying part of Black's remarks was that he indicated that he did in fact intend to charge the jury at a later time, and therefore did not appear to be entertaining a directed verdict at this point in the trial. Obviously there was still a lot of testimony to be heard, but this was certainly a positive sign.

Ambrose decides to move on. He decides to skip past discussions that Barone had with Mazzini following the death of Wayne Johnson. The Prosecution had already pressed Barone on these discussions.

"Alright now. Let's leap ahead a number of years. So when did the NYPD first question you about the murder of Wayne Johnson?"

"It's like I said to the lady *befaw* ... "

"To the prosecutor, Ms. Higney?"

"Yes to *dat* lady *dere*." He points at Higney. "Like I said to her *befaw*, I first started *talkin'* to the cops about this a long time ago. *Nuthin'* much happened, until a few years ago ... in late 1994 ... I heard from the cops again because *'parently* someone called *dem outa* the blue and told them that Babcock had confessed. At first I didn't know who this Babcock guy was, but then I *jus'* started *piecin'* it all *togetha*."

"So at that time you didn't know who Babcock was?"

"Dat's what I said yeah."

"You had never even heard of Babcock before?"

"Befaw that? Nope."

"But Mr. Barone earlier today ... on direct testimony ... you indicated that one time in 1980, you heard Mazzini 'slip up' ... I think your words were ... and refer to your benefactor not as the 'Mystery Man' but as Babcock. Are we now to believe that from this one hypothetical 'slip up' in 1980 until the police asked you to resurrect your phantom confession in prison in 1994 that you remembered the name of the defendant?"

"*Dat's* what I'm *sayin'* yeah."

"Oooookay then, let's move on." Ambrose drags out his affirmation word to demonstrate that he finds the witness's testimony on this topic less than credible. He emphasizes his incredulity with a subtle head shake. Meanwhile Helen Vereen keeps her eyes on the jury and notices their rapt attention.

Ambrose is a master of timing. He doesn't rush. He simply walks back and forth as though he is trying to find something in his notes while the jury ponders Barone's statement. Finally he moves back in front of the witness and continues his cross.

"Oh, yes. Just a few more questions, Mr. Barone ... In your testimony about *teaching Wayne Johnson a lesson* you indicated that you knocked out one of the victim's teeth. You also said that you used gloves with brass knuckles to do this. Is that correct?

"Yes."

"The Prosecution has not presented any fingerprint evidence in this crime. Is that because you were careful enough to use gloves?"

"I guess so."

"Then how was your DNA recovered from the victim's mouth and broken tooth?"

## *July 1996*

Barone simply shrugs as if to say, *how would I know?* Ambrose accepts the nonverbal answer before Judge Black can instruct the witness to put words to his opinion.

"No further questions, Your Honor."

∞∞∞

# XXXVII

## Early August 1996

"The State calls Simone Muirchant."

Every eye in the courtroom is glued to the figure of the tall attractive middle aged woman who is now approaching the witness stand. The focus on Simone could not have been more intensified if she were walking amidst spotlights on a fashion show runway. Every eye follows every step until she is asked to raise her right hand and gets sworn in. They are all about to hear from the woman who has had sexual relations with both the defendant and the departed. Everyone is expecting the testimony to be riveting. They know they won't be disappointed.

"Ms. Muirchant, Are you currently married?"

"Yes I am married to Jeff Levine, and we live in San Francisco."

"And how long have you and Mr. Levine been married?"

"We were married three years ago this past March."

"So March of 1993?"

"Yes."

"And were you ever married before your marriage to Mr. Levine?"

"I was married two times before ... both times to Frank Babcock."

"And when did those marriages take place? Ah ... let me restate my question ... Can you tell the court, for what period of time you were married to Mr. Babcock on each of these occasions?"

"We were originally married in October of 1965 and we divorced in October of 1970. We were remarried in October of 1975 and then we were divorced a second time in February of 1981. But we were separated a good deal of the time during both marriages."

## Early August 1996

"And these three marriages are the only marriages you have had?"

"Yes."

"Can you tell the court how many biological children you have had and when you had those children?"

"I have had two children. Foxy was born in March of 1966 and Maureen was born in 1967 ... in May."

"So both of your children were born during your first marriage to the defendant, Frank Babcock?"

"Yes."

"Were both of your children Frank Babcock's biological children?"

"No. Maureen was Frank's child. I was pregnant with Foxy ...eh ... Fox, when Frank and I got married the first time. But I was pregnant with another man's child."

"And did you tell the defendant about this other man?"

"No, not when we were first married."

"So you allowed the defendant to believe that Francis X Babcock Jr, or Fox, or Foxy Babcock as you have referred to him, was his biological child. Is that correct?"

"Yes, but I wasn't sure whether or not he was the father at the time. He could very well have been the father ... that is to say that there was a possibility that he was the father."

"And just how many other *possibilities* were there? How many other men could possibly have been Fox Babcock's father according to your estimation?"

"It was possible that either of two other men could have been the father."

"So three altogether?"

"Yes."

"Could you tell the court who the other two prospective fathers might have been?"

"During the period nine months prior to Fox's birth I had had sexual relationships with three men, Frank Babcock, Wayne Johnson and Mickey Johnson."

"And did each of these men know about one another?"

"At that time no. Frank did not know about either of the Johnsons and Wayne and Mickey didn't know about each other. Both Wayne and

Mickey *did* know that I was engaged to Frank. They *did* know that I was having sex with the man who was my fiancé at the time."

"With Frank Babcock?"

"Yes."

"I see." Máire Higney pauses long enough in her interrogation of the witness to allow Simone's testimony to sink in with the jurors. She turns around and walks back toward the Prosecution desk and picks up an index card and reads something from it quickly and puts it back down. It's all simple theatrics. She just doesn't want to gloss over any of the testimony that might suggest a distinct motive for the defendant. After she regroups she approaches the witness once again but stays far enough away so that Simone Muirchant can be seen clearly by all of the jurors.

"And so, at some point in time did you come to realize that Frank Babcock was not the biological father of Fox Babcock? And if so can you tell us in your own words how you discovered this fact."

"Yes. Wayne Johnson took a blood test and he told me that it showed that he was the father."

"When was that?"

"It was shortly after Foxy ... that's what we called him then ... was born. Maybe the following January or February."

"So then you were still seeing Wayne Johnson at that time?"

"For a little while. Remember we had the testing stuff to coordinate, and we were still friendly."

"Were you still having a sexual relationship with Wayne Johnson?"

"Not right after I got married to Frank. But we talked regularly. Wayne wanted to know how Foxy was doing. Frank and I separated for a while soon after Maureen was born and for a brief time during the separation I renewed the sexual part of the relationship with Wayne. But that all ended in 1968 ... the sex part that is."

"Why did it end?"

"His wife found out? I guess that's why."

"So your sexual affair with Wayne Johnson ended 12 years before he was brutally murdered?"

"Yes."

"When did Frank Babcock find out about your affair with Wayne Johnson?"

## *Early August 1996*

"I'm not sure exactly. I do know that he had his security people following me around, almost from the first time we separated in 1968."

"So technically he *could* have known about Wayne Johnson for quite some time before he took any action?"

"Objection Your Honor. Totally inappropriate. There is *no* evidence that Mr. Babcock *ever* took *any* action of *any* kind whatsoever ... with respect to anything he *may* or *may not* have known about Ms. Muirchant's relationship with the deceased, Mr. Johnson. The witness has already testified that she didn't know what Mr. Babcock knew and when he might have known it. So whether that was a declaration or a question from the Prosecution ... it was unsuitable either way. I move to strike this entire line of questioning as rank hearsay."

Judge Black listens and then casually says, "Strike the last query. The witness will not answer the question. And, Ms. Higney, I would hope that you will soon be moving to the time of the murder. After all, even *that* day is now nearly 16 years in the past."

"Your Honor, our intention is to demonstrate intent to do harm on the part of the defendant. This background is necessary in that intent."

"Then let's get on with it. But let's steer clear of premature attempts to draw conclusions and stick to the facts of the case. You will have an opportunity to present your summary to the jury at the appropriate juncture. Move on."

Higney is aware that eventually Simone did confront Babcock with the fact that Wayne Johnson was Fox Babcock's father. However that confrontation took place *after* the murder, so it isn't helpful. Higney wants to save the testimony about Babcock's confession until a little later to ensure the maximum impact. For now she decides to bridge to Simone's relationship with Mickey Johnson.

"So then, Ms. Muirchant, you have testified that you also had a sexual relationship with Mr. Michael Johnson, the man you referred to as Mickey Johnson. Is that correct?"

"Yes."

"Is Mickey Johnson in the court room here today?"

"Yes. He is seated right over there." She nods toward him sheepishly. Mickey stares ahead stoically. Syd Johnson looks embarrassed by everything, and simply clutches her husband's arm.

"Please tell us the time frames ... the date parameters if you will ... with respect to *this* relationship." Clearly Higney is insinuating that Simone has a rather promiscuous history. However she still needs to have the jury believe Simone's testimony. Higney knows that the Defense will try to make her look like a liar. So Higney's insinuations are simply a way to let a little air out of the Defense balloon before the cross examination takes place. It's a delicate balance to strike.

"Originally it lasted for several months in the spring and summer of 1965. Then Mickey left for Vietnam and I didn't see him again until January of 1969. I only talked to him once or twice after he came home from the war, until the summer of 1974."

"And what happened then, in 1974?"

"We renewed our relationship."

"Sexually."

"Yes sexually and ... er yes sexually."

"Was there something else?

"No. We renewed our sexual relationship for a few months before I went back to living with Frank."

"And then a year later you remarried the defendant?"

"Yes."

"Did Frank Babcock know about your affair with Mickey Johnson?"

"It wasn't an affair. Neither Mickey nor I were married at the time. But yes I believe Frank knew about it. I think his people were still following me, and there was a certain intensity to our relationship for a few months."

"Do you want to explain that in more detail?"

"We saw a lot of each other ... frequently more than once a day ... in the city and on Long island ... usually in hotels."

"You mean that you frequently had sex more than once a day. Is that what you meant by 'a certain intensity?' "

"Yes."

"And you believe that Frank Babcock knew about this?"

"That's what I believe, yes"

"Ms. Muirchant, I recognize that you have previously given us the time frame for your second divorce from the defendant, but would it be accurate to say that although that was five years after your second marriage, the marriage was not harmonious during most of those five years."

"You would have to define what you mean by harmonious."

## *Early August 1996*

"Did you live in the same household ... under the same roof with your husband and your children throughout that five year period?"

"No, I lived at *Babcock Manor* for about a year and then I moved into my own flat in Manhattan. The children lived with Frank and I took them into the city on a regular basis to spend weekends with me."

"Were you engaging in marital relations ... sexual relations ... with the defendant during the period after you moved out of *Babcock Manor* up through the period of Wayne Johnson's death?"

"No, not after I moved out. No I was not ... we were not ...eh ... we didn't."

"Did you have a sexual relationship with either Wayne Johnson or Mickey Johnson during this timeframe?"

"No, that was completely over prior to my second marriage to Frank."

"You mean the sexual part of the relationship?"

"Yes."

"But you still had some kind of a relationship with the Johnsons. Is that right.

"Yes."

"Will you explain these relationships to the court?"

"At this time, in fact from the time shortly after my son's birth in 1966 up until 1981, I believed that Wayne Johnson was Foxy's father. Wayne believed this also. In fact he went to his grave believing Fox was his son. But Frank didn't know this at that time. He believed that my affairs with Mickey Johnson and Wayne Johnson both took place *after* we were first married. He did not know that these affairs dated back to 1965.

"Anyway, Wayne stayed in touch with me regularly until just before he died, because he always wanted to know how his son was ... or at least the person he thought was his son ... you know Fox ... was doing."

"And would you tell the court when you finally learned the truth about Fox Babcock's paternity?"

"Around April of 1981, I learned that Mickey Johnson was Fox's father."

"This was ten months after the murder of Wayne Johnson. And for 15 years prior to that time it had always been your belief that Wayne Johnson ... not Mickey Johnson ... was Fox's father. Is that correct?"

"Yes."

Higney let that fact settle in. She avoided asking questions about Frank Babcock's beliefs during this time frame, and she simply allowed the jury to assume that the defendant's knowledge and beliefs would be somewhat similar. And she knew that the Defense would not allow Babcock to testify about what his actual beliefs may have been.

"Let's move ahead a bit then. We would like the jury to understand some of the facts of your relationship with the defendant. You both suffered a common tragedy with respect to your other child, who died from disease in July of 1982. Although that tragedy is now well over a decade in the past we do extend our sympathies. There could be no greater suffering in life than the death of a child."

She pauses for a moment.

"We also understand that following the death of your daughter, you spent a significant period of time in India working with the poor and indigent people of that country. Is that correct?"

"Objection your Honor. We might understand a little latitude for background purposes, but almost all of this testimony is totally irrelevant to the facts of this case. This was well after the time of Wayne Johnson's death."

"We are establishing the character of our witness, your honor. The jury will be called upon to evaluate her testimony on substantive issues. They deserve to know a little about her background as well as the background of the relationship between the witness and the defendant.

"I'll allow the testimony but move along more directly to the evidence in the case please Ms. Higney."

"After your time in India, did you at some point establish a business relationship with your ex-husband?"

"Yes. Frank invested in MBF."

"MBF?"

"Yes, MBF Digital Haven & Harbor.... That's the company that my partners and I established late in 1989. Frank became an early angel investor in our company, three months later."

"And so as a result of this business relationship did you have occasion to have dinner with you ex-husband during August of 1991?"

"Yes we had dinner in New York City at Ecco Restaurant in the lower Tribeca area of Manhattan."

## Early August 1996

"And did you discuss your ex-husband's investment in great detail at that time?"

"No. Truthfully very little business was discussed at all."

"Can you tell us what was discussed?"

"Mostly personal stuff. Frank wanted to discuss what happened to Wayne Johnson."

"Were you surprised by this?"

"Yes, certainly, I was very surprised. I thought that he wanted to talk about MBF."

"So when did you realize that Frank wanted to talk about the murder of Wayne Johnson rather than the financing for your company?"

"Shortly after we got there."

"And what did you do when you realized that your dinner conversation was heading in this direction?"

"I excused myself for a few minutes and went to the ladies room to gather my wits about me and to gain some emotional control. I also turned on my handheld recorder and left it in the record mode when I returned to the table."

"Do you always carry this recorder with you?"

"Yes, almost always ... I usually use it for personal dictation."

"So then you recorded your conversation with the defendant?"

"Yes I did ... most of it anyway"

"And did the defendant confess to playing a part in the murder of your ex-lover, Wayne Johnson?"

"Sort of, but not really. Frank told me that he had arranged to have Wayne 'taught a lesson.' I think that's how he put it."

"And did the defendant tell you who he hired to assault Wayne Johnson?"

"He told me that one of his security guys, Tony Mazzini, hired two men who were ex-convicts."

"Do you recall the names of these criminals?"

"Richie Barone and Malcolm Johnson."

"I see. Now, Ms. Muirchant ... Wayne Johnson's murder took place 16 years ago, and the dinner conversation that you had with the defendant took place nearly five years ago. It might seem odd to the jury that you can recall the names of these assailants so readily after so much time has expired. Can you tell the jury how exactly you are able to recall these names?"

"As I said, I taped ..."

"Objection your Honor." Phillip Ambrose was on his feet immediately in an effort to protect his client. His associate Helen Vereen carefully observed each juror's reaction. "The testimony that the State is trying to elicit includes an unsubstantiated claim that ..."

"Overruled. Counsel please approach the bench."

"This issue has already been decided. The witness is testifying to a confession that she has heard directly. The fact that she is also stating that she taped this confession is part of her testimony. The State also intends to present evidence that another witness has also listened to the same tape. Mr. Ambrose you will have ample opportunity to cross examine these witnesses about the whereabouts of the actual tape, and I'm sure that the State fully expects you to do so. Ms. Higney, please proceed with the questioning of the witness."

Ambrose is certain that this is a flawed ruling on the part of Judge Black. He thinks that at a minimum it could provide a basis for an appeal.

The lawyers all return to their previous positions and Higney asks her question once again.

"Ms. Muirchant, you were in the process of telling us how you were able to recall the names of the men who had beaten Wayne Johnson to death?"

"Objection."

"Sustained, strike the question. The Prosecution will refrain from drawing conclusions while making its inquiries."

"Ms. Muirchant, you were about to tell us how you were able to recall the names of Richie Barone, Malcolm Johnson and Tony Mazzini, so long after your dinner with the defendant ... the dinner at which you have testified that the defendant confessed to hiring these men to 'teach Wayne Johnson a lesson.' Would you please complete your answer to this question?"

"I remember the names because I heard them many times when I replayed the tape of my conversation with Frank."

"So, again to be absolutely clear, you are testifying that you taped Frank Babcock's confession to you at the Ecco Restaurant in August of 1991?"

## Early August 1996

"Yes."

"Did the defendant know that you were taping your conversation?"

"No. He did not."

"Did you tell anyone else about this recording?"

"Not for a long time, but I eventually told a business colleague of mine, Betty Barrymore."

"Did you actually play this tape for Ms. Barrymore?"

"Yes."

"When and where did you play the tape for her?"

"It was August of 1994. I told Betty about the tape when we went to a concert together in New York, but I didn't play it for her until we returned to California a week or so later."

"And what was Ms. Barrymore's reaction to this tape."

"She said I should make a copy and then take the tape to the police department."

"And did you do so?"

"No. I didn't do either of these things."

"Then how did the police department learn about the tape?"

"I assume that Betty told them."

"Had you ever told anyone else about the tape *before* you disclosed it to Ms. Barrymore?"

"No I didn't."

"Have you disclosed the tape to anyone else *since* you told Ms. Barrymore?"

"Well yes, I have discussed this several times with police investigators over the past year and a half."

Simone is now getting antsy about disclosing the only other person who may have heard the tape. She wants to be very careful about her choice of words. She doesn't want to commit a crime herself by lying under oath.

"Let's disregard the police for a moment. Let me ask you this. Have you ever played the tape for any other person or persons – besides Ms. Barrymore?"

"No. I only played it for Betty."

The actual question and answer are ironically very satisfying to both Máire Higney and to Simone Muirchant. Higney is satisfied that she has given the jury the impression with that the police have at least heard the tape at some point, which they have not. Simone is happy because she doesn't have

311

to disclose the fact that Fox Babcock has probably heard the tape, even though she didn't technically *play* it for him. More than anything she does not want her son dragged into this sordid trial.

"So did Ms. Barrymore ever confirm for you that she had told the police about the tape?"

"No, in fact she denied it."

"So where is this tape at this time?"

"I don't know. And if Betty didn't tell the police about the tape then I don't know who did."

"So was it your intention to keep this tape to yourself forever? You have just stated that you concealed it for three years."

"I'm not sure. I don't know what I would have done eventually. I guess I never came to a decision about some things. I didn't want to testify in this trial, but my lawyers have advised me that I have to obey the subpoena."

"Did you ever tell Frank Babcock that you taped his confession?"

"No, in fact I have only talked to Frank Babcock once since the dinner at Ecco. It was in Pittsburgh in August of 1992. It was at Fox and Evelyn's wedding."

"And at that time you did *not* tell the defendant about the tape?"

"Correct. We *did not* discuss our dinner conversation at Ecco at all. We didn't talk much about anything other than Fox and Evelyn and how happy we wanted them to be."

"Okay, let's talk about Fox, then. Did you ever acknowledge taping your ex-husband's confession to your son, Fox Babcock? Did you ever actually play this tape for Fox to hear?"

"No, I never played the tape for him. After the indictment we talked about the Ecco dinner conversation but not about the tape."

"What was his reaction?"

"He was disappointed. I assumed he was shocked. I mean ... I was telling him that the man he treats as his father ordered his genetic grandfather to be attacked. He was also hearing this from his mother. Fox never did anything to deserve any of this. And I feel horrible for whatever shame or anguish this trial has brought to him."

Simone has realized for some time that she was likely to be asked this question. She is able to answer it without perjuring herself. This is gratifying because she doesn't want to have Fox dragged into the case. The

## Early August 1996

judge has already ruled in pretrial hearings that only Simone would be able to testify as to the content of the tape. She had actually heard the confession first hand as she was taping it. However the tape is not now available to be placed into evidence. Therefore Judge Black has ruled that the testimony of anyone else who may or may not have heard the tape would be regarded as hearsay and therefore disallowed.

"Did Fox have any advice for you regarding how you should handle yourself at this trial?"

"He just told me to tell the truth, that he was tired of all the lies. He said he felt like he has been living someone else's lies since the day he was born."

"Did you take that to mean that Fox wanted you to testify that his step-father ordered the killing of Wayne Johnson?"

"I believe that he just wanted me to tell what I knew."

"And because you heard Frank confess to this crime, you knew that he had ordered the killing of Wayne Johnson. Is that right?"

Just as Ambrose jumps up to make an objection, Simone answers the question in a way that favors the Defense.

"No, that's not right. I don't believe that Frank ever intended to kill Wayne. In fact I know he didn't. That's not who Frank is. He may have wanted to rough up Wayne but he certainly didn't want him killed. And that's what he told me at the Ecco dinner; that's what's on the tape and that's what I believe."

"Order in the court. Order in the court." Judge Black bangs his gavel as the murmur level in the gallery begins to crescendo. Although Simone is technically the State's witness, her last answer is devastating to the Prosecution. Higney waits until there is silence in the gallery again and then continues in an even tempered manner.

"And so, where is this tape at right now and why isn't it available for this trial?"

"As I answered before, I don't know." Simone is perspiring as she pushes her hair back away from her face. "I don't know the answer to either of those questions."

"When was the last time you physically saw the tape?"

"I can't remember that exact date. However I remember the first day I knew it was gone. That was Valentine's Day last year."

"February 14th, 1995?"

"Correct."

"So how did you come to realize that the tape was missing?"

"I always kept it in the bottom drawer of my dresser, buried under some clothing that I wore infrequently." I had a red top in that drawer also and when I went to get that top to wear on Valentine's Day for dinner, I noticed that the tape was gone."

"Who had access to that drawer besides yourself?"

"No one. This was my home." She hesitates and adds, "I guess you could say that my husband Jeff would technically also have access, but Jeff never goes through my things and he didn't even know about the tape. He has his own room in the house."

Jeff is looking on from the back of the courtroom, He wants to tell his wife that she is offering "TMI – too much information." He is reddening as he wonders what others may think about his relationship with his wife. He shouldn't care. But he does. It's just his way.

"Was there ever any indication that your home was broken into?"

"No, nothing like that."

"Do you have guests over frequently?"

"The normal amount for any couple I would say. Jeff has a card game occasionally with friends. I sometimes have had some of my students stop by. Nothing out of the ordinary."

"If you had to venture a guess as to what happened to your tape, what would you say?"

"I just don't know. That's what I *would* say and that's what I *am* saying."

When Simone has completed her testimony for the Prosecution it is very late in the day ... actually early evening. The Defense has agreed to begin their cross examination the following morning.

∞∞∞

# XXXVIII

## August 1996

The Defense begins the cross-examination of Simone Muirchant. Lead attorney Phillip Ambrose is handling the questions.

"Good morning, Ms. Muirchant."

"Good morning."

"You know, after listening to your description of your marriages to the defendant yesterday, I thought that it might be prudent to begin by asking one very simple and straight forward question. He makes this statement in a loud voice but then asks the question softly. "Did you ever actually love, Frank?"

It's a loaded question to level at the witness at the outset, but Ambrose is looking to subtly establish some ground rules. He wants the witness to think before she answers his questions. And so she does – for about 10 long seconds.

"No. I don't think I ever did."

Ambrose is thrilled with Simone's response but he doesn't follow up directly at this point. Instead he merely pauses for effect and then goes after the facts.

"You have testified that you twice married Frank Babcock ... and twice left him. Estimating by your previous testimony, I have calculated that during the fifteen year span of time that encompassed these two marriages, you were actually married for approximately 11 years. Is that right?'

"Yes, but we were often separated during those 11 years that you calculated."

"And during these periods of separation ... those within the marriage and those periods when you were legally divorced ... did Mr. Babcock leave you or did you leave him?"

"I left him."

"And the children?"

"Foxy and Maureen always lived with Frank, but they visited with me quite frequently."

"I see. So on all of these occasions of separation and divorce it was you who walked out ... on Frank ..." Ambrose again pauses for effect but never takes his eyes off Simone. "... and on your children."

"Yes, but I would say ..." She stops herself and returns to a single word reply, "Yes."

"And at any time during this 15 year time span, including both marriages and your time living apart from your husband and children, was Frank Babcock ever violent with you or with his children?"

"No, never."

"Not even once?"

"No, Frank is not a violent person by nature."

"During the time of your marriages to the defendant, did Mr. Babcock ever physically *threaten* you or your children?"

"No. He was never violent with me and never threatened any physical violence."

Ambrose walks back to his desk. He allows this testimony to sink in before he continues this vein of inquiry.

"Now Ms. Muirchant, another fifteen or so years have passed since your second divorce from Frank Babcock. However you have maintained a more or less sporadic but continuous relationship with him throughout that period of time. And that relationship is both personal and professional. Is that a fair statement?"

"I guess it is. The personal part of our relationship is strictly as it involves my son, Fox."

"And this relationship has endured even though for the vast majority of this time you have lived in California with the exception of the two years that you lived and worked in India. Is that also true."

"Yes."

"Now allow me to ask a similar question to the one I previously asked you, but I am simply changing the timeframe. During the time since the *end*

## August 1996

of your marriages to Frank Babcock ... basically the most recent 15 years ... during this time ... has the defendant ever been violent toward you or either of your children?"

"No."

"Did he ever threaten physical violence toward you or your children?"

"No."

"So then is it fair to say that over the past thirty some odd years that you have known Frank Babcock, he has never – ever – committed any violent act toward you or your children and that he has never even threatened an act of violence?"

"Yes, that's fair."

"So then do you believe that Frank Babcock ordered anyone to kill Wayne Johnson?"

"Not to kill him ... no."

"In this so called confession ... the one which was supposedly taped ... but we can't find the tape ... in this so called confession, did Frank Babcock tell you that he ordered Wayne Johnson to be *killed*?"

"No."

"But you have testified that you believe that Mr. Babcock ordered Wayne Johnson to be 'roughed up.' Is that it?"

"Yes, I think so."

"Did Mr. Babcock actually tell you that he ordered someone to 'rough up' Wayne Johnson?"

"Not in those exact words."

"Yes, I think your testimony was that Mr. Babcock told you that he wanted Wayne Johnson to be 'taught a lesson.' I think those were the words you used. Is that right?"

"Yes."

"And you have also testified that the defendant never physically harmed you or even physically intimidated you. Is that also correct?"

"Yes."

"Then isn't it possible that when the non-violent Mr. Babcock told you that he wanted Wayne Johnson to be 'taught a lesson' it could very well have been a non-violent lesson that he wanted imparted?"

"I don't know. I guess it's possible, but that's not what happened."

"Yes, sadly that's why we're all here today, sixteen years after the tragic murder of Wayne Johnson." Ambrose pauses long enough for that to settle in and then suggests an alternative possibility.

"If we are to believe Mr. Barone's testimony … he was hired by an ex-police officer to kill another police officer." Another pause is allowed as Ambrose hopes the jury will be speculating along with him. "But you knew the victim. He was your former lover … or at least one of your former lovers …isn't it possible that Wayne Johnson had other enemies besides Mr. Babcock?"

"I don't know. Wayne never mentioned anyone like that to me."

"Isn't it probable that in the line of his police duties, Wayne Johnson might have incited the ire of a different person or persons with either a criminal history or a criminal intent?"

"Certainly that's possible, but I only know what Frank told me about what happened with Wayne. I don't know about any other possibilities and Wayne never mentioned any to me."

"Objection your honor." Máire Higney appears truly angry, but she allows Simone to answer before raising her objection. The tactic seems to work.

"Counsel is speculating not cross examining the witness. Outrageously he is offering his own unsubstantiated version of an alternative killer. There is nothing in the record to suggest that anyone other than Frank Babcock and his co-conspirators had anything whatsoever to do with the murder of Wayne Johnson."

"Sustained. Mr. Ambrose would you restate your question to the witness without leading her to any uncorroborated or speculative places. The trial of this defendant will be decided on the jury's interpretation of the facts as presented, not on any hypotheticals. The jury will disregard the last question from the Defense and the answer given by the witness and both shall be stricken from the court record."

Ambrose doesn't mind this mild judicial rebuke. His colleague, Lincoln Pierce had already hinted at these possibilities when cross examining the State's NYPD witnesses earlier in the trial. The Prosecution didn't react at that time because of the inherent weakness of the testimony supporting an investigation that had evolved and diverged from its original conclusions. However the testimony of Frank Babcock's ex-wife is much more crucial to the trial. Therefore Máire Higney is disinclined to allow the Defense's

## *August 1996*

"alternative killer" theories to develop any roots whatsoever. Ambrose is satisfied that he is able to at least resurface this thought process.

"Alright then, Ms. Muirchant, I want to move on to another line of questioning. I'd like to skip ahead to your testimony about the Ecco dinner in 1991."

Judge Black interrupts Ambrose and says, "Counselor, we have been going for quite some time now without a break. Would this be a good time for a short recess without interrupting your examination of the witness?"

"Yes."

All are in agreement and the judge orders a twenty minute recess. There are at least seven members of the press in the room who are also eager to get word back to their respective news outlets. The progress of the trial has received gavel to gavel coverage in the New York area for the last several days. It has also garnered a good deal of attention in news outlets throughout the country and even internationally. It is the most sensational trial since the Simpson acquittal.

There are also many in the courtroom who need a hygiene break and immediately head in the direction of the restrooms. Simone has no such urge. She merely steps down from the witness chair and stretches her legs. She takes a few deep breaths and thinks about Fox. She believes that she is doing exactly what he asked her to do: to tell the truth.

∞∞∞

Almost exactly twenty minutes later Ambrose resumes his cross examination of The State's witness.

"So Ms. Muirchant, I know we are moving quite some time into the future from the time period that we were discussing prior to the break. But I would like to at least keep to the topical thread of your relationship with your ex-husband who is the defendant in this trial."

"Okay."

"So before we move to some clarifying questions about the Ecco dinner in 1991, I would like to ask a few brief questions about an engagement party that you hosted for your son and daughter-in-law in October of 1989."

"Objection, your Honor. What is the relevance, here? This is beyond the scope of the direct examination. There has been no previous testimony about events that occurred in 1989."

"Your Honor my questions here will be very brief and to the point. They are relevant. They help characterize the relationship between the defendant and his ex-wife. The Prosecution has relied upon this relationship heavily in trying to *create* motive both in the testimony of this witness and prior witnesses."

"Overruled. However, the Defense will quickly focus its questions to its stated purpose."

"Did you arrange an engagement party for your son in October of 1989 at which the defendant was present?"

"Yes. But that was the night of the earthquake."

"The Loma Prieta Earthquake?"

"Yes, most people call it the San Francisco earthquake."

"And who were the invitees to this engagement party."

"It was supposed to be a small dinner party. Frank and his previous wife Diane were invited ... "That would be Diane Heath-Babcock?"

"Yes but Diane didn't show up. Fox and Evelyn were of course going to be the Guests of Honor, but the earthquake hit before they arrived."

Simone pauses reflectively and then adds, "Mickey and Syd Johnson were also invited and they did arrive ... as did Frank ... before the earthquake hit."

"Did you have a personal guest ... or date of some sort? Was the dinner intended to be for four couples?" Ambrose asked the question as though he truly didn't know the answer.

"No, I didn't want to complicate things by inviting anyone else. I was comfortable with that. It was only supposed to be seven of us."

"But it turned out to be just the four of you ... the Johnsons and you and Mr. Babcock. Is that right?"

"Yes, as I said Fox and Evelyn were on their way to my home when the earthquake hit."

"Alright then ... were you or any of your guests injured in the course of the earthquake?"

"Frank had a heart attack, almost exactly as the quake hit. My home was pretty much destroyed, but thanks to Mickey and Syd, we were all able to get my car passed my twisted garage door and drive Frank to the emergency room at the hospital."

"So then you and the Johnsons actually saved the defendant's life?"

## August 1996

"Objection. The witness is not a medical expert. She is not qualified to make any such determination. And this whole line of questioning has no relevance whatsoever to the ..." Higney is perplexed. She knows she should have objected more strenuously. It was a mistake but not a devastating one. Now she just wants to slow things down.

"Sustained. The jury will disregard the last question."

"That's all I have on that topic then for you, Ms. Muirchant. Let's move on to a few last questions about your dinner in 1991 ... that would be about two years after you and the Johnsons heroically drove the defendant to the hospital following his heart attack."

∞∞∞

The point is not lost on the jury. Regardless of whether or not Simone and the Johnsons had actually saved Frank Babcock's life, there was definitely a caring relationship among the Johnson and Babcock families at the time of the engagement party. And this was nine years after Wayne Johnson had been murdered by someone. Obviously this was before the time of Babcock's alleged confession to Simone, but nonetheless it shed plausible doubt about the theory of ongoing animosity between the families.

As Ambrose is cross examining Simone on these points, his colleague Helen Vereen, takes careful notice of the rapt attentiveness of the jurors. It appears as though they all have a thirst for more information about the mayhem that took place during the earthquake. But Ambrose has adeptly taken advantage of Judge Black's instruction to be brief and to the point. He has left the jury with something else to debate. After all he is simply chasing the specter of reasonable doubt.

∞∞∞

"Moving on to the 1991 dinner at Ecco ... Ms. Muirchant ... you indicated that you can recall your ex-husband's statements because of your repeated playing of this ... this missing tape. Between the 1991 dinner and when you somehow lost this alleged tape recording, how many times do you believe that you replayed the tape?"

"I'm not sure, but many times."

"More than 25 times?"

"No definitely not that many times."

"More than once?"

"Yes, I played it soon after it was recorded ... maybe two or three times."

"After those two or three times ... then ... did you play this 'greatest hits' tape every week? Every month?"

Ambrose's sarcastic double entendre reference to 'greatest hits' is meant to discredit Simone's testimony. However it's a fine line he is treading with his derisive questioning. He wants the jury to believe some of her testimony but certainly not all of it.

"No. After my original playing of the tape, I put it in my drawer and didn't listen to it again for a long time."

"And what prompted you to again listen to this alleged tape?"

"Betty Barrymore and I went to the Woodstock '94 festival and began talking about many personal issues and about times we had shared together in the past. I told her what Frank had told me at the dinner a few years earlier and that I had taped it. After we went home I played the tape again for myself ... and then about a week later Betty came over and I played it for her as well ... twice, I think."

Ambrose is aware of the risk that he has just taken. He knows that by questioning Simone Muirchant about the tape and allowing her to testify that she had played it for Betty Barrymore, it might lend credence to the existence of the tape. But he feels strongly that he has not opened up the opportunity for the Prosecution to later ask Simone's friend about the existence of the tape and certainly not about the tape's contents.

∞∞∞

*Judge Black had ruled on a pretrial motion in limine that there should be no testimony about the tape's content other than Simone's first hand testimony. She could testify that she made the tape. Ambrose was quite dissatisfied with that less than comprehensive ruling. Yet he knew that it gave him the opportunity for an appeal should his client receive an adverse verdict from the jury.*

∞∞∞

Still at this point in the trial, with Simone Muirchant already testifying about the existence of the tape, Ambrose feels he has no choice but to attempt to discredit the witness and the tape.

## August 1996

"So then, Ms. Muirchant, in your earlier testimony, you said that you never played this phantom tape for the defendant or for any law enforcement officials; that you never even played it for your son, Fox Babcock. You also said that to your knowledge the only person that has ever heard this tape … if it indeed it exists … the only person besides yourself to hear it is your longtime friend and business colleague, Betty Barrymore. Is that correct?"

Simone hesitates and answers the question in a slightly modified way.

"I only played the tape for Betty and I don't know where the tape is now, so I am uncertain whether anyone else has ever heard the contents."

"So then this list of people that has *not* heard this recording includes every law enforcement official." He hesitates and then adds "And can we assume then … that to your knowledge … the entire Prosecution team has also never heard this tape?"

"Yes."

"Really, Ms. Muirchant? Now really?" As he says this he doesn't look at Simone but instead Ambrose chooses to glare at the Prosecution bench. Then his face loses its anger and is modified to sadness as he turns toward the jurors and simply shakes his head desolately. His colleague Helen Vereen notes the jury's reaction and is thrilled by Ambrose's performance.

"Yes, really," Simone replies meekly. Ambrose continues to shake his head slowly.

"No further questions, Your Honor … uh wait. I'm sorry I do have one more question if I may."

"Yes, alright go ahead ask your final question."

"Ms. Muirchant, you testified earlier that you never really were in love with Frank Babcock. Then why exactly did you marry him … twice?"

"I don't know. I guess there could be lot of answers to that question." Simone seems reflective.

"Yes, I'll bet there are billions of answers." He pauses and then turns to the bench and says, "Now I *really* do have no further questions, Your Honor.

∞∞∞

## Techies, Trials & Terrorists

On redirect Máire Higney is very brief and to the point as she looks to reestablish the fact that her witness did in reality make and maintain a tape recording of the 1991 dinner conversation.

"Ms. Muirchant you have testified on both direct examination and on cross examination that you did in fact tape your conversation with the defendant at the dinner in 1991, and you also testified that you played this tape for Betty Barrymore sometime in early September of 1994. Is there any reason for you to change that testimony now?"

"No. Of course not."

"Do you need to modify that testimony in any way?"

"Not at all."

"Good. Now we can move on your testimony about the 1989 engagement party. In light of the fact that you have testified that you had previously had sexual relationships with two of your guests, many years before the time of the dinner party, I need to ask you to clarify the status of those relationships in 1989. Is it accurate to say that you did not have an ongoing sexual relationship with either Mr. Johnson or with the defendant in 1989?

"Yes that's absolutely accurate and had been that way for more than a decade in the case of the defendant and even longer with respect to Mickey Johnson."

"Just so the jury understands the nature of your relationship with the Johnsons and the defendant at that particular time ... would you tell the court exactly why you invited the guests whom you invited?"

"Certainly. I invited Mickey and Syd because Mickey is Fox's father and Syd is Mickey's wife. I invited Frank because Fox had always regarded him as his father as he was growing up. They have always been very close. In the case of Frank's wife at the time ... Diane Babcock ... I think her maiden name was Heath ... well I invited her because ... as I said, she was Frank's wife at the time. I didn't know that they were in the process of getting a divorce."

"And at the time you didn't even have a business relationship with the defendant. Is that correct?"

"Uh ..." Simone thinks briefly about the timeframes in question. "Yes, that's true."

"All very logical then? The party invitations ... maybe some difficult or awkward relationships but nothing that mature adults couldn't handle. Is that a fair characterization?

## August 1996

"Yes. I'd say so."

"And therefore this event has no real relevance in this murder trial. Would that be your opinion?"

"Yes."

"No further questions, Your Honor."

There is no re-cross-examination.

∞∞∞

After Simone's testimony the judge declares a half hour recess. Simone returns to her gallery seat momentarily and speaks softly with her husband while the others slowly file out of the gallery. She wants desperately to go to the ladies room and freshen up, but she doesn't want to be ambushed by the awaiting media who will undoubtedly besiege her with questions that she cannot answer.

There are additional larger public bathrooms in the hallways of the courthouse building but the ladies room at the rear of the courtroom is only accessible from the courtroom gallery itself. It contains two booths and two sinks and an area for changing baby diapers. After most of the gallery has emptied into the external hallway, Simone walks directly into the empty ladies room.

By the time Simone exits from her toilet stall there is one other woman in the restroom area. It's an older woman that Simone doesn't recognize. However the woman waits silently as Simone proceeds to wash and dry her hands. Simone realizes that the woman is staring at her but she is not troubled by it.

Finally she turns away from the sink and toward the doorway, but the woman is in her way. As Simone looks up and makes eye contact with the older woman, the septuagenarian rears back and smacks Simone hard across her face.

"That's from my daughter, you worthless slut."

Then Kathy McDonough turns around and leaves the bathroom. She keeps walking clear out of the courthouse. Simone does not know what to say or do. Her face hurts. However when she cries the tears are tears of frustration rather than tears of pain. She has done just what Fox had told her to do. She told the truth. But she feels as though her integrity has been impugned.

∞∞∞

# XXXIX

## August 1996

"The State calls Betty Barrymore."

"Counsel, please approach the bench."

After her long grueling testimony that morning, Simone is very surprised to see her old friend Betty Barrymore in the courtroom. She is aware that Betty has been listed as a potential trial witness. However discussions with her own attorney have led Simone to believe that it would be highly unlikely that Betty would testify. Simone is aware of the pretrial legal wrangling about testimony from a tape that was lost and unavailable as corroborating physical evidence. Her lawyer has told her because of Judge Black's ruling on the pretrial *motion in limine* that Betty will not be able to testify about the contents of the tape, and that therefore her testimony would likely have no substantive impact on the trial.

Meanwhile at the bench Judge Black is issuing fair warnings to Máire Higney to remind her of what has already been decided about the breadth of any potential testimony from Betty Barrymore. He informs her that not only is a discussion of the tape contents disallowed, but also he would disallow any testimony about the discussion that took place at the Woodstock Concert grounds with respect to the accused supposed confession. That kind of a third party report would be considered hearsay and Judge Black doesn't want to have to make that point in open court.

∞∞∞

"Ms. Barrymore, it is my understanding that you have known Simone Muirchant for more than twenty-eight years, and that your initial

## August 1996

introduction was as students at Harvard Law School. Are those facts correct?"

"Yes that's accurate."

"And I understand that you have had an intermittent business relationship with Ms. Muirchant for most of those years as well. Is that also correct?"

"Yes, that's true."

"During all of this time that you have known Ms. Muirchant, have you always found her to be honest in her business dealings as well as in her words and deeds?"

"Yes. I don't know a more honest person than Simone."

"Objection Your Honor. The Prosecution seemingly is presenting a character witness for another witness. This is unduly prejudicial and has no bearing on the facts of this case."

"Sustained. Ms. Higney, I am assuming that your witness will have substantive factual evidence to divulge and I expect that you will move in that direction immediately."

"Yes, Your Honor."

Higney turns back to her witness and heaves a long shot that is entirely unexpected by the Bench or by the Defense. She even worries that she might be cited for contempt.

"Did Simone Muirchant ever play a tape for you that involved a conversation between herself and her ex-husband?"

"Objection your honor!" Phillip Ambrose is on his feet immediately trying to nip this line of questioning in the bud.

Judge Black is apoplectic. "I will see counsel for the Defense and the Prosecution in my chambers immediately."

There is animosity now among all parties and Judge Black is particularly incensed. However when they arrive in chambers, both the Prosecution and the Defense are eager to make statements ahead of the Judge's instruction.

"Judge Black, you have ruled that testimony about the content of any purported missing tape is inadmissible and that any attempt to put forth hearsay in a circuitous manner is also verboten. In light of your ruling the Prosecution's question is simply outrageous."

"Your honor, clearly counsel for the Defense has opened the door for a rebuttal to the fact that he has called the tape 'phantom'; 'mysteriously lost'; and even sarcastically referred to the tape as 'the greatest hits.' The Prosecution does not intend to probe the content of the missing tape but we feel the obligation to confirm that Ms. Muirchant did provide a tape ... some kind of tape ... to Ms. Barrymore and that this tape is now missing."

"Well Ms. Higney we are certainly not talking about a movie tape or a song tape of some sort. Ms. Muirchant has made a reference to a conversation with her ex-husband. She testified that she had tape recorded the conversation and that the tape is now missing. Any further discussion of this missing tape by another party is superfluous overkill and could prove to be prejudicial. It will not be allowed in this court. The objection will be sustained and the jury will be instructed to disregard your last question."

Back in open court that is exactly what Judge Black does. He sustains the objection and instructs the jury as he said he would. However Phillip Ambrose pushes forward in trying to protect his client.

"Your Honor, the Defense moves for a mistrial on the grounds of prosecutorial misconduct. The State has attempted to place previously banned, unsubstantiated, prejudicial evidence into the court record and in the presence of the jury."

"The court will adjourn for the rest of the day and evening. We will reconvene at 10 AM. I expect written briefs with respect to the Defense motion to be on my desk by 9 AM. We are adjourned."

∞∞∞

At home that evening, Mickey Johnson is unusually quiet. He is sitting alone in his study trying to read Robert James Waller's bestselling novel, *The Bridges of Madison County*. Syd read the book the previous week, found it interesting, and suggested that Mickey read it before they go to see the movie, which has just come out. Mickey finds the book boring.

They both know that Syd keeps suggesting movies they might see or books to read or anything else that might distract Mickey from the constant tension of the trial of Frank Babcock. A couple of weeks earlier Syd's brother, Jermaine Spataro, had helped out by taking Mickey to see the summer's hit movie: *Independence Day* a mind-numbing film about invading aliens that starred Will Smith and Randy Quaid. But even this type of diversion only serves as a temporary distraction. Syd knows that she will not be able to get her husband back to any sense of normal until after the trial is over. She decides that maybe it's better to just face the problem straight up. She is worried about the man she loves.

## August 1996

Syd walks into the study and Mickey looks up from the book.

"How are you holding up, Mickey?"

"Okay, I guess."

"Do you want to talk about it?"

"The trial?"

"Yes."

"I don't know. Do *you* want to talk about it?

"It might help."

"In what way?"

"I'm not entirely sure. But you know that I love you very much and I am very worried about you. You haven't been expressing yourself to me very much, during all of this. I want to give you space but I want to give you support as well."

"I guess I'm worried more about the kids than I am about everything else lately."

"The kids? That's crazy, Cody, Noah and Jessica are all doing fine. Mom has things under control and she even gets occasional help from Jermaine. She knows that Kathy wants to be at the trial, as much as possible.

"Interesting that you should say that. Kathy was just in here a half hour ago. She apologized and told me that she couldn't take the stress of watching the trial any longer and that she will be helping out at home again starting tomorrow."

"See that? So why are you worried about the kids? We've got all the help we need."

"I hope so. But you know how kids are, in school and all. Their friends are probably hearing all about this trial from their own parents and from the media. I'm sure our kids are getting teased about it in school. We've had issues about things like this in the past. Remember?

"Yes, I know."

"But our own kids aren't asking us anything at all about the case. That bothers me. I don't want to lose their trust."

"That can never happen, Mickey. You are too good a man for them ever not to trust you."

Mickey wonders about his all-consuming craving for vengeance. Will this trial make it go away? He will find out soon enough, he knows.

∞∞∞

# XL

## August 1996

The next morning after Judge Black reviews the written briefs submitted by both the Defense and the Prosecution, he decides to allow the trial to proceed. He has confidence in his jury. They appear to be following the details of the case much more closely than some other juries he has worked with in the past. He will allow them to decide this case. However he warns Máire Higney and gives her strict instructions to steer clear of eliciting any further testimony regarding the missing tape.

Higney feigns frustration but decides to move on. She knows that she has dodged a bullet but is now dancing near the edge of a knife. She does not want to lose her chance at a conviction on this point.

∞∞∞

"So then Ms. Barrymore, is it true that you and Ms. Muirchant have not been on speaking terms since the indictment of her ex-husband?"

"That's true. And I find the circumstances around our rift to be quite hurtful."

"And why is that?"

"Objection!"

"Simone believes that I told the police about the tape ... Am I allowed to say that ...? About the tape?"

"Objection!"

Barrymore doesn't wait for an answer but just plunges ahead. "Simone thinks that I told the police that she had this taped confession from her ex-husband. I swear under oath that I didn't do it."

"Objection, your honor. Objection, objection, objection."

## August 1996

Before Judge Black can respond, Betty Barrymore adds, "And I didn't say anything to anyone, the police or a lawyer or anyone. I just gave Simone my advice and tried to maintain our friendship. That's all."

"That's enough, Ms. Barrymore!" Judge Black turns toward the Defense table. "Your motion for mistrial has been previously been denied, but your objection is sustained."

Then Judge Black turns his attention to the jury box and says; "The jury should disregard the dialogue about any tape that may or may not exist. There is simply no tape in evidence and therefore the alleged contents of this missing tape are mere conjecture and should not be considered relevant in any way whatsoever."

The judge had exhibited a lethargic manner in the early stages of the trial. He is now bordering on anger. Finally he turns back to Prosecutor Higney and gives a one word direction, "Proceed."

"Your Honor, in light of your rulings, I feel that justice might be best served if we ask no further questions of this witness."

Betty Barrymore is so nervous that she begins to rise out of the witness chair as though she has finished testifying.

"The witness will remain seated. The Defense may commence its cross examination." Judge Black's voice is ominous.

∞∞∞

"Good afternoon Ms. Barrymore. Thank you for your sincere statements ... All of your testimony of course is under oath." Lincoln Pierce lets this statement sit for several seconds before asking his next question.

"Have you ever had occasion to use illegal drugs in a recreational setting while in the company of the previous witness, Ms. Muirchant?"

"Objection, your honor. This line of questioning is entirely irrelevant to the matter at hand and thoroughly inappropriate."

"Quite the contrary Your Honor. Not only is the question relevant to the character of the witness but we believe the honest testimony of this witness may well shed light on the veracity of the previous witness's testimony. On direct ... The State appears to have had no other reason to present this witness other than as an attempt to boost the character of its main witness, Ms. Muirchant. Meanwhile, Ms. Barrymore has provided no other meaningful testimony or evidence for the Prosecution of these charges. She not a first-hand witness to any consequential event pertinent to this trial. She represents a misguided attempt on the part of the

Prosecution to introduce a character witness. The Defense merely wants the ability to cross-examine the character of such a witness."

"The objection is overruled. I'll allow the question in a narrow context, Counselor. However demonstrate relevance with your next few questions. I will not allow a fishing expedition."

Judge Black then turns toward Barrymore and adds, "The witness should be aware that the answer to the question may result in self-incrimination and that she is protected by the fifth amendment of the constitution from any requirement to answer such a question. If the witness choses to invoke her rights, then the court will direct that the Defense move on to another line of questioning." Judge Black looks directly at Barrymore to make sure that she understands his ruling. He fully expects her to invoke her Fifth Amendment rights. So does Pierce.

"Your honor, allow me to withdraw the previous question and rephrase it in a way that might get us past the self-incrimination issue."

"You can try that Mr. Pierce."

"Ms. Barrymore, when Ms. Muirchant first told you anything whatsoever about her relationship with the defendant, was *she* using illegal drugs?"

"I invoke my Fifth Amendment rights." She snaps out her answer before Higney is able to gain the floor.

"Objection. This is a totally irrelevant and non-specific inquiry ... yes ... a total fishing trip question. This question has no relevance whatsoever to the testimony that has come before the court so far."

"Your Honor the Prosecution has tried to tie the relevance of a non-existent tape to the testimony of this third party witness through surreptitious innuendo. The Defense is merely attempting to counter such a questionable practice by demonstrating that perceptions both by *this witness* and by *the previous witness* may have been influenced by other factors."

"Counselors, approach the bench."

The jury watches as the hushed discussion takes place with an animated flair. It has been a morning of sheer fireworks, with one objection after another – all seemingly connected to a tape that they have already been instructed to ignore. It is unclear what exactly Judge Black's ruling will be now or how he will arrive at it. But it is becoming readily apparent that the line of questioning about drug use is probably off the table. Yet there are

## August 1996

no specific instructions to the jury about how they should treat the previous line of questioning and objections. In reality Judge Black has granted the Defense some latitude in countering the Prosecution's ill-advised attempt at using Barrymore as a character witness. When the lawyers go back to their respective positions the Defense goes back to questioning the witness.

∞∞∞

"Ms. Barrymore, you have testified that you have known Ms. Muirchant for many years and that you have known the defendant for almost as long. Is that correct?"

"More or less."

"Yes or no would be a more appropriate answer to the question, Ms. Barrymore. Have you known Mr. Babcock for as long as you have known Ms. Muirchant?"

"Yes. Give or take about a month ...yes."

"I see. You have said that Ms. Muirchant is a very honest person. If you have known Mr. Babcock for an equally long period of time, then you must have formed some opinion of his honesty as well. Would you say that Mr. Babcock is an honest or a dishonest man?"

"I'm not sure ... I can't say."

"You were a partner and co-founder along with Ms. Muirchant in MBF Digital Haven & Harbor. Were you not?"

"Yes, that's true."

"So, I would imagine that you trusted the defendant when he provided seed funding for your business."

"Truthfully I never spoke to the defendant about it. Any discussions that took place between MBF and Mr. Babcock would have been handled by Simone for obvious reasons. If she trusted him, then I trusted him and so did Howard."

"Howard?"

"Our third partner in MBF is Howard Feldman."

"So then just how well *do* you know the defendant? When exactly did you first meet him?"

"I first met Mr. Babcock, briefly, when his wife and I were in law school together."

"And when did you last personally *speak* to Mr. Babcock?"

"I don't recall but it was a long time ago."

"More than five years ago?"

"Yes."

"More than 10 years ago?"

"Yes, I have had no personal interaction with the defendant since the late 1960's."

"Wow, is that so?" Lincoln Pierce acts amazed but then sheds that demeanor rapidly and asks; "Would it surprise you to hear that the defendant has no idea who you are?"

Pierce knows this certainly isn't true, but the jury doesn't know that.

"Yes, it would. I would think that he would certainly know who I am. Even though we haven't spoken in many years, he still would know who I am. If nothing else, I'm sure he knows who the principals are of a business that he has invested in."

"I see. So let's go back to the last time you actually *spoke* to the defendant … I believe you said that was the late 1960's …"

"Yes. When Simone and I first became friends she was somewhat separated from Mr. Babcock. They still got along but they were living apart. But they also had two kids."

"Did Simone live with you at that time?"

"Yes. Simone had moved in with me. I met Frank Babcock one time when he came to our apartment to pick her up. Other than that time, I have never spoken a single word to him. However he was certainly a frequent topic of conversation between Simone and myself. Mr. Babcock and I just never had another occasion to have a face to face conversation."

"Did you at least talk with him occasionally on the phone? After all, you and Simone were such good friends throughout these years."

"No. At least not that I recall."

"Then is it reasonable to presume that you might not even know his voice if you heard it somewhere?"

Betty paused for a few seconds and then answered Lincoln Pierce's question. "I guess that's reasonable." At the Defense desk, Helen Vereen smiled slightly. Several of the male jurors also smiled in unison.

"No further questions your honor."

∞∞∞

Ambrose, Pierce and Vereen, the elite Defense team for Frank Babcock, didn't want to lend credence to the testimony of Betty Barrymore. The witness had come across as bumbling. Even though she might appear to be honest, it would be easy for the jury to assume that Barrymore was trying

## August 1996

to force fit her beliefs and loyalties into the narrative of her testimony. Again, at the very least there should be reasonable doubt about her testimony.

Phillip Ambrose was particularly happy that his second chair, Lincoln Pierce, had managed to get Barrymore to acknowledge that she might not recognize Frank Babcock's voice if she heard it. This was accomplished without any allowance for testimony of anything that Barrymore may or may not have heard on a tape that may or may not even exist. The admission more or less rendered Barrymore's testimony useless to the Prosecution. Ambrose was also happy that Pierce was able to suggest the possibility that she had used drugs with Simone Muirchant, thereby throwing some question over the rest of her testimony as well.

∞∞∞

There were a few other witnesses that the Prosecution might call but they decided to rest their case on the basis of the witnesses that they had already called. Long before the start of the trial they had decided that calling Fox Babcock as a witness was much too risky. He would have no firsthand knowledge in the facts of the case, and he would be highly unlikely to testify against his father in any other manner. To the contrary he might provide some exculpatory evidence that they were not yet aware of. If Fox was to be called as a witness, then the Defense would have to call him.

"The Prosecution rests its case, Your Honor."

Judge Black assesses where they are in the prosecutorial process along with the fact that it is now close to 4 PM. He is about to suggest that maybe they should adjourn before the Defense team begins its rebuttal to the charges and their defense of their client. But before Black can speak from the bench he notices that a young man has been allowed quiet entry near the rear of the courtroom. The young man moves quickly so as not to be disruptive and sits down in a back row seat. The seat just happens to be directly next to Simone Muirchant – his mother.

Before anyone in the gallery turns around, Judge Black addresses the Defense.

"It is now 3:55 PM, counselors. Would you prefer to begin your defense after a short recess or should we adjourn until the morning."

"We are ready to proceed immediately, Your Honor, but are prepared to follow the wishes of the court in whatever it determines to be most prudent." As he says this he almost inadvertently raises his right hand in a partial stop sign and then quickly lowers it so as not to seem disrespectful. Then he launches into his motion.

"However Your Honor, before making that decision please consider a directed verdict. The Defense moves for a dismissal of all charges. The Prosecution has failed to make a case beyond a reasonable doubt on any of the three charges. Their case is merely predicated on the scurrilous and contradictory musings, assumptions and unverifiable accusations of an ex-convict and an ex-wife. There is no testimony or physical evidence that puts our client anywhere near the murder scene and there is no direct first hand evidence of any conspiratorial meeting or mandates on the part of Mr. Babcock. Your Honor, there is just no evidence. No evidence, period! And therefore the Defense moves for a speedy dismissal of these charges.

"Your motion is noted counselor. Decisions on such motions and are not made lightly. I will rule on it in the morning. For the benefit of precision, please make your motion in writing by 8 AM. I will also entertain any written arguments by The State against this motion at that time. For now this court is adjourned until 9:30 AM tomorrow." After he articulates this decision he looks up briefly to see Fox Babcock and Simone Muirchant hurrying out through the rear gallery door.

∞∞∞

# XLI

## August 1996

9:30 AM the following morning comes more rapidly for some than others. Throughout the prior evening the Prosecution had been wringing their hands in dismay. Judge Black was a hard jurist to read. While he had allowed more freedom to probe the missing tape than they thought he would, he had also allowed a certain latitude to the Defense in their characterization of the State's evidence. They worried that there was a definite possibility of a summary judgement and they knew that they had had a tough case to prove right from the get-go. Now it was a matter of waiting to see how the judge would rule.

∞∞∞

The State doesn't have to wait long. Promptly at 9:30 AM the judge makes a simple declarative statement and ruling. He is careful not to add any protracted rationale for his decision. He doesn't want to prejudice the jury one way or another, but he is indeed going to allow them to come to their own decision.

"I have carefully read the Defense's motion for a directed dismissal of the charges against the defendant and have considered this motion in the light of the testimony that has taken place thus far in this trial. My ruling is that the motion is denied. Mr. Ambrose, are you prepared to begin your defense in these proceedings?"

Phillip Ambrose does a perfect job of acting totally non-impacted by Judge Black's ruling.

"Thank you for considering our motion Your Honor, and we understand fully your ruling that it will be up to the jury to determine innocence of our client. We are prepared to commence our defense and would like to begin that defense by presenting several character witnesses on behalf of Mr. Babcock.

"As our first witness the Defense would like to call Father Thomas Dunham."

As was already clearly evident from the Prosecution's debacle with Betty Barrymore, calling character witnesses had its risks. The witnesses can only be asked questions germane to the elements of a defendant's character that are pertinent to the crime or crimes at hand. In this case the witness can testify that he has never known the defendant to exhibit any violent tendencies, but questions expounding upon his philanthropic endeavors would be considered out of bounds. The character witness is also subject to cross examination. Another jeopardy exists in that the Prosecution can potentially call witnesses to show *bad character* in rebuttal of the *good character* witness. It obviously can get risky.

Specifically calling Father Thomas Dunham, the Jesuit President of the Shenandoah High School community, had additional points of intrigue associated with it. Both the defendant and the two sons of the victim are Shenandoah High School graduates. In addition Dr. Fox Babcock, the man whose paternity had been at the center of the controversy is also a Shenandoah graduate. Three of those men are currently in the courtroom.

The final intrigue is that the Prosecution's most evocative witness had at one time worked for Father Dunham as his administrative assistant. That was in 1965, precisely the year in which Simone Muirchant became pregnant with her son and married Frank Babcock. Fascinatingly Father Dunham had actually fired Simone from her position at Shenandoah not because she dressed much too suggestively for the all-male student body, but because she presented too great a temptation to him personally. But only Dunham knows for sure how most of these pieces fit together.

Father Dunham is himself a graduate of 1937 class at Shenandoah High and he has known the Johnson family since 1961 and Frank Babcock even longer. He has prayed a lot before coming to court on this occasion.

∞∞∞

"Father Dunham, how long have you known Frank Babcock?"

"Let's see, Frank was a member of the Shenandoah Class of 1953, so that would mean that he was a freshman in September of 1949. So I guess I've known Frank for almost 45 years."

# August 1996

"And besides knowing Frank as a student at Shenandoah, did you maintain a relationship with the defendant since that time?"

"As a matter of fact, I have."

"Would you characterize that relationship for the court?"

"Certainly. In all honesty, I don't remember Frank so much as a student at the school as I remember him as an alumnus. Frank was a good student though. He didn't go to a Catholic college like so many of our graduates did then … and still do even now. But Frank went off to Dartmouth. I remember that much for sure. He was one our Ivy League guys. Frank went to Harvard also … for Law School. The earliest memories I have of our relationship are somewhat sad ones. Frank's father died when Frank was a sophomore at Shenandoah and then his mother died a few years later when he was up in New Hampshire at Dartmouth.

"Other than those sad occurrences many years ago, what were your other early impressions of Frank Babcock?"

"Well for sure I wasn't blind to the fact that Frank came from a very wealthy family. His parents were both very generous with their gifts to our school. But Frank had first-hand experience of what it meant to be a Skylark, so when he became an alumnus he was even more generous with the school … both with his financial support and his personal time."

Higney wants to object to these statements as being non-evidentiary, but she knows that the Bench will often grant a little latitude as long as the Defense gets to the point relatively quickly. She also realizes that the Defense's open ended questions are not the issue but rather the witness's expansive answers that are causing her angst. She remains seated and does not issue an objection citing the no-bolstering rule, because she knows it will be overruled. She is still planning on how she should question Dunham with her cross examination. She hopes that the Defense will not skip past the fact that Father Dunham knows all of the players and not just Babcock. To her surprise Ambrose doesn't skip any of it.

"So then you became more familiar with the defendant as an active alumnus prior to the time that he became engaged to Simone Muirchant. Is that right?"

"Yes, in fact Frank Babcock became the youngest member ever of our Board of Trustees in the early to mid-1960 and he remained active on our Board for more than 20 years. I'm not sure of the exact dates. But I believed he stepped down sometime in the late '80's."

"You said that Mr. Babcock stepped down from the Board 'in the late 80's.' As a matter of full disclosure, isn't it true that a few years after Mr. Babcock stepped down from the Board of Trustees, Mr. Michael Johnson, the son of the decedent, then also became a member of your Board of Trustees?"

"Yes that's true. We are also very happy to have had Mickey Johnson as a member of our board for the past four or five years. Both men are Shenandoah graduates and have served the school admirably and generously since their days as Skylark undergraduates."

"So going back to the defendant... after Frank became a board member in the 60's did he ever suggest that you employ a personal acquaintance of his?"

"No, technically we didn't *employ* her. I assume you are referring to Ms. Muirchant. She was engaged as my clerical assistant for several months in 1965, but we did not pay her for her services, directly. Mr. Babcock may have paid her. I don't know those particulars. I was aware though that Mr. Babcock and Ms. Muirchant were engaged to be married at the time."

"Did there come a time when you thought that it was best to let Ms. Muirchant go? In point of fact, did you fire Ms. Muirchant from her non-paying job?"

"Yes."

"Did you fire her because she was pregnant?"

Now even Judge Black is mystified. This is supposed to be a Defense character witness and counsel for the Defense is asking his witness if he had at one time committed a discriminatory hiring practice violation. No one objects. The judge just listens along with everyone else.

"No. At the time I didn't know that she was pregnant. She wasn't showing ... at least not that I knew about." Father Dunham's face reddens in obvious embarrassment at a memory he would rather not recall.

"How did Frank Babcock react to the firing of his fiancé?"

"Oddly enough to this very day Frank has never mentioned it to me. Although I guess it's obvious that someone mentioned something to someone ... or you wouldn't have asked."

"Why *did* you fire Ms. Muirchant then?"

"I think that saying that I fired her might be truthful but still an overstatement. Remember she wasn't being paid by Shenandoah. Yet to answer your question as specifically as I can, I would say that I let Ms.

# August 1996

Muirchant go because she dressed too suggestively for the job she had at an all-male high school."

"Could you be more specific?"

"She wore mini-skirts and was often braless."

*Oh my God,* Judge Black thinks. *I have allowed Ambrose to turn my courtroom into the Harper Valley PTA!*

"We appreciate your candor Father Dunham." Ambrose also feels that this line of questioning can blow up in a second. He quickly pivots to a more direct question. "Father Dunham, in all of the forty-five years that you have known Frank Babcock have you ever known him to be a violent man?"

"No, never."

"Have you ever heard him scream or yell or get in someone's face in a fit of anger?"

"No, I have not."

Ambrose has quickly covered the basics so now he decides to wander back over the history of the two men to derive whatever additional mileage he can get from this interrogation.

"You must have been aware of the controversy surrounding the parentage of Fox Babcock that led to court decisions in 1980 and 1981. Did that have an impact on your relationship with Frank Babcock?"

"It was a difficult time for Frank, I'm sure, but I was not privy to what was happening in the court case. You have to understand, while Shenandoah is a unique school in many ways, it is much like other schools that frequently have to work around the problems that surface when marriages break down and families get fragmented. This often has an impact on our students, who are our main concern and responsibility."

"But you were aware of the family difficulties at some level. Were you not?"

"The most concern that I had for the Babcock family at the time was for their collective loss of Frank and Simone's daughter, Maureen. She died a tragic death and her brother, Fox was a student at our school during these most trying times, and he was very close to his sister, as I recall. So, Fox was my biggest concern with respect to the Babcock family at that time. But he adjusted admirably, eventually graduating at the head of his class and honoring us all with his valedictorian speech at graduation a few years later."

"And during all of this time, did you ever ... even one time ... know Frank Babcock to lose control of his emotions ... to grow angry and bitter or to blame anyone else for his difficult family life?"

"As I indicated in response to your earlier question, the answer is no ... not ever. In fact I don't think I know of anyone who might have exercised more self-control under similarly trying circumstances."

"Thank you, Father Dunham. I have no further questions."

∞∞∞

The courtroom drama moves on very quickly from this point. The Prosecution chooses not to cross examine Father Dunham. The Defense then presents two additional character references for Frank Babcock. The first witness is a long term client, who vouches for Babcock's honesty and even-temperedness. Again the Defense chooses not to cross examine the witness.

The final character witness was James Robinson, who is described as the caretaker and property manager for *Babcock Sea Breeze Chateau* in Southampton, N.Y. Máire Higney realizes that this a blatant attempt to appeal to the black jurors, but there is little she can do about it. Ambrose chooses Lincoln Pierce to conduct the questioning of Robinson. The jurors listen as Robinson offers his opinion about what a fair and trusting boss Frank Babcock has been. Robinson describes Babcock's equanimity under duress as he dealt with various neighbors and with a sometimes nasty local press. Robinson says that he "never once saw Mr. Babcock lose his cool."

Máire Higney is impressed with the order in which the witnesses had been brought forth by the Defense. She knows that if she asks questions only of this last witness, she may engender thoughts of prejudice on the part of the black jurors. She decides it's worth the risk. She too has been impressed by the attentiveness of the jury during the latter stages of the trial. She has a plan and she thinks she knows how to expose black jurors to the obvious pandering on the part of the Defense.

∞∞∞

"Mr. Robinson, thank you for your precise and insightful testimony. It is clear that during the time that you have known the defendant that he has treated you with the dignity and respect that everyone has a right to in an employer/employee relationship. And thank you for telling us clearly that you believe that the defendant never 'loses his cool.' I think that's how you put it. I have just a few clarifying questions for you. I promise I will be brief."

## August 1996

Higney speaks quickly but softly. Her demeanor is all about kindness. Robinson smiles and nods that he is ready to answer her inquiries.

"I think that you testified that you met Mr. Babcock and began working for him in 1988, but that you didn't work for him full time until about six years ago in 1990. Do I have that right?"

"Yes. Those are the right years."

"So then, Mr. Robinson, you had no idea who Frank Babcock was back in 1980 at the time of the murder of Wayne Johnson. Correct?"

"No ... I mean yes ... I didn't know him then."

"So then is it fair to say that you would have no idea of what kind of temperament, Mr. Babcock might have had nearly a decade before you ever met him or went to work for him?"

"Yes, that's fair."

"Interesting. Have you ever wondered why the billionaire, Mr. Babcock chose you to be his character witness, Mr. Robinson?"

Robinson paused and then answered slowly, "well, yes I have wondered."

"I'll bet you have!" She looks at the witness long enough to make him blink but not so long as to make him worry. The jury notices. Helen Vereen notices the jury noticing.

Higney says, "No further questions Your Honor."

∞∞∞

After the testimony of James Robinson, the Defense rests its case without calling a single witness for rebuttal of any of the evidence that the State has provided. Like the Prosecution, the Defense had briefly considered calling Fox Babcock. But they knew they would only do so if the proceedings had gone somewhat differently. But they were satisfied that they would not have to play that trump card with all of the risks associated with it.

Now the Defense simply provides no further defense, period. There is no testimony from police officers about their original finding of a random mugging. There is no testimony from any DNA experts to dispute the findings of the Prosecution's experts. They call no witnesses from the corrections department to further undermine the character of Richie Barone. The Defense believes they have already covered their base on these issues through their own thorough cross-examination of the Prosecution's witnesses. And finally and rationally, they do not call Frank Babcock to speak in his own defense.

## Techies, Trials & Terrorists

The Defense simply wants the jury to see the case the same way that they do, and to return a not guilty verdict based upon the shallowness of the State's evidence and its inability to prove guilt beyond a reasonable doubt.

∞∞∞

The closing argument for the State is full of vitriol. Máire Higney spends a good amount of time recapping the police work that was done in piecing together the crime scene. She underlines the certainty with which the investigators can prove that Richie Barone was actually at the scene of the crime when it occurred back in 1980. And she quickly dismisses Defense efforts at suggesting an alternative killer. She argues that it was entirely speculative and that not one name had been offered up by the Defense for consideration as an alternate killer. She terms these Defense efforts "desperate and absurd."

Máire Higney is aware that prior police work had been spotty, but she herself now has no doubt that Barone was there at the scene of the crime. Higney has more concern about the thin link that brings Babcock into the conspiracy. If it weren't for Simone Muirchant's testimony, their entire case would rest on the shoulders of a lifelong criminal. That scares her. Eventually Higney's closing argument devolves into a scathing character assassination;

> "... furthermore although the defendant's motive for murder has been clear all along, it might be prudent to understand his motive for *confessing* his murder. Here's how it all went down:
> "Pathetically, Mr. Babcock was still seeking the love of his first wife. This pitiable reality was actually pointed out during cross examination by the Defense. Ms. Muirchant told the court that she didn't love Mr. Babcock and that she *never* did love him. Tragically, Mr. Babcock didn't understand the principle that money can't buy him love. Then ... wretchedly he reached out to the woman he can't have; the love he can't buy, and tries to pry her affections loose by earning her pity.
> "Ridiculously, this very wealthy man ... this heir to generational wealth ... believes that nothing at all will

## August 1996

come of this confession. He believes this because he believes that he controls everything and everybody with his money. But he is wrong. The defendant doesn't realize that the NYPD never gives up on a case when one of their own is savagely murdered.

"So the police investigation team keeps beating the bushes for years on end. They are aware that there is hatred between the defendant and the deceased. They know the motive is clear and early on they attempt to interview Mr. Babcock. But the defendant provides an alibi for his physical presence on the night of the murder. He surrounds himself with legal protectors and never grants an interview with respect to the murder.

"Yet behind the scenes the police finally uncover a man who says that he knows who killed Wayne Johnson. Admittedly it takes a while before Richie Barone is willing to cooperate and confess his *own* involvement. The investigative team follows up with the incontrovertible DNA evidence affirming Barone's presence at the crime scene. Still there are some who feel we still need more evidence. The hard work continues on.

"Sometimes fortune finds frenzy. Some might call it luck. However you choose to view it, in September of 1994, the NYPD receives an anonymous call regarding the murder of Wayne Johnson. The caller says that we need to interview Simone Muirchant because she now knows who killed her ex-lover Wayne Johnson. To this day we don't know who that caller was but we are all now grateful that the call sent us in the right direction.

"In all fairness, Ms. Muirchant is not very forthcoming at the outset. But please understand that for many years she has been under the spell of a control freak ... a sleazy billionaire who has had private investigators following her every move throughout her life. Frank Babcock is pathetic. He is a man with billions of dollars and no friends; four marriages and no contemporary soul mates. He was born with proverbial silver spoon in his mouth but it is a mouth Simone Muirchant wouldn't kiss. After some anguish … I'm sure …Simone chose the righteous and honest path. She chose to testify honestly against an ex-husband who was currently invested in her business. She simply knew that she couldn't let her ex-husband get away with murder.

"So it all fits together rather nicely. The Defendant had the motive, the means and the inclination to murder his adversary and he colluded and conspired with Richie Barone and two other men who have since died. They all colluded to kill Wayne Johnson. Justice must be served. We can't allow a hard working police officer, a patriot, a Marine Corps veteran, a loving father, an America citizen… to be savagely murdered without punishing his killer. Members of the jury we implore you to return a verdict of guilty of $1^{st}$ Degree Murder and Conspiracy to commit murder for this despicable premeditated act."

After she sits back down at the Prosecution desk, Máire Higney begins to worry immediately about the Defense's closing statement. She knows that they are very talented and that her own case has holes that can be exploited. She knows that she has attempted to create a very sinister picture of the defendant and that she believes that she has done a good job of establishing motive. As a very experienced prosecutor, she also realizes that motive alone amounts to nothing. She knows that Judge Black probably erred by not granting a summary judgment and by leaving it in the hands of the jury where anything can happen.

∞∞∞

The closing argument for the defense is a good bit briefer. Ambrose decides that Lincoln Pierce will present their side of the story.

## August 1996

"Ladies and gentlemen of the jury, let's get right to the point. Regardless of the ribald and sundry stories of marriages gone bad and sad sexual liaisons without love, the very serious matter that is before us transcends those salacious details. Intriguing though they may be these tawdry tales do nothing to diminish the fact that the defendant Frank Babcock had absolutely nothing to do with the violent death of Wayne Johnson."

For the next ten minutes or so Lincoln Pierce recounts some of the evidence of investigators who gave their testimony early in the prosecution's case. He demonstrates how the many contrasting opinions of that evidence over the intervening sixteen years still do not in any way implicate the defendant. There is no eyewitness testimony, there is only contradictory opinions about forensic findings. He refuses to call these findings 'evidence.'

Nevertheless Pierce tells them that they should consider the magnitude of the inconsistencies within the investigation over the years. He says that it would be natural to wonder how the government's "assumptions and conclusions were changed to fit the narrative of their case ... a case based upon scurrilous accusations made by the victim's former lover."

Pierce also points out that Simone Muirchant's testimony about a supposed confession is entirely uncorroborated. He dismisses Betty Barrymore's testimony as an absurd attempt to add "third-hand balderdash" to validate this false testimony. Pierce points out that Judge Black has understandably ruled that the court should not be subjected to this kind of testimony. Pierce then winds down his closing argument by bridging back to his own opening statement.

"So as you can see ladies and gentlemen of the jury, the Prosecution has simply focused its efforts on creating an overly assumptive rationale for a motive. Why would they do this you ask? Because they have no hard evidence with respect to any of their charges. They have not put the defendant at the scene of murder. They have not provided any evidence whatsoever to demonstrate the defendant's collusion, collaboration or conspiracy with Richard

Barone or anyone else. Conveniently after all of these years, those who could easily refute such an allegation have passed away in the interim.

"So with absolutely no hard evidence whatsoever, the Prosecution has attempted to create a felonious crime out of motive alone. And as you have witnessed they have failed in this attempt as well. They have ineffectively attempted to cobble together a motive against a man who they have mischaracterized as violent and vindictive. Yet their own main witness to this supposed motivation, the defendant's ex-wife, has testified that he is ... and I quote ... 'not a violent person by nature.'

"And so there you have it, just as the Defense has intimated in our opening statement. *No evidence; No motive; No case*.... No, no, no.

"We ask that you do the right thing after considering all of the facts, and the lack of facts as well, and return a verdict of 'not guilty' on all the charges against this innocent man."

∞∞∞

# XLII

## September 1996

As day one of jury deliberations passes, the Defense begins to worry. But it is a normal worry. The jury has been deliberating for about three hours and has not reached a verdict. Naturally the Defense hopes for a quick exoneration of its client based upon the pure lack of compelling evidence presented by the Prosecution. Ambrose, Pierce and Vereen realize that their decision not to offer an extensive defense for their client certainly has the potential to backfire. However they also know that some juries are just more methodical in their approach especially at the outset of their discussions. They all go home for the night assuming that the acquittal will come sometime on day two of the jury's caucus.

When day two of the deliberations comes and goes without a jury decision, the Defense attorneys begin questioning each other about what they think could be going wrong. Helen Vereen assures her colleagues that at least four of the jurors will never vote for a conviction. She is the only one of the Defense team that feels 100% confident that their client's freedom is assured.

Meanwhile the Prosecution grows ever more hopeful of getting a conviction. Privately they realize that their case is weak. Getting by without the granting of the Defense motion for a directed verdict was monumental. Once the trial outcome is in the hands of the jury they know that anything can happen. With each passing day they grow slightly more confident.

Day three of the jury deliberations comes with a request from the jury about the conspiracy charge. They question whether this charge can apply to either first degree murder or second degree murder. This raises hopes even higher on the part of the Prosecution. But there is nothing definitive in the wording of their request for information and clarification.

Astoundingly there is a day four to the deliberations. The Defense is now quite concerned. What can possibly be taking so long to render a not-guilty verdict? They must therefore be trying to decide between first and second degree murder. The mood among the Defense counsel is decidedly somber.

∞∞∞

It is now the seventh day of jury deliberations. Several times the jury has asked for clarification of Judge Black's charge to the jury. They have also asked about specific differences between $1^{st}$ degree murder and $2^{nd}$ degree murder. Originally these inquiries led the Prosecution to be hopeful that they might at least get a conviction on the lesser included charge of murder in the $2^{nd}$ degree, which could mean that they might also return a guilty verdict on the conspiracy charge as well.

But as time dragged on and the jury sent its first message that it might not be able to reach a verdict on all of the charges, the Defense became more hopeful. It was quite probable that they had already taken $1^{st}$ degree murder off the board and were still hung up on the other two charges. Then again it was quite possible that the jury had decided that the defendant was guilty of murder but hung up on whether it was first degree or second degree. But all of the lawyers for the Prosecution as well as for the Defense had been at this stage of suspense in other trials before this one. They knew that regardless of how well they had presented their cases, juries were unpredictable.

∞∞∞

Throughout the trial Judge Black seems to be particularly motivated to have the jury reach a consensus on all three charges. But after more than a week of deliberations, he accepts the fact that this will not be the case.

"The jury foreman will read the verdict on the two charges that have been decided. The defendant will please rise."

Frank Babcock stands up and he is joined in this movement by the three Defense attorneys who have been working his case. The Prosecution team is already standing but they now come to standing attention. Babcock looks directly at the jury foreman. Inscrutable the foreman reads his verdict.

## September 1996

"On the count of murder in the 1st degree we the jury find the defendant: not guilty. On the count of conspiracy to commit murder, we the jury find the defendant not guilty."

Judge Black then tells the court that the jury has deliberated for more than a week and examined all of the pertinent evidence and is unable to reach a verdict on the 2nd degree murder charge. He then declares a mistrial on the second degree murder charge. He informs the Defense and the Prosecution that the State will have the right to retry the defendant on this charge if it intends to do so. Both sides are well aware of this fact and most of the gallery audience also understands his instructions.

The verdict doesn't elicit a dramatic reaction from either the Defense or the Prosecution. Phillip Ambrose, Lincoln Pierce and Helen Vereen are obviously pleased that they have managed to get their client exonerated of the most serious charge of "Murder One" as well as on the conspiracy charge. However Frank Babcock hardly feels exonerated.

The Prosecution feels that they gave it their best shot. There are not many things they would have done differently. But now they have the opportunity to do just that.

∞∞∞

Fox walks outside of the courtroom and is immediately swamped by reporters. He has left the trial without acknowledging either of his fathers. His mother was not in the courtroom for the verdict. Fox is alone but he is a powerful young man. He pushes his way past the shouted questions.

"Dr. Babcock, are you satisfied with the verdict?"

"Fox, why didn't you acknowledge the Johnsons or the Babcocks after the verdict?"

"Dr. Babcock why didn't you testify in the trial? Would it have made a difference one way or the other?"

"Dr. Babcock, do you want to see a retrial?"

"Fox, are you happy?"

Fox pushes towards the waiting limousine that will take him to LaGuardia Airport for his flight back to Pittsburgh. He pretends not to hear all of the questions. In reality he hears each question clearly, especially the last one. He has no answers for any of them.

∞∞∞

Back inside the courtroom, Jack Birdsong turns to Mickey Johnson and says, "Stupid verdict ... they'll definitely retry him Mickey. Don't worry about it." But Mickey shakes his head slowly. He doesn't answer his friend. He knows that Jack wants the best for him. However Mickey is not so sure another trial is any kind of solution to the long term bitterness that he has felt for Frank Babcock. He turns toward Syd. She opens her mouth as if to say something in reply to Jack's statement. However at first the words don't come out. Finally she allows her answer to flow forth.

"We don't want another trial, Jack. Everyone has suffered enough already."

"Except Babcock, he deserves to be in jail for the rest of his life."

"In a way he will be, Jack. He will be forever tormented by the anguish he has caused everyone. We just don't want to be in that emotional confinement along with him. Mickey and I have talked about it over the last few days. God has his reasons for doing things the way he does. We'll just have to accept those reasons and the outcomes that go along with them."

"God might have had his reasons for leaving me in the Hanoi Hilton, but that didn't mean I shouldn't try everything I could to get out of that hellhole. We need to see his through until Babcock goes to the slammer."

"I'm with Syd on this one, Jack. I'm not going to fight it anymore."

Jack Birdsong realizes that this is may be a turning point in his bond with Mickey Johnson – his closest friend in the world.

∞∞∞

Upon hearing the verdict, Frank Babcock's first reaction is significant relief, but it is followed shortly by apprehension, anxiety and even remorse. The mix of emotions is unsettling enough that he struggles to maintain his blank stare. He does not see the jury. He does not see the Judge or even his lawyers.

Physically Babcock feels exhausted. More than anything else he realizes that he has spent the last twenty months of his life fighting for his freedom. And although his lawyers had indicated that if he beat one rap he would likely beat them all, that outcome has not yet come to fruition.

More than anything else, Frank Babcock wants his old life back ... the life that allows him to do pretty much whatever he wants to do without worrying about the consequences. He fully realizes that he has not achieved that on this day. He turns around to face his wife, Margot. She is smiling through tears of joy and relief. Standing next to her Hadassah Silver is

## September 1996

grimacing through tears of woe and grief. Technically she is the defendant's mother-in-law although she is actually much younger than the billionaire. But Hadassah Silver wants her daughter to be free of Babcock's clutches and believes that Margot should have earned reparations for her forbearance along the way.

∞∞∞

Simone Muirchant's StarTAC cell phone is ringing. It is a clamshell mobile phone recently released by Motorola. The signal is crystal clear and she can hear her son perfectly.

"A split verdict ... Dad got a split verdict. I'm relieved. I don't think he should have to go to jail."

"Tell me what happened. The jury was split?"

"No ... at least not on two of the charges. Dad was found not guilty of first degree murder and of conspiracy to commit murder. He can't be retried on either of those charges. However the jury was deadlocked on the second degree murder charge. He could be retried on that charge and that would mean another trial and all of this might go on forever. I hope they give up on it. The damage is already done. Dad is a different man than he was two years ago."

"Will you and Evelyn come out here to California and visit with me, now that this phase of everything is over?"

"We'll see Mom. Right now we're really busy, but we promised ourselves an extensive sabbatical a few years back and we haven't taken it yet."

"Why not?"

"I'm not sure Mom. I guess that recently life has just gotten in the way of living."

∞∞∞

# XLIII

## September 1996

After he arrives back at his Pittsburgh residence, Fox Babcock makes sure that the very first thing he does is to tell Evelyn that he loves her. He knows that it is important to constantly reinforce the emotional pillars that support a person. Just saying the three little words is as healthy for the person who says them as it is for the person who hears them. He knows that much.

Evelyn has been waiting for his arrival and has a fire going in the living room fireplace, and a bottle of Fox's favorite Merlot ready for consumption. Their son, Mikey is sleeping upstairs.

"So are you glad that you went there?"

"Yes. You were right. I needed to be there for my own sanity."

"I'm sorry I missed your call. By the time I got your voicemail you were probably already on the plane."

"That's alright. I'm here now and it's over."

"Are you sure. The TV reporters keep saying that the Prosecution may retry your dad on the lesser murder charge."

"That's not going to happen. They just don't want to say that right away. The media would like this to go on forever. Me? I've had enough."

"What does your dad think of the verdict? And how about your mother? And Mickey? What do they all think?"

"The only one I've talked to is my mother. She asked me to call her because she is back in California and even that conversation was brief. I think that she was satisfied with the verdict. No one really expects a new trial. I'm pretty sure this is over. She wants us to come out there by the way."

## September 1996

"To San Francisco? Did you tell her it wasn't on our near term list of places to go?"

"Yea, sort of."

"There's one thing about the trial that is still a mystery to everyone, though."

"You mean the tape?"

"Yes."

Fox walks over to the computer case that he had brought with him to New York. He unzips it and pushes aside his laptop so that he can access another compartment in the bag. He takes out a six year old cassette recorder and removes the tape from inside the recorder and throws it into the blaze in the fireplace.

"End of mystery."

∞∞∞

*Jeff Levine, left Long Island and flew back to California, shortly after his wife's testimony. Simone waited until after the closing arguments but left before hearing the verdict. She flew home separately from her husband.*

∞∞∞

After she hangs up from the call with Fox, Simone feels a little let down. It isn't the result of the trial that bothers her. It is the way things went with Fox. She knows that he is troubled by her testimony. She tried to follow his instructions and simply tell the truth. The only time she hedged on that was when she was asked who she had played the tape for. Her shaky answer left two questions unanswered and therefore a bit of a mystery for the jury.

If Simone had added Fox's name to the list of those who had heard the tape, then all parties in the courtroom may have logically concluded that Fox was in possession of the tape. Obviously the whole proceeding could have turned on such a revelation.

But the other question is one that Simone herself cannot answer. Who actually tipped off the NYPD in the first place about Babcock's confession? Heretofore she had believed that the only real possibility was Betty Barrymore.

Now Simone is rethinking her assumption. Barrymore has repeatedly denied calling the police over the last two years and now she has denied it under oath. Simone suddenly feels very guilty about the way she has treated Betty. She decides that she will give her a call to apologize and let her know that she now believes her. Simone knows that this will be a very hard call to make especially since she still doesn't know who did make the call.

∞∞∞

Simone is still thinking these things through as she walks into the Tadich Grill on California Street in downtown San Francisco. She is meeting Jeff for a late lunch at the stately old landmark restaurant. Her husband is already waiting for her and they are seated immediately.

"Frank was found not guilty." Simone gets right to the point.

"I just saw that on the news at the bar while I was waiting for you. So ...?"

"It's pretty much what I expected. The second degree charge is still open for a possible retrial, so that's a wrinkle."

"How do you feel about it?"

"I don't know to be honest, Jeff. I think I have been numb about the possible outcomes since before the trial even began. So when I testified I just tried to do what Fox advised me to do ... to tell the truth."

The waiter comes by for their orders. Simone orders a mesquite broiled Chilean Sea bass. Jeff orders a Hang Town Fry. His dish is a local specialty that is in essence an oyster and bacon omelet that has a history going back to the California Gold Rush days.

"And so you did ... you did tell the truth. If you ask me they should have convicted him. The man belongs in jail. From what you've told me, his confession was very believable. I wish I could have heard it. Why didn't you tell me about the tape when you first told me about his confession?"

"I guess I felt a little sheepish about what I did. Maybe, I just didn't want you to think that this was how I did things with everyone. I don't know Jeff. I guess I'm not really sure about a lot of things. I'm sorry I didn't tell you right away. Please forgive me."

"As long as we are asking for forgiveness, I also have something that I need forgiven."

"You called the police, Jeff. Didn't you?"

"Yes, it was me."

"But how could that be? I never told you about the tape. I only told Betty."

"That's right. The investigators only knew about the confession. You assumed they knew about the tape. You inadvertently told them about the

## September 1996

tape yourself, when they came out to interview you. That's when I first learned about it also. And by the time we finally discussed it, it was gone. Do you know who actually took it?"

"I have no idea." It is the first lie she had told in weeks.

∞∞∞

# XLIV

## October 1996

Frank Babcock is on his way to see his lawyers in their Manhattan office. He is dressed casually in jeans and a baseball cap. It's a new look for the billionaire but it gives him a modicum of protection from the stares of strangers.

Babcock's attorneys have told him that the Prosecution is not likely to retry the charges of second degree murder. Although this is somewhat relieving to Babcock, he is annoyed that it has taken this long to have some of the travel restrictions removed. His lawyers have reminded him that unfortunately the finding of not guilty on the first degree murder charge was not a finding of complete and total innocence. However they also told him that they were working diligently to get the final charge dismissed by the court. Meanwhile some onerous constraints remain in place.

The unusual agreement to allow Frank Babcock the restricted use of his passport is a constant reminder that his innocence has not yet been completely proclaimed. Phillip Ambrose and his team claim that they will be able to get this limitation removed very soon.

Near the corner of 5th Avenue and 59th Street, Frank is approached by a short man with a van dyke beard. As soon as the young man makes eye contact with Babcock the billionaire suspects trouble.

"Mr. Babcock, my name is Seward Charles and I am with the CIA. I would pull out my credentials and show you right here, but neither of us wants to make a scene. Would it be alright if we just walked together in the

## October 1996

direction of your attorney's office and talked a little more? That way I can demonstrate my position rather than flash my identification?"

Babcock has not fully stopped to talk to this man Seward Charles, and the CIA agent is already walking unobstructed by his side. It was simply another reminder that Frank should have his personal security with him at all times. The tradeoff for his personal privacy just isn't worth the hassle.

"So you know who I am and you know where I'm heading. What do you want?"

"That's a terrific open-ended question. Over time there will be some excellent answers that I will be happy to provide. For the moment I would just like you to listen to me as we walk. It will be my responsibility to ensure that our conversation is not overheard in its entirety or in meaningful soundbites."

They are now walking rapidly. However they are still five blocks from the offices of Ambrose, Lincoln and Vereen. Babcock doesn't want to talk to anyone but his attorneys and he picks up his pace rather than get into further discussion with the supposed CIA agent.

"Before you decide to involve your attorneys in our conversation, I will underline its importance by saying that you will probably not want your intimate affair with Masira al-Haddād known to a lot of people. It could prove dangerous to you and your lover."

"I don't know what you are talking about."

"Alright then, would you rather discuss the murders of William Beaumont and his transgender whore friend Harriett Aristide? I'm sure those names ring a bell to you."

Frank Babcock feels a new sinking feeling, not unlike the one he felt when he was originally arraigned on murder charges two years earlier. He slows his rapid pace to a half step and then stops completely. Then he turns quickly on the little man with the beard and asks, "What the hell do you want from me?"

"Cooperation, Mr. Babcock. Trust me we can make certain impediments disappear overnight. All we want is the cooperation of a man who we assume loves his country."

∞∞∞

*1998*

# Techies, Trials & Terrorists

# XLV

## May 1998

Simone is returning from her first trip to India since September of 1984. But her accommodations in India are very different this time. She has been traveling first class through her two weeks on the subcontinent and her business colleague and former student Lynette Kemp is also traveling in relative luxury as well. Their new business is not even a year old and already they are doing more business than they could ever have imagined. Lynette actually started the business after taking a business class in entrepreneurship at Berkeley. Simone had taught that class. As part of her initial foray into business Lynette has been dutifully studying the IT marketplace that her mentor Simone has already conquered twice during her business career. She quickly discovers that there is one huge time-bound opportunity that could reward those who recognize it with a significant return on relatively minor investments. The opportunity is commonly being referred to as Y2K.

∞∞∞

Y2K is a composite acronym that represents the year 2000. Whenever business people began talking about Y2K they were generally referring to issues around the "millennium bug," a software glitch that resided in the IT bowels of a lot of business software and hardware. This didn't seem to be such a daunting concern to many business executives until they learned that retrofitting the IT systems of their businesses could cost tens of millions of dollars. In some cases even nine figure estimates were not considered to be outlandish assessments.

## *Techies, Trials & Terrorists*

*The rudimentary issue at the heart of Y2K was a formatting glitch associated with the storage of calendar data. A predominant number of computer programs only used two digits to represent the actual year on their internal calendars. This was not a problem in the early days of business computing because a date in 1960 could easily be distinguished from a date in 1961 by the simple retention of the final two digits of the year. However as the end of the century drew near the large and growing concern was that programming would not be able to distinguish the year 2000 from the year 1900. This could obviously result in significant sequencing issues, if left uncorrected. The sequencing issues could then result in very practical business breakdowns, and in some situations, even dangerous conditions could ensue.*

*In a matter of months large American corporations were desperately in need of programming help to retrofit their outdated hardware and software. Not only was such talent in high demand but it was also in short supply. The clear and obvious answer to this dilemma for many companies was outsourcing. Many large and small companies alike who had never even considered outsourcing were now lining up to use this tool as a way to cut their projected IT costs. And the rapid expansion of the internet and its World Wide Web was facilitating the acceleration of this phenomenon.*

∞∞∞

Simone and Lynette started their new business, shortly after Simone and Jeff Levine decided to terminate their marriage and go their separate ways. The lack of true passion in the marriage had made it less painful a breakup than it might have been. The stress of the Babcock trial certainly hadn't helped. Yet neither Simone nor Levine blamed the events surrounding the trial for the dissolution of their nuptials. On the other hand, turning to a new business venture somewhat lessened the melancholy for Simone.

∞∞∞

**Synette Systems** has been created as a middle man play. Simone Muirchant and Lynette Kemp are placing US based business with Indian outsourcing companies and taking a healthy commission in the process. But as their clientele begins pursuing these opportunities directly on the subcontinent, the ladies begin looking to open up their own center in one of three cities in India, Mumbai, Bangalore or Chennai. They are also looking

## May 1998

for third partner – ideally an Indian citizen who knows how to grease the skids in India.

On her first trip to India Simone had been in quest of a spiritual meaning to her life; on this trip she is in search of business opportunities. However she is not as interested in these opportunities for herself as she is to secure economic success for Lynette, her youthful business partner.

Lynette Kemp clearly possesses that strong drive and Simone appreciates the fact that Lynette has pursued the idea of acting as an agency rather than an actual outsourcing company. This allows *Synette Systems* to operate with very little overhead while learning the business. Fiscal year one revenues look as though they will exceed three quarters of a million dollars, almost entirely predicated on delivery of outsourcing revenues to Indian production centers. But Simone knows that they will have to dramatically change their business model in order to take full advantage of the final year and a half before the start of the new millennial. Hopefully they will then be positioned for expanded possibilities if they successfully handle the near term opportunities.

∞∞∞

After they arrive back at the San Francisco airport, Simone retrieves her car from the airport parking lot and the two female entrepreneurs begin their ride into town.

"This has an amazing trip, Simone. Thank you for everything you showed me. I never would have believed that things are so amazingly different in other parts of the world. In all of the cities we visited the poverty is just unbelievable."

"It does take a little getting used to."

Lynette allows Simon's answer to linger for a few seconds and then makes a deeper seated inquiry.

"Can I ask you a personal question?"

"Sure, why not?"

"How did you manage to live among all of that poverty for nearly two years?"

"Funny that you should ask, because we didn't even go to the poorest areas, when we visited these cities. Our hosts wanted to show us the best of their cities. But where I was in Calcutta, the people are much more destitute. But at the same time, they gave me a reason to live, after the loss of my daughter. I wanted to help. In fact, I think that if there is one thing I've always wanted to do ... it's to help people."

"That's a wonderful attribute, Simone. You have certainly helped me a lot."

"Be careful, Lynette. I said I've always *wanted* to help, but too often I just screwed things up for those I've tried to assist."

"Don't be so hard on yourself. I mean ... I'm very grateful that you agreed to join me in our business, and I know we wouldn't be doing anywhere near what we're doing without you. And I'm not worried about you messing anything up. You just need to put yourself first in some things. I'm certainly thinking about what's best for me. You should think about what's best for you."

"Thanks for your thoughtfulness, Lynette. But at this stage of my life, I am who I am."

"Sometimes you don't seem as happy as you should be. You qualify as a genuine serial entrepreneur. This is your third gig. People admire you."

"You seem to forget, I also have three divorces, and no family to talk about."

"You have Fox and his family. What about them."

"They seem to be doing OK with or without me. They're pretty busy and never come out to California. The only time I see them is when I make a point to go back east."

"Well the new millennium is just around the corner. Let's hope the next century will be good to all of us."

∞∞∞

# XLVI

## November 1998

The terms of their agreement had been relatively simple. The CIA has ensured that New York State wouldn't pursue a retrial. The State did not, in fact, fight his attorneys' motion to dismiss the hung jury charges, and the charges were subsequently dropped. For his part Frank Babcock would never know whether or not it was the CIA who actually made this happen. Yet he was on the hook to tell the CIA what he knew about the interactions of the al-Haddād family with the bin Laden family and/or the Royal family of Saudi Arabia. In one sense it was a nothing for nothing deal. The NY State government had very little chance of gaining a conviction on a retrial and Frank Babcock knew very little about the inner workings of the Saudi government or the two prominent Saudi families.

The tricky part was that Frank Babcock was unsure what the CIA, the FBI or the NYPD knew about the murders of his daughter's tormentors. And Babcock's handler Seward Charles made sure that Babcock knew that future efforts at discovering the truth in that matter were wholly dependent on Babcock's continued cooperation. In a way Frank Babcock had a new set of handcuffs and he had no idea how long he would be restrained. Now two years later he has worked diligently to stay out of the hot media spotlight with some modicum of success.

∞∞∞

*The CIA's interest in the al-Haddād family is entirely linked to its business dealings with the bin Laden family. In fact it is focused primarily on*

## Techies, Trials & Terrorists

one rogue son of Mohammed bin Laden. Usama (A/K/A Osama) bin Laden is regarded by many in the Arab world as a combination freedom fighter and spiritual leader. Others regarded him as somewhat of a pariah. One thing for sure is that Usama bin Laden is extremely well financed. The CIA believes that Usama was born in Jeddah, Saudi Arabia in 1957, but that he is currently considered to be a stateless person. He had formed a terrorist network with operatives throughout the Middle East known as Al Qaeda. Bin Laden had originally formed the group while fighting with the mujahideen in trying to extricate Afghanistan from the throes of the Soviet Union through a holy jihad.

In the late eighties when Usama bi Laden had returned to Saudi Arabia after defeating the Soviet efforts in Afghanistan, he believed that he was chosen to also fight the holy war against the infidels to the north in Iraq. He believed that Suddam Hussein was masquerading as a Muslim but was in reality a tyrannical dictator purely pursuing an aggrandizement of his own self-interest without regard to the teachings of Allah. Usama was infuriated by his own country when the House of Saud chose to get in bed with the United States to defend itself against Suddam Hussein. It was a role that Usama believed he was called to fulfill. Furthermore it was his belief that the United States had a colonial interest throughout the Middle East and was interested in spreading Christianity to the detriment of Islam. He vowed to fight this sort of incursion. In August of 1996 bin Laden declared a fatwā against the United States.

∞∞∞

Frank Babcock wasn't thrilled by the fact that his life had taken a turn in this direction. He had never before felt subservient to any person or organization. But now he was clearly conducting his affairs subject to the approval of a United States intelligence agency. And he felt like he was continuously digging himself in deeper. He felt that his new cloak and dagger life style had been foisted upon him before he ever knew what was happening. Now he is once again meeting his handler in a noisy crowded mid-town eatery near Grand Central Station. It obviously isn't his choice.

"So how are things going between you and your friend Masira?"

Seward Charles and Frank Babcock were being referred to as: "the Odd Couple," by a few of the other agents who knew about their relationship. That outlook even earned Frank his code name "Felix" to reflect the way they conducted business.

## November 1998

"We'll be seeing each other again soon. She is happy for me that other things have cleared up."

"I'm sure that *you* are happy for *you* also."

"Not so much. Remember it was not my idea to get this all started up again. Besides she now has a husband."

"And you have a wife ... see ... no one would suspect!"

"You know what, Seward, your sarcasm is grating on my nerves."

"Come on Frank, you're doing great. Remember we haven't asked you to do anything that you haven't done before on your own. Besides I'm very impressed that a guy your age has the libido of a young Lothario. But I hope your loyalties are more in line than Rowe's character."

"Funny, I don't think of you as an English literature kind of guy, but nonetheless I doubt you will need to worry about me filling the role of Calista as *The Fair Penitent*."

"Sorry you underestimate my education, Frank. Did you know that Nicolas Rowe actually stole the name Lothario and all it implies from an earlier writer?'

"Yes, I did. Lothario appears in Cervantes' Don Quixote, does he not? Perhaps it is *you* who underestimates *my* education. Anyway, let's get down to business shall we?"

"Yes, so here's what we would like to know? Where is the money coming from? We know that Usama is generally well funded by family members and by some extended family assets. But even though this guy lives like a pauper, he manages to feed an ever growing army that worships his every word. If the guy were a Christian we would look at it as a miracle of loaves and fishes, but he is a Muslim so we are looking for a more practical rationale."

"Your analogy sounds somewhat racist, I'd have to say."

"It is. And I don't give a flying fuck about it. Remember Jesus didn't go around blowing shit up."

"Now that's more like the Seward Charles, I've come to know."

Charles ignores Babcock's dig and begins to lay out the details of various financial transactions and financial institutions that he would like to know more about. He then hands Babcock a manila envelope containing some of the same information in more detail.

"The long term goal here is to try to cut off bin Laden's financial spigot so that he and his al Qaeda buddies go to their graves as indigents without influence."

"If you're counting on me to unravel the financial intricacies of the Arabian Empire, you've got the wrong man, Seward."

"It's Oscar to you Felix. And don't be so naive. Also puffery will get you nowhere. We have myriad resources working round the clock to get things done."

"Good then maybe you don't need me anymore."

Seward ignores Babcock's remark and replies. "So far you haven't provided us with very much and we're enabling you to get back in bed with your paramour. I don't want to hear any complaining. Just get us whatever you can get on the finances of the three members of the al-Haddād family that are in the file I just gave you. That will be a decent start."

"I'll see what I can do."

"Good and the next time you're jumping her bones, ask Masira if any of her family members were hurt in the August embassy bombings. Our intelligence indicates that a few years back some members of Abdulrahman al-Haddād's family were involved in a construction project in Kenya just outside of Nairobi. We didn't find anything similar near Dar es Salaam in Tanzania. However we already know that some bin Laden money helped fund the bombing of our embassy there."

"You can't assume that just because there is bin Laden family money involved, that the Abdulrahman al-Haddād's family is also sponsoring these terrorist attacks. The families are separate and in some way even rivals."

"Look Felix, leave the strategy stuff to the big boys, just see if you can find out if Masira knows of any family members who might have been in the area."

Frank Babcock is chagrined by Seward Charles' put down. He has never had to deal with anything remotely like this ever before in his life. From the time he was a child, every person he met was sooner or later deferential to the Babcock fortune. Seward Charles is treating him like a schoolboy and it stings. But in some small way he also finds the work stimulating. He doesn't know how long he will be counted on to be a snitch but for now he at least knows what his job entails.

"Ok, so after my next meeting with Masira in Spain, how do I get in touch with you."

## November 1998

"You don't. I'll find you ...like always."

Charles stands up from the booth where they have been seated and starts toward the door leaving Babcock to pay the check. He then looks over his shoulder and says, "Oh, by the way, I see that the FDA has just approved Viagra. You see ... our government is always giving us the tools we need to get the job done."

∞∞∞

# XLVII

## November 1998

Mickey and Syd are finally at a point in life where they can enjoy raising their children together without being overly reliant on other people. Both of Mickey's mothers-in-law are getting older and are also growing more dependent. Sydney's brother Jermaine is now doing well and is living in Manhattan. He has a new partner and both Mickey and Syd like him.

The Johnson children are growing up so fast that it's hard to keep track of their progress. Cody is a sophomore at Shenandoah and Noah is a freshman there also. Little Jessica is not so little any more. The young beauty is in seventh grade. All three children seem to be adjusting well to their fast advancing lives.

The other good news on the personal front is that Fox and Evelyn and their son, Mikey, are moving closer to Long Island. It is a very welcome surprise. They will now be living in the leafy town of Bernardsville, New Jersey, not far from the home of Mickey's good buddy, Kevin "Leaf-Eater" Kislinger.

∞∞∞

It's now been more than two years since the end of the Babcock trial and Mickey has been able to put most of it behind him, but not without Syd's loving support. They don't talk as much about it lately and when they do, the discussion is rather dispassionate.

Discussion of their personal travails have been displaced by two frequent topics: a renewed interest in national politics and a growing interest in breakthrough technologies that may very well launch a very

## November 1998

different century ahead. The Johnsons both wonder and worry about how these issues will affect their children.

The Johnsons like very many Americans have been glued to their television sets in recent months, transfixed as reporters unravel and expose the sordid affair between the cigar-wielding President of the United States and a young female intern, who has managed to lend her surname to the public as a new sobriquet for oral sex.

For the first time Mickey Johnson like many other Americans has started paying closer attention to world politics as well. Mickey is driving Syd to the New Jersey to see Fox and Evelyn, who have invited them out to see their new home that they closed on just that week.

∞∞∞

"You know, Mickey, it's hard to believe how far along technology has come. This GPS navigation system is absolutely amazing. I can't believe it can tell you turn by turn how to get someplace. And it does it all while you're moving. It's just incredible! I never knew something like this was so close."

Syd stares in amazement at the small screen in the dashboard of Mickey's new Lexus 400. She finds this novelty feature to be an absolutely fascinating invention.

"With the way things change so fast, I'll bet that in three of four years these navigation systems will be standard in every car." Mickey responds. "And how long after that do you think it will be before the cars simply drive themselves?"

"I don't know but that sounds as though it will take all of the fun out of the Indy 500."

"Who knows? Maybe not the fun. Maybe only the danger. The drivers can sit back in a room someplace and drive these things like Cody and Noah do on their video games."

"Doesn't sound like much fun to me."

"Tell that to our boys."

The GPS System has guided them across Staten Island, over the Outerbridge Crossing and up Interstate 287 toward their Bernardsville destination without missing a turn. Syd flips the radio over to an all-news station. They listen to the latest update on the Clinton-Lewinski scandal and a terse commentary on some of the fallout from the American missile strikes in Sudan and Afghanistan a few months earlier.

373

# Techies, Trials & Terrorists

One reporter details how some other countries are calling out the US airstrikes as: "a Hollywood response from a scandal ridden presidency." They point to a recent American movie entitled: "*Wag the Dog*," and intimate that Bill Clinton is demonstrating a facility for having "life imitate art."

∞∞∞

*Wag the Dog played in theatres earlier that year and starred Dustin Hoffman and Robert De Niro. In the movie in the fictional US President attempts to distract the public from a sex scandal of his own involving sexual advances made in his oval office against a girl scout. The movie shows how the President's staff has created a war in Albania to distract attention from his misdeeds.*

∞∞∞

"Do you believe this stuff? What a mess this jackass has made of the presidency? He has the whole world laughing at us. Can you imagine if it's true?" Syd is more incredulous than angry.

"Well, that's definitely not the case. Besides this Lewinski bimbo is no girl scout."

Syd laughs a little bit, then shakes her head and laughs a little harder. Soon she has launched one of her familiar rippling laugh tracks that makes Mickey laugh along with her.

"Come on Syd, this stuff is really not all that funny. The President taking advantage of a young intern is one thing. Allegations that it is effecting his foreign policy is something else altogether."

Syd stops laughing for a moment or two and then responds to her husband.

"You are right, Mickey. Terrorism isn't funny."

Syd and Mickey drive a little further and then Syd adds another commentary.

"It's amazing, I don't think most people ever heard of this guy, Osama bin Laden before. And now he is mentioned in the news almost every day. Some people call him Usama and some people call him Osama. But everyone calls him a terrorist. Why don't we just demand that his country arrest him and extradite him to the US immediately?"

"Can't just do that Syd. He's a stateless person."

## November 1998

"What country is he from again? I always get those Arab countries confused – like twenty years ago when Ayatollah Khomeini held all those Americans hostage in the embassy. I kept getting Iran and Iraq confused. Now there are all these 'stan countries' that we have to deal with, Afghanistan, Pakistan, Kazakhstan, and a bunch of other 'stans. It's hard to tell one 'stan from another. They all sound alike."

"Interesting phrase. Sounds like racial stereotyping to me."

Syd laughs at Mickey's dig, and punches him softly in his right shoulder even though he is driving. "I didn't say they all *look* alike."

"Ok, if you say so." Mickey keeps his right hand on the steering wheel but reaches his left hand across to rub his right bicep. Syd has barely touched him so he is not in any pain, but it is merely a reflexive action of protecting the arm that suffered a war wound in Vietnam – well before the 'stans became an issue. Then Mickey reflects back on Syd's question.

"You asked why we can't get some of these terrorists extradited. Well many of them are a kind of stateless people. This guy bin Laden is a classic example. He was originally a Saudi Arabian citizen. Then he went to Sudan and Afghanistan and Pakistan. He's been all over the Arab countries. Things have changed. We are no longer fighting countries, we are fighting ideologies. The enemy combatants have changed also. We are no longer fighting armies, we are fighting terrorists."

Just as Mickey finishes his statement, the computer generated female voice in his Lexus GPS system tells him to "take the next exit to the right."

Mickey says, "Clinton could probably use one of these systems in the *oral* office to show him turn-by-turn where to go and what to do."

Syd starts up one of her rippling snicker/giggle/laugh/hoots. "Maybe in the 21st century we will have one of these electronic ladies in our homes and we can let the computerized voices tell us how to do everything."

∞∞∞

# XLVIII

## December 1998

Father Thomas Dunham had been an educator at Shenandoah High School in Garden City for all of his adult life. He also spent four important years of his teenage youth at the institution when he was a Skylark in the class of 1937. More than any one person Dunham represented Shenandoah and everything it stood for. Now he was suddenly dead at the age of 79, and the Shenandoah community can feel one of its pillars crumbling. Yet the strength of the institution is clearly evident at the cleric's funeral. From all over Long Island, greater New York City and some of the neighboring states, people have traveled to Garden City for Dunham's funeral services.

The funeral mass is taking place at the Shenandoah's 1200 seat auditorium, because the campus chapel is way too small. Even in the more expansive auditorium all of the seating has been taken. There are close to 150 additional people standing in the back. More are standing past the open doors in the auditorium foyer, which serves as the narthex on this occasion. Nearly half of the current student body and many of their parents choose to attend the services on a day that the school is officially closed. However the students are not seated in any specific seats and are accorded no special preferences over the other mourners that included numerous alumni and multiple special guests.

∞∞∞

The Mass of Christian burial is presided over by a Father Declan O'Brien, the Jesuit successor to Father Dunham's post at Shenandoah High School. After Mass an uncommon eulogy for Father Dunham is given by

## December 1998

Fulsome Thatchley, Dunham's close personal friend. Thatchley is a reclusive man of letters. Despite his 43 best-selling novels and numerous op-ed pieces published in a variety of national and international newspapers and magazines, Thatchley has not made a public appearance or given a speech in more than thirty-five years. His book covers no longer carry his photo. Thatchley lives quietly at the northern tip of New York State on a small island in the St Lawrence River. As childhood friends Thatchley and Dunham had known each other for 75 years. They had corresponded consistently and frequently throughout their respective careers and got together in upstate New York for a weekend every summer. The occasion of Father Dunham's funeral was only the first time in forty years that Fulsome Thatchley had set foot on Long Island.

"There are so many events and achievements that catalogue the remarkable life of my friend Tom Dunham that it's wasteful to merely stand here and list them. It is not necessary anyway because I realize that I stand before a group of people who knew our departed brother very well.

"In a world of good and evil, Tom Dunham helped edge the world toward good. He did this more than any man I know. His work with, and for, the young men of Shenandoah High School has impacted the world in so many positive ways. He used his brilliant mind to enlighten the minds of others. He was an astute businessman as well as a creative scholar and a cutting edge educator. These personal attributes allowed him to build Shenandoah into the unique educational colossus that it is today.

"At the same time I can honestly say that I have never met a more authentic human being than Tom Dunham. The only possible breach in that authenticity was his humility. A man who accomplished so much may have actually been disingenuous simply by being so humble. But I will leave that for others to decide. To me, Tom was a friend, a sounding board and yet also an intellectual adversary. We didn't see certain

> fundamental things in similar ways. Tom staunchly believed in God ..."

As Thatchley stands in front of the large audience certain members of the assembled group had their own recollections of interactions with the priest.

Mickey Johnson recalls a different man than the person that he hears Thatchley eulogize. Mickey remembers a man who was powerful in his own right and who ran Shenandoah High with a domineering adherence to the mold of the *Shenandoah Man*. It wasn't that every graduate had to be a carbon copy of one another. Quite the contrary Shenandoah produced a vastly diverse set of high achieving graduates. But it was a fact that Father Dunham insisted that every alumnus of his educational institution was imbued with a passion for excellence as well as a commitment to compassion and social contribution. These were the "twin caissons of character" that he required every graduate to build upon.

But Mickey also recalls that Father Thomas Dunham testified on behalf of Frank Babcock at his murder trial. He never understood why Dunham chose to do that. He wonders if Dunham truly believed in Babcock's innocence or if he was merely standing up for one of the school's largest benefactors.

Syd had not accompanied Mickey to the funeral services but he is happy that his son, Fox is sitting there next to him. There are also many familiar faces among the alumni of Shenandoah, but those faces do not include Frank Babcock, who is traveling abroad. Mickey's longtime friend, Jack Birdsong is also traveling outside of the United States. But Mickey does spot his buddies Pudd'nhead Watson and Kevin Kislinger near the front of the auditorium

Mickey puts his scattered thoughts aside as he listens to the famous recluse author continue his reflective intimate eulogy of his cherished friend.

> "Our friendship was one that allowed us to talk to each other about our life's work in an open and honest way. Tom was the one person outside of my team of literary assistants, with whom I ever discussed my work. He wouldn't allow me to credit him with any printed acknowledgement in my books,

## December 1998

but he was an integral part of nearly every book that I have published. And Tom would discuss his life's work with me in great detail as well. That is why I agreed with his challenge from an earlier date. We agreed that whichever of us died last, would speak at the other guy's funeral. So Tom, you win again and here I am.

"My own work as a novelist has often been criticized by others because my plots never end in a neatly wrapped package. By design, they always have more than a few loose ends. Some of my critics believe that this is merely a marketing ploy to sell the next book. Others just find it an annoying attribute of my style. Once Tom asked me very directly about this and I told him that it intrigued me why so many people believed that life comes in such gift wrapped packages, when in fact real life is always loaded with loose ends. Meanwhile all I have ever tried to do was simulate lifelike realisms. Not all storylines reach their conclusion simultaneously.

"And so it is that Tom's death did not sync up with world events that he so hoped to influence. He fondly hoped that one of his beloved Shenandoah alumni would find the cure for cancer ... would reenergize space exploration ... would become President of the United States ... would solve the energy crisis ... would be a global unifier-in-chief ... would find world peace ... would discover a mathematical formula for happiness ..."

Thatchley pauses briefly to allow the congregation to draw abreast of his rambling eulogy. He then adds: "Yes, we all know how much he loved his math." This draws a tittering of laughter from the current student body and a more rounded laughter from those alumni who knew Dunham when he was directly involved in the educational endeavors of the student body. To the very end of his days he was the moderator of the Shenandoah Math Club.

"So now that we jointly recognize these incongruities, allow me to share one other item that remains uncompleted as Tom passed away much too early at the age of 79.

"Tom was working on a book that he believed could be foundational for many of his other aspirations for his Shenandoah family.

He was working on this book for almost two years that he has simply titled: 'Forgiveness.' He said that the subtitle had yet to emerge. Tom graced me with the privilege of previewing the work which he had nearly completed and that he wanted to be his millennial gift to all of you.

"Not being a fan of critics, I imagine there is a bit of irony that I'm left to appraise the written word of my friend and confidant. I will not do so. But at his request I will very inadequately summarize his message.

"Tom firmly believed that there is nothing more important in our emotional makeup than love – and that in order to truly love – we need to be free of all spite. In order to be free of spite we must forgive. Tom's treatise is full of scriptural references and it also draws upon the scholarly wisdom of sages from many periods in history including robust reference to the polymaths of the Renaissance. Of course, Tom also references the Greek mathematicians who so fascinated him with their intellectual prowess. As you might expect, Shakespeare also plays a role in Tom's musings about forgiveness. In fact Tom's references and citations are so robust that he might leave the reader thinking that he doesn't have an original thought on the topic that he can claim as his own. But that's just not so. It's there and you will find it.

"Tom boldly suggests that finding a mechanism for simple forgiveness will be an absolute necessity for

## December 1998

21st Century progress. Forgiveness is needed in the Middle East to stop the endless bloodshed. Forgiveness is needed in marriages to stem the uptick in the dissolution of those unions. Forgiveness is essential between a child and his parents and between a brother and a sister. Forgiveness is needed between generations to effectively build a better world in spite of the sins of our predecessors and the sins we now ourselves commit.

"Can Pakistani's forgive the Indians? Can black Americans forgive white Americans for the oppression of their slave ancestors? Can Native Americans forgive Europeans for misappropriating their continent? Can Christians forgive Muslims? Can Muslims forgive Jews? Can the Jews forgive the Germans for the Holocaust? So much sin and transgression … So much depravity, decadence and debauchery … So great a need for forgiveness.

"If Father Thomas Dunham were here today, I believe he would call upon all of his expanded Shenandoah family to understand forgiveness and to let it begin with us."

Thatchley speaks for another ten minutes promising to get his friend's book finished and published posthumously. But overall the eulogy is unusual. It is not so much a reflection on the life of Thomas Dunham as it is like an otherworldly directive from the cleric himself and delivered to his apostolic family with the assistance of his reclusive friend.

After the services there is an extensive reception in the Shenandoah Arts and Athletics Center (commonly called simply "The SAAC".) Mickey and Fox walk in that direction and begin to talk about the services they had just attended.

Fox asks Mickey, "What did you think of Fulsome Thatchley's eulogy?"

"I'm not sure. He's a weird old duck. Not hard to see why he was friends with Dunham. The eulogy was a bit bizarre, I think. Somehow I expected a bit more … maybe a bit more about their friendship for over 75 years ... some personal insights or something ... I'm not sure what. How about you? What did you think, Fox?"

"I actually liked the eulogy. I liked the whole concept of forgiveness. It certainly has been valuable to my relationship with Evelyn. After all she has forgiven me and has provided collaborative support with my daughter in West Virginia."

"One of these days I'd like to meet her. After all, little Miss Dolly Swift, *is* my granddaughter? Right? And it would be nice to meet Dolly's mother, Maddie, also. Do you think that would be okay with Evelyn?"

"I *know* it would be okay."

Mickey thinks for a while and then says; "About this forgiveness thing, I'd like you to know that I'm trying hard to forgive Frank. Syd is on me all the time about it. Sometimes she sounds as though she might have had an advance copy of Dunham's book."

"Would you be able to forgive him if you knew he actually *was* responsible?"

"It depends, I think."

"On what?"

"Maybe, on *how responsible*."

"Interesting."

"Have you talked to my wife about this?"

"No, why?"

"Syd has asked me pretty much the same questions. And I've told her that it's not just about forgiveness, it's also about regret. It's pretty hard to say, 'I forgive you' when I haven't heard the words, 'I'm sorry.' And it's not like we're talking about something trivial, here."

"After the indictment first came out ... that's four years ago now ... we were in your house when you told me that you believed that Frank had something to do with the death of your father – my grandfather. Now two years after the trial, what do you believe really happened?"

"I believe that it happened exactly the way your mother described it in court. And I also believe, crazy as it sounds that Frank actually confessed all of this to Simone at the Ecco dinner and that she actually taped it. Knowing all of the parties involved, I believe that is exactly what happened. Simone can drive a person crazy at times, but she is incapable of making up a story like that and testifying to it in court. Impossible."

"You are right. That is what happened."

## December 1998

"Don't tell me. You have the tape!"

"Not any longer ... I took it from my mother's home long before the trial. She never knew for sure that I took it. But I burned it immediately after the trial."

"That explains a lot."

"Do you forgive me for not telling you sooner?"

"You are my son, Fox. I forgive you, yes."

"How about my mother? Can you forgive her too?"

"You know something. In your mother's case, there is nothing for me to forgive. Simone was honest. She told the truth as best she knew it. Simone has always abhorred violence. There is a certain consistency in her personality that led me to believe that she told everything truthfully."

"Can you forgive Frank Babcock?"

"That will take a lot more time. I'm working on it."

"I hope they publish Father Dunham's book soon."

∞∞∞

# Epilogue

In San Francisco, Simone Muirchant goes to bed after watching a news report that talks of ongoing violence in the Middle East. She is troubled by the fact that her ex-husband, Jeff Levine is considering a business opportunity that could station him in Israel for the next two years. What is so compelling about the Middle East? Her first husband, Frank Babcock is now spending more time in the UAE then he is in the USA and now Jeff wants to move to Israel for a couple of years. To Simone this is insanity. It's crazier than her ideas about setting up a base of operations in India.

She rolls over in bed but still doesn't rest. Just as she begins to nod off, thoughts about Fox startle her into a restless state. What is he doing? What does he think? Why doesn't he visit me? What about my grandson, Mikey? I barely know him. I've never met the other one, the other grandchild … what's her name again? Oh yeah, Dolly. What kind of name is that? Dolly, hmmm? What does the future hold for Dolly? She rolls over and over a few more times. The year 2000 is getting closer.

∞∞∞

In Bernardsville, New Jersey, Fox Babcock can't quite get to sleep. As usual Evelyn has fallen asleep within minutes after they had sex. It is almost like a sleeping pill for her. Although he loves Evelyn and Mikey, he also cares about his daughter in West Virginia. He hopes that he will see more of her this year. He knows that Maddie would like that as well. But this will be a big year coming up. Fox and Evelyn Babcock have recently celebrated their sixth wedding anniversary. Happily they have finally made plans for their big trip. Originally they were going to make the trip as a newly married couple. Now they were making the trip with their son in tow. He wonders if Maddie would allow them to bring Dolly as well. Never happen … he realizes … way too long a trip … He continues to toss and turn, now thinking about his new job that he doesn't have to begin for 6 months. Life is good. Evelyn has also managed to delay the start of her new job for a period of time. More tossing and

# Epilogue

turning. He sees Sergei Zubkov in his dream as light sleep begins. He wakes up and tries to shake it off. It takes a while.

∞∞∞

In Garden City on Long Island, Mickey Johnson is sleeping better. Vengeance no longer obsesses him. He still dislikes Frank Babcock intensely, but he no longer thinks about revenge on a daily basis. What keeps Mickey awake at night these days is unusual for him. Mickey is worried about bigger things. He is worried about world politics. Increasingly he is concerned about the upcoming 21$^{st}$ Century and what that will mean for his wife and children.

As he rolls over in bed he thinks that these were the things that always concerned people like Simone. In the past these were simply academic issues to Mickey. Now he understands, or so he thinks. Still he wonders what's ahead for his own country. *I'm only 51 years old. Once a Marine always a Marine but maybe I should do more. Thank God I have Syd* he muses. *She'll be at my side as we raise our family. The future will be better for all of us.*

These thoughts allow Mickey to finally find sleep. Oddly, his dreams incorporate thoughts of times earlier in his life; angry thoughts of Vietnam; sad thoughts of his first wife, Barbara; confusing sexual thoughts about Simone. He wakes up briefly, and then goes back to sleep soundly. He rolls over and throws his good arm around Syd. Thank God for Syd, he thinks, again. He is smiling as he falls into a deeper sleep. This time he sleeps until the morning sun rises.

∞∞∞

In Spain, Frank Babcock is laying in a huge emperor-sized bed. His head is nestled against the oversized naked breasts of Masira al-Haddād. Masira has gained a little weight and she sleeps more soundly than she should. The canopied bed curtains are all that stand between them and the salted sea breeze. The Mediterranean coast now serves as their rendezvous location. But Masira is no longer just his lover; she is now his mark. Every whisper she makes gets reported to his handler, Seward Charles.

Babcock also thinks about Margot's undersized breasts and wishes he was resting his head against them instead. He also thinks about his adopted son Fox, but he doesn't worry about him at all. He is doing well for himself. Nor does he worry about his grandson, Mike. They are Babcocks but

# Epilogue

not blood Babcocks. There is love and respect but there is just not enough time.

On the other hand, his biological son, Jedidiah Babcock, is now 8 years old. He is smart and respectful. Margot is doing a wonderful job with him. She is only 29 years old. Frank is 63. What will their future together be like? There is much talk now about the next millennial. It's less than 13 months away. What kind of world will these children of the millennial generation experience. God knows. Life doesn't always have storybook endings, Frank muses. Sometimes you just have to suck it up.

∞∞∞

Gradually across the world the Babcocks and the Johnsons find rest for the night.

∞∞∞

# Other Novels by Jim Lynch

**Communists, Capitalists & Cokeheads:** *The Connecting Generation* (2017)*

**Boomers Bastards & Boneheads:** *The Wasted Generation* (2016)*

**Flunking Chemistry Class:** *The Baseball Players* (2013)

**Seekers, Sinners & Simpletons:** *The Spirituality Players* (2013)

**The 2020 Players:** *A Futuristic Account of the 2020 Presidential Year* (2011)

**The Rhapsody Players:** *The Sensuous Pursuit of Health, Happiness and Longevity* (2010)

*These books are part of the **Generation Series**

*Book Four of the **Generation Series** entitled:

**Madmen, Millennials & Malcontents:** *The Social Media Generation*

Will be coming later in the fall of 2020

Jim Lynch is a novelist, who has written literary fiction on an eclectic set of topics. His previous novels include:

Prior to his writing career Jim was engaged as a visionary business executive who spent more than 35 years leading other professionals in both entrepreneurial pursuits as well as big business endeavors. He started his career with eight years' experience as an investigator for James J. Lynch Investigation and Security Services. He then spent the core of his business career (22 years) as an executive with AT&T. After retiring as an officer of AT&T, Jim returned to his entrepreneurial roots and founded a thriving sales consulting business, and co-founded a successful IT outsourcing business. Then he was one of four entrepreneurs who founded Rhapsody Holdings in 2007.

In addition to his career as a business executive Mr. Lynch also gives back to the community through his interaction with several nonprofit causes. He is an active member of the Board of Trustees for the Hunterdon Healthcare System as well as the Hunterdon Medical Center. He has also served as a member of the Board of Trustees for SOAR, a Washington DC based charity that assists aging members of the clergy.

Jim and his wife Debbie reside in Hunterdon County in western New Jersey, where they have raised eight children together. They are also enthralled by the budding young lives of 15 grandchildren.

Made in United States
Troutdale, OR
04/14/2025